I, Jacqueline

To
CHERRY KEARTON
with my thanks

About the Author

Hilda Lewis was one of the best-known and best-loved of all historical novelists, known for her authentic application of period detail to all her books. She was born in London and lived for much of her life in Nottingham. She wrote over 20 novels and died in 1974.

I, Jacqueline

HILDA LEWIS

TORC

Cover illustration: © John Foley/Archangel Images.

This edition first published 2008

Torc, an imprint of Tempus Publishing
Cirencester Road, Chalford,
Stroud, Gloucestershire, GL6 8PE
www.tempus-publishing.com

Tempus Publishing is an imprint of NPI Media Group

British Library Cataloguing in Publication Data.
A catalogue record for this book is available from the British Library.

ISBN 978 0 7524 4564 9

Typesetting and origination by NPI Media Group
Printed and bound at Nutech Photolithographers

AUTHOR'S FOREWORD

Our story opens in Holland in fourteen hundred and seventeen—nearly two years after Agincourt.

In England, the victorious Henry V is on the throne; in France the mad King Charles VI is soon to be succeeded by Joan of Arc's Dauphin.

Count William VI, hereditary Prince of Holland, Hainault, Zealand and Friesland, is nearing his death. His heir is his young daughter Jacqueline; and his last days are tormented by this question: Will she be accepted as undoubted prince in his place?

The land is torn in two by quarrels. Certainly his own party, the *Hooks*, will support her; but what of the *Cods*, enemies of his house?

The sudden death of Jacqueline's husband—the heir to France—leaves her without her natural protector. A new marriage must be made at once. Whom shall the young princess marry?

With this death and with this question we begin the story of Jacqueline.

Epitaph for Jaqueline

L'amour pour quatre fois me mit en mariage,
Et si n'ay sceu pourtant accroistre mon lignage,
Gorrichem j'ay conquis contre Guillaume Arklois,
En un jour j'ay perdu presque trois milles Anglais.
Pour avoir mon mary de sa prison delivre,
Au Duc de Bourgoingnons tous mes pays je livre.
Dix ans regnay en paine; ore avec mon ayeul
Contente je repose en un mesme cercuil.

Four times in wedlock heart and hand I gave
And though my ancient line ends in this grave
Gorcum I won from William Arkels' host.
Three thousand English in one day I lost.
My husband from his prison to set free,
My kingdoms all I gave to Burgundy.
Ten years I reigned in grief; content am I
In my ancestral tomb at last to lie.

PRINCIPAL CHARACTERS

IN HOLLAND

The Countess Jacqueline, Hereditary Prince of Holland, Hainault, Zealand and Friesland.

Count William VI, her father.

Margaret of Burgundy, her mother.

John of Touraine, Dauphin of France, her first husband.

John the Fearless of Burgundy, her mother's brother.

John the Pitiless of Bavaria, bishop-elect of Liége, her father's brother.

John of Brabant, her second husband.

Philip the Good, her cousin; son to John of Burgundy.

Beatrix van Vliet, her half-sister.

Frank van Borselen, stadtholder of Holland; leader of the Cods.

William van Brederode, captain of her forces; leader of the Hooks.

IN ENGLAND

Henry V, King of England.

Catharine of Valois, his wife.

Henry VI, their son, the infant King.

John of Bedford, brother to Henry V, commander of the English forces in France.

Humphrey of Gloucester, his youngest brother, Protector of England.

Henry Beaufort, half-uncle to Henry V, bishop of Winchester, Cardinal of England.

Eleanor Cobham, Gloucester's mistress, later his wife.

IN FRANCE

Charles VI, the mad King of France.

Isabeau, his wife.

Charles VII, their youngest son; Joan of Arc's Dauphin.

I

It was my mother who thought of the black ribands. She had always a strict sense of what was proper; habit would lead her to seemly behaviour though the heart remained cold. That my young husband was suddenly, shockingly dead seemed to weigh less with her than that no one had thought to find me a black gown or even to tie a mourning riband about my arm. As for myself, I was so bewildered by the suddenness that I had had no time as yet to feel my loss.

But it is like me, impulsive as I am told I am, and as I must believe I am—though the years have disciplined me more than a little—to plunge into the middle of my tale without telling my name or my parentage.

Well then, I am called Jacqueline—of Bavaria, or of Hainault, or of Holland, whichever you choose. Yes, I am that Jacqueline who, ill-fortune pursuing, set all Christendom by the ears with scandal in high places.

My father was William VI, Count of Holland, of Hainault, of Zealand and the free Islands of Friesland; my mother, Margaret of the house of Charolais, from which are sprung the great dukes of Burgundy. My father, lively and loving with his friends, could yet lay a heavy hand upon his enemies. He was renowned for his prowess in the fight—and with women. He was a friend to scholars and to poets; and in his court the laws of chivalry lingered still.

My mother is a true de Charolais—hardheaded and ambitious; she has always put the honour of her family first—the de Charolais. And she is a true de Charolais in her looks; of low stature, the eyes pale grey, not overlarge nor lustrous; but the mouth is thin rather than full and she holds it tight-pressed and did, even when she was a young woman. Whether she ever loved my father, I don't know. She did her wifely duty but without generosity. And, perhaps one cannot blame her; for she never forgave him his women. A gentler wife might have won him; but her pride was set hard. Everyone knew about his mistresses and his bastards—and she with one child and that one a mere girl!

She never quite forgave me, either, that I had not been born a boy.

She was no unnatural mother but she was not a loving one. When I behaved ill I was not only whipped but threatened also with the name of the great duke, her brother. *Your uncle of Burgundy will be after you!* she would cry out. Or, *I am sending to my brother John.* And that was worse than any whipping. For a whipping is soon forgotten; but fear breeds in the dark places of the heart. John of Burgundy was my childhood bogey and so remained throughout my life ... and good cause, too. Although it was the last thing my mother desired, it was she herself that had bred in me this fear and distrust.

I feared my mother and I loved my father. He was my sun that shone. Whatever disappointment he may have felt that I was not a boy he never showed it. He loved me because I was his child; he enjoyed my childish company because my answers came pat, and my laughter, too. But most of all he was pleased because I was pretty in the Dutch style rather than in the Burgundian. When I was nine years old or thereabouts, Master Jan van Eyck painted a picture of me and my father wore it about his neck. It is lost now, like most of my treasures; but like many a lost treasure it is safe in my heart.

I see it as clearly, as though I held it before me—the round-faced child with rosy cheeks and light-brown curling hair. The eyes are dark blue—and Master van Eyck has caught the expression marvellously; they are trying not to laugh and the little mouth is buttoned up with the same desire. The small creature is well aware of the seriousness of the occasion; but for all that it is certain that the laughter must come bursting through. The chin is round and very determined for so young a child; the nose is delicate, a little tip-tilted. Altogether if I may say it of that far-off child—a pretty creature.

I cannot remember when I was not an important person. I had arrived late in the married life of my parents, though my mother was barely thirty; but sixteen years is a long time to wait and they had given up hope. I was three years old when my father succeeded to the throne of the Counts of Holland; and so I became *Daughter of Holland* and his sole heir.

In any court, even a small court like my father's, a young prince is flattered and fêted; and so it was with me. Sycophants would run fawning with presents and with pretty speeches; but they turned their backs quickly enough when the wind blew cold.

I must mention one other person who played a great part in my life—Beatrix van Conengiis, my favourite woman and constant companion. My mother disliked her and would have sent her packing; but Beatrix held her position at my father's command. He told me himself, when I was eleven or twelve perhaps, that she was his daughter—and, indeed, she had his handsome look. He desired, he said, at least one loving heart about me during his many absences; and he desired, also, her own advancement. And so it turned out. She had not been about my person but a little while when she caught the eye and the heart of the Lord of Conengiis—a match for which even my father had not dared to hope; and it did not make my mother any sweeter. From the time I was old enough to understand anything I knew that Beatrix cherished me with a never failing love ... and that my mother hated her.

I cannot remember further back than my fifth year—the year of my betrothal. I was carried by mother to Compiègne to be betrothed to the second son of the King of France. There were feasts and music and masques though, shut away in the nursery with Beatrix, I never saw any. But, one thing I do remember, and that was a fit of passion in which I screamed because my father had not come. He had promised; and he was not there. It was only afterwards that I knew why he had not kept his promise to me, the only promise he ever broke. He had been bitten by a dog on his way thither. Always a lover of beasts, he had stooped to a strange mastiff in the courtyard of an inn and the creature had sprung and bitten him in the leg. And, though he sent me pretty gifts and loving messages, I would neither look nor listen but still cried out and beat upon the floor and would not be comforted.

There were many to whisper behind their hands that nothing good could come of this betrothal, for my betrothed's father was absent as well as my own—Charles VI of France had been left behind in Paris to howl in his madman's cell. The excitement had been overmuch for his frail body and the ever-dreaded sickness had fallen once again. But I knew nothing of that. I only knew that my father's place was empty; and that Madam Queen Isabeau sickened me with her smell of stale perfume and sweat. My mother used no perfume at any time; and she had fallen into our good Dutch habit of soap and water. Courageous as I was and high-spirited, I was frightened of Queen Isabeau for all her handsome looks. It was not only the smell that went with her—at the French court my mother was almost alone in the sweetness of her body—but because she was tall and heavy and towered above me like a dark tree; and because her mouth was red as blood and it shut down like a trap, and her eyes flicked like a whip to make you do whatever she commanded.

John Duke of Touraine, my betrothed, was seven years old; that is three years older than I. He was good and gentle; and he showed no sign of his elder brother's weakness in character. Louis the Dauphin, in spite of his tender years was already known for stubbornness and for spiteful ways. But John did, alas, show signs of that other weakness that would not let Louis ride a horse or even sit long in a litter without swooning. But our good Dutch food would make all well, my father used to say.

When we returned home after my betrothal John went with us to learn the ways of the people he would one day help me to govern; and I was the happiest child in the world. I did not know what a betrothal might be; but I did know that it had given me—a lonely child—a most loving companion. He would do whatever I wanted. It was I that suggested our games and he that followed. When he did not follow quickly enough I would stamp and catch hold of his dark hair; and he would gently uncurl my fingers, careful not to hurt me rather than to spare himself. When we did things that were forbidden—walk in the river when the March winds blew cold from the sea, or chase the sheep so that they ran in all directions, bleating madly—it was John that took the edge of my mother's tongue, and the whipping, too.

I was fourteen and he seventeen when we were put to bed together. There was a great ceremony in the Hague chapel and a great feast to follow. My mother had hankered after the French custom of putting the bride to bed, seeing that John was of France and she, herself, of Burgundy. But my father would have none of it, and that was a weight off my heart.

So John and I went to bed soberly. I was old enough to understand the nature of marriage; but surely marriage with John was different. For ten years we had played together, lain together in the hot sun and beneath the cool shade of trees. We were brother and sister; why should marriage alter that ... for the present at least?

But when I was waiting in the great nuptial bed, I was not so sure. John stood there his too-thin body trembling beneath the bedgown, and there was a new look in his eye. I would not let myself be afraid of this new John.

'All this playacting!' I said. 'Dear God, how tired I am—half-asleep already. Come to bed. Heaven be praised it's wide enough for half-a-dozen.'

I saw how he flushed; but the old habit of obedience to my whims, held good. He came quiet into bed and lay brotherly next to me. The long day had been much for him; he was a delicate lad, and soon he was asleep. I knew perfectly well—even if my mother had not seen fit to remind me—my marriage duties as *Child of Holland*. But I was not yet ready. I was fourteen and just beginning to learn the nature of my own body. Had John been a stranger, excitement might have driven us together. Or, had I been given time, I should, I think, have come to love John the husband as dearly as I loved John the brother. But we were not given time.

The next day, seated in our chairs of State, we received the gifts of our nobles and churchmen and burghers. And then at last, our thanks being given, we were allowed to depart for Hainault, to spend what we Dutch call the *white bread nights*. And glad I was to leave the searching eye of my mother and her blunt questions. I had feared to the very last she would come with us.

In Hainault, among the childhood haunts where we had played as brother and sister, it was not hard to keep John from his husband's rights. *Soon*, I would say, *soon*. He was not a lusty youth and soon he came no more to my room than to say *Good-night*. We were both of us young and time seemed to stretch endless before us.

And so the pattern of our new life was established before we returned to the Hague; and, for all the blessings of the church and the sharp tongue of my mother and the encouraging jests of our friends, there was no bedplay between us that first night or any other.

And so our pleasant life meandered on. John was gentle as ever. Sometimes it seemed to me that he was lower in spirit than he should be; but then, I told myself, he was delicate and easily tired. The truth is I was too young, and too selfish, to understand the strain I put upon him. Now that I understand the nature of the bond between men and women, I grieve—though it is all of twenty years ago—that I showed so little kindness.

I wore my new title *Madam the Duchess of Touraine*; but it meant little to me. I am Dutch in my ways—though there's little more than a trickle of Dutch blood in me. For the rest I am Burgundian through my mother and Bavarian through my father. But I am Dutch in my thinking; and so I never thought of France, that it might one day be my home and I its Queen.

There was little to disturb these pleasant early months of my marriage except the usual quarrels between our noblemen which took my father away from home. Hooks and Cods the parties called themselves. *Hooks and Cods*. The very names are all-but forgotten now, though for years they spelled bloodshed and heartache; and to no one more than to me.

I must tell you how the quarrel began. My greatgrandfather was the Emperor—Louis of Bavaria; his wife was Margaret Countess of Holland from whom I inherit my lands. Many Dutch lords—*Cods* they called themselves because of the grey speckled livery they wore—hated the Bavarian blood of my family. But the *Hooks*— hooks to catch the Cods—stood loyally by my family.

For three generations now there had been continual quarrels between the two parties. My grandfather had managed to keep the Cods down; and so did his son after him. But it was a great annoyance to my father and a great worry, too. From the time I was a little child he worried about me, wondering what I—a woman—would do against the rebel lords when my own time came.

And then, suddenly, the pleasant order of my life broke; and everything was changed.

Louis, heir to the throne of France, died suddenly; and no trueborn child to inherit the crown.

John was utterly cast-down. It was not so much affection—the brothers hardly knew each other. I doubt whether they had met since my betrothal ten years ago; and Louis had never been easy to love. It was an unwillingness, yes and a fear also, to step into the empty place. France was dark with bloodshed; not only the blood shed by Henry of England, but with that spilt by noble against noble; bloodshed and treachery. Treachery; there were ugly tales that Louis had been poisoned. And then, too, there was the mad King and the wanton Queen to reckon with, each incalculable; Louis might well have been poisoned between them! If John was afraid, it was no wonder.

In trying to rouse his spirits I had little time to think of myself and what Louis' death was going to mean to me. But soon I began to notice deeper bows and curtseys and a greater running after me with compliments and gifts. Moreover my mother treated me with a new formal courtesy; but for all that I should not cease to be her obedient child. It was the prescribed respect paid to the future Queen of France—even though that Queen happened to be one's own daughter. My mother rarely transgressed the rules of etiquette.

It was my beloved Beatrix who first spoke the words.

'So now the Daughter of Holland becomes Madam the Dauphine. One day she will be a Queen!'

'No!' I cried out. 'No! I don't want to be a Queen. I don't want to go into France. I'm afraid of the mad King—though I pity him, too. Oh he's gentle enough when he's well but when he's sick—and the sickness comes without warning—then they take him away snarling and howling like an animal. And I'm still more afraid of the Queen; she's in her right mind all the time; and it's a wicked mind. If she didn't like me she wouldn't hesitate to put me out of the way; or if she found a better match for her son—then, Jacqueline goodnight!'

Beatrix put a finger to her lip; she went over and opened the door, looked into the next room and then slammed the door hard.

'They say she poisoned Louis,' I went on. 'Louis, her own son! And, true or not, it shows the kind of woman she is! But most of all I'm afraid of my uncle of Burgundy. When he comes here, he's a cloud over everything! He doesn't come often—but often enough for me! But in Paris ... in Paris ...' and I began to tremble.

She came over and put her arm about me. 'Don't let him trouble your heart. You forget your father.'

'I could face it with my father; I can face anything with him. But he won't be there. I don't want to leave my father, Beatrix, I don't want to leave him!'

She smiled at that; she was his daughter too.

'I feel safe when he's here.' And I remembered the times he had stood between me and the worst of my mother's tongue. 'And I cannot, cannot leave him! Nor I cannot leave Holland where I was born and bred. And how shall I leave Hainault with its woods and its hills?'

And when she tried to comfort me with the woods and the hills of France I would not listen, crying out that I was a Hollander by birth and a Hainaulter by heart; and that I would not go into France to be among strangers that would not love me.

My mother, that ambitious Burgundian, could not understand my unwillingness to take possession of my fine new title. She would have bustled me into France then and there, but by father reminded her that we must wait until we were summoned; and that alone held her back.

Since my mother might not carry me into France until the summons came, she busied herself with new jewels for us both; and there were new gowns, new shoes, new gloves. My father, though he admired rich fashions in a woman, protested. I was but fourteen and growing fast. I should grow out of my clothes before all was ready. She did not, however, trouble herself to listen. She had the de Charolais love of display—though she could be mean enough where none could see.

And so, when the summons came at last to show the people of France their future King and Queen, everything was ready. And once again I was for France. And once again my father was not with us. He was in France trying to smooth out the quarrels between his brother-in-law of Burgundy and King Charles. And once again I longed for him, fearing his absence a bad omen. But my mother feared nothing—except that the spring winds might roughen my skin. We could not know, either of us, that soon my cheeks would be roughened with tears.

And so I come back full circle to where I began—back to Compiègne where I had been betrothed as a little child; and where now my young husband lay dead, and where my mother stood regarding me with annoyance, the black ribands in her hand.

II

Beatrix took the ribands; and even in this moment of grief, I saw my mother send her a look of dislike.

'See that your lady has at least this much sign of grief about her,' she said, severe; and, even while Beatrix was at her curtsey, slammed the door behind her. Beatrix came over and stood by me at the window. Did I, indeed, show no grief then for the loss of my dear companion? I had shed no tear; my heart was heavy as stone and as cold. And now, seeing the ribands black between the whiteness of her fingers, I was suddenly stabbed by my loss. She put her arms about me; but there was no comfort for me anywhere except in my father. For I was sick to the heart of Queen Isabeau's wailing and I feared they would bring the mad King from Paris. At the thought I was shaken with fear. *Father come quickly and take me home, home to my own Holland...*

I watched Beatrix tying the ill-omened ribands. 'When will my father come?' I asked.

'At any moment now. He will have heard that Monsieur the Dauphin is sick ...'

'But not dead, not dead!' And even that word on my own lips could not bring the tears to my eyes, the tears I badly needed to shed.

'John is dead.' I nodded, driving the words home to my dull brain. 'We came into France to show ourselves to the people. Well, John has shown himself for the last time.'

'And you will never be Queen! Does that grieve you, sweetheart ... a little?'

'It's the one good thing in all this heartbreak. I was not meant to be a queen. The smallest island of Friesland is dearer to me than the whole of France. And now, now I can go home!' The longing in my voice shook my heart though it could not bring the tears. And I remembered my mother only this morning trying, no doubt, to comfort me—and her tongue all unused to gentleness. 'It is not as though he were ever your husband,' she said.

I think I must have shown some anger then; for I felt the colour burn in my cheeks and her own anger burst through; she could never endure being crossed or criticized. 'You may well grieve! Had you done your woman's part, your son would have sat upon the French throne. You slept with the man a full year and never a sign of a child. It's hard to believe Isabeau's son so backward! Even young Charles has got himself a bastard—and he but thirteen!'

'I did love John,' I told Beatrix now and it was as though I spoke not to her but to John lying unhearing in the next room. And then, since one must not lie in the face of the dead, added, 'And yet I don't know ... Beatrix, I don't know.'

'You loved him,' she said softly. 'You loved him as a sister loves a dear brother.'

'But he was my *husband*! And no desire! Tenderness, yes; but no stirring of desire. Am I like my mother, a niggard in love?'

'You are all your father's child,' she said. 'And a child, indeed! Fourteen. It was over-young for the marriage-bed.'

'My mother was wed at fourteen. And Madam Queen Isabeau, too.'

'The one's a miser in love, the other's a wanton.' Her shrug dismissed them both. 'You're a more delicate breeder and must take your time. For all your fifteen years you're a child yet! When the time comes you'll give your heart and your soul; and, never fear, your body, too. You'll get great joy from love; or great sorrow—and God alone knows which it will be. So don't be in a hurry, child. And certainly this is no time to talk of love.'

She spread the loops of the ribbon and pinned the knot in the bosom of my light gown.

The gown looked more unsuitable than ever. The black knot set off the whiteness of my breasts. Isabeau herself, wantoning, could have done no better. I pulled it viciously from its place. Had I no better way of mourning John whom I should miss in every place? I should turn to show him this or that, but he would not be there; not in the garden where we had played, nor in church where we had prayed; nor yet in the bed where I had denied him.

'Beatrix,' I said, 'I wish I had been kinder; before God I do wish it! I am stubborn and self-willed—so my mother says; and you, yourself, at times. I set my will against John often and often ... and not only in the matter of our bed. And many a whipping he took for me. My heart breaks for it now.'

'Little cause for heartbreak,' she said. 'Never think you bent his will to yours. Did you know him so little, Jacque, my dear? He did not bend his will to anyone—not to your father, not even to your mother; and certainly not to you. Weak his body was; but his spirit was strong. He gave you your way because it pleased him; it was his own will to please you always; yes and to take your whippings, too. And the things you wanted were harmless enough—to hunt rather than to sit indoors over the chessboard; to dance rather than to play upon the lute; to chatter rather than listen while he read. Had you wanted anything wrong, why then you would have seen. You would have seen a man!'

'Yes,' I said. 'Yes. Of all Isabeau's sons, he alone was pure, he alone was good ... and I think he sits at God's footstool. Pray that he will put in a good word for me.'

'God judges for Himself, my heart.'

'Then I am lost. Oh Beatrix, I do desire to be good; to be obedient and gentle and serviceable. But I am my mother's child and my Burgundian blood is too strong. It defeats me; it defeats me, Beatrix. And so I must pray that John will whisper in God's ear.'

And then I remembered that though his gentle spirit was certainly in Heaven, his body lay cold in the room beyond. And remembering the gentleness of his eyes, and the kindness of his mouth; and the hands and feet so quick in my service that were now still for ever, 'I cannot bear it!' I cried out all wild with my grief, 'I cannot, cannot bear it!'

I swung round at the opening of the door.

It was my father. He knew. I saw it in his face as I ran into his arms.

'So the rumours about Isabeau have started again,' my mother said.

My father nodded. 'They say she poisoned John as well as Louis.'

'And I say so, too!' And she bent her hawk's eye upon my father.

'They're saying other things as well!' He outstared her with a cold blue eye. 'They're saying your brother of Burgundy poisoned John because the boy wouldn't jump to the whip, wouldn't agree to sell France to the English. Your brother has a pact with the English ... very secret.' He turned to me. 'I don't think your uncle had a hand in John's death, though he would have – had it suited him. As for Madam Isabeau, her reputation isn't sweet. Yet you saw her; cheeks raw and chapped with tears. Were they true tears, do you think? Is she a woman, for all her whoring, to poison her own sons?'

I said, 'Louis was weak enough to snuff himself out if he breathed too hard; why should she burden her conscience with him? And John.' I stopped, remembering my mother-in-law wailing and her voice all roughened with tears. *They took him from me ten years ago and he but seven years old. Ten long years. And I did not set eyes on him again until I saw him in this same Compiègne ... and he was dying. Sweet Christ save us such a death!*

'No,' I said, 'I don't believe it.'

'Then you show a sound judgment. For the truth is John died of a discharge in the ear.'

I nodded. And I remembered now, John sitting in the charette and cupping his ear with his hand. He had looked pale and heavy but he had not complained; he never complained.

'I am glad you show good judgment,' my father said. 'God knows you'll need it; and perhaps sooner than you think!'

There was something about him, a sadness strange to his gay spirit, so that even my mother turned a startled eye. 'What's on your mind?' she asked and her voice had lost some of its sharpness.

'Nothing,' he said and shook his head. 'Nothing.'

We were home again and I missed John at every turn. I could settle to nothing. My mother, impatient at seeing me downcast would rally me. 'Do you miss the French crown? We'll find you another as pretty, never fear!' I would do my best to smile, she had no love of a whey face; and the sting of her tongue could quickly turn white to red. So I never told her that I had dreaded nothing more than the French crown, the French court—the mad King, the bad Queen and my dark uncle of Burgundy. For the crown of France was gone and all its terrors with it. I was the Daughter of Holland. I asked nothing better than to rule when my time came—let it be long in coming!—in peace and in justice and in prosperity. John was a heavy price to pay for freedom; the French crown a light one.

These days there was a tenderness between my father and me; a tenderness on his side the deeper because it was to be so short—

though I did not know that then; a tenderness on mine because he looked so ill. He would walk a few steps and then stop, his face pale and shining with sweat; and then he would force himself on with dragging feet.

I knew he was sick; but I never believed that he was going to die—a man in the flower of his handsome manhood. Of course he would get well again! He *must* get well again! God would not take my father from me, too.

Nor would my mother admit things were bad. Once she came upon me, weeping; and when I stammered out that it grieved me to see him in pain, she cried out that he was well enough; and would recover soon. Girls with too much time on their hands were apt to grow fanciful! And I did not see that her sharpness covered her own fear.

'We must find you a husband,' she ended. And now it was my turn to cry out. It was too soon, too soon! But she pooh-poohed my nonsense. '*Daughter of Holland*—certainly you must marry again; and quickly. Besides, it's right for every woman to marry as soon as may be—unless she choose to bury herself alive in a nunnery. And that, I fancy, would not suit you at all!'

'I must marry, I don't question it,' I told her at once. 'But not yet; not just yet.'

'Fruit that's over-ripe rots quickly,' she said. 'There's no market for it.'

I said no more and so we left it. I must marry again; but I would not shame John's memory with a hasty marriage. On that I was determined. My mother must leave the matter for the present. I would ask my father to command it.

I remember I was standing by a window at the Hague Palace watching the birds flying and crying over the lake when I told him what my mother had said.

For a while he did not speak but stared out over the water as though the swooping and darting of birds were his sole concern. He turned at last and said slowly, 'God forgive me but I must speak ... while there is time. Don't trust your mother, Jacque. She's a de Charolais. To advance the honour of her house—her own house—she'd be without pity, without faith. One day you must stand against her. Your mother and your uncle of Burgundy! You must stand against them both ... and it may be, alone.'

I should have known then how near to death he was, but his

meaning was lost in surprise that he counselled me to defy my mother, I that had been trained to immediate obedience.

'This talk of marriage is no surprise,' he said. 'They've been plotting together—your mother and her brother—ever since John died.'

'It's too soon,' I told him as I had told her. 'Too soon.'

'Princes cannot stand upon niceness,' he said gently. 'For the sake of this country, its peace—its very existence as a free people—you must marry again and soon.' He took my hand. 'Those two have chosen your husband; and it is not the one I have chosen. If you wait too long I may not be here to speak in the matter.'

And now he had spoken so plainly of his death my heart turned over. He was my father; he had always been there. What should I do lacking him?

'The groom they have chosen is your cousin of Brabant,' he said.

'No!' I cried out at once. 'He's too young.'

'Too young, too feeble-mind and body. A bad marriage; and you must not make it. You must not make it, Jacque. Marriage must secure the succession to you and to your children. The Brabant marriage will do neither. Brabant is under the thumb of Burgundy; and it is Burgundy that will rule, not you, Jacque, not you. Dutch necks beneath the Burgundian heel! It would haunt me—heaven or hell.

'As for children, I doubt Brabant will give you an heir—he's rotten stock. And he'll never make old bones! He's riddled with the sickness that comes from loose living. He'll die long before you, as far as man can see; and he'll hand you and your inheritance over to Burgundy. If you take Brabant then you are lost; and your inheritance is lost, all, all lost.'

'I would not marry Brabant if he were the last man in Christendom; and you may set your mind at rest. But if I must marry—who shall it be? Who?'

He said slow and doubtful, 'There's been an offer from England. King Henry offers his brother.'

The King of England's brother! There was a marriage, indeed! And I remembered a young man who had come to our court, a debonair young man, bowing over the hand of a solemn child as though she were a woman and a beauty.

'Gloucester!' And I hardly knew I had said the name.

'Not Gloucester. Not Gloucester,' he said at once. 'The Brabant marriage would be bad; but marriage with Gloucester, worse. Oh he's charming; clever, too. But there's no principle of good in him. He'd split this land in pieces like an orange and suck each piece dry. Not Gloucester. Bedford.'

'No!' I said at once. I had heard of Bedford—a great fighting-man, hard hand, hard head, hard heart.

'He's a good man; but not for you, perhaps ... not for you. No foreign marriage—be the man never so true—would hold this land together. Jacque, my child, I have been thinking and thinking long. You must take one of our own nobles.'

One of our own nobles! A come-down, indeed, from the royal house of England.

I said quickly, 'That would not suit my mother at all.'

He looked down into my face. 'Nor you neither, it seems—not so glorious as the English marriage, I admit. But it would suit Holland very well. It would be a good marriage, a right marriage. Think, child! A strong man, respected alike by Hooks and Cods. He would keep the land in peace for you and for your children.'

I could not speak for disappointment. At last I said, slow and grudging, 'And which gentleman have you in mind?'

He looked at me very steady. 'Van Borselen,' he said.

The Zealander, more bitter than most against our Bavarian blood! Van Borselen, leader of the Cods, a hard man; a most harsh pride. *Van Borselen!* I could not believe it.

'You would give me into the hand of the *Cods*?'

'I would join your hands,' he said, 'to keep the land in peace.'

I said bitter, 'And if van Borselen refuse? Do I offer myself to his brother? Or to van Arkels? Or to whichever Cod will take me? I am a woman—do you forget it?'

'You are a prince,' he said. 'And I think you forget it. For what is a queen, even, but a piece to move here and there as best suits the game. And if the queen is not played shrewdly then she is lost—and all is lost. Think of it, Jacque; but do not think too long. Time passes ... it passes.'

III

My father was a very sick man; even my mother could no longer deny it; now he could not endure the coming and the going at the Hague, nor yet the bustle of the smaller court at le Quesnoy. He longed for Bouchain and the quiet house he loved.

I shall never forget that journey. He tried to ride; but soon he let them carry him to the charette. He lay back on the cushions, his teeth clenched so that there was blood upon his lips; and, as the carriage jolted him this way and that, his face that had been white, took on a blue look and glazed.

At Bouchain he went straight to bed and his surgeon was summoned. I was waiting in his dressing-room when I saw them take the bloody cloths away. It was late evening and a blackbird singing, and the hawthorns shaking their scent into the Maytime air, when my mother came out of the bedchamber.

'That old bite!' she said, brisk; but her eyes were troubled. 'They have lanced the swelling to let out the poison, and soon he will be well again.'

'Please God!' I said. If only my father would get well, I would build a chapel here at Bouchain. And I would furnish it with gold and silver; and I would endow it ... but one must not try to buy God. My confessor had told me that when I was a little child, running to God all eager with my requests and my offerings. Then dear God, I promised, I will build You a chapel whether my father gets well or not ... but let him get well!

When I saw him next day I knew he was not going to get well.

'Come, never look so sad,' he told me smiling, and all the time his teeth clenched against the pain. 'A bite ... a little bite ... long ago.' And there was wonder in his voice.

The old bite. Those that had called my betrothal ill omened had been right. My young husband was dead; and now my father was dying of the mishap that had befallen him riding thither.

The next day I did not see him at all; but there was a constant procession, not only surgeons and priests, but nobles and councillors summoned to his bed. I knew then that all hope was hopeless.

'My father left the Hague for peace,' I told my mother all angry with my grief. 'Why do they trouble him with all the coming and going in his bedchamber?'

She hesitated; she said, and her voice had lost its sharpness, 'He is calling upon his nobles and his burghers to give their loyalty to you.'

'Loyalty? I am the Daughter of Holland! Who can withhold it?'
'Those that are anxious for your shoes. Your father's brother for one. He's had a greedy eye on your inheritance this long while.'

'But he's a priest ... a bishop!'

'Bishop-elect only. And itches to change a mitre for a crown.'

'I am Daughter of Holland,' I said again, 'I am my father's heir.'

'It's not as simple as that,' she said. 'Would God it were! Your father holds his countships under the Emperor; and the Emperor may count it a male fief. In that case it is not you that would inherit ... but your father's brother.'

That, I, Daughter of Holland, might be set aside was a new thought; and a frightening one. With his death, I lost, it would seem, not only a beloved father but maybe my inheritance as well. I had been brought up from babyhood as my father's heir; my whole training, my whole mind, had been directed to that end. To lose that inheritance would be like losing a hand or a foot—my whole life maimed.

I had no more tears to shed; stony-eyed, this early summer's day, I watched the stream of men passing in and out of the sick room. Some I knew well; others not at all.

First and foremost, my father's brother of whom my mother had spoken—John of Bavaria, bishop-elect of Liége, with his dark, cruel face. My father had summoned him to swear protection to me, his young niece and hereditary prince. Oh he would swear and swear again, but would he keep that promise? I looked into his face and had my answer.

I saw him as he came from the sick room. His cold eye picked me out where I stood in the shadow of an alcove. He came over and bowed over my hand and smiled as if to comfort me. But his smile frightened me more than his scowl—a dog's grin. Hard to believe the same loins had sired this man and my father.

A little later my mother's brother, my uncle of Burgundy, strode in. I had not even known he was expected; my mother must have sent for him days ago; yes, even while she was making little of my father's sickness.

I stood up as he came out but he gave me neither word nor look. Perhaps he did not see me, for his lips smiled a little, which was not fitting, coming as he did from a dying man.

Between my Bavarian uncle whom men called *the Pitiless* and my Burgundian uncle whom they called *the Fearless*, I was likely to fare ill. *Blessed St James intercede for me* ... I found myself praying to my patron saint that my father might even now be spared; and this time I prayed for myself, too.

These bitter days I could not bring myself to leave the anteroom. If my father had strength to see all these strangers, surely he must send for me, his child!

Half-hidden in my corner I would watch them go into the room; and through the half-open door I could see my father's face as the chamberlain spoke their names.

First came the great family of van Brederodes that are sprung from the same stock as myself, loyal to the core—Gysbrecht, the fighting bishop of Utrecht that had both christened and married me, Reynolde Lord of Vianen, and between them William Lord of Brederode head of their house, that grim fighting-man and my father's dear comrade in arms. I saw my father's sick face lighten as he went in. Then followed Renald Duke of Juilliers, a most turbulent man, with his kinsmen the great van Arkels, father and son; and, on their heels, the Lord of Egmont. Rich men these, of ancient family; men of weight with burgher and with peer. I prayed St James that their hearts would turn to me; but I saw the sorrow in my father's face as they went out and had no hope of them. But my heart lifted a little when Everhard of Hoogtwoude and Lewis of Flushing went in together and I saw the tenderness in my father's face. His own sons, these; begotten when the blood was hot and his stamp was upon them both. Fine men, upright and true. My brothers—and I thanked God for them.

And so the days wore on; and the long procession came and went. Didier van der Merwen came with the old Lord of Sevenbergen, and Arnold of Eienburch and many another I had known from child-hood, good Hook nobles all. But my heart knew its enemies too. William Lord of Ysselstein and William of Lochorst, and other Cods with them; and all of them whispering together ... and nothing good to me.

It was the evening that my father died and summer dusk darkening the room when two men came in together; tall men with a cold, grave air—brothers it was well-seen. That they were great lords was not to be doubted; there was power about them and pride. Many of our nobles wear something of this look; but in these it was deep-ened, as though their very being was distilled from pride. Who they might be I did not know; that they were not friends, was certain. They did not carry themselves like friends come to bid their dying lord *Farewell*.

If there was great pride in them, there was, I fancied, great integrity, too. I half-put out a hand to them as they went by; but they did not see me hidden in my place.

If I had gone forward, shown them my tears and my need, would my life have been different? Who can say? They were hard men and proud; and they were set against my father and his house ... and I stayed in my place and I let them go by.

I heard the low murmur of voices in the next room; my father was trying to persuade them to friendship. But it was all useless. I heard the clear *No!*

Who were they, these proud men, these men of power? Outside the anteroom a page lounged, wearing a livery I did not know.

'Who are those two that went in just now?' I asked.

He looked at me in contempt; and that was not surprising. If I did not know his master, he did not know me, unkempt as I was and stained with my tears, my plain gown crumpled where I had fallen asleep in my chair.

He said, insolent, 'It is not to be expected you should know them. They are no friends to this house. The taller is my master the Lord Frank van Borselen, Seigneur of Zealand, and the other, his brother Floris.'

Lord Frank van Borselen. The man my father desired for my husband—the cold, proud man. I felt my heart shrink within me. As a husband—no, no! But as a friend—? And I remembered the way he had carried himself, an air, it seemed to me of triumph, that his enemy lay dying and he, himself proud and strong. And I remembered the sharp *No*. Neither husband nor friend here! Living or dying, neither my father nor I would ever win his favour.

'You may well stare!' And the boy was contemptuous as though he spat. 'My lords come not in friendship—though the Bavarian seeks to decoy them. And the decoy?' There was a lasciviousness about him. 'A hen. A plump white hen for my lord Frank. Well that cock's particular. He'll not step this hen and you may tell your mistress so; and, moreover ...'

The words died in his throat. He stood staring, mouth slack, high colour faded to a sickly green.

'You'll end your days without a tongue if you put it to such foul use,' Frank van Borselen said. It was a low voice, no trace of anger in it; yet frightening by its very quiet.

'This is a house of mourning—or soon will be. You shame me with your loose talk. Your pardon, mistress,' but his eyes did not see me. I might have been any serving woman, save that our wenches are neat and fresh. 'It is a low fellow and has much to learn—if he have the wit!'

The brothers strode off without a backward look and left me standing there.

I stood looking after them. And now my hand was held out towards them. Enemies to me and mine. But there was a justice in them and a courtesy and I coveted them for friends. But it was too

24

late. They neither turned nor slackened and I was left standing with my empty hand.

He'll not step this hen, this plump white hen ...

My hand fell to my side. I knew now what the boy meant.

Beatrix coming in to call me for supper found me crouched in the dark. She put out a hand; her fingers lifted my chin, felt the wetness of my face. 'Jacque, my dear, my darling! This is a time of sorrow for you ... and for us all!'

I turned away my face and she said no more; only her hand stroked the tangle of my hair.

I said, 'Do you know the tale of the cock and the hen, the plump white hen?'

'No,' she said, 'is it a good tale?' and she was puzzled. 'It depends if you're cock or hen.'

She said, 'I was never good at riddles. Come, Jacque, speak plain.'

'A barnyard jest—' and I began to tremble.

She said, 'When we're overthrown with grief so very little hurts us! You had best tell me, Jacque.'

So then I told her, sitting there in the dark and she stroking my hair.

'You are not clever, Jacque,' she said. 'This van Borselen refused not you, but your father. Why, he never set eyes on you in his life! Come, sweetheart, do a few words from a foulmouthed boy distress you? The Lord of Borselen showed how all clean men must think, friend or foe! And, if you were yourself, you'd see that plainly. Your father thinks of you; your happiness, your safety, your greatest good. And that's the good of the country; the two go together. Van Borselen leads the Cods. Gain him—and you gain the Cods. Your father sought to make an enemy into a friend. Is that so shameful?'

'It is shameful to be offered to a man and be refused.'

'Nonsense,' she said, crisp. 'Princes are bartered every day; they are the common coin of affairs. If shame there is, it isn't yours. It rests with the man that values enmity above his country's peace, that grows fat on bloodshed ...

'He's a lean man,' I said. 'Very cold and proud.'

'Would you have taken him if he had said Yes?'

'As a friend—with all my heart! As a husband—I should have obeyed my father. But I should have wished myself dead first.'

'You cannot have it both ways,' she said. 'And this is the best way.'

I nodded. 'He was my father's enemy and now he is mine. It is good to know enemy from friend.'

I was eating my supper, and every mouthful fit to choke me, when my father's summons came.

He lay white in the warm glow of the cressets; and their flickering light moved upon the hollows of his cheek. Already he wore a remote, cold look.

The physician stood up and came to me where I stood in the doorway. 'You must let him say what he will, my lady. Do not try to stop him. Until he has finished he will not allow himself to die ... and he is very tired. His mind is clear and he has saved himself for this purpose. Every now and then you must moisten his lips.' He nodded towards a cup with a feather lying across it. 'I shall be in the next room if you need me.'

He went out and I crossed over and knelt by the bed.

For a while my father said nothing, only he searched my face with his eyes—eyes that had been so gay and were dark now with the shadow of death. They clung to my face as though they could never be done looking.

'Child,' he said at last, 'little Jacque.' His voice was faint but the words came clear. 'Friends are gathering. Enemies ... enemies, too. The Emperor ...' He shook his doubtful head. 'Your uncles ...' he shrugged wearily—a shadow of that quick shrug of his. 'Poor child! My brother has promised; but ...' he shook his head again from side to side. '*Watch the bishop.* Once we played together you and I ... but it's a game no longer. Watch the bishop, watch my brother, Jacque. And watch the knight—the knight that doesn't jump straight; that's your uncle of Burgundy. Never trust him. Oh he'll promise, promise—but never trust him. Our lands march too close with his ... too close ...'

For a while he said no more but lay there, his face twitching with pain; at last he spoke again. 'Your mother and her brother ... stand against them both ... you *must*. Hard ... hard ... but you must do it!'

His eyelids fluttered down and I moistened his lips with the wine. At last he spoke again.

'You cannot stand alone. Listen ... do you *listen?* You must marry as I said ... you ... must ... marry...'

I took in my breath knowing the name that must come.

'Van Borselen,' he said and his eyes were fixed on me. 'He has refused,' I said.

'Ask ... again. *You* must ask.'

I said nothing. *Offer myself? Be refused again?*

'Hard,' he said. 'But not too hard ... nothing too hard ... for the people. Your duty, Jacque ... your *duty!*' And his eyes besought me.

'England?' I entreated him. 'What of England?'

He shook a fretful head. 'No foreign hand ... even the just hand. I know ... I know ...' He was murmuring now, no longer clear. 'I fought ... for peace ... all my life. But—' he lifted his own hand, looked at it, let it fall again. 'No foreign hand ...' He lay there whispering to himself.

Suddenly his voice came clear—for the last time clear. 'Ask, ask van Borselen,' and fixed me with his darkening eyes.

'Yes,' I said. 'Yes.' And then, 'If he refuse me?'

The lids had fallen. I knelt down and whispered urgently in his ear, 'If he refuses me—what then?'

But there was no answer. He had my promise; it was enough.

It was very late now but I could not go to bed. My heart was full of grief and burdened with its troubles. I knelt beseeching heaven for the passing of my father's soul.

Sunlight was full in the room when Beatrix' hand upon my shoulder awakened me.

'You should come now,' she said, very gentle; her eyes were sunk deep into their sockets with grief—she was his daughter, too.

My father lay flat upon his back, the nose sharpened in his face and the dreadful sound of his breathing rattled like chains—chains he would soon cast off. My mother knelt by his side; he did not know her and he did not know me. His fingers were plucking; and between the rattle of his breathing I caught his muttering ... *crooked knight ... crooked bishop ... crooked ... crooked.* His hand moved dimly as though to take a piece from the board—and it was as though he took my heart in his hand.

The hand dropped.

'Bouchain ...' he muttered ... 'Bouch ... ain ...' And all the time the dreadful chain rattled in his chest.

I did not know what he meant but my mother did. She bent over him in the great bed—the bed she had once shared with him. 'Yes,' she said; and it was a voice I had never heard in her before ... or since; very gentle. 'At Bouchain. I promise.' And she bent and kissed his cold mouth.

IV

May thirty-first, in the year of grace fourteen hundred and seventeen my father entered his rest. His body was carried back to the Hague and through the towns as we passed and along the countryside, the people came out to pay their last homage. 'Their true homage is to stand by his daughter,' my mother said, grim. 'Well, God be praised you have your uncle of Burgundy! Give thanks for my brother of Burgundy.'

And knowing my mother, and knowing her brother, I felt more desolate than ever. In six short weeks I had lost both husband and father. My mother I had never found easy to love; now, since my father's dying words, I distrusted her. What did a mere daughter matter, or the whole of Holland for that matter, against the glory of the dukes of Burgundy?

My father's heart enclosed in a casket had been sent back to Bouchain; it was there he had been happiest. To send his heart home; that was the promise my mother had given when, breathing the word *Bouchain*, he had died. She was always one to keep a promise—if she lost nothing by it!

And now my father being dead and done with, she lost no time in busying herself about my marriage. The Brabant marriage. The marriage my father had warned me against. But how could I, an ignorant girl, stand against my formidable mother and her terrible brother?

Beatrix van Conengiis showed me the way.

'You must send for the Lord Frank van Borselen,' she said.

I stood there flushing and paling, remembering how I had been offered ... and refused; and the coarse jests the young lad had learned, maybe of the master himself, for all my Lord's fine talk!

Beatrix said, 'I would give my life to serve you, Jacque. But not my life nor a thousand lives will serve while Cods and Hooks tear the land in pieces.' And then, when still I did not answer, she said softly, 'It was our father's wish.'

It was the first time—as it was to be the last time—she ever mentioned her relationship to him or me. This gentle heart of my own blood seeking nothing for itself, moved my hard pride. I said, 'I will send for him.'

Frank van Borselen came at my summons. He stood before me, upright, arrogant and solid as a rock. My father had been right—a man to lean on. But he would not take me though it made him Lord of Holland and all my lands. Steel against steel and the bright blood flowing was more to his mind.

'It is an honour I must decline.' He bowed stiffly. 'It is a pity so fair a lady should ask twice.' He bowed again and I saw the mockery in his eyes. If ever he came into my hands he should pay for that!

My father's brother, my priest-uncle of Bavaria, came and knelt, offering homage. His lips were cold and dry upon my hand. I thanked him for his love. At the word his pale eyes glittered. My mother said when he had departed, 'He's not called *the Pitiless* for nothing—the good bishop-elect! If you're not careful—and very careful—everything you possess and you, yourself; also, will be crammed into his maw.'

My uncle of Burgundy came offering his protection. I listened while he spread before me the advantages of the Brabant marriage. It was as though he held before a child a honey-cake. And all the time I remembered how my father had said that the young duke was under Burgundy's thumb.

I thanked him too. 'I will think over what you have said,' I promised. 'But I do not mean to marry so soon. It would show poor respect for my husband's memory and for my father's, too.'

'You show poor respect for your own commonsense,' he answered, rough, and deliberately turned his back and left the room.

My mother at once took up the tale. 'We think only of your good,' she said. 'We are persuaded you should marry my godson, your cousin of Brabant. His land marches with ours—a stepping-stone between Holland and Hainault.'

'A stepping-stone may slip from your feet and land you in the water,' I said.

She flushed; her right hand made a movement I knew well. But I was no longer a child to be punished. I was Madam the reigning prince. In my hand lay gifts of land and gold; even in anger her thrifty soul remembered it.

She said, pleasantly, 'This stone would not slip from your feet; it would hold them firm.' And then her Burgundian impatience broke through. 'Oh,' she cried, 'we do not talk of stones but of my godson—a fine young man. See for yourself!' And she held out a little painting on a riband.

'A pretty boy,' I said, careless, 'but over-young!'

'And how old are you, young Madam? Sixteen—and he already fourteen! Two years—what's that? Listen, my girl! It's no bad thing to have a husband younger than yourself; to have an obedient husband is useful—as you may find!'

'My father commanded me to marry a *man*; a man to carry my affairs. He hated the Brabant marriage. He warned me against it.'

She lost her look of smiling good nature.

'He was not capable of judging. Listen! He *wanted* the Brabant marriage. It was his idea from the beginning. *He* wanted it and then he turned his back on it. Why? Because sick men are inconstant. And then he wanted the English marriage—I expect he told you about it; and he turned his back on *that*! This Dutch marriage was his last whim—a sick man's whim. And, given time, he'd have turned his back on that, too. Will you offer yourself for a third slap in the face from van Borselen?'

My cheeks burned as though he had, indeed, struck me. But I could not believe her tale of a sick man's whim. I told her, 'He knew well what he said—and you know it. If not, why did you send his heart back to Bouchain?'

'It was a thing long understood between us.' She seized her chance. 'I have always obeyed your father's wishes. But in this matter of your marriage he did not know what he said—he was too sick. Besides ... there's a thing he didn't know. There's another husband for you—and one you may not be able to escape!' She stopped; she said slowly and clearly, 'Your uncle of Bavaria!'

I stared at her and my flesh crawled.

'I could not lie about such a thing,' she said, 'could not even think it for myself. By Christ and His Sweet Mother, I speak the truth.'

'My father's brother!' I said at last. 'A *priest*!' And could not tell which set my flesh crawling more. 'It isn't possible!'

'It's possible enough; and may well happen—unless you yourself put it out of the question by marrying first. Uncle-priest will cast off his priesthood; his envoys are even now in Rome. And the next thing will be a dispensation for the forbidden degree of blood. You will see!'

I saw ... I saw. An old man. Cruel eye, cruel heart. *The Pitiless*. A man so near in blood ... incest.

'Uncle and priest!' I said as though the words were a talisman against threatened horror.

'Pin-pricks, merely. The Pope will make short work of both. But

an old man pickled in blood and a handsome youth! Even if everything else were decent and clean it shouldn't be hard to choose
between them. And further; if you take Brabant, my brother will
stand by you.'

I said nothing. Between *John the Pitiless* and *John the Fearless* I was
likely to fare ill.

'Van Borselen has refused—twice refused,' she reminded me softly.
'The English marriage has fallen through; and your uncle of Bavaria
means to thrust you into an incestuous bed. So you see there is no
one, no one at all but your cousin of Brabant. And he's ready and
waiting.'

'Then he must wait a little longer,' I cried out. 'I must think. I
must *think*!' And I wanted nothing more at this moment than to be
rid of her. I was shaken to the soul by this new horror. If I married
my cousin of Brabant I should be safe from that! But my father had
warned me against the marriage, he had *warned* me ... But then he had
known nothing of this new suitor—this incestuous uncle of mine.

'Don't keep Brabant waiting too long, unless you are anxious for
your uncle's bed!' she said.

I did not answer. I went over and held the door for her. For the
first time in my life I dismissed my mother.

I came back into the room sick and shaken. From the table the
little picture smiled at me—a young face, delicate and fine. The grave
eyes looking steadily out upon the world reminded me of my young
dead husband; and that was no wonder, seeing they had been cousins.
The mouth I thought girlish with its pretty red; girlish, too, the light
curling hair falling about a high collar of rose tissue. A very pretty
young man. But would those pretty hands be strong enough to hold
my inheritance fast? Well, if they were not, my uncle of Burgundy
would strengthen them. For the rest, young or old, handsome or
plain, I would take any man before my father's brother. But still I
walked about the room crying within myself, I must think ... I must
think!

You must stand against your mother. Even now I could not easily cast
away my father's warning. And while still I walked thinking first this
way and then that, the door was flung open and my mother burst
into the room.

To dispense with ceremony was unlike her; but her grave look, and
the way the quick breath came and went, were excuse enough.

'Your marriage must wait a little,' she said. 'First things, first; and
the first thing is to take homage as hereditary prince. There's no time

to lose. The Emperor means to reject your rights. He means to name a new prince in your place!'

So there at least, she had spoken true! Was it possible I might trust her?

'I hear,' and she fixed me with her eyes, 'he's about to name your loving uncle of Bavaria.' And the way she said *loving* turned my blood cold.

'Well,' she said, very brisk, 'if we move fast enough we may yet put a spoke in uncle-bishop's wheel. We start on your progress at once. We take the oath first at Hainault and work our way north.'

Of all my subjects the Hainaulters were the most loyal; of all places, Hainault the most dear. My father had warned me against her, this most subtle woman; but I forgot his warning when she spoke.

'Yes,' she said thoughtful, as though she had not already worked it out step by step with her brother. 'The first homage is Mons; we set out tomorrow, as soon as it's light. Every day lost is a day gained to the enemy.'

'Twelve days since my father died,' I told Beatrix busy about my clothes. 'Twelve little days, and no time to weep—time only to busy myself with affairs.'

'They were his affairs too,' she said. 'Hold fast to your inheritance; it was his dying wish.'

'Does a man see clearer for dying, or does death cloud the clear mind? He foresaw evil from the Brabant marriage. But the more fearful evil—marriage with his own brother—he did not foresee.'

She crossed herself.

'I don't know which way to turn or what to do. If I obey my father and refuse Brabant then I'm in the worst danger of all, danger to my soul. Marriage with my father's brother! Would the Pope allow so vile a thing?'

'If the Pope allows it, then it's no longer vile—or so men will tell you. But the heart knows its own law. By that law it would be a most wicked marriage.'

'Then I must take my cousin of Brabant.'

'He's in the forbidden degree, too,' she said. And when I protested that a cousin is not an uncle and more natural to take to one's bed, she said, 'Still there must be a dispensation for that, too; and so you are forced to leave the matter a while. Make your progress. Things may take another turn, a new suitor, who knows?'

'My uncle of Burgundy will not stand by me unless I take Brabant,' I said.

'Do you trust him to stand by you? Your father warned you against him.'

'Who else is there? And my father was a sick man.'

'You've looked too long at a pretty picture,' she said. 'Jacque, don't make light of your father's warning. I think he forgot nothing.'

We rode out on a gay June morning in the midst of an armed escort, lest the Cods attack, or my bishop-uncle break through like a wolf to carry me off. We avoided cities for the most part, and so on Sunday morning, June thirteenth in the year of our Lord fourteen hundred and seventeen we rode into Mons.

A great procession had come out to meet us and to bring us within the city—the burgomaster and the bishops, and behind them the churchmen and the knights, the merchants and the gild-masters. The sun shone upon jewelled crosses and gold chains, upon cloth-of-gold and the rich furnishings of horses. But—and here is a strange thing!—at the moment we rode through the gateway, the weather suddenly changed. Dark clouds blackened the summer sky, rain began to fall; not the warm drops that are welcome and soon dry, but a sharp and bitter rain. Thunder growled and lightning broke. And, as we rode in, banners that should have flown, dripped limp; and the garlands stretched across the streets from window to window, were ruined; flowers fell broken, colour streamed from ribands, and our horses slithered upon cobbles all slippery with rain and crushed petals.

But, for all that, the church bells rang out; and we rode on, I smiling and bowing through streets so crowded that I must hold my breath against the stench. Yet, in spite of the joybells and the cheering, I knew the thought that spoiled the pleasure of all, gentle and simple alike; I knew it by the sinking of my own heart. *Ill-omen: ill-omen*. And though I tried to laugh it away for what was this but a trick of weather we should not have noticed any other time?—still I felt it in my bones.

Ill-omen.

And so dripping in our finery, we reached the church; one must pay one's duty first to God. And as I knelt at the altar of St Waltrude and made my vows over the sacred relics, my heart lightened a little.

I was to make other entries—greater cities, more gorgeous processions ... and finer weather; but this, in my own beloved city of Mons was the first and dearest. I was shaken to the soul, as I vowed to God that of all His servants, I would be the most obedient, the most faithful, the most humble.

It was a vow, alas, I did not keep.

When we rode out from church the rain had stopped but the sun not yet come from behind the clouds. The day was cheerless as our procession rode to the stadthouse.

I sat in my high place while, offering homage, came the Chancellor of Hainault leading his Privy Council; the princes of the church followed in all their splendour, abbess and prioress richly gowned as any lady of the court, though more sober in hue; thereafter came my nobles, each in his degree. And all sealed their homage with a kiss.

And now it was the turn of the burghers. Our burghers—by old custom—do not kiss hands. The Burgomaster reads the oath aloud and each man raises his arm in assent. So there I sat, a waving forest of arms saluting me—and it was the most moving moment of all. For though nobles and churchmen strengthen a sovereign, it is upon the goodwill of the people that the crown rests; we Dutch have always known it.

And now it was my turn to pledge my faith. I rose and read aloud my promises, reciting the privileges and rights of Mons.

And this oath made between sovereign and people upon the *Joyous Entry* is not to be broken except by death; and, if it should be broken, then ill-luck follows and the wrath of God.

Then followed the feast where we sat far into the night; and, after a few hours in bed where I was unable to sleep for weariness and excitement, we took horse for Soignies.

And so it went on, city after city. At le Quesnoy where I had played with John, I gave him my tears ... and I forgot him again as we rode on.

The Joyous Entry. Day after day I played my part, smiling and gracious, thrusting down my tears and my fears—there was little time for either. My bones would be aching long before Beatrix could put me to bed. But I was happy. How could my uncle of Bavaria harm me when my people loved me so? I laid aside my grief for father; and I forgot the gentle boy that had been my husband; he belonged to the child Jacque; the woman was dreaming of another John—John of Brabant.

I was not quite sixteen, and in the springtime of my pretty looks. I was fêted, I was loved. I, that had been a child beneath my mother's thumb, was now meeting my people face to face; I was learning my cities and their customs. Sometimes I would be led to the belfry where, with my own hands, I must ring the bells; and the joyous sounds ringing out from under my hands sealed the contract of love between the city and me.

Sometimes I was made to sit in the judge's seat according to old custom, to show that from me and me alone came the law. But though my mouth pronounced sentence, the words were whispered in my ear by those learned in the law.

'You have done not so ill,' my mother said in her grudging Burgundian way. 'It is no bad thing for a sovereign to be young and not uncomely—as long as she submits herself to those that are older and wiser. And be not puffed up. It's a love easy to win; easier to lose. Be careful that you keep it.'

And then, suddenly, my dream of the people's love was rudely shattered.

The Emperor, though he had not yet chosen my uncle in my place, made public his refusal to recognize me; and the Cod nobles supported him. They would not accept me—my father's daughter. In the Ysselstein fortress the Cods were gathering.

I sat listening to the messengers, quiet, as becomes a ruler; but anger getting the better of me, I sprang up crying, 'Let them stay there till I come! With God's help I will teach them a lesson they will not soon forget!'

Through the hot summer weather my messengers rode out to summon my friends—south through loyal Hainault; north to Holland and to Friesland whose homage I had not yet taken. And, I myself, following northward, would not allow myself to be cast down; as we rode my courage strengthened. From city and from castle my Hook nobles streamed to meet me—the Lord of Brederode that had been my father's captain and was now mine; a heart as wide as a church door and the cunning of a fox. And with him his son Reynolde Lord of Vianen that was to shelter me in my dire need; and the young Louis de Montfort faithfullest of knights and his kinsman the Stadtholder of Holland himself. And more fighting-men than I can name here, though their names are written in my heart—Philip son of Claes that fine soldier and Hubert of Culambourgh with his wily tongue. And best of all Gysbrecht the fighting bishop of Utrecht to give us the blessing of the church. Strong arm and loyal heart, all!

So from Mons to Ghent we rode and thence to Delft and Leyden, to Amsterdam and Haarlem. Already the summer fields were scarred with the sickness of war—fire blackening the green corn, trees bearing deadly fruit of hanged men; ravages of the enemy, and that enemy my own people. Tears would spring to my eyes; anger dry them before they fell. I would put an end to the quarrelling and the ravages, so help me, God! And turning in the saddle, I would look back at the swelling numbers of my forces—at my brothers Everhard and William and Lewis riding ahead of their men, not holding against my father's child the bend sinister in their shields as lesser men might have done.

And with my father's bastard sons, his bastard brothers, honourable men, great in heart and in dignities—Adrian of Dordrecht, William of Medemblik, William Lord of Schagen and Albert his brother. And I honoured them all, honouring in them my father and my grandfather that had bred these men to be my strength and my courage.

V

My mother had been wrong about my uncle of Bavaria, or so it appeared. I was to learn—and in no long time neither—that her wits were sharper than my own. Now I could see nothing but that he had come marching from his estates in Zealand, and his fighting strength behind him.

'You see!' I told her. 'He's loyal! He was the first to take the oath; he takes his stand with us! As for the other thing ... marriage—' and I could hardly bring myself to name the abomination, 'gossip and scandal! He's not free of his priest's vows nor asked to be free.'

'Not yet,' she said and nothing more.

These days I would ride about the camp encouraging my men and thanking them for their love of me. And, night and day, I would kneel beseeching God—not for my own sake that was all unworthy, but for the sake of my people that they might live in peace—that He would be with me in this first trial of strength between me and my enemy and give us the victory.

And He heard me. Ysselstein fell. It was mid-July and high summer, just before my sixteenth birthday. But, even while I knelt, thanking God for his mercy, the stench of burning rose to trouble my heart.

It was my first glimpse of warfare and the beastliness that takes hold of men.

They had given the city to the fire. When I saw the flame lick upward with a thousand tongues, and the masonry crumble like a castle of sand, and the woodwork flaming like banners to heaven; when I saw the poor wretches that had not been able to escape and were left to burn, I could no longer endure to look but turned and fled, my ears stuffed against their crying.

'A man must use the victories God sends him,' my priest-uncle said, his cold eyes wild with excitement, his hands slippery with blood. And, with those same wet hands, he forced my fingers from my ears and turned me back again. And there I must stand, staring upon the burning fortress, though my heart turned over with the stench of burning flesh ... but afterwards I was not so squeamish.

We had won our first victory; but I was too green to see it was my uncle's victory, not mine, and that he would know well how to use it.

We rode joyfully northwards. And now it was not only nobles that came to join us, but the common folk—prentice and ploughboy, eager in my defence; and craftsmen offering the skill of their hands; and farmers and fisherfolk offering such food as they could spare. From Enkhuisen, from Hoorn, from Monnickendam and Volendam, loyal hearts followed us all the way.

But, back again in the Hague palace, for all this first victory, my heart was sore. I had seen a noble fortress given to the flames; now I must hear the names of those fallen in my defence. I found Beatrix in a black gown, pale-faced and drawn. Her husband Gillis van Conengiis had fallen at Ysselstein. 'Stop weeping like a fountain!' my mother said, contemptuous. 'You'll take another husband soon enough—and a better one maybe!'

I found her harshness intolerable; yet she spoke with a shrewd tongue. Beatrix wept bitter tears for Gillis, and then, tears spent, took the Lord van Vliet to husband and bloomed afresh.

It was not only for the destruction and the slaughter that I grieved; it was for the punishments I must decree—the scourgings and the maimings and the hangings; yes and for the burnings and the buryings alive. I was still a few days from my sixteenth birthday, and must bow to the will of those wiser than I. My uncle, the pitiless priest, told me that neither he nor any man would fight for me if I threw my victories away. And good men like van Brederode, assured me that mercy was no mercy when it encouraged my foes and wasted the sacrifices of my friends.

So I ordered the punishments and argued no more. But the scourgings and the hangings drove away sleep. In my dreams I would see a man that had been upstanding and strong, dragging his broken bones upon the ground and I would cry out and wake to find my cheeks wet with tears. Or the stink of burning flesh would come between me and my food and I would turn away sickened. Or I would stop my breath to know how it must feel when they cast the earth upon the living body; and when it seemed my eyes must burst from their sockets and my heart crack in my breast then I would open my mouth and thank God that I might breathe still of His sweet air.

No, whatever men say of the cruelties commanded in my name, I swear by Christ that my heart was unwilling.

'Rebellion must be put down with a hard hand' my mother would say, hearing that I cried out in my sleep. 'You'll get used to it. You take it harder because you've nothing else to think about!'

'What else could I think about?' I asked, shaken still with the punishments my lips had spoken.

'Marriage,' she said. 'It's time—unless you long for an unnatural bed. At any moment your uncle of Bavaria will be free of his priestly vows; I have private words from friends in Rome. And you know what his next step will be! But we must work fast. My messengers wait to ride to Rome with letters praying for dispensation between you and your cousin of Brabant; they wait only for your nod. Give it; and you can be safely married before the renegade priest can move in the matter. And if what's done doesn't please him, you'll have your mother and your uncle of Burgundy to stand by you.'

Then, seeing that I hesitated still, she said, 'How long will you wait? If once the Pope declares that marriage with your uncle of Bavaria is for the peace of Christendom, then neither I nor my brother can stand by you; no, nor the Hook lords neither. All, all must bow to the Pope. You'll be left, I'm afraid, to stew in your own broth.'

I stood there wondering why I hesitated. I would die rather than marry my uncle and I was already half-in-love with Brabant's picture. But ...

She knew my thoughts. She said, 'Your father told you I desire this marriage because your lands and the Brabant lands march all together and because both are convenient to my brother's eye. Well, that's true. I do desire it. But for your sake—for yours alone. Where there's union there's strength. But, if it were not so; if there were no need of union for strength, still, as Christ hears me, I would urge the Brabant marriage to save you from an unnatural bed.'

I lifted her hand and kissed it; and it was only afterwards that I was able to disentangle the half-lies from the truth. And then it was too late and I was taken in the snare.

The month of July, my birthday month, wore on. The midsummer sun beat down upon the flats of Holland and I longed for Hainault with its cool woods and the hills where a breeze forever stirs. But my mother and I were in Biervliet with all my family to consider my marriage.

My uncle of Burgundy was not there; busy about the French wars he had sent his son in his place—my cousin Philip, young and smiling, his face smooth as a girl's. He looked gentle and honest, he that was neither; a seasoned fighter, a hard liver and a lecher. And there were gathered also the leaders of my party and all that wished me well ... and one that did not wish me well; my uncle of Bavaria like a hungry beast.

I trembled when I heard of his presence; for now my heart was wholly set upon the Brabant marriage—part in fear of him; part in love for a pretty face. My father's warning I had cast aside. If my family and my friends approved friends that were ready to die for me—then the marriage was right. My father had been wrong ... a dying man!

Wildly I besought my mother to use her wits to keep my father's brother from the council but she said, 'We cannot keep him out. He's your uncle; but what else he would be to you none but ourselves knows as yet. He was the first to pay you homage; he came with his fighting men and took Ysselstein for you. To keep him out would give the thing a crooked look. He must be there. But have no fear. If he sets himself against the Brabant marriage we shall ask him to make another choice. And there *is* no other choice. And if there were he would not make it, seeing the very different groom he has in mind. No, today he will approve our choice. But tomorrow? Tomorrow he'll go quickly to work; and if we don't move faster, sweet Christ alone knows what will happen.'

My family and my friends approved the marriage; not one word of dissent; not even from my father's brother where he sat smiling like the tiger men named him.

'I cannot think there'll be any difficulty,' my mother told them, speaking no word of the envoys she had already sent. 'There was none made about my daughter's first marriage and she and her husband were first cousins. Such marriages you know well are made every day.'

'But still the Pope may refuse,' she said to me later in the privacy of my chamber. 'He may well refuse if uncle-priest demands it—his Holiness isn't so secure on that new throne of his! But then uncle-priest must give his reasons; and he cannot speak openly till he's free of his obligations to God. With ordinary luck we'll see you safe-married before he has time to raise his voice.'

And now, like any young girl, I looked forward to marriage with my handsome cousin. I was sixteen and marriage-ripe. And I had the strangest feeling that marrying John of Brabant I kept alive something of John of Touraine—they had a look of each other; and that being a loving wife to the second John, I atoned for some of my unkindness to the first. I think I was quietening my conscience for disobeying my father. He had been dead three months now and in those three months much had happened that he had not foreseen. And besides, the country was quiet for the moment. It's true that Hooks and Cods waited to fly at each other's throats but since their defeat at Ysselstein the Cods had been wary.

And so I gave myself to dreams of my marriage—a handsome husband obedient to my will; my uncle of Burgundy standing strongly by me; my uncle of Bavaria powerless; my country settled in peace.

How young I was, how ignorant!

Quite suddenly my uncle of Bavaria showed his hand.

'I expected treachery from that quarter,' my mother said, thoughtful, 'but not quite so soon. He's clever that man! He says the husband you've chosen is too young. He says that he himself came from Liége to restore peace between Cods and Hooks; and that he has restored it. He says you and Brabant lack experience to keep the peace he has won. So—are you listening, daughter?—he demands to govern for you until ,you're old enough to govern for yourself!'

I sprang up at that. 'And that will be—*when?*'

'When cows roost in trees—since you cannot change your sex. That's the string he harps on. *A woman holding the reins at such a time!* You must fight back, my girl; and you must fight now. If that man gets a finger in your affairs, it'll soon be his whole hand, and the rest of his body will follow. You'll be completely in his power. There'll be no Brabant marriage for you nor any other—except the one he plans.'

'What can I do?' And I beat my hands together. 'If I set myself against him he'll withdraw his armies and throw me to the Cods.'

'You may leave that to my brother of Burgundy,' she reminded me. 'Your uncle of Bavaria is clever; but we are cleverer still. He makes your sex a weakness; we make it a strength. Call a full assembly of the Estates—the governments of your countships meeting together. Declare yourself of age. It's risky. But you're young and not ill-favoured ... and a girl. A girl putting herself upon the love of her country—that's a strong card! And, besides, there are many who remember the cruelty of John of Bavaria and the slaughter he made at Liége.'

These days, in spite of my father's warning, I turned to my mother for advice. What else could I do? Who else would have counselled me to call the great Assembly and turn my girlish weakness into strength?

I had reason to be glad that I had taken my mother's advice when I faced the Assembly at Schoonhoven. My mother—whose eye missed nothing—saw that I was dressed for the part. I wore my hair free-flowing beneath my father's crown like any virgin; a white gown stressed my youth and my simplicity; and a knot of black ribands reminded them of my loss and my need.

And so I came into the great room alone; and I went to my high place and stood there; and my mind was a blank. All the things I had been told to say had gone; I stood there dumb and my hand went out like a child that asks for help. I made the gesture all unknowing; but my mother told me afterwards how the childish gesture had moved them all.

'Sirs,' I said, 'I am my father's daughter; you were his friends and some of you have nursed me upon your knees. He was your lord; and a good lord that spared himself no hardships for your sakes. To him, dying, you swore love and obedience to me, his child. To you, now, I swear *my* love, *my* obedience. I am turned sixteen which is considered manhood in princes. But sixteen I know well is full young. Sirs, I am very willing to be guided in all matters by any council you may choose for me. But I am not willing to be commanded by any one man. For who can look into the heart of any man to trust him? A man—though he be one's nearest and dearest—may be driven by ambition and by greed and by his own cruelty. And who shall call a halt when his hands are upon affairs? Therefore I will take no *Ruward*. I will take instead the love and good counsel and comfort of my people.'

God I think put the words upon my tongue; I had moved them all. Their hearts I had softened; but they were still hard-headed Hollanders; they must weigh and sift and weigh again. I offered my love and my duty; my uncle of Bavaria offered peace.

My mother and I were requested to withdraw. We sat together in the warm sunshine of the anteroom but for all it was high summer I trembled.

'John of Bavaria is much hated,' my mother said. 'It was shrewd to remind them of his cruelties. Let them remember the massacre he made at Liége. Feared he is; but our Hollanders are not to be bullied. Besides, there's great advantage in a young, obedient sovereign.'

How long we sat there I cannot say; nor whether the sun still shone. I only know I could not get warm again and that my hands trembled still. But when they summoned us again I walked steady enough.

I found my uncle of Bavaria standing by the Sovereign's chair which is the *Ruward's* place ... when there is a *Ruward*. He had no doubt at all of the decision; and the way he stood, proud and impatient, a hand gripping the carved crown of my chair, showed the way his thoughts ran. It was a step—and a small one—to the throne itself.

I seated myself in my place, he standing beside me; and together we heard the decision that meant so much to us both. He heard it without a change of colour; not a muscle moved. But, as I stood to thank my people, he turned his back upon them all and strode away, only, as he thrust his way out, he turned to throw me a look of hatred.

'Let it not disturb you,' my mother said. 'He was always your enemy! Well, you have the goodwill of the Assembly; and you have my brother of Burgundy.'

'God be thanked!' I said. And I forgot it was against Burgundy himself my father had warned me.

VI

'The reverend father in Christ, your uncle, loses no time,' my mother said, and she threw the paper she was holding upon the table. 'We took it from the messenger on the road from Dordrecht.'

Dordrecht. The very name spelt trouble. It was the one city that had refused homage. To Dordrecht flocked the Cod nobles and their followers; to Dordrecht flocked every man with a chip on his shoulder—and there were plenty in our troubled land. My uncle's bitter tongue had seen to it!

I took up the paper.

It was a letter addressed to my people at the Hague calling upon everyone, gentle and simple alike, to lay down their allegiance to me, the so-called countess, and to hand over the city, together with full homage, to its true lord, my uncle of Bavaria.

'The messengers are posting north, south, east and west,' my mother said. 'Every town will have received its orders.'

'Then we must take Dordrecht; smoke out that nest of hornets.'

'You had best wait for your uncle of Burgundy,' she said drily. 'Don't let that little success at Ysselstein go to your head. Remember it was the Bavarian won it for you!'

I must have made a movement of impatience, for she said, 'You can't afford to behave like a child. There's very much to consider before we take the field. Your uncle-bishop is a proved soldier; his pockets are lined with gold. Every mercenary in Christendom will swarm to his banner.'

'Our pockets are not empty!' I said.

'We haven't enough; not near enough! And, if we had? Why should any mercenary serve under a green girl, unless he were in love with death?'

'Then I will fight with those I love behind me!'

She shrugged, as though I compared mice with lions.

'And,' I said, 'God will not turn His back.'

'You haven't got God in your pocket,' she answered. 'You must wait for my brother of Burgundy.'

'I haven't got him in my pocket, either!'

'He has his commitments in France—' she began.

'—fighting with the English against his own King!' And I have never learned to control my tongue.

I had stung her de Charolais pride. 'A reigning sovereign you may be,' she said, 'but you'll not be one long if you don't keep a wise tongue in your head.'

Summer moved into autumn; and autumn into winter. My uncle of Bavaria was making ready. We heard the reports on all sides. But still there was no word from my uncle of Burgundy. Each day added to my fear and to my impatience. Was he waiting for the result of our embassy to Rome? If His Holiness refused dispensation for me to marry my cousin of Brabant would Burgundy turn his back and leave me to fend for myself? Had my father been right in saying the de Charolais thought only of themselves and their house; and all kindness, all honour, even, must give way to that?

God, I had said, would help me. But God helps those that help themselves. The last week of November I called my captains together—the van Brederodes, and with them Anthony, Stadtholder of Holland, and Louis his nephew; and Arent of Ghent-by-Geldrois, and many another.

Together we listed the towns we could count upon, the nobles and the men under their banners, our engines of war and the gold at our disposal. They shook their heads over our resources but to me, ignorant as I was, they seemed ample. I had stout hearts about me and loyalty and love; and the right was with me. My courage, fretted by waiting, rose again.

Gorcum was the place we chose for the first clash with the enemy. It is an important town—the junction of waterways. My mother troubled me with no more warnings. The time had come to fight—she knew it as well as I. She knew also—though she never said so—that my loving uncle of Burgundy would not lift a finger until I was safe-married to Brabant. Until that time I might stew in my own juice.

These days I spent much time on my knees; and God put a thought into my heart, but I said nothing about it to my mother. She came into my tent the day before we were to ride out and there, across the pallet, lay a heavy woollen cloak such as soldiers wear and upon it a breastplate, a helmet, and a sword. She stared at them for a moment and could not speak—a rare thing for her.

'I lead my forces,' I said.

'Into *battle*?' she cried. 'You're crazy. Whoever heard of such a thing?'

'There were Amazons ...

'And shall you cut your breasts off, also?' she asked sardonic. 'You're to be married—if you live so long.'

'The Queen of the Amazons married, so we are told. And I shall marry also, in God's good time. Or let us say in the Pope's good time.' I picked up the helmet and fingered its shining crest. 'The English King rode into Agincourt with his crown upon his head,' I said.

'And it was hacked in a dozen places.'

'But the helmet stood firm! Fetch me my crown, Beatrix.'

My mother said nothing. She took the helmet from my hand and herself set it upon my head; she took the crown from my woman and set it upon the helmet.

'You are a wild and headstrong girl,' she said; but there was a softness in her scolding. 'As your mother I forbid you; as your subject ...' she made a deep curtsey and it was only half mockery; I could have sworn to tears in those hard eyes.

I had won obedience from my mother; I took it as a good omen.

And a good omen it was!

Truly God does help those that help themselves! Where my crowned helmet shone, the press was thickest. I am no braver than

44

the next woman; but that day I knew no fear. There is, I think, a madness in the fight that works in the blood.

Our plans were sound, our need dire, our cause just. Before sunset my uncle of Bavaria knew the day was lost.

It was the proudest hour in my life. Without de Charolais help I had won the day. Not even the lists of our own dead could quench my triumph. 'They came to their death with honour. God will reward them,' I said.

'And will He raise up men to take their place?' my mother asked in that dry way of hers.

And she was right. Too glib, that speech of mine, unfitting in a girl that should have been upon her knees. I see that now I have learned a little wisdom.

The victory was to me. But, green as I was, I knew this was only the beginning; the fighting must be long and bloody. Losses on both sides had been great and we both needed time to make them good. So there was an unspoken truce between us. I returned to the Hague with my captains to confer with my council ... and to await the answer from His Holiness.

These past weeks I had had little time to think of marriage; now, with a lull in the fighting, like the Amazon Queen, I welcomed the marriage-bed. Our envoys had been in Rome since the summer, beseeching the Pope's favour; and their prayers were accompanied by the pleasing jingle of Burgundian gold.

Towards the end of December they rode back. Since this marriage would prevent the shedding of Christian blood, dispensation was granted. I might, in all Christian honour, marry with my cousin of Brabant.

I was happy these days in my fool's paradise; and, perhaps it was as well, for the sorrow that followed was long and bitter.

And then, suddenly the preparations came to a standstill. My mother and my uncle went about with black looks. There had been, it appeared, a hitch. I was not to worry my head about it, my mother said; all would soon be set right. And set right it was. Preparations were once more hurried forward; my mother was all smiles again, yes and that sour man her brother, also.

'We must keep the celebrations quiet,' my mother said. 'Your uncle of Bavaria has already been at the Pope to revoke the permission.'

But however quiet one may hope to keep the marriage of a reigning sovereign, nothing will prevent it from being bruited abroad. The Emperor himself spoke now. He forbade my marriage.

'The Emperor has come out into the open at last!' my uncle of Burgundy cried out, bitter. 'You have no right, my girl, to your father's crown! The Emperor, God damn him, names your uncle of Bavaria heir to all your lands to hold for himself and for his male heirs for ever.'

So it had happened; the unjust thing, the cruel thing my mother had feared; and which I, myself, had never quite believed.

Disinherited.

My people mine no longer.

'So—do you listen, daughter? the Pope has released uncle-priest from his vows. He's free to marry.' Her meaning look added disaster to disaster. 'It's as well you're out of his reach ... or are you?' She swung about to face her brother. 'Will Brabant take my daughter now?'

'By God, he'd better! The marriage goes forward. As for the other—we don't accept the Emperor's decree.'

My uncle of Burgundy ground his teeth and swore to deal with my father's brother. My mother, not less grim, promised I should be married on the day fixed. I need trouble my head about nothing.

And so the preparations went forward. My mother came with arrangements for the ceremony; my steward with his lists of food, my chamberlain with the names of our chosen guests. Those that had not been invited knew only that we gave a feast; that it was a marriage-feast they did not know.

As for myself, seeing me absorbed in the fit of a gown, the selection of a jewel, you might have been pardoned for thinking there was peace throughout the land; that Cods and Hooks were not waiting to fly at each other's throats; or that my uncle of Bavaria was not gathering forces to rob me of my inheritance. I was that same girl that had led her troops at Gorcum; but I was not yet seventeen. I was to be married and I was in love. And there had been so much bloodshed and so many tears.

And so the days rushed by; and it was the first week in March and my groom not yet come. 'Patience,' my mother said. 'Be not so hot. The day that is coming, comes.'

And come it did! I was married the tenth day of March in the year of our Lord fourteen hundred and eighteen; and it is not a day I am not likely to forget.

I did not see my groom until I met him in church. He had arrived late the night before and was fatigued with his journey. The excuse for his tardiness was good enough; I know, none better, that princes are not their own masters. But, for all that, I lay restless on my wedding-eve, tossed this way and that between delight in my handsome groom and disappointment in his unloverlike sloth; between the approval of my mother and the warning of my father. Now that I was to be married on the morrow his warning came back clear and sharp. I was disobeying my father's last wish to me.

Across the press lay my wedding-gown. In the moonlight it glistened ghostly, as though a spirit lay there ... or a dead man, perhaps. And then—a trick of moonlight or a small breeze from the window the thing stirred. I cried out before I could stop myself and Beatrix came hurrying, my mother at her heels. My mother sent her away for a posset and sat down on my bed ... and it was the first time I could remember her doing so intimate a thing.

'Well!' she said brisk and cheerful. 'You lie awake like most young brides! It's a pity. You'll want to be in looks tomorrow. Such a handsome groom! No doubt you're remembering your father's words; well, remember also he was a sick man! I'm your mother and your happiness comes first with me. Never let it be said that I forced my girl into an unwelcome marriage. If you're unwilling, why then the thing's finished! It's not easy to send my godson of Brabant back insulted; and certainly it would add to the list of our enemies—and they are sufficient already! Still you have but to say the word and I will send my godson packing!'

I looked at her amazed by this sudden turnabout. I knew her for a cunning woman but I did not read cunning in this. I read only her love for me.

'You need have no fear!' She was all affection. 'I will stand by you against Brabant and all his kinsmen; yes, even against my brother of Burgundy himself!'

I took her hand and kissed it. And I forgot the times I had been harried and driven by this same mother. 'Weddings are the times for gifts. Name any estate of mine you favour and it's yours. Before I marry tomorrow, I'll have the documents drawn.'

In an instant her face changed; the look I knew so well was back again the calculating look, the greedy de Charolais look.

'Thank you, child,' she said warmly. 'Now here is that woman with the posset.' She took the cup in her hands and gave it to me. 'When your lady has taken her drink,' she spoke to Beatrix, cold as always, 'leave her. See that she's undisturbed.'

But for all the posset I could not sleep. The calculating look on my mother's face—the look I knew so well—disturbed me. My father was back to haunt me again.

I suppose I must have slept. For, suddenly it was full daylight and the birds tearing the air with their sharp calling. Beneath half-closed lids I saw Beatrix kneeling at my own prie-dieu and I knew she was praying for me. She finished her prayer and rose and came over to the bed; and there she stood looking down with what might have been pity in her eyes.

But ... pity! Why should she pity me?

VII

I knelt beside my groom. Looking sideways between my fingers I thought him smaller, slighter than I had believed; but in the dim light of the chapel I could not be sure. His face I had not yet fully seen; and now it was shadowed by his devout hands. I longed to see those features I knew by heart ... by heart, indeed!

I brought my thoughts back to the service that was making him and me one flesh.

And now my groom and I were exchanging the vows and the priest received them. And I was a wedded wife for the second time.

There were few guests in the little chapel and my uncle of Bavaria was not present; I doubt he knew I was being married. I was glad to be free of his fierce hawk's face. My uncle of Burgundy was absent also and his son Philip. Both had been recalled to France and of that I was glad too; the sour face of the one and the secret-smiling of the other, would have spoilt the wedding-feast.

And now all seemed set fair. Our guests pressed forward to offer their good wishes; my mother showed smiling satisfaction, and I thanked her in my heart for having saved me from the wickedness of my uncle of Bavaria.

And then, suddenly, in the press of our guests, I came face-to-face with my husband.

John of Brabant was of low stature and very slight-overyoung to take a woman. But it was not only his body that filled me with dismay.

It was the face. How true the painter had been, yet how false! I could trace the picture line for line in the living face—the delicate nose, the fine upper lip, the lower red and full; the dark eyes and the bright curling hair. Yet the living face was different; hatefully different. The nose was sharp rather than delicate; the upper lip thin rather than fine, it dragged at the corners giving the face a sour look. The lower lip pouted red and swollen as though it had been stung—a greedy look. The eyes, overlarge in the face, and set deep in bruised sockets gave him a dissipated air. The yellow skin, the peevish, greedy mouth, the dissipated eyes, the whole sickly look of him filled me with dismay. And he had been drinking; it was evident in the vacant look, the high, giggling voice. I saw now why I had not seen this husband of mine before we were fast-wed. It was a trick of my mother's. She had feared that, even at the last moment, I would refuse the marriage.

And only last night she had talked of my free choice, of sending an unwelcome groom packing! *Do not trust your mother!* My father's warning fell too late upon my heart.

But now the thing having been done, I must play my part. I allowed my wretched groom to take me by the hand and lead me to my place beside him at the table.

And there I sat miserably crumbling my bread. Now and again I would carry a morsel to my mouth or sip at my cup. But what I ate, what I drank, I did not know. It was all I could do not to put my head down on the table and weep like a child.

Nor did my groom seem in better spirits. He stared down upon the table and would not raise his eyes. He sent away the soup and then the meat with a surly gesture. While our guests drank their soup, ate their fish and meat, he could not wait but crammed his mouth with sweetmeats like a greedy child. Nor was he any better with the wine; he thrust out his cup to be filled before it was well empty, tossing off one after the other with all the ease of a drunkard.

Suddenly he jerked to his feet and went stumbling from the room. His departure was greeted with a great burst of laughter—full-bellied from seasoned men; light, sly laughter from no less seasoned women.

I sat there cheeks aflame. I knew the cause of their jesting ... The groom could not wait. Too hot for the marriage-bed.

I longed to run and hide myself from the lewd laughter; yet when the nod came from my mother, how gladly would I have delayed ... a little longer, longer, longer. I rose and the pages lifted the great train of my gown; unwilling as a thief to the gallows I walked the length of the room. I had disobeyed my father and there was no help for me anywhere.

At the head of the stairs I would have turned towards my old rooms but my mother motioned me towards her own apartments—the sovereign's suite she had taken as my father's bride and used ever since. Now, with her eye for decorum she had vacated them for me. She would have entered with me but I shook my head forbidding her.

The anteroom already showed evidence of its new occupant. A lute, ribands trailing, lay where it had been cast, upon the floor; wine from an overthrown goblet dripped upon the table—my father's table and a fine piece of craftsmanship. It is strange that with so much to fear, anger should have burned so hot at so small a thing.

I stepped into the next room—my mother's dressing-room and now mine. That, too, was empty and it surprised me; I had expected to find Beatrix. It was hardly more orderly than the anteroom. A dish of comfits lay scattered upon a table; a woman's gown lay thrown upon the floor ... and the gown was not mine. Through the half-open door I could see the bedchamber with its garlanded bed, empty and waiting; from this a door opened into my husband's dressing-room—the room in which my father had slept as long as I could remember.

And, so standing in the littered room, I heard the sound of voices, of tipsy laughter. I stopped short.

I stood and listened. There were, it seemed, but two voices—the light girlish tones of my husband and the deeper voice of a woman.

Suddenly I knew, but would not know; would not let myself believe the insult offered me on this my wedding-night.

I took a step into the next room and stood there in the middle of my bridal chamber not knowing what to do. The sound of a laugh decided me—a woman's laugh, light and rich and infinitely sly.

I pushed open the door.

My husband sprawled upon the narrow bed, my father's bed, half-naked and wholly tipsy. A woman—in her shift—sprawled there with him, a young woman I did not know, but was soon to know only too well. She struggled to rise; she at least was shamefaced a little. But the vicious boy pulled her down again, fumbling at the large white breasts; the nipples, I saw with disgust, were budded with gold.

He lay there hiccupping and laughing in my face. 'I present to you, Laurette T'serclaes,' he said. 'And, truly, I present her—a gift, a bridal gift—lady of the bedchamber. Chief lady, mind that!' He turned to pinch her cheek. 'Now then, my girl,' he told her, 'be about your business. Prepare Madam here for bed!' And he hiccupped again.

I was taken by so cold a fury I thought I must die of it. Anger, good hot anger I knew well, it is my nature; but this cold fury that all but stopped my pulses—never! I did not look at the woman, though I was well aware of her—the strange eyes sea-green beneath a tumble of pale gold hair; and the voluptuous look of her like an overblown rose.

I said, very quiet, 'Sir, my ladies are chosen. There is no room for Mademoiselle ... or should it be Madam?'

'It's Madam.' And he patted her thickened belly. 'Wife to my good friend Everhard, my very good friend.' And he belched in her face.

I said, and I would not look at her, 'Then be so good, Madam, as to withdraw.'

The red came up into his face, empurpling the tipsy flush as though, for all his youth, he must fall into an apoplexy. His mouth opened and shut.

Laurette T'serclaes said in the rich voice that went so well with her overblown splendour, 'Turn and turn about! Everhard has been patient long enough!' She pulled herself from his clutching hands, smiled to me with insolence and went from the room.

I looked at my husband, the vicious boy that was not ashamed to share his mistress with his friend. There was nothing I could say; it needed more experience than mine to deal with this. I turned about and went back through the bedroom to my dressing-room; he followed me, smiling and tipsy.

I sank down upon a stool; I was surprised to find myself shaking—every limb.

'Where's my woman?' I asked him very sharp.

'No need of that old hen!' he hiccupped. 'I've found you one that won't offend your eyes nor—' he hiccupped again, 'mine.'

I made no answer. Outside the anteroom, the pages lounging half-asleep, stiffened at the sight of me, sped to find Beatrix. I went back into the dressing-room. 'This chamber is mine,' I said. 'Be so good as to go away.'

'But the bedroom is ours!' He grinned. I kept my eyes upon him and the grin died in his face; he looked frightened; a little boy about to be whipped. He backed a step and went from the room.

Beatrix when she came at last looked unexpectedly old; as though these last hours had put new lines in her face.

'To send you away was none of my doing,' I told her. 'You must never leave me again.'

To my distress, Beatrix the staid, the wise, began to cry. And now our positions were reversed. Always it had been her part to play the comforter, now it was mine. She knelt weeping; and comforting her I found my own comfort ... such as it was.

'Madam,' she said. And then, 'Jacque, oh Jacque!'

'Beatrix,' I said, 'what must I do?'

'God knows!' she said. And then she said, very slow, 'You have a warm heart and a strong will; and you're all of a woman. Jacque, you could ... win him.'

'Can you write in sand?' I asked. 'As for winning him, as God hears me, I have no desire for it.'

We said no more for a while. She put off the crown and caul and took out the head pins.

'When you put my hair into this net,' I said, 'I was happy. I would not have changed place with any soul in Christendom. Now there is not the meanest soul but I envy him.'

'Hush,' she said, 'hush, Jacque my dear, my sweet, my poppet.' Her tongue found the sweet, silly name of my childhood. 'It's over-soon to talk like that. All will be well. You have the courage to make it well!'

She was unlacing the back of my cote when my mother swept in.

'Not abed yet!' And she threw up her hands. 'The guests grow impatient.'

'For what?' I asked; cold; and I would endure no more than I must.

She laughed out loud. 'Must I teach you your manners? It's the right of your guests to see you bedded—as you well know.'

There was justice in that. I am no prude; had things been different I might well have admitted them. One might be proud lying next to a proper man.

'Hurry!' she cried. 'The guests are waiting.'

'Then they must go away at once—and you with them!' And while she stared, not believing her ears, 'Put back the laces in my gown,' I told Beatrix. I turned again to my mother, 'Not a button unlooped nor a tag untied until this door is bolted upon you and your friends.'

The colour came up into her face and then left it. She said, very quiet, 'You have no head for wine, that much is clear. When the wine's in the wit's out. Tomorrow you will be sorry to have insulted your guests. Well, if no eye may profane your love-play, see at least it's well done.' She paused at the door. 'The land is full of troubles.

Get yourself with child as soon as you may and put an end to them.'
There was an odd sincerity about her and I was ashamed a little.

'Good-night,' I said and swept her a curtsey—she was, after all, my
mother; but she could have taken it for mockery.

I kept Beatrix as long as I dared; but, in the end I was forced to
let her go.

Bedgown about me I went into the next room. My husband was
already in bed. Had I been less unhappy I must have been sorry for
him; he looked so sick, and so shamed. But I was in no mood for
kindness. I looked at the flushed sick face and I remembered how
he had tried to force his mistress upon me that they might laugh
together over my marriage-bed. Had I shown him kindness that
night the story of my country might well have been different ... and
my own story also.

VIII

I stood by the window and looked out upon the unfamiliar garden—
unfamiliar from this strange angle of the bridal chamber. The flickering candle light made yet more strange this strange chamber. It was
the first time I had slept with a light since childhood. I found pleasure
in the healing dark but the boy in the bed was afraid of it.

Dawn came up red, the light broadened; the candles guttered and
went out. I had been standing by the window for hours, a bedgown
about my nakedness in the cold March night. I would not get back
into the bed though my teeth rattled like stones in a sack. I had done
my duty; I had got in beside him.

He was stupid, he was clumsy, he was useless. Nor was I helped by
the stale smell of wine. Drink one must at a feast; but he had taken
altogether too much, nor had he thought to sweeten his breath before
coming to bed. He had fumbled me while I lay stiff with disgust;
then he had heaved himself about and presented me with his back.
He had lain restless a while, whimpering like a small dog. And then,
suddenly, he was asleep.

I stood looking out of the window and seeing nothing but the
long procession of days ... and nights. This creature was my husband;
I was his wife. They had caught me in a dirty trap.

I was startled, suddenly, by sunlight bright upon my face. In the
next room I heard quiet movements—Beatrix making all ready for

me. Soiled and dishonoured I could not face even Beatrix. I pulled myself together. I went into the next room.

At the sight of my face she cried out.

I said, 'They have wedded me to a sot, a fool, a vicious boy. As God hears me I'll never bed with him again.' And I began to shake as with a palsy.

She opened her mouth to speak and, as though she thought the better of it, shut it again. She said at last, very low, 'No need ... maybe.'

No need! But I was married to the man; and she was a woman to respect the duties of the marriage-bed. There was, I thought something odd about her—an indecision, an excitement foreign to her quiet.

I said, 'You know something, Beatrix.'

'I don't know,' she said, surprisingly, 'I don't *know*.'

I flew to her then, pulling at her arm. 'Can we undo this thing, can we? You must tell me; or by Christ's Virgin Mother I will end it—and myself, too!'

She crossed herself. 'You're too good a Christian, I hope!' But I must have looked wild enough, for she said, troubled, 'There's gossip, Jacque. But—gossip!' She shrugged. 'It is wise not to repeat it.'

I said, 'You must let me judge.'

'It could be my death,' she said, slowly. 'Your mother always hated me.'

'Your name shall not be spoken in the matter.'

She sighed. 'Your happiness is dear to me; your honour dearer. Listen, Jacque. The Pope gave a dispensation for your marriage; all the world knows that. But there was a second letter ...'

A second letter! I stared at her.

She nodded. 'Early January when it came. That's when the preparations stopped. Remember? Your mother and her brother tried to keep it a secret—but these things will out. Certainly there was a letter. What was in it, I don't know ... but enough to stop a wedding.'

'Dress me, Beatrix,' I said and made myself quiet under her hands.

... A letter. And the wedding preparations stopped. Some little hitch—my mother had called it. What hitch? My mind leapt. *Had the Pope revoked his permission in that second letter?* Impossible! Wed me within the forbidden degrees—and no permission! Even my mother would not have dared. But ... backed up by her brother? It would not be beyond them to swear the letter came too late, and to prove it, too! Whatever the truth, how should I come by it? How match myself against my mother?

I found my mother at her prie-dieu; in spite of folded hands and closed eyes, there was a satisfaction all about her.

I waited until she had finished her devotions. At last she stood up, smoothing first her bedgown and then her dark hair. Without the head-dress she looked strangely young; there was no grey to her hair nor is there to this day.

I said, 'You may well pray! But God is no de Charolais; He may find it hard to forgive you.'

She tried to stare me down with her look of surprise. She had yet to learn that last night's work had made a woman of me.

'Madam,' I said, 'mother I cannot call you since you have not played a mother's part by me. Nor shall I ever call you so again until you undo the mischief you have done.'

The expression in her eye showed surprise—mild surprise and a little amusement. 'It is the way of men!' she said. 'You make too much of it.'

Her natural surprise, her faint amusement, shook my faith in a tale I only half-believed. But I went steadily on.

'I am no child to complain of that!' I said. 'God will damn your soul—and mine, also—if you do not make amends. You have disobeyed God's Vicar; you have married me within the forbidden degree of blood.'

She said, very cold, 'Have you lost your sense, girl? How dare you come to me with this poppycock?' But I saw how she moistened her lips; and she showed no surprise at my question. The accusation was not new to her.

'I am not to be beaten down by your scolding,' I said. 'His Holiness revoked permission for this ... this *marriage*! I know the truth but I'll have it from your own tongue. Let there be one word—is it *Yes* or *No*?'

She smiled a little. 'The answer's both *Yes* and *No*. Nothing's so simple as simple people think. The Pope gave his permission; and, as you saw for yourself, it was signed and sealed. He did revoke it in a second letter; but that letter was not sealed.'

'But it was signed!' I said very quick; and I was thanking God in my heart.

'But not sealed. And what's a papal bull without a seal? It was not *sealed*. And why? Because it was not meant to be obeyed. It was written to hoodwink your uncle of Bavaria, to keep him quiet: At this moment the Pope can't afford to offend anyone—he isn't too safe yet on that very new throne of his! Your uncle of Burgundy desires the marriage—very well, it's granted. Your uncle of Bavaria desires it shall be stopped—very well, it's stopped. But there's still your uncle of Burgundy! So the revocation's left unsealed. We're to read between the lines—the marriage goes on. And your uncles can fight it out afterwards. No, my girl, your marriage is fast!'

I looked into her subtle face and my heart turned over. Was she speaking the truth? It sounded like it. But she was a clever woman, very cunning. I said—and it was hard to speak for bitterness of disappointment, 'Am I fast-married?'

'As fast as church can make it!'

'Then God forgive you! You have wed me to a sot and a boor and a fool.' And then, remembering the fumblings of my wedding-night, 'An impotent fool.'

She laughed but her laughter did not ring true.

'A sot. A bore. A fool. Where's the man that isn't one or the other, or all three? As for the last, you haven't given the boy a chance to show his mettle, you with a face to frighten the most lusty man.' She made an impatient gesture, 'What's this nonsense about impotence? The man has his mistress—pregnant so I hear! That ought to satisfy you! Don't stare at me, child! We're not living in paradise but on solid earth. Your father had mistresses in plenty before our marriage … and after. It was a sport he rarely denied himself!'

'And did he send his mistress to undress you on your wedding-night?'

'God forbid!' And now she was shocked at last. 'I should have spoilt her beauty with a whip! No, I never clapped eyes on one; he kept them out of sight. But not his bastards. His bastards I have endured.' She closed her eyes as though upon remembered pain. They flew open again; she sent me a searching look. 'This woman of Brabant's. He sent her to put you to bed? I thought he had gentler manners.'

She had me fast-bound to an impotent fool and she prattled of manners!

'I will not take him for my husband!' I cried out.

'You *have* taken him!' she answered very sharp.

I shook my head. 'I could not take him. His Holiness forbade it.'

'The marriage stands; must I tell you again? If you cast doubts upon it then you are dishonoured. A wife and no wife; a soiled half-and-half.'

The scarlet came up into my cheeks at the insult; but I could not deny some rightness in what she said. I looked at her. I said, 'Answer me this and speak the truth as God and His Sweet Mother hear you. Did you know the man to be impotent?'

She spread her hands. 'No,' she said. 'Not I, nor you, nor anyone. You've seen his mistress!'

'Pregnant—yes; but not by Brabant, that I'll swear. He's not one to do a man's work.'

'You're in a hurry!' And she actually mocked at me. 'The boy's young.'

'Old enough to marry—so it seems. Many a man his age and less has begotten a son. You may spare your breath. The man's impotent and you know it. You knew it before ever you put me into his bed. And you were glad to know it. That's why you pushed the business on. Let your brother inherit my lands and titles; and his son after him. Good de Charolais both. Before God you have caught me in a filthy net!'

She said, 'Jacque, you wound me to the heart.'

'A de Charolais heart!' And I laughed. 'You knew the truth; and my uncle of Burgundy knew the truth. Yes, and all Christendom likewise. All Christendom laughing at the shame you have put upon me.'

Again she would have spoken but I would not listen. 'You may move back to your old rooms,' I told her, bitter. 'I will not set foot in them again till I bed with a full man.'

And now I was surrounded by enemies. On the one side my mother with her brother of Burgundy determined to keep me to my hateful bargain; on the other, my uncle of Bavaria gathering his armies to rob me of my inheritance.

And, in the background, my sulky bitter husband, eager to pay back my public slighting of him.

There was, however, one person whose advice I could trust. Not Beatrix; her heart was good and her truth perfect, but no more than I could she weigh the full matter. It was to William van Brederode I went. He would not advance himself by siding with one or the other of my enemies. He would advise me—not for his own good—but for mine. He was my father's kinsman; he had lifted me, a baby, to his knees; he had comforted my childish tears, kissed my infant cheeks. When he had sworn homage to me the truth in his eyes could not be mistaken. He would tell me what to do.

'Dear child,' he said, ' —and child you are, for all you are my Liége lady—between two enemies you are lost and cast aside, unless you match cunning with cunning. Your marriage must stand; for the present at any rate. I see no help for it! No, say nothing, Jacque my child, until I am done. Your uncle of Bavaria—more shame to him—claims your inheritance. The Emperor declares that you keep both lands and titles to the injury of the rightful heir. He calls upon your cities to support your uncle.'

'No!' I cried out. 'No. To me the oath was sworn; to me ... to me. Not one city will obey so wicked a decree.'

'Will they not? They will think the matter over and certainly some will obey—the Emperor is your overlord. Even the loyal ones will turn against you if you give them cause. The dispensation to your marriage was sealed; the revocation was not sealed. You were married by holy church and married you remain. Repudiate it—and the tongue of scandal wags; you cannot afford it. And one thing more. Even if you accept the marriage as it stands, still tongues will wag. Never was the marriage of princes like this one; hasty, hole-and-corner. The people are confused; there's gossip everywhere; and you must put an end to it. There must be a second ceremony in the eyes of all the people.'

'No!'

'Remember your enemies. You risk your inheritance ... and that of your children.'

'Don't you know the truth about Brabant?' And I heard myself laugh.

'No. Nor do you. Nor does anyone as yet. If you liked the boy better you'd know it!' He met my glance squarely. 'Jacque, my dear, you must show you mean to do your best in this marriage. Then Burgundy will support you; and Brabant's troops also. Deny the marriage—and between your two uncles you're lost!'

'I cannot endure the man. My flesh creeps at the sight of him.'

He said, 'If you cannot accept the marriage, then make a show of accepting it. What takes place in the privacy of the bedchamber is your own affair.'

'Who would think it?' I cried out bitter.

'My dear,' he took my hand. 'I speak to you as though you were my own child. There's only one safe way for you. Get Burgundy's help and get it now. When you're safe on your throne, petition the Pope to annul the marriage.'

'And if he refuse? Am I bound to that vicious boy for life?'

'He's bound to consider the matter afresh; after all, the dispensation was revoked. You can claim the marriage was never legal. And you'd have another card to play; Brabant's impotency—if it's true.

Meanwhile if you want the goodwill of Christendom you must show that you acknowledge your Christian duty.'

'I don't acknowledge it!' I said.

He did not answer. He looked at me very steady.

'A few short days ago,' I told him, 'I was an innocent girl—innocent and ignorant. And those that should protect me took me in the net. Is there no way now to break free save by guile?'

'It's a wicked world,' he said.

'So I see!' And then at the love in his face and the pain in his face, I said, 'I talk like a child that should face things like a woman. Match guile with guile—why so I will!'

A month later my marriage with Brabant was solemnized for the second time in the church of the Hague where I had married my first husband and where from time immemorial the Counts of Holland have been married and buried. And I wished, that day, they might bury me, too.

So there I was, married to a sot—and no hope of a child by him to sit on the throne of my father; and, if there had been, I would not have suffered him near me. Well, I was safe from my uncle of Bavaria, though I doubted sometimes I could have done worse with him! And he—that reverend father in God—since he could not have me, married with all speed to raise up heirs to the lands that were mine. And the bride? None other than the Emperor's own niece.

The net was closing about me.

IX

I was fast-married to my sot. And, for my own sake, I must acknowledge him the length and breadth of my dominions. We were back in Holland that he might make his progress and take homage as my husband. It was not only usual; it was necessary in view of my uncle's claims.

If I could keep him sober, he might—with his pretty face and a certain boyish charm he had when he chose—make a good enough showing. He had brought with him a pack of favourites to bolster his self-importance; they roistered and they swaggered and they cost me a pretty penny. And the most noisy, the most extravagant of them all were—need I say it?—the T'serclaes couple.

My mother advised me to come to terms with Brabant's mistress. 'You can't endure Brabant—and she can. You can get no favour out of him—and she can. Welcome her; for, welcome or not, wherever you go, she'll go, too: Maybe she'll help you to keep him sober. Get her on your side; better to make a friend of her than an enemy.'

'I prefer her as an enemy!' I said. And I was glad to show that I trusted neither my mother nor her advice.

'You're too headstrong, daughter.' She sighed; and set against her though I was, I could not doubt the sincerity of that sigh. That was the subtlety of my mother. One could never be sure of her. She could betray you over and over again to serve her own ends; and then, the hundredth time, she would betray those ends to serve you.

'I have been your obedient child too long!' I said quick and bitter.

'But not a gentle one. I see no gentleness in you. Had you been gentle with that boy on your wedding night, you would have won him. He had that woman with him to lend him courage—a boy's bravado to hide his fear. Had you been a little kind, a little clever, he would have sent her packing!'

A little kind; a little clever! And they wantoning half-naked! And yet she was right; I had known it when I stood by the window watching for the dawn and hearing his drunken breathing and hating and despising him.

'If he humiliates you now—you humiliated him then.' And she was right, right again! A thousand pities I could not trust her.

'It was not goodness drove you,' she said, 'it was pride and anger. I know you well! Brabant was soft metal and you might have stamped your pattern. Now the metal is hard and the pattern set. But it is not your pattern, my girl, and never will be! Oh Jacque, Jacque, what have you done? You're but seventeen and the whole of your life to be lived with the man; yet you choose to win not his love but his hatred!'

'The Pope will set me free! He must set me free!' I cried out, a little wild.

'Never think it. No one forced you into the marriage. You were willing enough. And for the rest there are no grounds ... no grounds.' She was silent, then she said, 'If you've nothing but contempt and dislike for the boy you've married, then you must hide it as best you can. Treat him with a show of respect. Daughter, I am warning you!'

At first it seemed as though my uncle of Bavaria would be sent packing. Hainault was the first to speak. Succession through a woman had always been allowed, it declared; and the Emperor had no voice in the matter. The oath had already been sworn to me; they could not and would not take it back.

Holland and Zealand followed Hainault's example. They stood by their oath to my father and to me.

My heart lifted at this love, this loyalty. Let Brabant be what he would-vicious, impotent, jealous-it mattered little! When I was secure in my inheritance I would set aside my useless husband. The Pope must declare my marriage void; he himself had revoked permission. I must marry again and beget myself an heir. My people would demand it.

So I hid my anger against my husband; and with it anger against my mother. To be at odds with them at this moment could do me nothing but harm. Through Holland, through Zealand, through Hainault we went all three; my husband and I smiling and handlocked. Who could guess that heart and hand were alike cold? And seeing us young and comely and friendly-seeming—and my mother all smiling-satisfaction along with us—the people cheered themselves hoarse.

Cheers and garlands, speeches and promises ... promises!

In spite of all the welcome and all the fine words little help was forthcoming—a small amount of money, a few men.

'What can you expect?' My mother shrugged. 'Oh they like you well enough—but take your side against your uncle of Bavaria! They'll need to think twice about it. It means civil war, of all wars the most deadly. And, besides, your uncle's no fool! He knows how to tempt people. Let the country accept him and he'll open his hand—privileges and easing of taxes for all. He can afford it. But, let them refuse—and it's the mailed fist. A man to fear—and they know it. The *Pitiless*, the *Tiger*, no bowels of compassion in him!'

'And my uncle of Burgundy?' I cried out passionate, 'where's he with all his fine promises?'

'He'll come; he'll come ... when he can. He has commitments in France as you well know.'

'We heard little of those commitments when you bribed me to marry Brabant with promise of his help.'

'You could have married your uncle of Bavaria,' she said drily. 'Come, child, this is no time to blame this one or that. When the time comes, my brother will be here.'

'Who can expect honesty from a de Charolais?' I said, bitter. The red came up in her face and her lips went thin. She turned about and left me.

If neither my uncle of Burgundy nor his son would keep their word, I must do the best I could for myself.

I summoned my captains. Old van Brederode came hastening, and my father's sons and many another. I besought my towns for help; I emptied my purse to purchase arms, to pay the men. My armies were growing—Hainaulters, Hollanders and Zealanders. The Cods flocked to the enemy standard. My uncle was a Bavarian, too, but he was a strong man to keep the peace, not a mere girl, But, strong as he was, he would be forced to rely upon them. The ruler upon the Cod side would be a new and pleasing experience for them!

But the hearts that rode with me were true; and a second army was marching from Brabant. My husband, unwilling though he was, must for shame's sake, support me. He had accepted the oath from my people and given his own. His honour was pledged.

Through the countryside marched my two armies. My husband and his brother St Pol led the Brabanters. I rode at the head of my own forces, astride like a man, gown pulled high through a leather belt; I wore the armour I had borne at Gorcum, the crowned helmet carried before me that all might see that, woman though I was, I would yet fight alongside my men. Before me went horsemen and lances, drums and flutes and tabors. But there was still no news from my uncle of Burgundy.

Our armies were making for Dordrecht, the stronghold of the enemy. We had sent men ahead to dam the rivers and build heavy blockhouses along the roads. We arrived to find the work well done—waterways and roadways alike useless to those within the city.

I was confident. Right was might; God would not forsake me. But my husband was sour. Only a fool, he said, would think the battle won before it was fought. I was not such a fool, but a captain's courage uplifts his men and I would not let Brabant's mocking pull me down. Wherever I went among my own forces cheers met me; but the Brabanters would not cheer. They were ill-pleased to be fighting in this foreign land; and they had no love of me that had no love of their lord.

A sit-down siege is harder to endure than the clash of battle. Yet I kept my patience equal and my courage high. I had defeated my uncle at Gorcum, I should defeat him again at Dordrecht. I should make an end of his claims to my crown.

Week after week. And still we sat outside the walls; the city was obstinate—gallant, I almost said. For all the blocked roads and water-ways and no food going in, we could not starve them out. *Patience ...*

and a little patience; and the city must fall. I said it over and over again to my fretful husband.

In the sixth week—and we were well into October—he came into my tent wearing that nervous grin I knew so well.

'I can't keep my men together,' he said. 'They want to go home. And who can blame them? This god-damned country of yours! Its winds are as cold as its heart. Look!' He pulled me to the opening of the tent. 'They're already striking camp!'

I looked at the cheerful bustle of departure and I could not speak. I said at last, soft and bitter, 'Hollanders are not so quick to run away.'

'Where could they run to ... but Holland?' And he grinned again. He flung himself out not ill-pleased; van Brederode came in, his face drawn.

'We must raise the siege. We haven't the men,' he said.

I looked at him. All our planning and all our patience ... and all our dead!

'Must we run away with victory in our hands?'

'Our forces cannot take this damned town alone. Arrows and gun-stones—I say nothing of quicklime or boiling fat—meant for two armies, would be diverted to one. Our men couldn't stand up to it and I wouldn't ask them. We should lose the town; and our men, too.'

'We need this victory, *need* it, to show the people I can fight, yes and win, too. A defeat for my uncle here as well as Gorcum—and maybe he and his friends will think again!'

'We'll fight again and win, I promise,' he said; but I would not be comforted.

And so we were forced to leave Dordrecht; and the enemy came from the city and fell upon us and killed many more than were lost in the siege. And they stole our baggage-arms and food; and they cast down the road blocks and they undammed the river. And for that I had to thank my husband and his Brabanters; and, as I rode, proud armour discarded, I heard that city after city was going over to the enemy. And for that, also, I must thank my husband.

Incalculable, irresponsible, he had suddenly changed his side. Pricked on by his stepmother—the woman that had married my uncle of Bavaria—without a word to me, he had sent letters to every city in my three lands declaring that same uncle my sole heir should I die childless.

And now, at this blow to Burgundian greed, my mother was alarmed.

'Go back to your husband,' she said—and she was half-pleading, half-commanding. 'Get yourself with child. What's the sense in fighting? Win or lose—still your father's brother takes all.'

'Still I will fight!' And then I said, very bitter, 'Do not fool yourself, Madam. The fine husband you have chosen will never get me—nor any woman—with child.'

And now with so much lost that he might well have saved, my uncle of Burgundy came hurrying with his smooth-faced son.

'Will you let your inheritance pass into the hands of that relapsed priest, that bloody monster?' he stormed, as though his own hands were clean; as though I had welcomed my uncle of Bavaria.

It was January and I half-way towards my eighteenth birthday. I sat in my high place at the head of the conference table; but I kept my eyes down upon the polished wood. Yet even there I saw reflected the dark face of my enemies—John of Bavaria and John of Burgundy. At each end of the great chamber stood a hundred nobles of each party. Velvets, furs and jewels. As though they had come to a wedding!

I sat there alone and forsaken, my husband unable to protect me; unable and unwilling ... useless. And I remembered once more, as I was to remember again and again, my father's warning. And I hoped, bitter, that my uncle of Burgundy who had not lifted a finger to help me, would be satisfied now he knew how much less my marriage would bring him than he had hoped.

For we had met together to sign the truce; the truce between me and my false uncle of Bavaria. I was to make over to him lands that were mine, lands for which I should have fought with my heart's blood; and for which I would have fought had Burgundy and Brabant stood by me.

I sat silent, while point after point was wrangled, conceded without my word.

' ... and to my uncle, the Lord John, Duke of Bavaria, all those lands which he has won both by battle and by oath, and of which he is now possessed...'

And I dispossessed ...

'... Dordrecht with South Holland; Rotterdam, Leerdam and Gorcum ...'

Gorcum town of my victory, lost to me now. Lost.

'... And all the territories between the Lek and the Longe and the Merwede ...'

Lovely lands, proud cities, goodbye. Yet it is not enough it seems, not enough.

'And the said Lord John, Duke of Bavaria, shall share jointly with the Lord John Duke of Brabant, the government of Holland of Hainault and of Zealand for five years ...'

... not enough to keep the lands he has stolen. He takes full government. Share, it says; share! Share with that drunken fool my husband! Brabant will drink himself to death while my country chokes within a bloody hand. And the five years over—will that hand unclose again? Never? And what will become of my poor country? And of me? Sweet Christ will you let this wickedness be?

And even now it was not finished. I must acknowledge him—the Pitiless—my heir. They were reading his new title aloud, 'John Duke of Bavaria, Son of Holland...'

Son of Holland. Never count your chickens too soon, uncle-priest! There's a condition, a little condition. You're heir only as long as I have no child. How if I bear a child? No not to my impotent fool but to another? By God's Mother my marriage shall be annulled and you may whistle for my sovereign's crown.

I brought my distracted mind back to the conference table.

... One hundred thousand gold nobles, minted in England, to be paid by me to this new heir of mine because he hereby renounced the rights of sovereignty bestowed upon him by the Emperor. *Rights!* God help us! And, *renounced.* Oh yes, he renounced with one hand to snatch them back with the other—and paid a king's ransom to do it! And where was so much money to be found? Never fear, he would bleed my poor country to get his gold.

I could not bring myself to sign; could not so betray my father's trust nor the love of those that held by me still. But, sitting there, I felt their pressure upon me—pressure of my enemies; pressure of false friends—of Burgundy and his son. Seasoned men all; and I, a girl of seventeen! I forced my mouth to the words. 'Is it your will that I sign?' At that, each man held up his hand in assent—a forest of hands; and each mouth cried out; and there was but one voice and it cried *Aye.*

Then my uncle of Bavaria came forward and my husband with him; and they set their names to the paper that took from me my right to rule and delivered my people into an alien hand. When that was done my cousin of Burgundy rose smiling in his place and bowed and brought me the paper and put the pen in my hand. And my hand moved; my name spelled itself upon the parchment.

And now the thing was done those at the table rose waiting for me to rise, to take the hand my cousin Philip held out to lead me from the room. I wanted to strike it from me, God knows; but I sat still and motioned to them all to go.

And so I sat while the great room emptied, each man walking in his degree and bowing towards me as he went while I sat unheeding. It was only when I was entirely alone and the doors closed, that I put my head down upon the shining table and wept.

And so it was that William van Brederode found me. I raised my tear-stained face; I tried to speak. I held out my hands; my empty hands spoke for me.

He went down, a little stiff, on one knee. He said, 'Dear child, it is bad; but not so bad. The Bavarian is greedy—he wants all. South Holland is his now; he may do with it what he will. As for the rest, he rules together with your husband. Lion and jackal; we know what that means. So your uncle's Son of Holland now and heir to all! God be praised for his greed!'

I raised my bewildered head. That last did not make sense.

He said, and he was smiling a little, 'Do you think your uncle of Burgundy will stand by his signature, Burgundy that hopes to gather all into his own hand? Never believe it. Soon the quarrel will flame up afresh. When two dogs fight, the bone must slip.'

'And who will pick it up? Myself surrounded by traitors? And what of the bone itself? What of my country torn and broken, my poor country? What must I do?'

He said, kneeling there, 'It ill becomes a man to tell a woman—and she not more than a girl—what she must do. But consider this! The Bavarian has sold those rights—rights, God help us!—bestowed upon him by the Emperor. He no longer calls himself Count of Holland but Son of Holland. Not sovereign but heir; heir only. And he's that until you have a child—and no longer. Give the people their true heir.'

He took my hand and looked at it. 'This little hand has lifted a sword,' he said. 'You have not shrunk from man's work, heavy though it was. But woman's work is heavier. Shall you play coward there?'

He kissed my hand and gently put it down; he rose, clumsy as old people do, from his knees.

X

Old van Brederode had given me my answer; and a bitter one. But it was the only answer—if my husband were capable. There was but one way to disinherit my uncle of Bavaria. A child of my own blood.

Simple commonsense; but I was not yet eighteen.

Between disgust of my husband and fear of my father's brother, I knew not what to do. For—whatever advantages I might secure if Brabant managed to give me a child—I should be chained to him for life.

'You're chained in any case,' Beatrix said. 'There'll be no annulment; too many interests stand in the way. There's only one way of safety for you. To regain all you've lost, you must honour your marriage; you must have a child of your own!'

'By *him!*'

'It's the natural consequence of marriage. Oh Jacque,' she cried out suddenly in a heartbroken way, 'it's a hard thing; but it's the only thing. Women have children by husbands they dislike and they love their children ... and in time they come to love their husbands, too.'

'You can put that last out of the reckoning,' I said. 'It isn't dislike I feel for Brabant; it's disgust. Well, suppose I do what you call my duty; and suppose he is impotent—as I truly believe—what then?'

'Then it will be the worse for you! You'll never be free and you'll never be safe!'

If she were right—and I feared she might be—I must try to win this vicious boy to my bed. I understood the urgency but I would not accept it. Flesh and spirit alike rejected it.

But look at it as I might, I saw nothing for it but to go back cap in hand to my wretched husband. I should have to humble myself, I knew that well ... and he cared not a fig for me except to humiliate me. But, maybe my mother was right. I was new-married and ignorant in the art of winning a man. It was an ignorance I must ask humbly to be allowed to correct.

I sent to ask that I might join my husband's court. He took his time to reply—I might please myself! Hardly a gracious answer and I must make the best of it. But even while my bundles were apacking, he had taken himself off, leaving no word where I might join him.

'Let him go where he will—to Hell, if it please him!' My quick tongue got the better of me again. Fortunately there was none but Beatrix to hear; so I bit back my anger and started off to follow my husband.

He led me a dance—as he meant to. I who had turned my back upon him must now come running. And it was not until I reached Mons that I came up with him.

I found him swaggering in my own house—*Count of Hainault*. I found him surrounded by his officials and his toadies, who browbeat my household. It was a clever way of adding to my punishment—a little on account and more to follow. Oh, I need have no doubt I should be paid in full.

It was van der Berg, my husband's treasurer, who showed his enmity most clearly; he was in a position to do so. As for myself, I could not look upon the fat Brabanter without my gorge rising. Beatrix hated him more than I did; hated him for his clumsy attempts at seduction, small eyes glistening in folds of fat; hated him for his stupidity in believing he had but to lift a finger to bring her running to his bed.

She said nothing at first, for fear of harming my desperate attempts at reconciliation. But then the thing grew too much for her and she burst out in a fury surprising in so quiet a woman.

'The fat pig must be put where he can insult no more ladies. I will see to it!' I promised, rash.

I swept in a fury to my husband's rooms and burst in upon him unannounced.

T'serclaes was with him. They were sitting very close, laughing together; my husband's arm lay about the favourite's shoulder, his hand toyed with the favourite's hair.

The fire leaped to my husband's cheeks.

'This is my chamber, Madam,' he said, reminding me, as once I had reminded him. 'And it is not the custom to enter without permission. Be so good as to take yourself away!'

I should have been wise to go, or to have made some attempt at placating him; but the favourite was there. My husband turned tittering to his friend and I let slip the last of my commonsense.

'Wantonness is, it seems, the fashion of your court!' I said. 'I should be obliged, sir, if you would order your treasurer to keep his paws off my woman Beatrix van Vliet.'

'Let her husband look to it!' He and the favourite laughed again.

'It's good to know that husbands have some duties!' I said, tart. 'Van Vliet is about my business at the Hague; I am not minded to send his wife back sullied to her lord.'

'My Brabanters sully no one, least of all dirty Hollanders!' My husband pinched the favourite upon the cheek and laughed for the third time. He had meant to sound manly; it came out shrill as a girl's.

I turned my back and left him. The sound of his high laughter followed me back to my own apartments.

Three days later van der Berg was found dead—strangled in his own bed.

One of my pages brought me the news—a small Brabanter appointed by my husband. Much as I disliked Brabanters for their insolence to me, I could not dislike this child. I should have remembered that for all his seeming innocence, he was yet a Brabanter, to look and to listen and to carry his tales.

Now I was unwise enough to laugh.

'There'll be no love-play in the bed where he lies roasting! Come, smile,' I told Beatrix. 'No need to look so pinched and pale; you're safe from that animal now!'

She nodded, dumb, and I went chattering on. The creature was safely dead—and a load off my heart.

In the midst of my chatter the door was flung open, and unannounced my mother came sailing into the room.

'You would do better,' she told me without greeting, 'to hide your joy in the death of a man!'

I was surprised at her unlooked-for appearance; I had thought her safe at le Quesnoy. She had come, she said, to keep an eye on me, an eye I clearly needed and that angered me more than her reproof.

'Why should I pretend to weep?' I asked as sharp. 'I have endured enough from that creature, enough and enough!'

'You may endure more, weep more, now he is dead!' She turned suddenly upon Beatrix. 'What do *you* know of the matter, mistress?'

I saw how the blood left my woman's cheeks. She said, very low, 'I, Madam? What could I know?'

'A great deal I should think!' My mother turned her harsh eyes on me. 'Your father left me burdens enough when he left you, my girl, without burdening me with the wickedness of his bastards!'

'What do you mean, Madam?' And my voice came out shrill and angry as her own.

'What do I mean, Madam? Surely it's plain, Madam! If you're in doubt question this woman of yours. And, when you've got your answer, then keep your mouth shut!'

'You forget, I think,' and I was stung by her tone, 'that I am your prince as well as your daughter.'

'How long you'll be anyone's prince, I don't know!' she said, drily. 'But my daughter you'll be all your life!' And she was gone.

It was then I saw that the boy had disappeared. How much had he heard? And when had he slipped away? I did not know; nor care ... not then. My concern was all with this good Beatrix of mine.

I asked no question; there was no need. She said, very quiet, 'It was my brothers.' And she might have said, *Your brothers.* 'They were not minded to see my father's daughter dishonoured.' And she might have said, *Your father's daughter.*

'Did you know before ... before ...?' I could not name the word *murder* in connection with Beatrix, my Beatrix with her gentle face and her loving heart.

She shook her head. 'They did not tell me before—or after. But I know.'

I was bitterly sorry that she, however innocent, should be involved in the affair. That it could involve myself I never dreamed; or that my position, such as it was, could worsen because of it.

I should have had more sense. I should have known that such a man is as dangerous dead as alive. Tongues that spared Beatrix did not spare me. Van der Berg had been murdered; and Madam the Hollander knew more than a little about it!

The Brabanters who had disliked me now showed open enmity. My husband haunted me with accusations and tears. 'You have robbed me of a dear friend—not the less dear because he hated you; as he hated all my enemies!' And he did not care who heard him accusing me of murder. 'Well, you shall not be one whit the better for it! There are others to step into his shoes to tread you down; you and your accursed Hollanders.'

Into the shoes of the hateful van der Berg stepped the more hateful T'serclaes. Now the venom of both husband and wife were turned against me. Between them they made my life a burden.

But I would not show it, not I! Each fresh insult seemed to glance from me, but it quivered long in my heart. And insults there were, in plenty. And not only were they wounding; they were mighty inconvenient. Did I desire a new gown, a new cup, a small gift for a friend, my Lord Everhard T'serclaes was forever enquiring why it was needed; and he made no bones about refusing. The treasury of his master was well-nigh empty, poured out in senseless fighting, he would tell me, all smiling insolence. And I would remember how the Brabanters had run away at Dordrecht—the only time they had mustered on my side; instead of victory I had been forced to treat with my uncle. Stripped of my rights, my treasure stolen, my purse grown lean—and my husband's fat—through their treachery, I must now come cap in hand. It was hard to keep my tongue still; sometimes there would be blood where my lip was bitten through.

As might be expected, the unchecked insolence of the T'serclaes couple did not escape attention—that she did not curtsey to Madam the Duchess but giggled behind her hand; that he scanted his bow as I went by and waited long enough to perform even that meagre attention; the whole court copied their example.

That I, my father's daughter, should be made the target of Brabantine buffoonery, filled me with anger; and not only for myself. I felt in this, the insult to my country. Never patient, there were times when I felt anger rise black as from a fiery mountain. But, though I kept a still tongue, the changing colour, the kindling eye, spoke for me; and, triumphant, my husband would pounce cackling with foolish laughter.

Day after day, week after week, month after month. And no kindness between us nor any courtesy. To get a child by him was not only repugnant to me, it was impossible, even had he not been impotent; we were never to be found in the same place, unless one of his cronies urged him to seek me out for the purpose of further insult.

At last, when I could endure it no longer, I hid myself in Hainault, where, deep in the country, I have a hunting-lodge; and there, in the joys of the chase—which I love above any sport—I would forget, for a little, my bitter marriage. And he, restless, would wander from town to town, from castle to castle, listening eagerly to the venomous tongues of T'serclaes and his wife. The more devil I, the more saint he!

And so we came to the summer of fourteen hundred and twenty. I was not quite nineteen and I had been married two years. I was unhappy in my marriage and cut off from all those things for which I had been born. I was frustrated, but I was not yet bitter. I tried to fill the empty days with small kindnesses. When I was at le Quesnoy, which was often, I would have the schoolmaster and the priests that sang masses for my father's soul, to dine with me. It filled their bellies and did not lighten too much my lean purse. And there would always be some gift I must make—a dowry for such of my women who, lacking it, must go unwed. And there were wedding-gifts; and how often I wished others happy that was so unhappy myself. And there were christening-cups; and how often I stood godmother that was not likely to be a mother myself.

But these small kindnesses were not enough; the purpose had been torn from my life and I languished, useless.

Between my two uncles I was undone. My uncle of Bavaria kept his stranglehold on the lands he had filched from me. He ruled with a strong hand and the people were cowed and quiet. My uncle of Burgundy had never lifted a hand to help me. And now he never would. He had been murdered in France. I did not weep for him, my childhood's bogey, but for the promise of help that never came. But I should have wept. For his son stepped into his shoes—Philip more dangerous with his sly smiling than the dark man his father; more subtle, more greedy, more ruthless. Philip the Good!

It is a strange thing. My uncle of Burgundy who had brought me nothing but misery while he lived, did me a kindness by dying. It came about in this manner.

King Henry of England—great Henry of Agincourt, had long been angling for my cousin Catharine of Valois; Catharine together with the crown of France. There had been haggling and disputes ever since she was twelve years old. She was not quite nineteen now—my own age almost to the day. Seven years of haggling! But the King of France, mad though he might be, he would never budge on one point. Almost entirely the slave of that strong wife of his, he would never, for all her persuasions, cut Charles from the succession—Charles the last son left to him. Now the murder of my uncle altered everything. Charles, as everyone knew, had had more than a finger in that pie; and, in the widespread anger that followed the murder, the King was persuaded at last to disinherit him. So Henry got Catharine and the Regency of France while the mad King lived; and the crown to follow when he died.

I have to explain this because I went to the wedding and met the King of England ... and altered the pattern of my life for ever.

XI

With every beat of horses' hooves I left some unhappiness behind me. I had stepped into the charette the unhappiest woman in

Christendom; I stepped out of it gay as any girl bound for a wedding.

Troyes was hung with banners and with garlands. The whole town was wild with excitement, bright with crowds in holiday clothes; the charette could hardly push its way along. The crowds, recognizing not me but a wedding-guest, cheered madly; nodding and smiling at the window, I waved back.

The Queen of France received me—Isabeau that had been my first husband's mother. The King was shut away, she told me; the excitement of the wedding had been too much for him. But others whispered that grief had brought the sickness again; grief because he had been forced to sign away his son's rights to this new son-in-law. But Isabeau showed no sign of grief. She played both Queen and King—and played them well. Dark eyes, bright-painted lips, she was all graciousness, all smiles; they said of her that she could take her pick of lovers yet ... and did. Now, for all her smiling, she was the same Isabeau that had frightened me as a child. She frightened me no longer; but I did not like her and I never would.

I found the bride in her chamber pale as a Christmas rose. *Catharine the Fair* they were calling her now; but it was a compliment, merely, to the King of England's bride. She was no beauty; she was too slight, yet she had a grace of her own ... until you set her beside a plump and rounded bosom. And her nose was a trifle long—the true Valois nose; but her youth and her pretty colouring disguised the fact.

At supper I had my first sight of the groom.

Like the best part of Christendom I was prejudiced against Henry V of England—a man whose harshness often hid his real love of justice. But, as he sat there, bending with courtesy towards the Queen, I was forced to admit he was handsome.

He looked older than his thirty-five years—face lined, grey in the chestnut of his hair. His eyes, of a true hazel, might have been beautiful, but for the coldness in them. And the straight nose and strong chin gave him a manly beauty so that one forgot, almost, the narrow line of the mouth. Yes, a handsome man, proud, strong, aloof; and majesty all about him. I remembered my half-man, my vicious boy, and could have wept there at the wedding-feast.

When we had done eating, while the tables were stacked away and the minstrels tuning up for the masque, Isabeau brought me to where he sat. Catharine was greeting her guests and he was alone; the chair in which he sat became him like a throne.

'I present to you, son of England,' Isabeau said, 'your kinswoman, my cousin and daughter Madam Jacqueline, Duchess of Brabant, Countess of Holland, Hainault and Zealand. She was wife to my son John, Christ assoil his sweet soul.'

His smile dismissed her. I rose from my curtsey and he nodded towards the chair that stood beside him.

'So!' And for all his grimness there was a faint smile about his mouth. 'Have you considered this, kinswoman? You would be future Queen of France and I, myself, elsewhere—but for the accident of death.'

'With God there is no accident, sir,' I said. 'My husband was good and he was gentle ... and he was very young. It needs a strong man on the throne of France. God give you long life and shield you from all ill!'

'I share your hope and return it again.'

'Sir,' I said, 'I thank you.' And so saying I saw my chance and leaped to it. 'Your wish, alas, comes too late. But we must not spoil your happiness, sir, with a sorrowful tale.'

'To help others is not to spoil our own happiness, but to add to it,' he said.

He did not mean it. It was a courtly speech and nothing more. He was about to wrap it up in some pleasant philosophy but I could not afford to let the chance slip.

'That is a kindness we might look for in you, cousin,' I said. 'We are true cousins; we stem from the same tree. But I make no claim to kinship. Yet, your grace, as all Christendom knows, is not one to forget a kindness. My father sheltered your father when King Richard banished him. For the sake of Henry Bolingbroke that came safe home to England and to a crown, will you help me now?'

He said at once—but he did not relish the reminder, 'I will repay my father's debt to your father's child.'

So I told him about my marriage that was no marriage—not in law since the Pope had forbidden it before ever we went to church; not in deed, because of my half-man.

'The Pope must grant me annulment,' and I was quiet as though I described some small business matter and not the great sacrament between man and woman. To ask pity of Henry of England would be useless; that was clear in his face. But set out my wares, drive a good bargain—and I might win him.

'I am to petition His Holiness; but it may be that, until he answers, I shall need protection. My uncle of Bavaria will be at my throat. He'll move heaven and earth to prevent the annulment. Nor will there be any safety in Brabant. I will endure the danger as long as I may; but I may need shelter until His Holiness answers. Shall I find it in England? If you will grant me sanctuary I will be your faithful friend and ally. Holland shall give you ships for your wars; not sell, but give. And there will be trade concessions—your wool for our weaving on such terms that you yourself shall name. I shall be an ally—such an ally!—when free of my half-man I come into my own.'

He looked at me thoughtful. Great soldier that he was he knew the value of a business deal.

He said at last, 'Should His Holiness grant this annulment, would it please you to marry in England?'

This question took my breath away. To be allied to England, to this great fighting King! I should be secure in my inheritance for ever.

'Sir, I say *Yes*. It is an honour as great as it is unlooked for.'

'It was not always thought so!' he said drily.

'Sir, *I* think so.'

'Why then,' he said, 'who knows but that we may change our kinship; no longer cousins but sister and brother?'

He drew a ring from his finger and said, very thoughtful, 'This could carry you through France where my word runs. As for the lands Burgundy holds, you may have luck there! Luck and wit—you'll need them both. Burgundy—' he said sharply, 'you did not mention him among the dangers!'

'To dot the *i* is waste of time when one can read!' I said.

He smiled a little sour. 'To give you this ring is to risk setting me at odds with Burgundy—a thing I cannot afford. Can you be trusted not to babble, kinswoman?'

'You may trust me,' I said. 'I swear it before Christ and His sweet mother.'

'A man's bare word is enough if he be honest,' he said; and I remembered that they said of this Henry that he never called upon God to be his witness, nor used an oath ever; his plain word stood higher than other men's oaths.

'I will give you the ring,' he said.

The thing I had never even dreamed could happen—had happened. The King of England stood my friend. Now I should sit again on the throne of my father. And it was as though a great drum beat in the place of my heart.

I was to marry the King of England's brother, his own brother ... when His Holiness set me free. And that he must set me free when great Henry stood my friend, I did not doubt.

I tossed sleepless in my bed.

...The King of England's brother. But ... which brother? John of Bedford and Humphrey of Gloucester were both unmarried. And the King had not said which one. I thought of Bedford as I had seen him this day—the great raw-boned, red-haired man with an eye as cold as that of the King himself, an upright man, unloving, unlovable. I had married twice; and each time to please others. Should I not marry this third time to please myself? The King's brother—why not? But Gloucester; not Bedford. Gloucester.

But my father had warned me against him. Worse than the Brabant marriage, he had said; and about the Brabant marriage he had been right, terribly right. But this was different. He had known Brabant well; he had not known Gloucester. I doubt he had seen Gloucester more than twice in his life.

Gloucester. And my mind left my father's warning, remembering again the delightful young man that I had thought the handsomest in Christendom, and the gayest and the cleverest. And when he had bowed over my hand as though I were the world's beauty and not a plump ten-year-old, I was sure he must be the kindest and the best.

Gloucester, Gloucester, Gloucester.

I had been married twice; and now, for the first time I was suddenly, surprisingly in love. I suppose the picture of Gloucester had always been in my heart—a child's picture, no more, and not within the compass of my dreams, much less my desires. He had been as remote from me as a knight in an old tale.

And now, suddenly, blindingly, he had materialized—a possible husband; the only possible husband. My father's warning I would bury with him. I had been obedient too long, unhappy too long. I knew full well that in the marriage of princes happiness is no consideration. Policy is all. If to marry in England were good policy, whether I took Bedford or Gloucester mattered to no one but myself.

And how it mattered! My whole life turned upon it.

Catharine's wedding-day. Trinity Sunday; sun and blue sky for a royal bride. Catharine looked beautiful. But where is the bride who, this one day, will not look like the Queen of Heaven? And certainly she had a handsome groom. Isabeau had whispered behind her hand that the girl burned for him. But to me she looked pale and a little frightened.

I remember how we undressed the bride that was now Queen of England; and would be Queen of France. And I could not but think how nearly I had worn that crown myself! We laughed and we jested but she lay there in the great bed and her face was white as the pillow beneath the bright flow of her hair.

Isabeau rallied us both. 'My daughter will beat you to it for an heir! She has married a full man. As for you, cousin, you'll get no child out of that husband of yours though you wait till Doomsday.'

Her words were an arrow to draw blood. So she, too, believed Brabant impotent. Suddenly it came to me that Beatrix was right—Beatrix and not van Brederode; this impotency must be the strongest chain to bind me to him. My uncle of Bavaria and my cousin of Burgundy would tolerate, neither of them, the possibility that I might produce a child of my own. Enemies they were; but in this, of one mind. There would be no annulment. They would see to it!

Let them do their worst! Did they think they had God in their pockets? God would speak through his greatest son. Henry of England would petition the Pope. God's Vicar could not refuse God's soldier.

I tossed between rosy future and bleak present. Twice I had been married and little good had come of it... I thought of this third marriage and my flesh trembled and stirred.

The wedding was over and I was returning home. Before I left I caught a moment with Catharine.

'Dearest Cat,' I said, 'be happy.'

She did not answer; only those grey eyes of hers clouded to purple.

'To be married to a full man might be heaven—if you will make it so. To be married to a half-man—there's hell; spite and distrust and misery, and nothing can change it. Thank God for your man and be happy with him.'

Spite and distrust and misery... With every beat of my horse's hooves my burden fell heavier. I was returning to my shameful bondage and not even the King of England's ring could help me. I should never escape because I had not the courage. To break with my husband without the Pope's permission seemed now too desperate a thing. His Holiness would command my return and back I must crawl like a beaten dog. And if I refused? Even King Henry himself could not shelter me. I should lose both my crowns—earthly and heavenly; I should live like a leper for the rest of my life.

I should have to be yet more unhappy before I dared court such disaster; and more unhappy I did not think I could be.

I did not even yet know the full extent of my husband's spite.

Things grew steadily worse. Everhard T'serclaes was making yet more trouble; now it was hard for me to get as much as a new shift. He was his lord's treasurer, he told Beatrix, and he could not make ends meet. Madam the Duchess was entirely too extravagant.

'Let T'serclaes look first to his harlot of a wife!' I cried out, all shaken with my anger. 'Let him enquire who pays for her gowns and her jewels and her furs.'

'No need!' Beatrix said, grim. 'My lord treasurer handles the gold himself.'

And so the days went by and lengthened into weeks and lengthened into months ... and lengthened indeed. But still T'serclaes pursued me with his insolence; and still I pretended to take no need. He was no more than a gadfly, I said.

But a gadfly can sting.

Beatrix came to me with a face grave rather than angry.

'T'serclaes declares that his lord can no longer support the expense of your ladies. He says we are eating him out of house and home. Oh he's *wicked*!' She was angrier than I had ever seen her. 'Not one of us eats more than we need to keep body and soul together. We know well that spiteful eyes are forever on our mouths!'

She was right. One had but to look at them at table. They ate little while the Brabanters swilled like pigs. 'Their good manners are their best defence if defence were needed,' I said. 'But it is not needed. It is my right to keep those women I choose about me.'

I was heartsick of the quarrelling and the meanness. I took myself and my own household from Brussels to Vilvoorde for a little peace. There in the quiet I thought I should never return to the bickering and the indignities. But—what then? Should I find courage to break free from my wretched existence? Even if the Pope held his hand, my cousin of Burgundy would be hot against me; and my uncle of Bavaria would raise heaven and hell.

And there was a third person I must consider—my mother.

If she stood by me, then her prestige might carry me through.

But would she stand by me? She would wait, I thought, to see which way the cat jumped and then she would come out on the winning side.

No, I could not count on my mother.

I was sitting in the garden at Vilvoorde pondering my problem and my ladies about me, some at their needle, others playing at ball. Quiet all of us, decent and well-behaved.

There was, I thought, a distant beat of hooves. I listened. Horses at the gallop. Suddenly the horsemen were on us, leaping the low walls, jostling through the gateway, my husband at the head, urging on his beast with whip and spur and not caring who might be hurt nor whether he broke his own neck or the neck of his mount.

I rose in the midst of my scattered ladies. Whatever contempt I felt for him I would not lower my dignity by lowering his. I greeted him with due reverence and my women, gathered again, dipped to the ground. My husband did not so much as incline his head, and the T'serclaes couple sat their horses, one on either side, smiling.

My husband lifted his voice—the shrill girlish voice that might have made me laugh had I not wanted to puke instead.

'Madam,' he said, 'you must dismiss your household at once—one and all! My purse can no longer support them. I have appointed others to their places and here are their names!' He flung a roll of paper at my feet and, turning, galloped away; and his party, following, churned the soft grass and broken flowers of my garden.

I put out my two hands and must have fallen; but Beatrix ran from one side and the demoiselle Ermgart van Rietuelt from the other and so they brought me into the house.

I sat within my chamber, the paper before me, and could not bring myself to touch it. My husband that had put so many shames upon me, had added this last, shaming me and my faithful women together; women I had known from childhood.

Suddenly before I well knew what I was about, I was on my feet, crying aloud for my horse. Let who would follow, I would wait for no one!

The dust rose on the white of the road. My lord Duke and his company had ridden in the direction of Fuhr, I was told. I galloped madly, dust in my nostrils, rage in my heart. Had he looked to see me he would have given orders to keep me out; he cared not at all what humiliations he put upon me. But he had not looked for me and so I found him in his chamber fondling his harlot; and, lest there be jealousy, his other hand fondled the husband. He was, need I say it? tipsy.

They had been gaming all three and the table was piled with the glittering spoil the precious couple had won.

It was upon this pretty scene I burst now. Never in all my life had I been so angry. I had a hot temper—and still have—though I was teaching myself to control it. Now the weeks of patience broke.

'Sir,' I cried out, 'you forget yourself, you and your wanton here, and the careful steward that counts the very shifts I wear, that watches every mouthful I eat! He makes his hay while the sun shines, he and the easy wife. Fool that you are, you load them both with treasure—my treasure. You have laid hands upon what is mine to give to these creatures that will turn their backs when you have no more to give!'

My hand swept the table and the jewels went flying. Even in that moment the prudent Everhard would have gathered together his spoil; but my hand uplifted, stopped him. I suppose I must have looked strange—frightening perhaps—standing there covered with dust from head to foot, hair wild, eyes ablaze.

'I will no longer endure this woman in any house where I am, no, nor the man, neither! And further, heed me and heed me well, I refuse to dismiss my women. Oh, I know well they are thorns in your flesh, well-bred as they are and of good conduct! Not one of them would stoop to the unashamed wantoning of this court of yours.'

'Wantoning!' Brabant said and he laughed. 'Overlong in the tooth, the lot of them. Skinny as old hens or fat as breeding sows. They must wait, my dear, till they're asked!'

'Hold your tongue!' I commanded and lost the last rag of my tattered temper. 'I am sick to the heart of your insults and will take no more. You're a child that should be whipped; you and your wanton and her husband, there. They, at least, are old enough to know better, and have been this many year. Listen to me. Your wife I may be—though I much doubt it. But I am a prince in my own right and I will maintain what state I please. I choose my own household as you do, yours—' my eyes flicked over the T'serclaes couple, who stared back unabashed. 'But let them not come in any house where I am; nor in any house where I may be. Remember it!'

And I turned about and away from his hateful presence.

XII

I had sworn to keep my women. But how was I to pay them? In south Holland my uncle of Bavaria collected the revenues for his own pocket. My husband had laid hands upon my jewels—and some of them I had seen upon the precious T'serclaes pair; and to him, direct, were paid revenues from such lands as were still mine. Sovereign of Holland, Hainault, Zealand and Friesland; yet poorer than the meanest servant—his wages, at least, were paid faithfully.

The women named by my husband came, all smiles. The T'serclaes in particular relished the position—I had refused to have her in the same house with me, yet here she was and here she would remain. I sent them from my presence, smiles on the other side of their faces ... but she went on smiling.

Christmas came and went; there was little goodwill in the season for me or for my women. Cheerfully they went unpaid; but I was sad for them, humiliated for myself. I was more than ever an object of dislike to the whole court. I had ignored my husband, their duke. I had scorned their wives and daughters—I had kept my own foreigners. Well, I should be punished! T'serclaes would see to it, the good treasurer! Madam the Hollander should hear more about it!

I laughed when I heard. What more could he do to increase my miseries?

I was soon to see.

It was the custom at the Brabant court to take the two light meals of the day in our own apartments, the two main meals in the great hall. T'serclaes began his persecution by sending meagre helpings of food to my suite, portions which, small enough to begin with, grew steadily less. Once I was foolish enough to play his game. I sent to the kitchens for more. Back came the answer, 'There is no more. Madam the Duchess supports two trains of ladies, we have orders to feed one train only.'

I did not ask again. But the persecution did not cease. Sometimes the door would be pushed open as though in error and we would see great trays piled high with bread, with meat, and great jugs brimming with wine and ale. And the servants, catching sight of a wistful eye or a watering mouth as they withdrew, would chuckle.

With hunger and humiliation we were in a state of misery I could no longer ask my ladies to endure. For their own sakes I must dismiss them; must lower my pride, eat my words.

'You must go, all of you, even you,' I told Beatrix. 'I cannot keep you here, half-starved, the butt of the whole court.'

'We will never leave you,' she said, 'not one of us—until you yourself want us to go.'

'You must eat or starve!' I reminded her.

'There's always dinner and supper!' she said. 'As for the rest—' she took from her neck the gold chain, Van Vliet's wedding-gift, and fingered the heavy links. 'This should keep us in food for a long time.'

'We are not come to that yet!' I said and put it back upon her neck. 'Bring me my jewel-box.'

There was, I well knew, little enough left. I picked up a ring of small value and looked at it doubtfully.

'It isn't worth much as a jewel,' I said, 'but it should buy quite a lot of meat.'

'Had it been worth more it wouldn't be here at all!' Beatrix laughed; and, laughing with her I felt my courage return.

After that ring, another; and then a brooch or two. Now my ladies, though not lavishly fed, had enough to support them between dinner and supper. When the last of my poor jewels had gone, my faithful women came, one by one, offering their own. I was grateful; but it was a gratitude heavy to bear.

It was a mode of living that could not last long. Yet I would not give way. I went about with a constant small gnawing of hunger; and that was easier to bear than the intolerable weight of humiliation.

The hope that had flamed high at Troyes was all-but dead. Poor and friendless as I was, and lowered by hunger, I should have given up all hope of freedom had not something happened; something so full of spite, of the passion to shame me to the depths, that it must either kill or cure my spirit.

Easter had come round again; a sweet April with gentle winds and the scent of violets; season of hope and joy. But for me there was neither.

No food had been sent to our rooms for days, save one portion only. Mouth watering, I sent it away. We could not go on much longer; there was little left in the way of jewels between us; and what there was would bring in nothing like their value—merchants have a nose for need! But today, at least, things could be borne. If we went hungry now, we should feast tonight. The Easter feast—and plenty for all. Tomorrow would be another day.

How we longed for suppertime. We would nod and sniff and, Duckling, we would say, or roast goose; or venison or pork. Like the story of old, each smelt her favourite food.

We had counted the minutes until it was time to go down; but we dared not appear too eager—a fresh butt for laughter. At long last I entered the hall attended by my ladies—and how poor and shabby we looked compared with the others—and took my place next to my husband at the high table. He did not so much as turn to greet me; he went on presenting his back while he leaned smiling towards the T'serclaes woman.

The guests were already seated and every table full; every table but one. The table set aside for my ladies and usually occupied by the Brabant women appointed by my husband, was empty. With thankfulness I saw my women take the vacant places.

It is not always easy to see what happens in other parts of the hall when a feast is in progress. There is much coming and going—servants carrying great dishes from the kitchens hurry backwards and forwards, pages dart to and fro offering meat, offering bread, offering wine, offering finger-bowls and napkins. Dogs leap and bark, falcons stir upon their perch with a great flapping of wings and raucous cries. Movement and noise are a screen between table and table.

And so it was that I helped myself freely from the dishes and ate with a good appetite. It was some little time before I knew what was happening. And then I did not so much see as sense; sense it by the odd behaviour of those about me—the tittering, the nodding and the smiling.

Under the cover of noise and movement, the Brabant women had come into the hall and were now seated at a table that had been set up for them. And they had been abundantly served—trenchers steaming, goblets brimming—they and everyone there except my own women. There they sat in that great hall before an empty board. And, as I looked, titters deepened into small gusts of laughter; laughter deepened, rose like a trumpet, rang through the whole court.

I made as though I neither saw nor heard. I ate and drank as though I did not know they sat there, my gentlewomen of Holland, bearers of proud names all, the target of mean laughter. At each mouthful the baseness, the spite, the insult to these dear friends rose to choke me.

They must go. I was beaten.

The feast was over; over at last the long, the bitter insult.

I rose and moved between the ranks of those that mocked with bent backs. And so walking, I found my hands tight clasped about my gown, lest I raise them to strike my smirking husband in the face. I went quietly by his side; and all the time I vowed that never again would I spend another night beneath the man's roof. And now, even in my mind I rejected the word *husband*; nor would I call him so ever again though I died for it. He had insulted me for the last time.

There was no sleep for me. I must get away. But how? Nothing was clear in the turmoil of my mind except that I must take no bundle nor tell a single soul. But Beatrix? Go alone—and not even a word of farewell? it must be so. It could be death for Beatrix if she had the slightest suspicion of my flight.

I sat moodily breaking my breakfast bread and drinking my wine, and rejecting plan after plan, when Beatrix came in much excited.

My mother was in Brussels. She had heard, it seemed, of the continual quarrelling between Brabant and me and was come to put an end to it. She had arrived the evening before and had put up at an inn.

My mother at an inn! She with her de Charolais pride and de Charolais parsimony!

'No doubt to weigh the gossip and come at the truth before going into action!' Beatrix said. 'And plenty of gossip she'll get!' she added grim. 'The whole town's agog with last night's tale.'

It wanted but this added difficulty in the way of my flight. Now I must wait—God grant my courage would not cool!—until she had betaken herself off.

'She spoke with my lord this morning. Never look so pale, Jacque my dear—she's gone!'

Gone! Without staying to see me, without asking my side of the story. 'It's clear she stands with Brabant in this,' I said, bitter. 'And no wonder. She cheated me into marrying him!'

'Could it be,' Beatrix said, gentle, 'that she was not minded to stay in this house where you have been so grossly insulted?'

'No,' I said. 'With her I'm always in the wrong! Too rash, undisciplined, she says. Well, be it so or not, I'm no longer her obedient child—and so she shall find!'

'Still, you should go to see her, she's at *The Looking-Glass Inn*. She's your mother, Jacque. She's a clever woman; and a proud one. I think she will not suffer this insult to go unchecked. I think she will find a way out of this unhappy affair.'

'I shall find my own way!' I said. And then, remembering the dire need of my mother's goodwill, I said, 'Still, you may send for a litter.'

There was no litter available—they were all being cleaned or refurnished or they were out on business. I called for a horse; it was the same tale—half-a-dozen excuses and not one beast available.

'Then I'll go on shanks's pony!' I said. 'Bring me my cloak.'

She would have come with me, but we judged it best not to anger my mother with the sight of her.

So there I was walking alone through the streets of Brussels, I that had never walked alone anywhere in my life.

It felt strange, walking there, pushed and jostled in the narrow street; but the very jostling brought me a sense of freedom, of security almost, so that unhappy as I was, and unwilling to meet my mother, yet I was lighter of heart than I had been since they had wed me

84

to my sot.

I had no difficulty in finding *The Looking-Glass*. My mother had commanded the whole house for herself and her suite. Jaw set, colour high, she looked so much like her brother, that childhood bogey, that my courage sank. But only for a moment. I have their blood in my veins.

I need not have feared; Beatrix had been right. But I had not been wrong either, thinking she would blame me. She had done so at first; I had after all fought bitterly against that second marriage service. But, once in Brussels, putting together this bit of gossip with that, it was plain that I had been grossly insulted. De Charolais blood had boiled. She had not stayed for breakfast; food would have choked her, she said. And there she was, in Brabant's actual presence—no man daring to bar her way—before he'd so much as heard of her arrival.

'He was having his riding-boots pulled on,' my mother said. 'There was a woman performing this womanly task. He was as full as a wineskin, early though it was. As a rule he's terrified of me; now he welcomed me for the pleasure of insulting me. Wine lent him courage; it didn't last long.'

'Madam, you come too late,' he had told her. 'The feast is over!'

'The woman at his feet grinned,' my mother continued, 'an overblown creature with his great boots clasped to her ridiculous breasts. By God I'll have her carried off and whipped, if she does not mend her manners, I care not who she may be!' my mother cried out. She took in her breath before she could speak again.

Suddenly Brabant had lost his temper. 'The feast is over,' he had cried out again. 'And all is over. I will no longer endure the insolence of this daughter of yours.'

She had looked at him then, the miserable boy trying to brazen it out.

'You're drunk, Brabant!' she had told him. And, indeed, he must have been drunker even than usual. He had not risen at her entrance but sat unashamed and fondled his woman. He had done better to treat my mother with respect. Now it was not only the insult to me—that might have been dealt with; it was the insult to her and to her house that had brought her over to my side.

'I will not waste my breath on you,' she had said, 'pickled in drink as you are. But I warn you; I warn you, Brabant. If you do not mend your manners, others will mend them for you.'

He had grinned at that. 'Meaning, dear mother?'

'You had best treat my daughter with the respect due to her—or you will find out!' And I can imagine how she stared him down with a fierce eye. 'You can, it appears, control your soldiers as little as you control yourself. Through their cowardice at Dordrecht more than half my daughter's inheritance is lost. Yet it was for you—her husband—to guard both her and her lands. You have failed miserably. Well, what's done is done. But there's still the future. I warn you, and I am not given to idle threats, if you do not behave properly—keep your whore out of sight to begin with—maintain my daughter in her proper state and treat her with all due respect, I do not say with kindness since kindness is not in you, I shall take her away.'

'You would not dare!' And she said he was white to the lips. 'She's my wife!'

'But not your dog!' my mother said. 'Remember it!' She swept him her curtsey—she was not one to ignore etiquette, however great her anger. And, indeed, it made her threat seem more formidable. And all the time she ignored Laurette T'serclaes as though she were—not a dog, for a dog is worthy of respect, my mother said—but as though she were not there at all. And was gone.

She had come over to my side. She was prepared to take me away; but only till such time as Brabant came to his senses. 'That you should leave him for ever, is a thing I will not and cannot countenance. His Holiness expressly said—'

'Never talk to me about the Pope!' I interrupted, 'my own conscience speaks louder.'

She looked about her, disturbed lest anyone overhear this heresy. She said, 'How can a Christian wife leave her husband? It's mortal sin.'

'It was the marriage that was mortal sin. When Brabant came to my bed my flesh crawled.'

She thrust out her hands and they trembled a little. For the first time in my life I saw her with a helpless look on that formidable face. And when she did not answer, I cried out, 'You have thrust me into this mess; now you must help me out!'

'That's easier said than done. There's Burgundy to reckon with!'

'An end to this loathsome marriage,' I cried out, 'or to my life.'

I looked at this mother of mine; for the first time her glance wavered before mine.

'I shall go to Hainault,' I said. 'And you must go with me. You must show Christendom you stand by me. Once in my loyal city of Mons you will see how little Philip counts.'

'Don't underestimate him,' she warned me. 'He is most subtle; more to be feared than his father.'

I laughed at that. The bogey that had darkened my childhood was dead. Unlike my mother I had not yet taken young Burgundy's measure.

XIII

Beatrix met me on my return; she had an odd look. 'You have a visitor, Jacque. She's waiting; has waited this long while. It is ... Laurette T'serclaes.'

The T'serclaes! I could hardly speak for his new piece of insolence. 'Turn her out and let in the clean air. How *dare* she?' I turned upon Beatrix. 'And how dare *you?*'

'I thought you should see her. I still think so,' Beatrix said very quiet.

The thought of admitting the woman into my presence turned me sick with anger. But Beatrix had a great wisdom where I was concerned.

'I will see her,' I said, at last, unwilling. 'But let her cool her heels; let her wait!'

When I summoned her at last, she actually made her curtsey and so remained until I gave her the nod to rise. She stood up then, head hanging, and did not offer to speak. 'Well?' I asked, very sharp.

She lifted her head and looked towards Beatrix. 'Madam the Duchess, what I have to say is between you and me.'

'There is nothing between you and me,' I said.

'Enough to cost me my life!'

'And is that so rich a treasure?'

'By God, it is not!' she burst out.

The outburst surprised me; but I gave no sign.

'And yet,' she said, 'we have but one life here on earth; and when I quit it, I am bound, I think, for Hell.'

I said nothing to that.

'Madam the Duchess thinks I am the Duke's harlot.' She shook her head. 'The Duke has no need of harlots; he has no use of any woman in his bed. He has his mignons ... and my husband is one.'

I sat there and gave no sign; but my heart turned over with disgust. That Brabant was impotent I had long believed; but that he diverted himself with mignons I had not known. And yet, had I not guessed it long ago; known and would not know? The way he looked at

Everhard T'serclaes and must finger him if he could; the way he had sat stroking the man's hair that day I found them alone; that day they had been gambling all three and he had fondled them both! Brabant's childishness, I had told myself. But it was I, I that had been the child, refusing to admit the things my own eyes saw. She spoke the truth now and I knew it. This was not the case of the complaisant husband—but the complaisant wife.

She said, 'I am no harlot but a most unhappy wife made to serve a shameful purpose. I am a blind to hoodwink the people—the common people; the others know well enough. *His mistress is with child!* the fools say. *If he has no children by his wife then the fault is hers.* It is *you*, Madam, they blame that he has no child. And they blame you for his whoring, too.'

I would not let her see how she shamed me with the truth about Brabant.

'If you are not the Duke's whore,' I said, 'what were you doing in my bedchamber—all gilded like a harlot from the east?'

'It was to rouse desire in my lord duke—if it could be done—that you might not know the nature of the man you'd married.'

'That was a kindness in you!' I said. 'And what do you get out of this pretty game?'

She pulled at the lacing of her gown; the low-cut cote slipped further still. The high full breasts I had last seen painted with gold were painted now with bruises.

'Madam, I loved my husband once. But, as God hears me, I am sick to the soul of him and his wickedness and the wickedness he puts upon me. I am sick and ashamed. Had he lent me to a full man in exchange for favour, I would have submitted myself. A good wife seeks her husband's good. It has been done before and will be done again. But to shame me in my womanhood with an impotent boy—it's a thing to make the flesh crawl.'

She had used the very words I had used this morning; I knew the moment's understanding. I saw her thickened belly and knew a longer envy. I had to hurt her, to plant my dart; she had planted too many in my heart.

'You are known for a liar, Laurette T'serclaes. They say you carry his child, say it to his face.'

'They flatter him to his face and laugh behind their hands. This—' and she touched her belly, 'is my husband's work. But he and his master would make my true-born child a bastard—the one for his pocket and the other for his pride. There would be more profit to me in Brabant's bastard than in T'serclaes' true-born son but I'm the fool that cannot take such profit.' She gave me the ghost of a smile. 'By the sweet Mother of God—' and she was suddenly passionate, 'I came as a friend. Because you are young and with a great inheritance, I tell you these things, that you may separate yourself from Brabant since he cannot be your husband; no, nor husband to any woman.'

She came a step nearer and held out her hands, 'Madam the Duchess, you hate me and with cause. Yet what I have said is true—and I think you must know it. You cannot live two years in this court and not know it. And yet, it could be that pride has blinded you ...'

I said, cold and quick, because she had hit upon the truth, 'Why thrust yourself into my presence to tell me what I know?'

'You know; but you have no *proof*. And no one dare give it but me. That proof I give you now that you may use it and go free of this marriage. But, Madam, do not let them call me as witness ... unless you must. Let them question others. I am not brave. I might take back the truth if they hurt me. But, if I must speak, then wait until my child is born and in a safe place. For it could be prison for me and the child would die. Give me that grace, Madam.'

She knelt and would have clasped me about the knees. I could not endure her touch. I struck her hands away.

The morning's surprises were not yet done. I heard Beatrix take upon herself to answer for me, her voice gentle to this woman as ever it had been to me.

'Madam the Duchess will not speak your name in this, unless you, yourself, permit it. You may set your mind at rest.'

Laurette T'serclaes dragged herself to her feet, her movements very careful, as though she thought for the child she carried. Beatrix went over and clasped her about the waist lest she fall.

Laurette T'serclaes stood and looked at me and her sea-green eyes were steady. 'Madam,' she said, 'you cannot forgive me and I could not expect it. There has been too much insult ... too much. So I will say only this. I am a woman driven between the will of men. There is that bond between us.'

'There is no bond between us!' I cried out, harsh. 'That I will not speak your name in this matter my woman has told you. You may go. And by Christ and His Sweet Mother, come again and I will whip you hence.'

She went slowly to the door; and Beatrix, my Beatrix, held it for her as if she were a queen.

'You forgot your curtsey!' I mocked when we were alone again.

'She deserved it; she has courage,' Beatrix said.

'Courage! It was nothing but another jest, another insult! Who could believe the creature honest?'

'I could; and do. Insult, do you say? She came because she was minded to see you insulted no further. Last night went beyond endurance she said. You were too harsh, Jacque, too harsh. You will be sorry one day.'

I did not answer. Already I was sorry I had behaved so ill; soon I should be sorrier still.

We were making for Hainault—my mother with her suite, I with my despised ladies and my little page. Surprisingly, he had begged to come with me. I had won, it seemed, one Brabantine heart; I could not afford to lose it.

We rode easy and unafraid. Had he desired it Brabant could not stop me. I was free to visit my own countship; and my mother's company lent me countenance. I think he was glad to be free of me for a while, hoping in his childish way that time would heal the insult; even he must have realized he had gone too far.

I have a natural gaiety and two years of misery had not killed it; now it rose again. And when from the distance I saw the walls and towers of Mons, I took in a deep breath of the soft April air. I had come home.

And home indeed. I was their lady; I had come to my own place again.

The peace; the dignity of being within my own house to command and to be obeyed. No more insults, no more humiliations, no more near-hunger. I was home.

Beloved Hainault. I rested upon its love. I rested upon its love; but not for long.

It was my mother, grim-faced, that brought me the news.

My uncle of Bavaria had moved again. He had taken a further stride into my dominions. You will remember he was to be paid a great indemnity of gold in exchange for the 'right' the Emperor had given him to my crown. Of that king's ransom fifteen thousand gold nobles, only, had been paid. Now my sly uncle offered to forego the rest of the money; yes, and to add another ninety thousand to it, on one condition. The regency he shared with Brabant must be extended from five years to twelve—and my uncle to be sole regent.

Brabant had agreed eagerly. He was always at his wits' ends for money. But, more than that, it was yet another way of getting even with me.

'Brabant has sold everything,' my mother burned with a white anger. 'Your right to govern, to receive dues, to levy forces, everything! For twelve years. Twelve years! And, at the end of that time—and who can look so far ahead? We might be dead, you and I—do you think he'll disgorge? Not he! You are set aside and made nothing—you, your father's daughter! The date's fixed. July the twenty-fifth.'

My birthday. There was nothing too great or too small but Brabant made it a whip for my back. I could not bite back my bitterness. 'You chose me a good husband!'

She threw out her hands. 'Such wickedness—who would have thought he had it in him? Obstinate, foolish, vicious a little, perhaps. But you would manage him, I thought. And so you might have done, but you did not choose! Some of the fault lies at your own door. Well, it's overlate to blame this one or that. Let us mend what we may! I don't know how your cousin of Burgundy will move in this. He might support your uncle—*if* Bavaria declares him his heir. And why not? He's got no son of his own. On the other hand, twelve years is a long time to wait and your uncle's in the prime of life. And now you must go complicating things by threatening to leave your husband; and that's certain to throw Philip into Bavaria's arms; no two ways about that! You'll have them standing shoulder to shoulder against you all three—the uncle that holds your lands; the husband that gives them away and the cousin ...' she stopped.

... *that means to have them all!* My mind finished the sentence for her.

I glanced at her. Was she honest in this? Or was it a way to coax me back into the trap?

'For the present,' she said, 'there's no great harm done. You're visiting your mother and that's natural enough. Keep quiet about intending to leave your husband; quieter still about this selling of your sovereign's rights. Make no move whatsoever. In July, when your signature to the precious document falls due, you must call an assembly of the Three Estates here in Mons; Mons is loyal and, I fancy, leads opinion. Meanwhile I'll write to my nephew of Burgundy. Of your decision to leave Brabant, I'll say nothing; of Brabant's treatment of you—much!'

'Three months,' I said. 'Three months to sit back and do nothing!'

'You were always in too much of a hurry,' she said; but she said it kindly. 'Three months is little enough to build up public opinion in your favour—keep firm your friends; sway the waverers; turn the hearts of your enemies. Make the most of them!'

She was right; I am not patient at the game of waiting. I called no council; I would not challenge my uncle before I must. I breathed no word about leaving my husband; my mother's protection, for the present, was enough. I remembered my friends, was gracious to waverers, courted my enemies. For the rest I spent my days between hunting and domestic duties. My house at le Quesnoy was shabby. I sent for an Italian skilled in such matters and had him clean and mend the tapestries. I had all the bedcovers examined for moth and I commanded the mattresses to be cleaned and set to air. So I played the housewife; but all the time my eyes were less upon domestic duties than upon events.

Van Brederode came to kiss my hand, and many another. Would they remain faithful when they discovered I meant never to return to the man they called my husband? I did not know; and I dared not think.

Things were going badly for Brabant. I was not the only one to throw off his authority. Brussels had risen against him and his favourites, and driven him away. T'serclaes had been killed and Laurette disgraced. About T'serclaes I was glad—one enemy the less! But for Laurette I grieved. My unkindness pricked me still; and I wondered whether her disgrace had followed upon that visit to me. What had become of the child she carried? And what would become of her? It was not hard to guess. All that beauty to end in the gutter!

And now it was July and the air sweet with summer. There was no signature of mine on the monstrous document; the indemnity of golden crowns was due.

I called a full meeting of the Three Estates.

'Sirs,' I said, 'you have before you a document in which I have had no part; nor has any man consulted me in the matter. I have not sold my sovereign's rights for gold, nor in any other way relinquished them; nor would I do so, except by death. And those that have set their hands to this wicked paper know it full well. I am your prince and you my loyal subjects; it is for you to declare the same in the ears of Christendom.'

I was prepared for their answer; my mother, that shrewd woman, had warned me.

'Madam and lady, we can say nothing, one way or the other, until we are clear as to the position between you and the duke your husband.'

'Since he is in Brabant and I in Hainault—where I intend to remain—the position is clear enough,' I answered, very steady.

They were shaken at that. They had heard rumours, of course; but this was my first intimation that I would never return to the half-man they called my husband.

'Yet, it is still our duty, as Madam the Countess knows, to send to Monsieur the Duke for his own word on the matter.' I bowed graciously; I could do no other.

Back came Brabant's answer at once. His greatest desire was to have me return to him!

'And he disporting himself with his lewd pleasures!' I told my mother. 'Well, perhaps he does want me back. It was always his delight to see how far he dared go with his persecutions.'

'It is the answer we have expected. He wants you no more than you want him! *My greatest desire is to have my dear wife and companion return to me!* So he gets the goodwill of Christendom; and you, its scorn. I see the hand of your uncle of Bavaria in this!'

'Let Christendom say what it will; I will never return to him!'

'Then you must be cleverer still!' she said, tart. 'You must call a second meeting of the Estates. You must put your case, make your appeal to them. We must consider together every word you are to say—and the way you shall say it. You must win them, my girl. It's this time or never!'

When I presented my case to the Estates I was well-primed and word perfect. Yet, when I stood before them, I threw away the wisdom of my mother and spoke from my heart.

'Sirs, you know me well, a woman bred to responsibility and to the performance of my duties. For this I was born and for this I was bred. But the duty we owe to God comes before the duty we owe to man. And, indeed, neglecting our duty to God, we cannot perform our duty to man. And so I have taken counsel of wise men that are also men of God; and they tell me my marriage is null and void. They have come to their decision upon these points.

'My Lord Duke of Brabant is my cousin in the first degree. Therefore we could not be united in marriage until we had received dispensation from His Holiness the Pope. This dispensation he gave and then revoked. *It was revoked before ever we were united in marriage.* But I did not know it. As I hope for salvation, I did not know it!

'Ignorance must excuse the fault; but to condone the fault, once known, is sin and a mockery before God.

'I say I did not know my fault. That is, my ears did not know it, nor my eyes see any wrong-doing. Yet in the secret places of the heart I knew. For God Himself has placed a monitor within us; so that when the man came to my bed the flesh crept upon my bones.

'Therefore, good sirs, I pray you very humbly, to consider the matter. For I cannot, in the name of Christian living, flout the laws of God and return to the obedience of my lord Duke of Brabant.'

And, having finished, I raised my head that I had kept low for modesty and looked at these men that held my happiness in their hands.

Then, without requesting me to withdraw, they whispered together, and Jacquemars Baudon my Stadtholder rose in his seat. 'Madam and Lady,' he said, 'there is not a man here but desires your happiness and is willing to pay for it with his own blood. But the petition you make requires the deepest thought. For, as you know—none better, being so virtuous a lady—that this is not a question of your happiness alone, but, as you yourself have told us, a question of upholding God's laws in Christendom.

'This much then is clear. If you are truly married, then being so Christian a lady, you must conquer the reluctance of the flesh and live with your husband as his true wife. But, if you are not truly married, then the happiness of us, your loyal and loving subjects, will be as great as your own.

'But this is too great a matter for us to decide. We will send to my Lord Duke of Brabant to inform him of your petition...'

And then, crushing even the little hope they had given, '... and as you know, it is our duty, also, to send to my Lord the Duke of Burgundy...'

Philip to stir the pot of my affairs! I had hoped to get the support of my own people before he got wind of the matter.

I put out a hand as though to beseech them and let it fall.

When I came again to my chamber I leaned my chin upon my hand and there I stood, like any stone.

'Come, child!' I jumped at the sound of my mother's voice. I had not even heard her come in. 'It's not so bad, believe me. They do right to consult my nephew; it will save time in the end.'

There was satisfaction on her. For all her will to help me, she could not forget her de Charolais blood.

'They set off within the hour; Baudon leads them. Philip's in

Ghent so we should get the answer soon ... but I suppose not soon enough for you. You had best find some way to occupy yourself.'

'Yes,' I said. 'Yes.' An idea had come into my head—an idea to use at need. 'Let me leave the matter a while; and the best way is to leave Mons, too. I shall go to Valenciennes. I love the house. I've not been there this long while.'

'A little change will do us both good,' she said at once.

I have wondered since if, even then, she guessed at my half-formed plan; I wonder whether she came with me to give me countenance and cover. Or whether, as I thought then, to see I played no tricks. Certainly I would rather have left her behind. For all her kindness she was still a de Charolais. I had rather—if it came to it—not have to trust her. But there was no help for it.

Philip was in Brussels. The news reached us when we arrived in Valenciennes. No need to discuss the significance of that! He had gone to Brussels to bargain. Support for Brabant in return for favour to come.

And the favour?

Philip count of Hainault, count of Zealand, Lord of Friesland.

Brabant to make him heir to all those countships my uncle had left to me.

There would be no annulment to my marriage. Philip would see to it.

Between kinsman of Bavaria and kinsman of Burgundy I was like to be stripped naked and bound to my disgusting partner for life.

If ever I needed help, I needed it now.

XIV

I felt in my bosom for the King of England's ring. Yet, even with the ring comforting in my hand, I made no move. Perhaps the miracle would happen—the Pope speak at last; or some quarrel between my cousin of Burgundy and the man they called my husband. Things might yet take a turn for the better. But if I ran away and were brought back again—what then? Henry of England would have no truck with a bungler; and I, myself, would be given no further chance to bungle. I must move with care. I told myself I showed a natural caution; the plain truth is, I showed a natural cowardice.

And so I let the summer months pass by. I hunted a little, hawked a little, played the country housewife. November came in, all fog and sleet; and December when the roads were frost-bound. I sat within doors and I made my plan.

I had brought with me from Mons—and not by accident neither—Jean Robbesart, Lord of Escaillon, young and brave, and a most true heart. He had travelled once in England; a fair land, he said, the men gallant and true, the ladies fair and kind. So now when I told him of my plans, I had not even to ask his help. 'Be very sure you will find comfort in England and strong arms to defend your cause. And I thank God that my own arm is the first in your defence.'

My mother provided the opportunity for the first step. January was half-way through. The sun was bright, she said, and I looked peaked. Why did I neither hunt nor hawk?

'I will not hawk,' I said, 'until I have new birds. Our falcons are lazy—overfed and spoilt. I must send into Italy for more; and young Robbesart shall go for me when the roads are easier.'

It was mid-February when he set out; and a week later I announced that my harper was about to make a journey to the shrine of St James—my patron saint; it had long been his desire. And, for his pleasant music, I was sending him into Mons that my treasurer should give him twelve golden crowns to help him on his way.

Jehan my harper was quick of wit, ready with his fists and my faithful servant. It was not to Hainault he went, any more than it was to Italy my young knight went in search of falcons.

I left the announcement of my own journey until a fortnight later. 'Since I cannot hawk,' I told my mother, 'I will ride to Bouchain to see how my altar-piece grows. The best of craftsmen need an eye now and then. I shall be gone three days or four.'

'No more?' she said and fixed me with a steady eye.

'No more!' I said.

'I am not as young as I was,' said that woman of boundless energy. 'I shall remain here.' I believe she guessed something of my purpose; Bouchain was taking me further from home. I fancy she thought I was flying to France whence Cousin Philip would soon have me home again with a flea in my ear. I should see once and for all how futile to try to escape! Had she any notion I was bound for England, she would have moved heaven and earth to prevent me from leaving.

Sympathy had always been imperfect between us; still I should have liked her blessing. Who knew if I should ever see her again? It grieved me to ride away with nothing but a light farewell. But greater still was my grief at leaving Beatrix. I could not ask her to put the sea between her and her new lord; nor would it be right to expose her to dangers that must only double my own. I dare not, for her own sake, confide in her even, lest I expose her to a most cruel punishment. My mother would see to it!

Out of Valenciennes I rode one sweet March morning with my little page and an escort of two gentlemen. They knew nothing of my purpose; I rode quiet and smiling as though fear did not knock in hammerstrokes upon my heart. If Robbesart had been taken! Or Jehan. Or both. If at the turn of this road or the next my cousin of Burgundy or my uncle of Bavaria waited!

Feigned courage often begets real courage. Who could fail on so sweet a day?

I put my horse to the gallop; my escort followed, even the little boy keeping up with his elders. My haste did not seem strange; we were all young with springtime in our blood. It was natural to gallop in the bright morning.

By mid-day we had slowed considerably; and now, above the beat of our own riding, we heard a sound; the sound for which my ears had long been straining.

When Robbesart rode up at the head of sixty horsemen I played my part well. 'Have you come from my Lord Duke of Brabant?' I asked. 'Or perhaps from my cousin of Burgundy? Do you carry me to Brussels?'

'We have our orders,' he answered, 'and they are not to be discussed.'

'Then I must go with you!' I said. 'For what can one do against so many? But, sir, my gentlemen have done no wrong, nor this child, neither. Let them return to Valenciennes to tell my mother what has befallen me.'

He nodded to that. 'But not just yet,' he said. 'I will tie them., very comfortable, in the shade of the trees; and I will tether the horses, too. And I will leave a man to guard them. In three hours he shall set them free. I regret it; but Madam will understand the need.'

So I sent a message telling my mother that I had been taken but she was not to grieve for I was in good heart. And I trusted she might guess what lay behind the words. And when we had seen the two gentlemen and the boy comfortably secured we rode on.

Riding, riding, riding.

Noonday sun beat upon us, afternoon dust rose acrid in our nostrils, evening shadows slanted.

Riding, riding, riding the long day through.

I would have ridden the dark night through also but Robbesart would have none of it. 'You have a great heart but a little body,' he said. 'You must rest tonight if you are to ride again tomorrow!'

At an obscure inn outside Fontenoy we found fresh horses. My harper had done his part with good sense. There was no private room bespoke for me—he had no desire to make me conspicuous. And they would have stared, indeed, at the dust-covered young woman so poorly attended, demanding that luxury. As it was no one gave me a second glance; and had they done so it would have been hard to discover Madam the Countess Jacqueline beneath the mask of dirt.

Of all the nights in my life that early spring night was, I think, the longest. I lay on the rough straw wrapped in my cloak. All about me men and women lay higgledy-piggledy and soiled the quiet night with their snoring. Had I been able to sleep through the noise the stench must have kept me awake—garlic and unwashed bodies and uncared-for hounds. And there was a constant movement—an arm thrown out, the soft rasp of scratching, a body turning, heavy, upon the floor, the sudden sharp wail of a child crying out in sleep.

Beside me Robbesart lay; when the moon came from behind a cloud I saw light run upon the sword ready at his hand, gleam upon his open eyes. At last, God be thanked, the darkness began to pale; through the window peered the dingy dawn.

I waited for the first cockcrow and I was up, smoothing down my crumpled habit and washing my face beneath the pump; the icy water, the draughts of clean morning air, gave me refreshment denied by sleep. Robbesart brought me a mug of beer thin and sour, a hunk of strong cheese and black bread; and went to saddle the horses. I looked at my young knight and thought of my good harper riding towards Calais bearing my message to the King of England. Between knight and harper there was little to choose for courage and loyalty.

Again the cycle of dawn and noonday of afternoon and evening; chill air and heat and dust, shadows and coolness. Once over the border we were halted here by the English, there by the French—Armagnac and Burgundian alike.

To both English and Burgundians I showed the King of England's ring. They were not surprised to find it upon the hand of one so poorly attended—war is no respecter of persons. Besides, it must be a day or two before news of my flight leaked through. Then, indeed, I should be hunted by Burgundy; and—if I were not safe in English hands—taken. Meanwhile the ring gave me safe-conduct through English and Burgundian lines alike. With the Armagnacs it could not help me. So to them I spoke the truth. Jacqueline of Hainault flying in secret from the tyranny of Burgundy. Then was help showered upon us—hospitality for the night, food, fresh horses and money. They were glad to put any spoke in Burgundy's wheel.

It was not yet daylight when we halted before Calais, English Calais; and safety.

The gates were fast shut but Robbesart trumpeted them open. And, trembling in every limb now that fear of capture was over, galled with long riding and scarce able to sit my horse, I rode into the castle.

Torches pricked the dark of the courtyard and there I found my faithful Jehan who lifted me from my horse. I looked from my young knight to my good harper. 'I shall never forget your kindness,' I said, 'nor the risks you have taken for my sake!'

'To rescue so good a lady from so bad a man is reward enough,' my harper said; and my young knight kissed my hand.

Walking between these two I took my first blow.

Henry of England had left for home; his brother would receive me in the King's name.

In the great hall, John of Bedford was waiting. We looked at each other, we two that might have been man and wife. I saw the big Englishman with his pale, cold eyes and I could not regret that those long-ago negotiations had come to nothing. As for him, no doubt he looked at my dust-grimed face and was glad not to be saddled with me and my rashness.

'Madam,' he said and he did not call me *cousin*. 'I have sent into England to know my brother's mind in this matter. Meanwhile you are welcome.'

'Sir,' I told him, 'I thank you with a full heart.' And though I knew I could never take him for husband, I recognized behind his coldness, the strength of the man; the uprightness.

The days I spent waiting for the return of Bedford's messengers seemed endless; and yet in all it was scarce a week. But by now news of my flight must be known all over Christendom and armed escorts—like good dogs—hunting to drag me home. True I was in Calais, English Calais. But was I safe? Burgundy had spies in every camp; and above all in this town of allies he did not trust. The knife slipped beneath the breast; the poison dropped within the cup. Cousin Philip would not hesitate if it suited his book.

I could not be moved from my place on the battlements. There I would sit, chin on hand, straining my eyes across the empty water; and, if a hand touched my shoulder, or a voice spoke in my ear bidding me to some forgotten meal, I would start, looking about me like a lost thing.

And so it was, when at last the sea's emptiness was broken by a sail, I slept where I sat and did not see it.

Bedford's hand upon my shoulder awakened me.

'Madam,' he said, 'it pleases my brother the King, to welcome you into England until your fortunes mend.'

It was a little time before I understood, all drowsy as I was with sleep. 'Now God be praised,' I said presently and smiled into the face that towered above me.

There was no answering smile. He was not pleased. But why? What harm could one poor, friendless woman do in so safe, so strong a land as England?

I watched the riband of heavy green water widen between ship and harbour. The weight of fear lifted. I was safe; safe from the snake of Burgundy, from the tiger of Bavaria, from the weasel of Brabant.

When we are full of fears we ask but one thing—safety. But, that given, the spirit ranges further; so now, sitting in the prow, wrapped about in my cloak, my hopes soared. The King of England would raise up an army to drive out Philip, to drive out Bavaria, to drive out Brabant.

That this was the last thing prudent Henry would do never entered my head; I should have remembered that he had said he would never quarrel with Burgundy for me.

I went on dreaming.

Yes, Henry would help me. He would not, of course, come himself; nor could he, perhaps, spare Bedford from the French wars. But I was not unreasonable. There was always ... Gloucester.

Gloucester.

Gloucester to command my forces; Gloucester to command my life. With such a captain, such a husband, I should be of all women the most blessed. And not only I. Our two countries would be blessed in this union, the one enriching and strengthening the other.

And again I put from me my father's warning. For now there flamed in me a passion for Gloucester against which I was powerless, all fed as it was with the tinder of my present need.

And now there was no thought in me of the land I had left nor the land to which I was bound; nor my griefs and perils. I had but one thought, and the thought was Gloucester.

The cliffs of Dover went up white into the sunshine. I could make out forests of masts in the harbour and the gay patchwork of square sails. And now I could make out the specks that were people going about their business.

I wrenched my thoughts from Gloucester. There were practical issues to be met. Who would be sent to conduct me to London? I could not be expected to find my own way there, penniless, unescorted, unannounced.

The ship grounded, the plank was lowered. I stood up shaking my creased habit straight, and stepped ashore. Standing there, feeling the English air upon my face, I was taken by so great a gladness, I could have knelt and prayed. But in all this turmoil it was not possible so I thanked Him in my heart.

I thanked Him still more when I looked up into the smiling face of Gloucester.

Ten years. He had altered, of course. The boy had become a man. There were lines about his eyes and mouth; but to me they were an added charm. I read into them experience, wisdom. Experience there was ... but wisdom?

He was different; yet he was the same. No man in Christendom with his handsome look, his debonair carriage.

I was taken by a passion of tenderness for him; taken and shaken.

XV

And so I rode through the English spring by Gloucester's side; and I rode as in a dream. Here was my master—if he chose. I prayed God he might so choose. I had struggled alone too long. I thought, as we rode, we were not unevenly matched. I was a great heiress and accounted a beauty. I had enough to offer even him, this prince among men.

'My brother is not in London,' Gloucester said, and it was the light and laughing voice I remembered. 'He's in the north, paying his duties to God in His holy shrines—and squeezing what he can out of his loving subjects to pay for the wars. Then off he'll go gallivanting to France again, leaving me to make everything smooth.'

I made light of the mockery, the edged jealousy, the rashness in talking so of the King to me a stranger; and one, moreover, that owed her present safety to the King. I could find no fault in him; I had fallen headlong in love and everything he did was right.

'I am sorry to miss the Queen,' I said, 'the only friendly face amongst all these strangers.'

'You'll see the Queen soon enough; she's at Windsor.'

'Is she sick?' Why else had the King left his young wife behind!

'Not she! She's well. Too well one might say. No sign of breeding. A disappointment to us all!' But it was clear from his laughing face that he, at least, was not disappointed.

So we rode side by side in the midst of the escort, he bending towards me, my face lifted to his. The country unwound before us—budded cherry-orchards, flowering blackthorn—the gay Kentish scene. Leeds Castle received us for the night.

After we had eaten we sat awhile and talked, Gloucester's handsome legs stretched to the blaze, and I holding my hands now and then towards the fire, for in this great house the spring nights were cold. We drank wine together; and his roving eye assured me that, for all my travel stains and all my griefs, I was not ill to look upon.

'Why did no one tell me I had so fair a cousin? I had expected something lumpish in the Dutch fashion. But you are more French; there's a quickness and a sparkle like the wines of Burgundy. Burgundy's wines are to my taste, but not its dukes. I find the de Charolais sour to my palate.'

'I am half de Charolais,' I said, in spite of myself, a little proud.

'Then I will learn to love them for your sake.'

'No,' I said. 'Keep your anger hot against cousin Philip; it would please me better!'

'Then I please myself, also. For the plain truth is—I hated old Burgundy; but I hate the young one more.'

'Then you are my true friend.'

'God grant it!' he said.

Oh Gloucester, Gloucester!

At Westminster I found my cousin Catharine come from Windsor to greet me. She looked well and very pretty. The Valois nose looked shorter in the rounded face; beneath the net the hair shone bright. She had matched her carriage to her new station; the Queen of England.

And, suddenly, I remembered how she had run about, a thin, shabby girl, uncared for in the gardens at St Pol. And I remembered myself the cherished child in the garden at le Quesnoy—Daughter of Holland that might have been Queen of France. Now the one was suppliant to the other—and it was Catharine that would be France's Queen.

I knelt to Madam the Queen of England. I felt myself lifted and kissed, both cheek and chin. I was ashamed of the moment's envy. I had never desired glory nor yet to reign a queen. I desired only to live safe in my own land and to rule lovingly those that loved me. And now I added one more thing—Gloucester.

And with God's Grace it would be so.

Within the week we moved to Windsor, Catharine's favourite house; and it was easy to see why. With its little hills and its clean shining river and its great trees, it reminded me of beloved Hainault. Her favourite house it might be; but she had brought me there to keep me from Westminster ... and Gloucester.

For the truth is there was more than friendship between us now. I had, he declared, taken his heart in my two hands in that first moment of meeting. And debonair that he was and all skilled in the arts of love, I longed to make an end to my hateful marriage and to know those joys of which I had long been cheated.

'I am glad, indeed, to have you, Jacque!' Catharine said more than once. 'It is good to hear my own tongue again—there's too much English spoken here!' She had a pouting, pettish look, as though it were not natural to find more English than French at the English court.

In spite of her good looks and her fine clothes, she was not well-pleased. Nearly a year since her marriage–and never a. sign of pregnancy. She was afraid of her husband, Gloucester said. And less than a year ago she had burned for him! Now she was cold with displeasure.

'Henry's annoyed because there isn't an heir. Well what does he expect seeing how rarely he lies at home?' Gloucester said to me more than once. 'Even now, riding at his pleasure, he hasn't thought fit to take his wife with him.'

I think he must often have pricked her with this same thought—if she needed pricking.

'These English want to see me, *me*. And so they should! I'm their Queen, their new Queen. And such a Queen! I've brought them France in my pocket.'

'A great jewel for England's crown,' I said. 'She could be the greatest country in Christendom—and beyond; I could bring her Holland together with Hainault and Zealand; yes, and Friesland and all its islands besides.'

'You're married.' She cast me and my offer aside.

'Not I! But, by God's Grace I soon shall be.'

'You had best leave God out of this till the Pope speaks. And what man will you marry?'

'Gloucester.'

'You're crazy!' And she had lost her, smiling air. 'Oh, I know you have a fondness for him. But—marry him, marry Gloucester! Madness. And madness, indeed, seeing you're fast-wed already. You had best not let this nonsense reach the King.'

'The King!' I said, softly. 'The King has plans for me, when I'm free. I'm to marry his brother. Didn't he tell you?'

'He tells me nothing!' She shrugged petulant. 'He thinks all women are fools; only tolerable in bed, he says; and even there he isn't encouraging. Well, a fool I may be; but not such a fool as to believe he'll give you to Gloucester. You've misread him. If he plans to marry you to his brother, then it's Bedford. Gloucester, never!'

I threw out my hands to ward off the thought of the big, cold man. 'I'll take no more Johns into my life. I've had enough, enough—John of Burgundy, John of Bavaria, John of Brabant. You may believe,' I said, bitter, 'I've had my bellyful of Johns.'

She said, 'A Dutch marriage could bring this country much good, if it's well-partnered; I see that. Bedford is such a partner; steady in his nature and a captain men fear. Our cousin Philip would sulk at such a match but he'd do no more; he needs Bedford. But Gloucester's another matter. Marriage with him could bring ill to us all—there's the old hatred between him and Philip. Philip would do more than sulk! Don't set your heart on Gloucester; you'd get no happiness from him, self-seeker that he is. Be sure that the King will arrange his marriage with the greatest care. Not to a hothead like you; but to some older woman, I'll swear; a woman cool and shrewd in judgment.'

'No,' I said. 'No,' and caught at her arm. 'I haven't had much happiness. Twice married—and never a husband. I loved your brother— and he was indeed a brother to me, gentle and kind. Even when we lay in bed together he was still my brother. And what could you expect? Like brother and sister we were reared.

'And the second time, what did I take to my bed? A drunken fool; impotent and spiteful with it. A half-man surrounded by women lest the world guess the truth.'

'Gloucester's no half-man, certainly!' she said, sour. 'I tell you, Jacque, his name's a byword. If you seek love, you'll not find it there.

There's no love in him nor faith nor constancy.'

'I will keep him faithful,,'

'Not you nor any woman. The man's greedy.'

'I have enough.'

'If you speak of your person, comely though you are, still it is not enough. If you speak of your inheritance—once it was rich...'

'And shall be again.'

'And *may* be again,' was all she would concede. 'Even then it would not be enough. Though you bring the whole of Christendom in your pocket, still it wouldn't be enough. There's never enough for a greedy man!'

'You can't frighten me with your sad philosophies.' And I remember how I laughed ... yes, I laughed. 'Handsome Gloucester is my fate. When you see him tell him I'm ready for my husband and my heir.'

'Carry your own messages, I'm like to see no one!' she said, pettish. 'Here I am shut up in the country when I should be riding English roads; and all England standing to see me pass. I should be at Leicester, at York, at Beverley—wherever the King goes. And here I am stuck fast in Windsor.'

'With never a man to amuse you?' And it was idle teasing.

'You are altogether too hot,' she said very quick.

Better than being too cold and so she might find! I held my peace; I said nothing.

Catharine was the luckiest girl in the world. She had but to wish a thing hard enough—and behold it was granted!

The King had sent for her. The people clamoured to see their new young Queen; and all his coldness could not stand against their warmth.

'Shall you come with me, cousin?' she asked.

'Not I! The King's kindness for me blows from the north—so I hear.'

'Are you surprised? There's been gossip. It behoves you to be prudent with Gloucester.'

'What have I done? Nothing that would anger a warm man. The King's too cold ...'

'Chaste!' she said, very quick. 'And you may wish yourself another as chaste.'

'It would seem your husband's chastity is too much for you!' I answered as quick.

She dropped her head; she had a desolate look. I was ashamed of my quick tongue.

'I'm afraid of him,' she said very low. 'Oh he's not without love, nor power to win it. But between him and me ... Oh you're right, Jacque, right! A coldness to freeze the blood.'

'Then you must turn cold hot—when you meet again. And, if you're to show yourself to your people, you had best be worth seeing. Let's go to the Wardrobe.'

She nodded at that; she was all smiles again.

I thought as we went together of the rich gown she wore and how there were plenty for her choosing—and I with nothing but the plain gown she had given me! She was not mean; but she had been brought up in a hard school.

'Cat,' I said and I thought the words would choke me, 'will you give me a new gown?'

'Why, yes!' she said at once. 'Take what you will!' And then, with de Valois caution, 'You may pay me back when you choose! The King is to make provision for you; one hundred pounds a month.'

I took in my breath. 'A great sum,' I said, 'and a generosity I could not expect.'

'Then pay kindness with kindness. Gloucester's not for you; must I warn you again? And thank God fasting it is so. You'd get nothing from him but a sore heart and a stained honour. Let him not near you when I'm gone.'

And, within a few days gone she was, riding beside Gloucester, in her fine velvet habit, with escort and highstepping horses, pennons waving, drums and trumpets. He was to take her part of the way.

Within the week he was back bringing me news from home.

Information had reached Mons the fourth day after my flight. It was dinner time; and the news cost my good councillors their appetite. My cousin of Burgundy, abusing me roundly, had hastened to the man they called my husband, to offer help. Well, I had expected that! My mother had not yet shown her hand.

'They may spare their breath to cool their porridge!' I told Gloucester. 'I swore before God never to call the man husband again and I never will! Philip's a snake, and Brabant's a weasel. But my mother's a good hunting-dog and I pray God she'll hunt on my side.'

'A snake and a weasel and a hunting-dog!' he said. 'And I? What am I?'

I looked at golden Gloucester. 'An eagle,' I told him. 'A golden eagle.'

'Prettily said.' He bowed. 'Well an eagle's more than a match for both snake and weasel. But, seriously, my dear, the gossips are busy about us.'

'And what do they say about ... us?' And it gave me pleasure, this linking of our names, if only in gossip.

'What they say about any man and woman who are never apart when they can be together. And,' he grinned, 'you can guess what that is! You've taken a proper man in Brabant's place—that's what they say.'

'I can't think I've taken any man!' I said.

'Whose fault is that? He's yours for the taking!' And he said it so lightly that for the moment I did not understand. Then, though my heart beat fit to choke me with delight in this comely man, this dear companion, I said, very sober, 'We are princes; and there are others to be considered in this. There's no plain taking between you and me.'

'Is there not?' he asked mocking; and took me into his arms.

I was not quite twenty. I had been married twice and not for love. I come from a family sensual and high-sexed, both sides. The de Charolais are noted for their appetites throughout Christendom; and my father had been no gilt angel. Now I felt the strength of a man's body next to my body; his mouth hard upon my mouth. And I was lost. These days joy shone through me and all about me, a clearer light within the eyes, a deeper cherry on the mouth. We met constantly and no tongue to forbid us. And there was excuse enough for our meetings. Every day brought news from France, news from my home.

Bedford was cold and disapproving—my duty was to my husband. Burgundy was hot and disapproving—he would come himself and drag me back! Brabant wept now for shame and cared not who saw him; now vowed a vengeance I was not likely to forget. My uncle of Bavaria was biding his time; he said nothing—always a bad sign with him. My mother also said nothing—and that could be a good sign. From King Henry no word. The gossip, perhaps, had not caught up with him. Or, may be, he was not a man to move for gossip.

And so we moved into April. The King and Queen were still away and I diverting myself as best I might at Windsor; it was dull enough when Gloucester was not there.

I came across him one afternoon as I walked in the garden; he was turning out of a pleached alley. I had not known he was at Windsor and my heart beat high for unexpected joy.

'I've been to see how the apricots are setting,' he said.

'It's full early, my lord,' I told him. 'We're not yet into May.'

'A prudent man looks early for his harvesting!' he said and looked at me sideways. 'And so it is with the King. Madam Catharine is with child.'

'Now God be praised!' I said. 'It is a great thing when a Queen carries the heir.'

He bent his hot look upon me. 'And for any woman,' he said.

XVI

Before April was out everything was changed; and there were no more snatched meetings between Gloucester and me.

The King and Queen had returned suddenly to London and were now at Westminster. Henry had celebrated St George's day rather later than usual, he had opened Parliament, and was busy, this first week of May, preparing for return to France.

About Catharine's news there could be no doubt. She had the look of a pregnant woman and it became her; she carried herself with an air of triumph. But there was no triumph about the King. He had changed so that in that first moment of greeting I hardly knew him. There was scarce a trace left of chestnut in the grey of his hair; and the eyes were sunk back into his head. He looked a man stricken to the heart.

And good reason.

Clarence was dead, slain in the heat of the battle. Dead at Beaugé, Tom, the brother dearest to his heart. If only the King might have come to terms with his grief. But he could not. Over and above grief for the dead man was anger and everyone knew it. Against all warning Clarence had rushed into an unnecessary fight. And now with him others lay—kinsmen and dear friends, captains and humble folk—uselessly slain. The King's heart grieved for this beloved brother ... but his head could not acquit him. So, like a man eaten from within, he was collecting his men, his ships, his engines of war. Now he would show France his metal! Only so could he assuage his anger and his pain.

The Queen came back to Windsor. We saw little of our men these days. She was glad it should be so; never at ease with her husband, she gave herself up to the coming child. But I missed Gloucester. For the first time in my life I was in love—and my love loved me.

That Gloucester was well-versed in the art of love-making I should have known had I, myself, not lacked all experience. He could make love as intimately in public as in private—and no one the wiser. He would give me a sidelong look that plunged deep into my heart, or his hand would move slyly to touch my hand or my knee, or my breast, even.

And it was not only his love-making. It was companionship—the joy with which he would throw himself into the hunt; the music he would make upon the lute; his wit, his spiced gossip; so that although Catharine could not approve his visits, yet she, too, welcomed them to break the quiet of our days.

I was still penniless. The King's provision for me had not yet been approved by Parliament and Brabant refused to allow me any of my possessions—not the meanest gown, not the poorest jewel. Not a pin's worth! he declared.

The rumours about Gloucester and me had pricked him hard, my mother wrote, though he declared himself well rid of a trollop.

But, she warned me, the anger of my cousin Philip was deep and it was constant. But, she trusted, without cause.

> ... for if there be anything at all in this gossip about you and Gloucester—which God forbid—and if your marriage to Brabant is declared invalid, then your cousin must bid *Goodbye* to our fine lands that march so sweetly with his...

I answered her at once. Yes, the gossip was true. As for my lands slipping from Philip's grasp it was what I prayed for day and night, though I could not expect him to relish it.

The King was shortly for France; Gloucester was to stay behind—the Regent; and my joy was beyond telling. I went to pay my respects to the King before we left, riding slowly with Catharine in the charette.

Whether he had heard the gossip about Gloucester and me he gave no sign; he was as courteous as ever—and as cold.

'England's your home, cousin, for as long as you require it,' he said. 'And I am glad not only for your sake but for the Queen's. It's hard for her in a strange land at such a time—even though that land be England. I leave her in your charge.'

And so he was gone, with his new ships and his siege engines and his gunners and his bowmen; and life, I could not but think, was the easier for his going.

If he had put the Queen in my charge, I was equally in hers; for she spoke more than once her disapproval of Gloucester's visits; but she did not forbid them. Trust him she did not; but she found him amusing; watched at every step because of her pregnancy, she could not help but relish his company.

But she was forever warning me against him.

'He thinks you're pretty and amusing; he thinks you'd be good in bed—and no doubt he means to try. But he'll take a wife for business and not for pleasure. But, mistress or wife—you'd get little happiness... It isn't in his nature to be faithful. Take warning before it's too late.'

'Let us marry and I undertake to keep him,' I said.

She shook her head. 'I know Gloucester! He's the youngest brother and he's ambitious. He thinks of nothing and no one but himself. He's Regent now—and you can see how he loves it! And, when the war's over and the King and Bedford home again, what power for Gloucester—except what he can buy with a wife?'

I nodded. 'He does long for a crown; but not his brother's—God forbid! Well, the crown of Holland is no mean thing. And I could give it to him.'

'It's hardly yours to give,' she reminded me drily. 'Put Gloucester out of your mind. If the King hears more of this talk—some he's heard already—he'll send for Gloucester; and you he'll pack off home to get out of your pickle as best you can.'

'He promised me shelter as long as I need it. He's not one to break his word.'

'He's exactly the one—if the reason's good enough. If you truly care for Gloucester then for his sake as well as your own, put him out of your head, I implore you!'

I made no reply. Twice I had married to please others; this time I should marry to please myself.

Catharine, though she knew little of affairs, knew her husband! It was towards the end of May and we were walking in the garden at Windsor when Gloucester came striding across the grass.

'Well, sister,' and he bowed to the Queen, 'I go to keep your French crown safe.' He turned to me. 'It seems they can't do without me in France!' And, for all his smiling, anger was hot in his eyes.

I cried out at that. Catharine sent me an *I-warned-you* look. Something about me must have touched her, for she turned away and, without a backward look, left us alone together.

What he said to me then I cannot remember; but I stood in the crook of his arm and the tears running down my cheeks. But the word was said at last, the one word I do remember ... and the word was Farewell.

He bent and kissed me. There was salt on his lips; but the tears were mine; they were mine, as they were always to be mine. He put me aside and my eyes followed him all the way. But he did not look back; I think he had forgotten me already.

I put a hand to my mouth to stop myself from calling him back. My hand came away red. He had caught my lips with his teeth, and I was glad of this so small wounding. I thought it showed how desperate his love; I did not recognize greed.

And so he was gone and all the joy of summer with him. I hid my desolation as best I might; I was companionable with Catharine, reading or singing or talking as she chose.

And so the long summer passed. We lived chiefly at Windsor and one day was pretty much like another. My birthday came and went and I was twenty. Catharine went heavy with child, wrapped from all the world so that news from France touched her hardly at all. Of course it was good! How could things go ill when she was to bear a son? That it would be a son she was certain. 'God is so gentle,' she said.

These lazy summer days my longing for Gloucester grew greater as the days went by. I importuned God—I cannot call it praying—day and night, for his safety.

Nor was I helped to a quiet mind by news from home.

I had ordered notices to be fixed to all church doors throughout my lands repudiating my marriage. By Philip's commands they were torn down, every one. And now he was demanding that I return to my wifely duties. How long would the King of England shelter me against the expressed desire of his most needed ally? It was a question that nagged forever in my mind.

Autumn dragged on. News from France see-sawed and my heart was always on the stretch. Clarence had come to his death in the fighting, and the King himself, all-but; then why not Gloucester? Sweet Christ, I prayed, not that, not that!

November winds were blowing cold when I urged Catharine to return to Westminster—Henry had desired his child to be born there; and he had left her in my charge. But, like a cat that will not stir from the fire, she would not leave until she must. And then, when she judged it time to depart—it was too late. The birthpangs were upon her. In the early hours of a December morning England's heir was born.

I was with her during her labour; the pains were short and sharp and she cried out, pitying herself excessively. But I envied her. She had borne her child; she was *safe*.

That was all I thought of until I saw her later. She lay in bed, the winter sunlight falling across her pillow and upon the fair head of the child in the crook of her arm. There was something infinitely moving about the pair—Catharine with a new gentleness and the child fair as the infant Jesus. And now it was not her safety I envied, nor yet her crown. It was her child.

This was a woman's life; it should have been my life. I should not have been driven into the thick of the fight and the smell of blood; I should not have been forced to fly my own land like a hunted animal. At that moment it was almost in me to resign my rights if I might live in peace and marry my dear love and bear his children. But, would Gloucester want me then? I thought, God help me, he would.

But the impulse was fleeting; my sense of right, of duty to my father and to my country, forbade it.

Catharine, that rather hard young woman, showed me a new kindness these days.

'Jacque,' and she looked at me above the fair head of the babe, 'I should wish you to stand godmother to my son.'

It was a thing I could not have expected. I could not speak at first lest I should weep. To be godmother to England's heir, his mother in Christ! That must silence scandal; it must give Philip to think; strengthen my cause in my own land.

But she would have her husband's anger to face. Already she had a reckoning to make because the child had not been born at Westminster according to his command; and at no time was she very brave.

I said, 'Dearest Cat, I am a stranger, homeless and dispossessed; penniless save for the King's charity. Would he welcome such a god-mother to his son?'

'You are our honoured guest,' she said with gentle obstinacy; I had not thought it in her. 'Set your heart at rest. I have asked Bedford to stand godfather and Beaufort, also. Bedford shall supply the protec-tion and the rich bishop the moneybags. The King's brother and the King's uncle! I chose them to please the King. I choose you to please myself.'

'Then I am honoured and content,' I said. I put my hand upon the tiny head and was surprised at the softness and the warmth. 'You shall not lose by it,' I told the infant, 'when I come to my own again.'

Many were angered at the honour given to *the foreigner*. Bedford and Beaufort tried to dissuade the Queen but she was obstinate. I was her own kin; godmother to her child I should be! So Catharine was churched and her child baptized, I holding the babe at the font.

And now she was to sail for France at the request of the. King; Bedford was crossing with new forces and would be her escort. She was so pretty these days, all bright with the joy of going home; she carried her head with a lovely pride because she had given England its heir. *Catharine the Fair.* It was no longer the compliment one pays to a prince.

We went to the Wardrobe to choose gowns for her journey. And I saw how her steward, the man Tudor, knelt as though he worshipped her. But she saw nothing. She pouted, as pretty spoilt women are apt to do, complaining of this and that; yet the gowns were rich and the furs fine. But she was going home; she meant to startle all Paris with her splendour.

'I can buy no more,' he said, very humble. 'Madam the Queen's allowance is not yet fixed by Parliament and there is no grant from the treasury.'

He spoke as though he himself were at fault. I looked at him. The man was in love with the Queen! A thing to laugh at. But I could not laugh. The love of a true man—however humble—a prince's life may hang upon it. I, a homeless beggar, knew it.

'Yet,' he said, doubtful, 'there *is* money; but I have not used it. I did not know the Queen's wish in the matter.'

'There's but one wish when it comes to a new gown!' she turned to me and laughed. And, when still the man hesitated, she said sharply, 'What money?'

'From the estates of Madam the Queen Johanne.'

'Spend it!' Catharine commanded.

I said nothing until we were back in the Queen's chamber.

'We heard about Madam Johanne, but rumours, rumours only. We couldn't believe it. The King's stepmother—and so good a step-mother. So it's true after all and she is in prison. Why? What has she done?'

'I don't know,' she said, troubled. 'I don't know. But she cannot use her gold in prison —that I do know. And that I shall repay the money—I know that, too.' And her face was bright again.

The Queen's chambers overflowed with rich stuffs, with furs, with jewels.

'Now I am friendless, indeed!' I said when the last chest was sealed.

'Come with me!' she said.

'Not I! I've no mind to meet cousin Philip! And it isn't for France my heart longs, but for Holland; and especially for Hainault that I love. It's hard to be a stranger in a strange land.'

'I know that, too,' she said.

'You're a Queen and I'm a beggar. You're a wedded wife and I am a woman forlorn; and my heart longs for its own. I long for my own people ...' and then driven by truth, I said, 'But there's one I long for more.'

She said, very earnest, 'Don't anger the King; he's an ill man to cross!'

'I'm not likely to come to grief on Gloucester's account,' I said, bitter. 'He's safe across the sea ... and I sleep in my chaste bed alone.'

But she had already forgotten me. She was wandering about fingering this and that and singing softly under her breath.

Easy for her to talk; everything was easy for her! But for me? Everything was hard, everything dark. I had petitioned the Pope but he had not answered my prayers. I had declared my marriage null and void and Burgundy and Brabant had been deaf. I loved Gloucester and had been offered Bedford instead. But, surely there was hope here! Surely the King of England must be hopeful that the entanglement with Brabant—marriage I would not call it—must be set aside. That he desired me to marry one brother rather than the other was a hurdle I would take when I came to it.

Catharine turned suddenly. 'I am glad I am for France,' she said. 'And not only because I am going home. It's because ...These English do not love foreigners—you have seen that for yourself ...'

I nodded. Yes, I had seen.

'I must have children, more children, Jacque, to keep me safe. The life of one little child is a frail thing! I am not strong like you. Driven between pillar and post I should die.'

'You'll have many children!' I told her. And indeed she was pretty enough to stir any man's blood; yes, even the cold blood of Henry. 'But—this talk of safety? From the Queen of England? What nonsense!'

'Is it nonsense? Henry's in the thick of the fight; at Louviers he was all-but killed by a gunstone. At this moment the future looks bright enough; but the next who knows?'

Did she speak with the tongue of prophecy? I have often wondered.

When we met again she wore widow's weeds.

XVII

Henry was dead; dead in the pride of his manhood—Henry that had stood my friend. I had thought of him as one might think of a god; now, at thirty-five, he had gone down to the grave. Once I had thought him cold; now he was cold, indeed.

Dead at Vincennes, his sickness kept from friend and foe alike, until Death himself spoke out loud. Riding at the head of his men, urging his sick body forward and failing; and dying in the dark of an August morning, head on his confessor's breast.

I thought of Catharine in her dark hours and of her strange prophecy. She had left England joyous as mayday; how would she return?

All England mourned; not only in palace and in town, but in far villages and scattered hamlets which high policies pass by. Every heart weeping for him who had been their hero and their King.

I looked down at the babe in my lap. He alone crowed and laughed. Yet he had lost most. Eight months old. Too young to bear the weight of a crown; younger still to be left fatherless. Yet he laughed while the country mourned. And, memory moving, I sent a woman, her face all blubbered with tears, for a black riband and tied it about the little arm.

But, the days passed and I walked in the sun in the garden at Windsor, the sharp edge of shock blunted. I grew used to the idea of the King's death; if I had lost a friend, there was one less to forbid my marriage with Gloucester. And there was a further comfort and hope. One of the King's brothers must remain in England to hold the reins until the babe was old enough. Bedford, as all Christendom knew, was England's finest captain. Now, more than ever, he would be needed in France. Surely they would not leave the command to my hothead Gloucester!

Gloucester would come home. Gloucester, sweet Gloucester—and no one strong enough to forbid our marriage.

Catharine had warned me that no woman would ever hold him— least of all a wife. I considered this, turning myself about before the mirror ... There were some that called me a beauty—the usual compliment paid to princes where they may hear. Yet, without overmuch stretching of the word, I could pass! Life in England, its peace and its safety, had put back some of the flesh I had lost. I was rounded now in the fashionable way of beauty—no more; there was a liveliness in the eye and in the mouth. And I favoured our Dutch headgear; an open net through which the bright hair shone—chestnuts in a golden basket. But looks alone would not hold Gloucester. I had taken him by the eye; now I must learn to keep him.

The King's death had darkened the face of England, but to me, it must bring my lover. I hid my joy beneath the decent mourning.

I forgot my joy when I saw Catharine again.

I rode to London to meet her. I had expected to see her sickly and sad—three months since the King had died, and she carrying out the heavy duties of a widow that is also a queen. I was not prepared for what I saw. She was very thin, and her face set in lines of misery—that one might expect. But now and again she seemed to listen to some secret thought; for I saw her mouth locked as though in anger, her face stamped with bitterness.

She asked about the child and, hearing he was well, wrapped herself in silence and listened no further, not though I told her how he laughed and crowed when he was pleased, and of his infant rages when they did not fly to his command—a true little King! There she sat and gave no more sign than as if she had died herself.

She would not rest in the Tower, even one night, so we passed through London. London; and a smoke-black sky pressing down upon shuttered streets; and in each doorway a man in black from head to foot, holding a lighted torch above his head. The black clothes, the dark streets, the orange torches flaming smoky into the black sky—a city out of hell you might think! The cortege moved on towards Westminster; and when we were clear of the smoky air and the night-sky clear again with frost-sparkling stars, she began to speak.

'The King has shamed me in the face of Christendom. When he lay dying he sent for those he loved ... but not for me. And there were messages for those he would never see again ... but not for me. I am nothing. I should have been named a regent but I am nothing. My child, my child even, given to the hands of others. Why do they take him from me? What have I done to merit such disgrace? I have brought France in my pocket to an ungrateful King; I have borne a son to an ungrateful husband. And what am I now but a stranger, disgraced, in an unkind land?'

And when I would have spoken—though, indeed, I knew not what to say—she cried out very bitter, 'Never tell me that the English love me ... though they should, they should! Love the foreigner! It was for the crime of being foreign that Johanne was thrown in prison; for that and that alone. Oh, I have heard while I was away; I have learnt. The King wanted her money and shut her up the better to despoil her. And no hand lifted to help the foreigner, no voice lifted to enquire into the truth!'

I said, 'You are ill with sorrow and with weariness. And who knows if the things you hear are true or false?'

'They're true enough. About Johanne—I had it from Exeter; and who should know but the King's uncle that had it from the King himself? When Henry felt himself sicken, he asked Exeter to have Johanne released without delay *for my soul's sake*. For his soul's sake! That says enough, I think. I wish he had been so tender of me. That I am to be shut out of affairs; that my son is to be taken from me—I had from Bedford himself.'

'Then ... Bedford is to be Regent?' And my heart sank like a stone.

She shook an impatient head. 'No Regent, no Regent at all. Protector. Protector only. But not Bedford, alas! Bedford's a cold man but he's just; he means well by me. It's Gloucester.'

My heart leaped again in my breast.

'But Gloucester's a mean man,' she said. 'Not just! He cares only for himself. The King has done me great wrong,' she said; and there-after—perhaps she sensed a coldness in me because of what she had said—was silent.

Life had changed indeed for Catharine. It had reversed the order of the game. The Queen had become a pawn.

When she saw the child for the first time since her absence, she snatched him from the nurse and clutched him to her breast and would not let go though the babe cried out and fought her off with his fists, and the nurse looked black as thunder. That the child did not know her was—as to any mother—grief to her heart. But with her it was more; much more. Without him she was reduced to nothing; and she knew it!

These days she was all a wildness and a despair; nor, though I longed, could I give her any comfort. There was a coldness between us. I could not forget she had called Gloucester a mean man. Unjust, unkind, self-seeking—those words I could forgive; but meanness stuck in my throat.

For her part she could not forgive me because I loved the man she now regarded as her enemy. He had, she was certain, worked upon the King with guile to push her from her rightful place. I tried at first to defend him; and that failing, tried to assure her that, loving Gloucester, I loved her none the less. As wife to the Protector I could—and would—serve her well.

But it was all useless; she was forever upbraiding me. 'Gloucester's wife you'll never be. The King would not have allowed it; nor will Bedford allow it. Never, never, never!' And she would repeat the word with a slow and irritating obstinacy.

'You yourself would set aside his dying wishes if you could!' I said once, goaded. 'But he laid no dying wish upon me. If he spoke with Bedford against the match, be very sure we shall hear!'

Now her distrust reached beyond Gloucester to me; she did not trouble to hide her dislike of me. By God's providence—or so it seemed—my kinswoman, Madam Johann, new-released from prison, desired my company; and I was glad to change the air of Windsor for that of Langley.

But not for long. The air at Langley was as cold as that at Windsor.

I found my kinswoman pale from imprisonment; and severe. The first thing she heard when she had been set at liberty was gossip about Gloucester and me; it was for that I had been summoned.

I grew weary of her complaints. I could not believe that marriage with Gloucester could harm anyone. On the contrary it could only—as King Henry himself had agreed—bring increased prosperity to his country and to mine. And surely I had the right to a little happiness! So when I could endure this second Queen's upbraiding any longer, I took to horse, and, the faithful Robbesart in attendance, was away to London. And there—and truly now Heaven did smile upon me—I found my lover new-returned from France.

Catharine came hurrying to Westminster and ordered me to her presence—Queen to subject. I went obedient and unafraid, I went with the intention of being gentle and kind; I had good reason. But the way she kept me waiting and the way she received me at last, cold and unsmiling, and the words she said, put me out of all patience.

'Yes, Madam,' I said; and I no longer called her Cat, or even cousin. 'It is true. We are living together at Hadleigh as man and wife—and there is no shame in the matter. My Lord of Gloucester and I are married.'

'Why this secrecy if there's no shame in the matter? Why these lies?' she asked, very cold. 'You are my friend and you deceived me.'

'There was no lying. I went to Langley and I meant to stay there. But I found the air too biting cold with Madam Johanne's tongue. I saw no need to endure it. As for the secrecy—my lord desired it!' I looked into her bitter face. I said, 'And wisely! You would have robbed me of my happiness, had you been let.'

'I would have saved you,' she said.

I shook my head. 'There was no more kindness in you ...'

'So you ran to the kindness of Gloucester. Gloucester's kindness! I wish you joy of it.'

'I thank you, Madam,' I said.

She lost her quietness then. 'You have disgraced yourself in the eyes of Christendom. Live with Gloucester you may—like any of his whores. Not as his wife; never as his wife. Have you forgot my Lord of Brabant?'

'I do my best, Madam, though it is hard. But Brabant is not my husband and never was. I have no husband but Gloucester. And, indeed—' and I heard my voice shake as though even now I might plead and she listen. 'It is no ill match. The King himself offered me marriage with his brother. He would have given me to Bedford—'

'I trust you will be happy,' she cut me short; her bitterness made mockery of the words.

I curtseyed to the Queen; I rose and stood looking at her. Her face did not soften; it was remote and cold. I went out leaving behind me our broken friendship.

In spite of the Queen I felt no shame; the only shame I felt was in having been tricked into Brabant's bed.

Bedford, that just man, knew the truth when he saw it. It was vital for him not to offend Burgundy, yet still justice urged him to our side. His letters, following my own, urged the Pope to declare the Brabant marriage null and void. Delay, he said, might well result in the shedding of Christian blood.

When my brother of Bedford, for so I could call him now, stood by me not because he wanted to—he had no joy in this marriage—but because justice demanded it, what need had I of shame?

And so I gave myself to my happiness. Madam the Duchess of Gloucester, second lady in the land and wife to my dearest love.

And I *was* happy. Whatever they said of his character no one could deny his charm. He was a gay companion, and delightful to women—until he tired of them. He was not tired of me; not yet.

I had all the charms of a mistress, he would say, and none of the shackles of a wife.

None of the shackles of a wife! I suppose I ought to have guessed then what was in his mind. If he regretted his bargain he could easily get rid of me; the Brabant marriage had not yet been declared null.

But how was I to have known? He was forever seeking me out; he could not, it seemed, let me alone. No sport, no past-time worthwhile without me. I rode, hunted, hawked and danced better than the best, he would say. And he was forever telling me I was beautiful, that I was charming, and that I was no prude. And he would tell me, laughing, that while other women emptied his purse I should fill it.

And so I should have done had he played his part. For I had made him master and ruler of all my possessions—when he should gain them for me. 'I am a woman,' I told him. 'I have no pleasure in policies nor in the battlefield; nor would they become me now I have a husband—a true husband—and I can rest.'

Yet it was little rest I had with Gloucester these days. We gave ourselves to pleasure of the sport, to pleasure of the table, to pleasure of our bed—as though there was no war with France nor any land of mine to win back.

It was my husband that tired first.

He loved me—he did love me then; I must believe it. But with him ambition must always come first. And now his uncle Beaufort, that cunning bishop of Winchester, was barring his way at every step.

My husband was Protector of England; but he was not Regent and he had not a Regent's power. He had managed—with the utmost difficulty—to secure the right to summon Parliament as though he were king. It brought him a little prestige but not much more. When it came to the vote, his was worth no more than the next man's. Nor had he the strength of his peers behind him. They distrusted him because he was forever seeking the goodwill of the lesser lordlings and squires that were flattered by his condescension and taken by his charm.

And, even more, he wooed the common people. In Holland we have long known the strength of the common people; sovereign and noble alike seek, before all else, their goodwill. But in England, without the great lords, a man cannot stand; and those Gloucester could neither break nor bend.

The anger between my husband and his uncle had been long, though hidden—more or less. Now, it came out into the open and the struggle promised to be bitter. Beaufort was the more subtle, the more tenacious; and, for all his belief in himself, Gloucester must have known it. I think it was in his mind, even then, at the beginning of the struggle that, if things went badly for him in England he would carve himself a kingdom in Holland.

But there was no such thought in my mind. Young, and very much in love, I thought it was for my sake he offered to return with me, sword in hand. I was a fool to believe he could think of others first; a fool to believe that, even to serve his own ambitions, he would stand firm in the face of difficulties.

Beaufort opened hostilities with the lightest of touches. My husband came bursting into my chamber one day, black as thunder.

'This thrice-damned bishop!' he cried out. 'This bastard uncle of mine! Yesterday he staged a pretty play and everyone applauded—except me, the fool for whom it was staged. The Chancellor resigns; and I'm summoned to Windsor. Fool that I was not to put two and two together! I got there to find the lords in Council—as many as he could scrape together—Ormonde and Talbot and Clinton and Poynings and a crowd of others. And the dear Archbishop-Chancellor, of course, surrounded by his covey of bishops, including beloved uncle Beaufort. And there was Madam Catharine smiling in the middle of them; pussycat with cream! And well she might!

'I saw now what was afoot—but even then I didn't see it all. Archbishop Langley was waiting to resign the Great Seal. I held out my hand, naturally; I expected him to hand it to me. But instead, he made as though to put it into Kinglet's hands—hands that couldn't even grasp the edge of it. So then my uncle Beaufort must needs come forward and put his paws round Kinglet's fingers lest the Great Seal drop. Then he called on me and, in the presence of them all, he guided that baby's hands towards me; towards me, Gloucester, Protector of the realm. And I passed it to that fellow that keeps the Chancery Rolls to keep till we'd chosen the new Chancellor.

'Oh it was a pretty scene and damnably significant!'

I needed no word of Gloucester to tell me how significant! It was to show him that he was not Regent but Protector; Protector only. All law came from the King and from the King alone—with Bishop Beaufort, of course, to guide him.

'Oh pretty, pretty,' Gloucester growled. 'Thrice-damned Beaufort. And thrice fool I. I should have known what was on foot. *Why Windsor and not Westminster?* I should have asked myself. I should have feigned sick. Madam Catharine makes common cause with the bastard bishop, does she? She shows her hand; let her wait till I show mine!'

I did my best to sweeten him. I pointed out that Catharine was but a pawn to be moved at the will of others. I said that no one could foresee this cunning step of Beaufort's. And though I did not tell him so, it savoured of a woman's cunning. And whose then but Madam Johanne's, the shrewdest brain in England? Obviously she believed in Beaufort's star. It was not comforting.

Gloucester went about furious; it was hard to talk to him without provoking a quarrel. And, as if that were not enough, I had my own difficulties. I say my own because they seemed to leave Gloucester unmoved.

Catharine had promised that I should be the scandal of Christendom; she was not wrong!

My mother's letter was the first harbinger of the wretched storm.

The whole land is full of rumours that you are married again. And, God save us, how can that be since you are fast-wed already? They say you have taken Monsieur the Duke of Gloucester for husband and that you are already with child by him.

You have ordered the Estates to meet; but you say no word whether these tales be true or not. God grant that they be lies! For I tell you plainly that Gloucester's strumpet you may be; his wife, never. I am in dire distress on your account.

My reply left her in no doubt of the matter.

The tales you hear are true; why should you doubt them? The contract—I will not call it marriage—between the Duke of Brabant and myself was, from the beginning, null and void; and this you know well.

By deed of gift I have endowed my husband with all my lands and titles. To the title of Gloucester he now adds Count of Hainault, Holland and Zealand, and Lord of Friesland besides.

You need be in no distress on my account. My marriage to Monsieur of Gloucester is recognized by the royal family of England, by the peers and the commons alike. The highest honour the King can bestow is to be bestowed upon me. I am to receive the Garter robes at the next investiture. When I tell you that I am the only lady in the land to be so honoured, you will understand the esteem in which I am held.

It is true, also, God be praised, that I am enceinte by my Lord Duke of Gloucester; and I ask Monsieur the Duke of Brabant that I may come to le Quesnoy for my lying-in ...

But, alas, I was too soon with my hope. For I miscarried early and a great grief it was to me, so that I envied the meanest woman in the land that had an infant at the breast; nor could I at first be comforted, not though England accepted me as Gloucester's wife; and in his letters to his Council the little King called me *our dearest aunt*; no, nor though the church received me with honour—my greatest triumph.

Indeed, we spent our first Christmas at St Alban's Abbey. My husband was received with joy as is fitting to a good patron, a good scholar, a good fellow. And the monks made much of me too, for his sake. It was there that I began to question what manner of man I had married. For now I sensed a harshness in him, saw for myself that instability with which men charged him. Now he would be angry and irritable, now his charming self; now he would set his heart upon a thing, now reject it. And, even in his kind moments with me, he was less kind.

I should have expected it. He was not noted for faithfulness to women; and, no doubt, his first raptures had begun to cool. And then, too, there was his disappointment over the child we had expected. He spared me nothing for my own disappointment; his chagrin fell heavy upon me that had raised his hopes. And one more thing. I fancy he was beginning to understand the censure he must face in Christendom for having married me—and no word from Rome to declare my Brabant marriage null and void. He was a man that did not take kindly to criticism; he liked to stand well in the eyes of the world.

And with this new lack of kindness went a weakness I had not expected beneath that gallant bearing. He could not—or would not—control his own bodyguard. He left them free to poach, to drink beyond decency, and to handle such wenches as had the bad fortune to stray across their path. Then he would turn suddenly upon these men of his and punish savagely the bad behaviour he had allowed.

I was crossing the courtyard of the abbey one evening when I halted at the sound of lusty crying. And there was my husband beating a man about the head; nor did he stop for all the fellow's bawling, nor yet for the blood that ran down from the man's head upon his own fine doublet. Well, to see a gentleman beating his servant is a common enough sight—though my husband laid on with more than common anger. But there was worse to come! Behind the man a fine greyhound dangled from a noose. I ran to rescue it—I have a great love of dogs—but Gloucester's fierce eye forbade me. And, indeed, it would not have helped; the poor creature was dead.

To hang an innocent beast! It was a thing hard to forgive. But it was an English custom he said; and who was I to argue against the laws of the country that had given me refuge? And so I put the wretched affair from my mind; but afterwards I remembered it ... I remembered it.

Gloucester was difficult and moody as I have said; but for all that he was a faithful husband—so I thought. But love they say is blind. And so it was with me in the affair of the Cobham girl.

My woman Agnes was retiring into the country and I seized the opportunity to invite my friend, Ermgart van Rietuelt, to take her place. I was actually writing to Holland when my husband appeared in my chamber. He was charming and sunny; and my heart melted at the sight of him. Would I, he asked, grant him a so small favour? To me—nothing; to the one for whom he asked—everything. He had a poor relation by marriage; a young woman well-bred and neat and of a pleasant humour. Would I give her the vacant place? I longed for Ermgart and for news from home; but I was pleased to serve him in this one small thing.

As soon as I set eyes on Eleanor Cobham I knew I had made a mistake; but I had no reason to go back on my word. She was everything my husband had said. She was well-bred and neat; she was of a pleasant humour ... too pleasant. She was slight and pale; she was quiet in her manner and assiduous in my service. There was no one to touch her in setting a gown to the figure; her quick fingers would coax the laces to narrow the waist and swell the curve of bosom and hips. And she was discreet. When my lord appeared in bower or bedchamber, then, with lowered lids, she melted away silent as snow. Sometimes he would question me about her; and, since I could find no fault, I was forced to praise the girl. But for all her nimble fingers I didn't like her; I longed to send her away. But how could I offend my dearest lord that looked so kindly to my comfort?

And so Eleanor Cobham came into my life. She had been there long, but I had not known it—Eleanor Cobham with her white face and her full mouth red as a dark rose and her curious eyes. I cannot remember that I ever saw them full-open; they gleamed dark beneath her slitted lids; they had a secret and a subtle look.

XVIII

But if there were clouds there was sunshine, too. If my husband was moody he could be kind also. And Madam the wife of the Lord Protector enjoyed great honour; as much, indeed, as any Queen. Gloucester delighted in pageantry; and since my dignity reflected his own, he saw I had my share. And then, too, I had been made a national, and my faithful Robbesart with me. If I did not feel less of a foreigner, I did feel an added security. The deed runs in the name of my godson the little King and I have it still by me.

> To our dearest kinswoman and aunt, Jacqueline, Duchess of Gloucester that she become a native free to enjoy all rights as though she had been born in England ...

... *Our dearest aunt, Duchess of Gloucester.*

That says enough, I think. For the truth is—though Burgundy and Brabant and my uncle of Bavaria, also, had raised a scandal in France and Holland, in Brabant and Bavaria—the English, by and large, cared not one way or the other about the matter. There were of course some here and there who genuinely disapproved; they did not count. But there were others who pretended to be scandalized to serve their own ends; and unfortunately these did count.

Bishop Beaufort would never like any woman my husband married, not though she were an angel from heaven. The struggle between those two for power was constant and bitter; they hated and distrusted each other, and it was natural, I suppose, that some of Beaufort's anger should spill upon me.

And there was Catharine who had been my friend and was my friend no longer. She was outraged by the marriage; not on any moral ground—but because she was afraid. There was our kinswoman Johanne forever at her ear with croakings of the evil this marriage must bring to that little child the King.

Johanne was talking nonsense. I knew my cousin Philip! He'd make as much trouble as he could for me. But, withdraw his armies in

France, leave the English to fight alone; weaken his ally and strengthen his enemy who called himself—and rightly—King of France; cast away careful ambition in a fit of rage—never! So I thought. I had done better not to measure my wits against the shrewdest brain in England.

We had believed, my husband and I, that the marriage accepted so quietly in England must bring me the longed-for answer from the Pope and put an end to the undesirable noise elsewhere. And, had I remained quietly in England, it might have happened so.

But Gloucester was fretting to be on the march for Holland; and the Pope importuned from all sides gave no answer. And no wonder! My husband and Bedford and myself were tugging one way; Brabant, Burgundy and my uncle of Bavaria the other. A wrong decision could plunge Christendom in blood. I see that now; but then it all seemed simple enough. It was a tangle; and for the peace of Christendom his Holiness must unravel it thread by thread.

My husband would have cut it through with his sword. It was I, longing for my own land though I was—for a fugitive however honoured is a fugitive still—that tried to restrain him.

'God knows,' I said, 'I would march today if I could. I have never shunned the fight nor would I do so now. I have ridden with my men and won my victories. But victory—as victory has taught me—is not enough. We must keep the love of the people warm towards us.'

'You are their prince,' he said quick and angry, 'to you the oath was sworn!'

I shrugged. 'Quickly sworn and quickly broken. Men love their lord but they love their belly more. My uncle is a bad man; but for all that he rules well. He encourages crafts and trade—a thing my father never did. The country is prosperous as never before. My people have forgotten me, I think.'

'All the more reason to remind them!'

'Not yet,' I said. 'Dear lord and husband, we are man and wife; but his Holiness does not say so; he has not yet admitted his grievous error.'

'How shall God's Mouthpiece admit to error?' His laugh was edged.

'God has His ways. Unless the contract of marriage between Brabant and me is declared null and void, the hand of the rebels is strengthened; and worse, some of my own friends will turn against me.'

It was not easy at first to persuade him to wait; but soon he came round to my way of thinking. He was a man easily moved by his impulses; he could covet a thing hotly today and reject it tomorrow.

And certainly, at this moment, there was enough to distract a more constant man.

First and foremost there was the unyielding struggle with his uncle Beaufort; and against that adversary a man must keep a single mind. And then there were his peers. Unless he could sway them he was powerless—and sway them he could not. Protector though he was, he had been forced to promise Parliament not to move in the matter of my inheritance until the Pope had spoken. And, at this moment, there seemed no good reason to break that promise.

But reason there was soon to be!

The blood pounding in my heart, I left the messenger kneeling, and shaken with fear and with anger, went to find my husband.

'Now are my two enemies joined!' I cried out. 'My uncle of Bavaria and my cousin of Burgundy. My uncle that cast away God's service to serve himself, and my cousin, that spits upon his own marriage, are shocked; shocked both of them at the insult we two have offered to God. My uncle names Philip heir to all his lands. And those lands—do you listen?—include *my* lands, every one; Holland, Zealand and Friesland, yes, and Hainault, too; my own Hainault!'

'The man's mad!' Gloucester declared red and furious. 'The lands are not his to give. He isn't sovereign, he's *Ruward, Ruward* only. He governs in your name.'

'Men give what is not theirs to give—and others take. Holland he filched by treaty and calls himself Count; Zealand and Friesland he took by force after I fled to England. As for Hainault, he swears Brabant mortaged Hainault and can't pay his debt.'

'It was not Brabant's to mortgage. It was yours. And now it is mine by deed of gift—your marriage gift. Holland and Hainault, Zealand and Friesland, mine to have and to hold for us and for our children for ever. Burgundy must refuse this iniquitous offer.'

I wanted to laugh at that; but the sound I made was more like weeping.

'Dear love, you married trouble when you married me! Why should Philip refuse the lands he's angled for so long—he and his father before him? Refuse the lands that march so sweetly with his because *you* object? There's little love lost between you; one more reason for him to accept!'

But he was not listening; he was away on some fantastic project of his own. 'I will write to the little Philip and put the matter plain. And, if he will not listen to the voice of friendship'—and the idea of friendship between him and Philip was yet one more fantasy—'and to the voice of justice, then by God he shall listen to the sword.'

If things did not move fast enough in Rome, they were moving fast in France and in Holland; too fast for me!

Brabant, styling himself Duke of Hainault, to my miserable fury, declared himself willing—if my Lords of Burgundy and Bedford would arbitrate—to stand by their decision in the matter of my marriage.

Gloucester laughed and his laughter was sour.

'A good suggestion—if the arbitrators were honest! The little Philip won't be biassed, not Philip, Bavaria's heir as well as Brabant's! Philip takes your lands and titles, my dear, as soon as the breath is out of Bavaria's body; and you may go whistle; unless you fight and fight now. It's no longer a question of your having a child of your own to inherit; not if you had a dozen children would your uncle budge. He claims everything by *right*; right of treaty, right of conquest, right of mortgage unpaid.'

'Bedford?' I said and as I said it I knew there was little hope.

'Never count on him. My good brother so lately wed to Philip's owl-faced sister! Let me tell you this. Bedford cares for nothing in this world but his country and his Kinglet. Rather than lose one hairsbreadth of advantage in France by quarrelling with Burgundy, he'd hand you over, lock, stock and barrel!'

'And they call him just!' My anger burst through. 'They insult me—vicious Brabant, greedy Burgundy, self-righteous Bedford. I am your wife; the King accepts me. To doubt my marriage is to insult the King. As for my inheritance—it's mine and yours; and I will keep it so. Before God, we fight and fight now!'

My kinswoman, Madam Johanne, came riding to Hadleigh. Like Bedford she cared nothing for Gloucester or for me. She cared only that not one hair of the little King be singed. But for all that her advice was sound.

'Son of Gloucester, I speak now for your good; and for the good of my kinswoman Jacqueline; and for the good of the little King. But most of all I speak for the peace of Christendom to avoid the spilling of Christian blood. You cannot afford to offend Burgundy now, at this moment, when we have such need of him in France. You must arbitrate; you *must!* And you may trust your good brother of Bedford. He himself petitioned the Pope to annul the marriage of

Jacqueline here. He will never deliver the helpless into the hands of the unjust. He is a just man. And, if he were not, still he would not give away your possessions. They have become *our* possessions; they will bring gold into our treasury, gold we so badly need. Be sure he will speak out for the right.'

'And while Humphrey and Brabant arbitrate,' I reminded her, bitter, 'my uncle takes all.'

She nodded. 'You can do nothing but wait. Waiting you lose nothing and gain much. Waiting, you put yourself in the right—and that must weigh with the Pope. And what weighs with the Pope must weigh with Bavaria; and with Burgundy and with Brabant.'

When she had gone to her chamber we discussed her counsel. On the face of it her counsel was good; but Johann was cunning to help those she'loved; and I could not think she loved Gloucester or me.

'Still it's good advice,' Gloucester said at last. 'So I keep my word to Parliament to wait awhile; so I remain in England to watch my uncle Beaufort—these cursed uncles! So I dispose His Holiness towards us. To wait can do no harm ... if we do not wait too long?'

'And how if the Pope's judgment go against us?'

'We'll take that hurdle when we get to it! I will write that I am willing.' And his mouth twisted as though with verjuice.

I can see him now, walking about the room, stooping to warm his hands at the blaze—it was a cold February day—his brows black, and bitter as the gall in which the clerk wrote.

I, Humphrey, son, brother and uncle of Kings...

He had always a sort of bombast when he felt unsure.

Duke of Gloucester, Count of Hainault, Holland and Zealand, Lord of Friesland, Grand Chamberlain, Protector and Defender of England, in order to avoid great peril and damages, consent to submit the discord between the Duke of Brabant on the one hand, and ourselves on the other, to our well-beloved brother the Duke of Bedford and to our well-beloved cousin the Duke of Burgundy...

For my own part I wrote,

I, Jacqueline, Duchess of Gloucester, Countess of Holland, Hainault and Zealand, Lady of the free Frisians, do pledge myself on the faith and oath of my body and the honour of a prince, to abide by the decision of my dear brother the Duke of Bedford, Regent in France, and our well-beloved cousin the Duke of Burgundy, on the difference between our Cousin the Duke of Brabant and our much revered lord and husband, the Duke of Gloucester, Count of Hainault, Holland and Zealand, Lord of the free Frisians...

I showed my letter to Johanne and her brows went up. 'You are either very clever or very simple,' she said. 'You promise to abide by their decision. Oh, you promise! Yet you call the one man cousin and the other husband. You make it very clear that Gloucester bears all your titles by right of marriage and that Brabant is lord of his own dukedom and nothing else. Your letter means that you are set on your own course; that and nothing more.'

'Yet it must serve,' I said.

The slow months passed. Gloucester had given them three months in which to come to a decision and we should have heard by May at latest. But May came and went; and June and July. It was full autumn when the advocates met in Paris to consider the case.

These days of waiting my husband was not easy to live with. Charm was turned off as with a spigot. He was rude, often, and sometimes violent. He would take himself off for days at a time and no word where he was going nor why; nor when he would be back.

I accepted it; I accepted it all. I had promised him lands and titles; I had brought him only trouble.

I rode over to Langley to visit Johanne. We had taken her advice and she was willing to be friends. And, indeed, I needed a friend. I was shaken with anxiety over the outcome of the arbitration. Would that vicious fool remain my husband, or Gloucester whom I loved? And I was gnawed continually about the fate of my country. Would my uncle take all while I sat by and lifted not a finger?

And then again—if things went against me what would Gloucester do?

'I have brought him nothing but trouble!' I told her, despondent.

'Never blame yourself!' she said. 'My son of Gloucester knows that if he wants your lands he must fight for them! He's always known it! The truth is he veers like a cock on the spire to every wind that blows!' And then without warning, asked abruptly whether I liked my woman Cobham.

I shrugged, surprised. Though I have as much jealousy in my nature as any woman, it had never occurred to me to consider Cobham—humble and, to my mind, plain—a cause for jealousy.

'She's well enough,' I said, careless. 'She's' obliging ...'

'Too obliging,' Johanne said. 'Too free with her favours by half!'

'Good luck to her—if she can find her market, poor thing!' And I remember how I laughed.

Johanne's plucked brows went up; they all-but disappeared beneath the coif.

'Would it surprise you,' she said, 'to know that men find her bewitching? Indeed there are some—cheated wives and sweet-hearts—that call her witch. Poor, did you say? Perhaps ... once. But not now. She's laid away some wealth, garnered, so they say, from the long line of gentlemen she's admitted to her bed.'

'Little chance of her admitting anyone to her bed now!' I said and I was careless still. 'She's forever about me.'

'Have you brought her with you?' Johann asked.

I was forced to admit I had not. She had asked permission to visit her mother.

Johanne said no more and I dismissed the matter, except that now and again I would look at that pale, pointed face, those slanted eyes, that meagre figure, and wonder that any man could be taken in the net of such slight charms. My mind was full of other things. In Paris they were still debating the matter that must bring me honour and happiness, or shame and misery.

And then something happened so that for a while I forgot even that.

XIX

I was walking in the garden at Hadleigh. It was a crisp autumn day and I walked thoughtful among the golden leaves thinking less of the sweet morning than of my own affairs. Gloucester was increasingly difficult; the strain of waiting for a decision upon our marriage weighed ever more heavy upon him. In council he was irritable, with his books restless, with servants harsh; and with me, all three.

And now, this morning, I had fresh cause for disquiet; there was news that might well cast a shadow upon my whole life. So I walked thoughtful among the autumn leaves, and, turning a corner, came upon my husband. He had plucked an apple; I saw him bite into it and cast it peevishly away. 'A maggot at the core!' he said. 'There's a maggot at every core—so it seems!' He cast a look at my thoughtful face. 'Well?' he said, impatient. And again, 'Well?'

'It's my uncle!' I said. 'Bavaria's a sick man; likely to die, they say.'

'God send it!' he said at once. 'A snake less in our path!' He shrugged. 'You cannot pretend to grief. You've wished him dead often enough!'

'A natural death; or a soldier's death. Not this death. Death by poison ... it's a cruel death.'

'This way or that, what matter? When heaven grants us our wish, give thanks—and no questions asked.'

'I fear the hand of heaven is not in this!' I said.

He looked at me sudden and sharp. I thought there was a secret look in his eyes.

'Meaning?' he asked.

'I fear the hand of one that loves me.' And for one hateful moment I found myself wondering whether his own hand had meddled in that matter. But that was not Gloucester's way. The sword, yes; the poison-cup, no. But for all that, whether his hand was truly in the matter or not I do not know until this day. But that my own name was not the sweeter for it, I know full well.

He said, careful, 'If you know nothing of the matter, what do you fear?'

'Harm to those that may suffer for love of me.'

'Those that love you will be glad to suffer for you!' And he laughed a little.

Would you? If princes were punished like common men, if they tore those handsome limbs of yours from your fine body—would you relish it? The thought turned me sick so that I put out a hand and stumbled upon the wet leaves.

'Come now!' And his hand tight upon my arm saved me from falling. 'You cry out too soon. Your uncle isn't dead yet, more's the pity!'

'Let him live or die, still the tale will follow us!'

'Do not flout God's gift,' and he smiled that charming smile of his. And then, very sharp again, '*Us?* Why—*us?*'

I looked into his eyes, the cold hazel eyes of the Lancasters. I asked the question I must ask.

'Do you know anything of the matter, my lord?'

'I?' And he laughed. 'We talk of *Holland.* Why should an English prince play poisoner there? He would have neither need nor opportunity. But a Dutch prince might well have both.'

A Dutch prince! It was as though he winged an arrow. I looked at him surprised. He was staring at me with an odd expression. *A Dutch prince.* The arrow found its mark. He meant ... *me.*

I stood there amazed and troubled. But surely this was some jest of Gloucester's; with him you could never tell. He turned and looked at me over his shoulder. 'Go into the house, my dear!' And now he was frankly mocking. 'You may find someone to elucidate the matter.'

Someone to elucidate the matter? He was teasing! I took in my breath with relief. But I was a little angry, too; he, my husband, did not scruple to wound me with his mockery. What of those that sought to discredit me?

I turned about and hastened indoors.

In my chamber a woman waited; a woman all in black. She fell on her knees as I came in; I hardly knew her at first—so old, so yellow, so stained with weeping.

I ran to Beatrix van Vliet and lifted her. Even before she spoke I knew the truth.

'Van Vliet!' I said.

She nodded. 'He did it for you!'

I felt my heart crack. I said, 'Do they know?'

She nodded again. 'They tormented him and he spoke. And now he must die.' Her fingers clutched at my arm. 'Save him, save him. You can. Only you ... little Jacque we have loved and served. And will serve to the end ... The end,' she said again and shook with tearless weeping.

I said, 'What can I do?'

'You are a prince!' she said.

'And what can I command? I am a fugitive.'

'You can beseech your uncle for Jan's life.'

'Do you think he'd listen? Even a saint racked by poison would find it hard ... and my uncle is no saint.'

'Then you must command. You are a *prince*,' she said again obstinate in misery.

'A prince may not set himself against the law.'

'Law comes from the prince. Have you forgotten your Joyous Entries, how you sat there in the judge's seat and said the word to punish or set free?'

'I did what I was told by men learned in the law. I did not set myself above the law. I obeyed it; though afterwards there was no sleeping because of the things my mouth had spoken. But it's all useless to talk. I have no power in Holland, no power at all. It's to my uncle you must go—and he'll not let his poisoner go free.'

She turned and paced backwards and forwards; every time she turned to face me, she looked at me out of her desolate eyes. It is a bad prince that sets his friends above the law; I thanked God I had not to make that choice. And then I remembered her devotion to me, this woman that was my sister; that had never asked a thing of me but to serve me with all her heart. She had lost her first husband in my service; now she must lose the second.

'Beatrix, Beatrix,' I said, 'I talk of the law and the duty of princes as though there was no heart in my body; but my heart is there and it breaks ... it breaks ...' and the tears ran down my cheeks.

She ran to me then and knelt, as so often in my childhood, and put her arms about me, forgetting her bitter need in my lesser need. I took myself gently away; she had the right to her own sorrow. I said, 'Jan van Vliet did this for me; and I am powerless to abate one jot of his punishment.'

I looked at her and she looked back at me. Between us lay the thought of a man hanged, drawn and quartered—the pain and the shame of that death!

'Oh Beatrix,' I said. 'My sister!' And I had never called her that before; but she did not even notice it.

'I love him,' she said. 'My first marriage—to please others. Oh, it was well enough. But this! Dear God, I ask no more of paradise.' She put out a hand as though to beseech me again; her lips moved, soundless.

I threw my principles to the four winds; I had done babbling of justice. I said, 'I love Jan for his love of me. I will help him if I may; though how, by God's Face I do not know! Tell me the tale. We might somehow, somewhere, find the hand of the great in this; a hand strong enough to reach out and save.'

She clasped her hands together. I saw how thin they had grown, how yellow, twisting upon the black stuff of her gown. For the rest, she sat very still, her voice quiet.

'It all began on Ascension Day. We were at Schoonhoven, supping with the Bastard of Langeraeck. After supper Jan walked by the river, a thing he loves to do ... he will not walk by any river again. There was a man following after him; and Jan, for the sake of courtesy—the man had been at supper—stopped to say Goodnight. It was a courtesy that cost him dear. For this man was an Englishman ...'

An Englishman! And I took in my breath. If Gloucester had had a hand in this, then he must reach out somehow to save the man he had brought to destruction.

'*Can you speak English?* the man said; he spoke very softly and his eyes went this way and that.

'Jan shook his head. The man had no Dutch but Jan had a little Latin and so they began to talk.

'The Englishman said he knew how we hated the Bavarian because of his treachery to our rightful lady. He said we could help ourselves and serve you at the same time; and we should be paid well; more than we could ever dare to hope. He said he served a great prince. *A great prince; and English.* What were we to think?'

I said nothing; I stared at her. I knew the name she meant.

'Oh we didn't know; we weren't meant to know. But we guessed; we were meant to guess. Your husband, Jacque ... we thought you wished it; we were *meant* to think it.

'So then Jan stood silent and thought awhile. He knew well my love for you ... and why I love you so. He knew how often I have lain awake and wept that you were far away; and how at times I would not come into his arms nor sleep, for thinking of you. So Jan—he's a soldier, a man of deeds and no great thinker—said *Yes.* And I swear before God that the thought of money was not in him; only how he might serve you.

'The man gave Jan English poison in a soft leather bag, lest the poison come through and corrode the hand.

'Jan went to the Hague; he got into the palace easily. His face is known and he didn't think to cover it with his hood. He found the Bavarian's chamber empty; the great chamber of the counts of Holland, that is yours by right. Before the prie-dieu a prayer book stood open. Jan says he remembered how this man had sold his God for a prince's crown; and that he was a hypocrite and cruel with it. *The Pitiless, the Tiger*—and his prayer book open for all to see how deep he prayed!

'Jan said his anger came up hot as blood. He smeared the pages of the book with poison. The man should die after he had prayed—so much grace Jan allowed him. He had no fears, he said, only a gladness that he had revenged treachery to you, his prince. His mind was quiet; thereafter he slept like a child. And who should know but I?

'The Bavarian fell sick. We waited for him to die that we might welcome you home again—our lady, our Jacque. We could not guess that it would be out of the frying pan and into the fire for you and for all loyal Hollanders. We could not guess that the Burgundian was already named heir—heir to all your lands and titles.

'So, simpletons that we were, we waited for the Bavarian to die;

and for you to come home again. But he did not die. The poison was strong; but he was stronger.

'One cannot poison a great duke and no questions asked—we should have remembered that. And all enquiries came back to Jan. Someone had seen him at Schoonhoven talking to the Englishman; a man on guard at the palace remembered him crossing the courtyard. A button had fallen from his coat; maybe they found it, who knows? They did not stop for proof. They came and took him from my bed and they carried him before the Privy Council at Purmerende, but they got nothing out of him. So the Bavarian had him carried back to the Hague and there, in the dark cell, with none to see—they tormented him. They broke his fine, straight bones...

She stopped while the long shudders shook her lean black-garbed frame.

'...Then, they carried him all broken as he was, before the Court of Holland. I was waiting in the courtyard to see him ... for the last time; to say a word of cheer ... for the last time. But when I saw what they had done to him...'

Again the long shudders shook her. I took her by the waist and would have made her sit but very gently she shook me off.

'This is a thing that must be said standing. He could not stand, yet he must stand. Oh Jacque, Jacque, it was then, seeing what they had done to him, my heart broke.

'So there they sat, the great lords, sworn to justice—the Lord of Egmont, the Lord of Cortgène together with his cousins the van Borselens.'

'Enemies all!' I cried out. 'There would be no mercy for any friend of mine. But,' I said, unwilling, 'there would be justice.' And I remembered how Frank van Borselen had this much justice in him that he had rebuked a page long ago for lewd words concerning a young girl.

'Yet their justice will not help you; you must fear it rather,' I said, very low. 'Your unjust man may be swayed by gifts, or pity even; but your just man remembers his duty to do it.'

'Yet,' she said, and fetched a sigh from the bottom of her heart, 'not one of those just men thought to ask *why* he had confessed; nor why he could not stand upon his feet; nor yet why so good a man had done this thing. It is a crime, so it seems, to put a poisonous snake from my prince's heel. And so the words were spoken ... and he is to die.

'To die, to die!' she cried out, 'unless ... unless ... oh Jacque, you are our only hope.'

'A poor hope,' I said. 'What am I but a stranger in a strange land? And I am driven this way and that! I love Jan for his love of me; but I know full well that poison is wickedness...'

'Wickedness, indeed!' my husband stood there in the doorway. He turned to Beatrix. 'Never seek pity where none can be. The man that uses poison is outside all pity. Stop wearying your lady with your useless tears—it's overlate for that! Go home again; I cannot welcome you here.'

She curtseyed first to him and then to me; she turned and left us without another word.

I would have spoken then but his hand, uplifted, stayed me.

'Your uncle's dying at last, God be thanked,' he said. 'And Brabant shakes in his shoes. He's lost his best ally and doesn't know when his own turn will come to make a forced exit. He blames you of course. Witch and bitch—he calls you both! You cannot afford, my dear, to keep that woman by you now, nor yet to show her any pity. The thing was done. It has no concern with you.'

'Has it not?' I asked. 'It disposes of one enemy and causes the other to shake in his shoes. Have we no part in it, no part at all, my lord?'

'We?' he said. '*We?* I have heard them call you rash, too quick of tongue, your own worst enemy; and by God, it could be true!'

He kissed me lightly—slightingly as it were—and left me.

XX

'My patience begins to crack!' Gloucester told me more than once. 'Your uncle's dying and here we wait. We wait for Parliament's permission; we wait for the Pope's word; we wait for this and for that! And all the time the enemy gathers strength. Behind the sot that calls himself your husband, Burgundy stands. If it weren't for thrice-damned Burgundy, your inheritance would return to you and no need to spill blood.'

'Even though the Pope hasn't spoken?'

'*Because* the Pope hasn't spoken. If he hasn't confirmed our marriage, certainly he hasn't denied it.'

'Yet there are some—and not a few—that call me your whore.' And, in spite of my smiling, my voice shook.

'Then I will cut out their tongues!' he promised, very pleasant.

And still the wearisome argument trailed on.

Backwards and forwards went the messengers; and my fears mounted lest I should find myself not Gloucester's wife but Gloucester's whore. As for him, his steady anger grew.

And now my fool of Brabant himself made things easier. He was ready to compromise, eager for what he could grab without fighting. If he might remain in possession of Hainault as long as he lived, he would renounce all claim to me as his wife. After his death Hainault could, for all he cared, come back to me and my husband. Philip was away, I fancy; certainly he was caught napping!

'Brabant ready to renounce all claim as my husband! A miracle, praise be to God, beyond our dearest hopes!'

But Gloucester would not smile. The mouth that could smile so sweetly——and kiss so sweetly—tightened.

'The promise comes from Brabant and from him alone. Do you think Burgundy will back up that fool? Not he! Well, I've no more patience! I'm going to take my rights. I'm no hairsplitting churchman; I'm a soldier.'

I was as eager as he could be; but for all that I put in a last word. 'We promised Parliament to wait; we agreed to stand by the decision from Rome.'

'There's *been* no decision, no decision at all!' He turned upon me, all carried away by his fury. 'When my rights are kept from me, why then I take them!' And his hand flew to his sword.

He was so handsome then, I took fire myself—dry tinder, I must own. I burned now to see my own land and to win back what was mine.

Parliament was not pleased. If my Lord of Gloucester wanted to fight in the Low Countries, no one could stay him! But my lord must understand that Parliament could not help him. Every available penny must go to furnish the French wars. For his own private fighting my lord must provide his own money, his own forces.

My lord was not unduly set back. Hope sprang easily in him and was as easily cast down. He could find both money and men. He knew how to win hearts—the hearts of his inferiors; and he was a good captain. Men would come willingly to his standard.

I went, reluctant, to make my farewells to Catharine. I knew she would shower me with reproaches; but I could not find it in my heart to leave without seeing her. I found more than I bargained for at Windsor. I found that formidable woman my kinsman Johanne.

It was Johanne—by arrangement evidently—that came to the point.

'Cousin,' she said, cold and quiet, 'restrain that hothead of yours! Even were he to succeed—which he never will—his first duty is to his king in France. Burgundy's a snake; and who should know that better than you? Anger him and he'll turn and bite. Oh, not only you—that's your own business. But the King—and that's everyone's business; and Gloucester's most of all; Protector of England; yet he endangers the King's French crown.'

'And such a little King!' Catharine broke in all soft and silly. 'Jacque, you're his godmother. You held him at the font. You have a special duty ...'

'I have a duty to my people and to my husband ...'

'Which husband?' Johann interrupted, sour.

'If you were younger, Madam,' I told her, 'you should pay for that!' I turned about; but at the door I paused. I could not leave Catharine in anger—she had been my friend; she had made me godmother to her son; she was twice my sister by marriage.

'Dearest Cat,' I said, 'we serve your son in this as well as ourselves. Gloucester's gain is England's gain. All my lands to be united with England for ever!' I ran over and kissed her averted cheek. It was cold beneath my kiss.

Nothing for it but make my curtsey and be gone.

And now, all being ready, we wasted no more time. It was strange to find myself riding to Dover, to make this first step on my journey home. But once in Dover, we must waste time whether we would or not. We would stand upon the castle ramparts now holding out a hand to catch the wind, now watching which way my scarf would blow. And always it was in the wrong direction.

Waiting came hard with me; harder still for my husband.

'My enemies would say heaven takes a hand!' he burst out once. 'Well, heaven or no, it's my own hand that counts!'

And now there was time—and time enough—to discuss a question that had long troubled me. I had not raised it before; it was a hurdle we must take when we came to it. Now the hurdle was near.

'I am asking myself,' I told him, 'where my mother will stand in this. Will it be with us; or with Brabant?'

I saw his startled look. I think he had not considered the matter seriously. He had a way of believing that the thing he wanted to happen must happen; though hope turn sour in one enterprise, up it would bob sweet and smiling in the next. No great judge of people, he had taken it for granted that she would support me, her child.

'She's a de Charolais—and you know what that means,' I said. 'On the other hand, she saw for herself how Brabant behaved. I don't think she'll soon forget her daughter walking in the dust of the streets to seek protection at a public inn. And, there's another thing—Brabant's impotent. She knows very well that for the peace of Holland I must have a child of my own ...'

'It's a matter you seem in no haste to remedy!' he said, and his sour glance reminded me it was not only my heir we awaited, but his own-heir to a royal naive and great possession. I tried to bring him back to the matter in hand.

'Of course she might say the peace of my people is safe only in Philip's hand—and believe it, too. She's a de Charolais and we must reckon with it!'

And we were at the beginning again!

'I will make my reckoning with Master Philip when the accursed wind changes!' He got up and went into the house.

The wind changed at last. We made a good crossing and landed at Calais. For all his impatience, Humphrey was anxious to vex Burgundy no more than he could help. Our men were ordered to march through France courteously, paying for food and injuring no man ... no woman neither. Did he really think to stay Philip's fury with a sweetmeat?

As soon as we set foot on French soil we found messengers from Mons. Mons was happy at my return; but I could not be welcomed within the city until my Lord of Brabant had been consulted, together with my Lord of Burgundy.

I should have expected it. Since I had run away there had been peace; and the great gift peace can bring—prosperity. It was clear that the thought of warfare made no appeal. Instead of being welcomed with joy—as I had confidently expected—there appeared to be nothing but dismay.

'Three years, since I ran away—it's a long time!' I said, disheartened and unwilling to show it. 'How can I expect them to receive me with a full heart, at the first?'

'By God, they had better!' Gloucester said.

'We must be patient, dear heart. Mine are a people not to be moved by threat or punishment. We must give them time. If I have lost something of their love, be sure I shall win it again. I am their prince. As for you—' and I smiled into his handsome, angry face, 'they have but to look at you—if you will but smile—to come running to our side.'

But it was not as easy as that! Mons—my own city—torn between love of me and fear of Philip, knew not which way to turn.

For the next step I was not prepared. We were at Crespin and well on our way to my reluctant capital—when my husband, all black with his anger, brought me the news. Mons had sent to my mother begging her to see that I did not enter the city; but, if come I must, then, until they had had time to consider the matter, I must on no account bring Monsieur of Gloucester with me.

Fortunately my mother was no longer at le Quesnoy when the deputation arrived. In the midst of our anger and dismay she walked in. She had come to join Gloucester and me. So there was one hurdle out of the way and I thanked God for it.

I had not thought to be so moved at the sight of her. Sympathy between us had so often failed. She had been hard and domineering both to my father and to me; and she had sold me to Brabant to serve the ambition of her house. Now that she had arrived, all unlooked for, I dismissed the past.

I ran to her, tears pouring down my cheeks and threw myself into her arms; and she, unwonted tears in her hard, dark eyes, held me close and then put me from her to see how I had fared, and then held me close again.

It was the first time in my life I had ever felt certain of my mother; it was as though victory were already in my hand.

When we had made an end of weeping and embracing, she turned to my husband. 'My hard head cannot approve of you, son of Gloucester,' she said, 'but my heart—my woman's heart—says, Here is a *man!*'

'I trust your heart will convince your head, Madam mother,' he said and bent to her cheek with flattery of eyes and lips.

And so it was at Crespin, with the three of us in loving friendship together, that the deputation found us at last.

It was hard to bite down my anger. I was their Prince, free to come and go as I chose. I saw Gloucester's fingers gripped about his sword, and, knowing the man and how all might be forever lost by one rash act, I put out a hand and laid it upon his sleeve. He made no move but let it lie; and, while I rehearsed in my mind the things I should say—whether to show anger but not too much anger, or friendship but not too much friendship—my mother was already speaking, gentle as any dove.

'It gives me pleasure to welcome old friends, Monsieur de la Loge and Monsieur le Peron ...' and I stood amazed that she remembered their names, for they were simple burghers and in no wise distinguished. 'Friends I call you, in spite of this unlooked-for message of which you are but the bearers—unwilling, as I believe. Your Council has forgotten something and it is this—your prince commands and not the Estates. She is free to set foot wherever she will in her own land; yes, and to bring her husband with her. Tell the Estates of Mons that we shall be with them in less than twenty-four hours.'

It was a desolate journey we made to Mons. We were almost into December and the wind blowing cold. I lay back in the litter huddled in my furs ... and my courage as cold as the weather. Valenciennes had closed its gates against me. Would Mons follow suit? And every town at whose gates I knocked?

My mother did her best to rally me. 'I remember your courage at Gorcum, and I cannot think you a coward. So, seeing you pale and trembling, I can only think and hope ... daughter, are you breeding?'

'This is no time for woman's work; now I must play the man.' And I could not endure to confess the depths of my disappointment.

'Woman's work is still woman's work—and women the stronger for it. You'll win more hearts carrying a child than carrying a sword.'

Whatever the Council of Mons might think, whatever the Estates might declare, our welcome was warm—my mother's hint had not been given in vain. The city fathers rode out to welcome us and to bring us within the streets all hung with tapestries, all strewn with garlands. At the Naasterhof where the Estates met, and where we lodged, my standard flew.

The Estates had been summoned for the third day after our arrival; and, while we waited, the careful city provided us with modest feasts. And there I would sit, smiling and nodding and hiding my fear lest, after all, Mons should not declare for us; and hiding another fear also—that the cool reception he had been given would cool my husband's ardour to fight should fighting be necessary.

His ambition I kept hot by showing him this part of his new dominions. He would wander in the valley looking upward at the city crowning the hill, its churches and houses riding above strong walls. 'A fine city,' he said more than once. And each time I would answer, 'It is yours; your good city of Mons!' And I was glad to give him so great a gift. And I would add, 'And there are others as great. The whole of Hainault is yours for the taking, and Holland and Zealand and Friesland with it.' And I prayed that I might lean upon this man, my husband. Let him take all. Let him govern in my place.

Let me be his dutiful wife and the mother of his children. I had been pushed from pillar to post long enough.

These days I feared not only for my inheritance; another more secret fear gnawed at my heart. That, too, I hid beneath a smiling face.

That first night in Mons, all happiness at being home again I went to my chamber expecting to find Beatrix. I had long looked forward to our meeting since I had written from England asking that she would come to me again. I knew that my husband had disapproved of her presence in England—and with some justice. It might help to keep alive the scandal that lingered with my uncle's sickness. But here it was different. My people knew me; they could not believe me capable of such wickedness. Beatrix had suffered for my sake. How could I turn my back upon her now?

So now I could not go fast enough to my chamber, longing for her kindness and her most comfortable arms.

I found no Beatrix. Instead, Eleanor Cobham, demure beneath downcast lids, slid forward.

I was all amazed. What was she doing here?

'We had not expected you, Cobham. We chose our women and you were not amongst them,' I said.

Her curtsey swept the floor; even in that moment I envied the grace, the liquid movement of that slender, high-bosomed body.

'My lord duke commanded me.' And I thought there was a shade of insolence curdling her respect. 'I was for home—as Madam the Duchess knows. But my lord duke said that, mindful of the comfort of all, you had forgotten your own. He requested my attendance on you—a favour to himself.' And now I could have sworn to slyness in those secret eyes.

I nodded. I made myself quiet under those long white hands of hers, though my own hands longed to strike her in the face. The words of Johann concerning this same woman pricked in my heart; Eleanor Cobham was known for her witchery over men. For all her downcast looks she was any man's harlot—that could pay her price.

And there, surely was my answer. Proud Gloucester would take no other man's harlot to his bed.

But, in spite of that, doubts of my husband began to stir.

XXI

The day had come. In the Naasterhof the Estates were assembled. Now I should know whether my people accepted me; whether I stood crowned before Christendom—a wife and not a whore.

I went down to meet my fate, scarce able to walk for the trembling of my limbs. White gown, white face beneath white coif, I had an untouched look. 'A virgin, one would swear, in spite of your three husbands!' my mother chuckled. 'Well there's nothing like it for melting men's hearts. The more lecherous a man, the more he values virginity—if only to deflower it.'

So there I was walking in my white gown, my hand resting upon Gloucester's blue velvet sleeve and glad of it to support my trembling. Behind us went my mother all in scarlet, erect, regal. Margaret of Burgundy. Beware!

The Estates received us, standing in silence. And, when we were all seated, I in the great chair of State, my advocate stood up—Jan l'Orfèvre, known throughout the land as a good churchman; the choice of him as my advocate had been my mother's.

'We are met here,' he said, 'to pronounce upon your willingness to receive your lady within this Countship of Hainault, and to enquire whether you will—or will not—support her cause. I could say you have no choice in the matter, since to her and to no other, your oath was sworn, your allegiance given.

'But I know well—as you' all know, and most of all our lady here—that we must first obey the laws of God, to which every other law must give way. And so it is on the question of our lady's marriage we now take our stand.

'If her marriage to my Lord Duke of Brabant be legal and binding, then we will give her no welcome nor any help until she return to him again. But, if that marriage be not binding, then it is our duty—as well as our pleasure—to help her to our uttermost against her enemies.

'Our lady has bowed herself before the advice of venerable churchmen and doctors foremost in the law; and their opinion is plainly set forth.

'They declare with one voice that there is no marriage between our sovereign lady and the Duke of Brabant; and there never was. It had been forbidden by His Holiness; at the moment of solemnization it was still forbidden; and it is forbidden now.

'The marriage of our sovereign lady to my Lord of Brabant is therefore beyond all question null and void. And so she has cleansed herself by confession, receiving forgiveness under three conditions— that she, at no time, share her bed with my Lord of Brabant; that she say the prayers prescribed in penance; that she give alms to the amount imposed. All these conditions she has obeyed.

'Being thus free in the eyes of the church and of the state, she gave herself, without stain, in marriage to the noble Lord Humphrey Duke of Gloucester. And this marriage, accepted by the church in England and by the royal house of England, has now lasted two years. Are we to declare it adulterous and wrongfully stain the clear honour of the lady we are in duty bound to cherish?

'Sirs, this is a true marriage and I demand in our lady's name that you receive her true, legitimate husband, Humphrey Duke of Gloucester, as Regent and Governor in Hainault.'

I remember how I sat staring straight before me and seeing nothing while he pleaded my cause. And, when the Stadtholder of Hainault stood in his place—Brabant's appointment and a man I did not know—my heart shrivelled to a pea.

'If Madam the Duchess will leave us to our deliberations, we shall make an end of the matter as soon as may be and make known our decisions.'

I stood up then and bowed to my Three Estates and left the Council chamber.

I sat within my own chamber while the short December daylight darkened to night. And all the time I was remembering that the Stadtholder whose face I did not know had addressed me as *Duchess*—as though I were Brabant's wife; not by my own title *Countess*, my sovereign's title.

'It isn't easy to say which way it will go,' my mother said, breaking the silence. 'There was many a kindly look thrown in your direction but you missed them all, sitting and staring at nothing. I think it should go well. And Gloucester's troops on their doorstep may also incline them to say *Yes*. Still, discussion will be hot; I think they will not give an answer today.'

And then she said, 'It would help you, I am sure, if—until the decision is made—Gloucester keeps from your bed.'

'He is not over-anxious these days,' I said.

'The Cobham woman!' She did not pretend not to understand. 'Daughter, mark me well. You had best send the creature packing!'

'It is enough, enough,' I cried out and was myself surprised at the passion in my voice, 'to have this long and terrible waiting, without this gnat to prick me—this light, slight woman!'

'Light, yes; slight, no!' my mother said. 'If you are not careful she'll break your courage and your heart.'

I said nothing; but I was resolved to endure the woman no longer, to sweep her from my path as a spider is swept from the corner of one's house.

Three days I waited for the Estates to speak, three long and heavy days. It was on December the fourth that I stood side-by-side with Gloucester to hear my answer.

'Madam, our countess and liege lady, we accept your marriage with Monsieur the Duke of Gloucester as a true marriage. And we reject the marriage with Monsieur the Duke of Brabant as null and void. Therefore we declare the bonds made between ourselves and the Duke of Brabant to be broken now and forever. And, that being done, we will accept as lord and governor the Duke of Gloucester, your undoubted husband.'

In that first moment I could not speak; my hand tightened upon Gloucester's arm as though I must fall. Yet I had known the answer early this morning and had already offered my thanks to God. I had thought, that being done, I could stand quiet and give no sign. I had not allowed for the feeling that surged within me now—the pride and the humility. To stand there in the capital of beloved Hainault, to hear my own people declare the marriage with my dear love true and binding! It was as though God's hand wiped away the dirt that spotted my honour. Speak I could not. Deeply, humbly, I bowed and left upon the arm of my husband.

The next day he made his Joyous Entry; standing by my side he took and received the oath. Seeing him there so handsome and so noble I could not but remember the mean and shiftless boy raging— or weeping perhaps—in Brussels.

I thrust him from my mind. I would not let him spoil the sacred moment. I had given my husband the first of the promised count-ships. I would give him my entire inheritance, I would keep nothing back. Surely then his angers would cease and we should be loving and gentle together.

And I forgot, until too late, my cousin Catharine's words. *A greedy man is never satisfied.*

And so we began our solemn procession through Hainault. I was shaken to the heart's core to be home again, to be accepted by my own people. Sometimes the thought of Eleanor Cobham rose to trouble me; but now she troubled me in a different way. I was ashamed of the jealousy that had left her languishing in Mons. I was sure, in the happiness of what I had to give, that I had done an injustice to them both; to the dignity of my husband and to the humble serviceable girl. I would make it up to her with kindness and with gifts.

It is an odd thing; in battle my will is iron but the kindness of my own people leaves me defenceless as a child.

Mauberge and Soignies, le Quesnoy and Valenciennes acknowledged us now, yes even Valenciennes that had shut her gates upon us; Avesnes and Chimay. Yet Gloucester was not pleased.

'I am Count of Hainault, true!' And his brows were black, 'but not in my own right. They accept me as Regent; but only for you; for *you!*'

'Soon they will accept you for your own sake. Who would have dealings with a woman when they can deal with you? Soon you will hold them all in the palm of your hand,' I told him smiling. But he would not smile back again.

Wherever we went bells rang, flowers were thrown, fife and drum added their note to the sound of cheering; men came flocking to our banner, yes, even Brabant's commander-in-chief, bringing his men with him. Everywhere faces smiled—the faces we could see. But what of the faces we could not see?

It was my mother that reminded me not to be misled by smiling faces. 'The struggle will be hard,' she said. 'The old bitterness between Hooks and Cods is strong as ever. Oh yes, the Hooks will come out on your side but they're sadly diminished—some dead in battle, some in prison, some fled to foreign lands, and some too poor—few enough to take arms. As for the Cods, they supported your uncle of Bavaria and naturally they expect to enjoy their reward. And don't make any mistake. Your uncle, sick though he is, is still strong enough to command them. Brabant's a weakling, that's true; but a weakling in a most strong hand, the hand of my nephew of Burgundy. And one more thing. I've no wish to cloud your happiness—God knows you've had little enough! But the tales that named you in the poisoning of your uncle are by no means dead. They will be heard louder than ever when it suits your enemies.'

It was true and I knew it. But how could I be unhappy when Hainault had accepted my husband and me? Brabant screamed when he heard the news—so we heard—running wildly through room after room to find his comforter. I was a bad wife, he wept into the bosom of his mignon, but I was still his wife and by God I should know it! Hainault accept adulterous Gloucester! It could not be done. The oath of the Joyous Entry had been made to him, Brabant, and it could never be broken. He would punish an adulterous wife and put the Englishman to death!

I could imagine the tears, the sulks, the fits and the frenzies!

My uncle of Bavaria took the news differently. For all his faults he was a man and no grizzling child. I had defied God, putting aside my true husband, and I must be taught my duty.

He was by no means free from the poison; but in spite of the vomiting, the loosening of the bowels and the constant weakness, his spirit was in no way diminished. He was gathering his forces; he would stand by his nephew of Brabant.

And Cousin Philip, whose name was a byword for lechery, was also God's champion to punish me.

Certainly the broken reed Brabant had strong supports.

And then, suddenly, my uncle of Bavaria was dead—dead in the midst of his preparations and his threats. I had hated him because he had worked me evil in plenty; but he had been my father's brother. Now that he had sent so many down into the grave was gone there himself. A whole year a-dying; and the quarters of van Vliet long fallen to pieces no longer corrupted the air of four cities.

But still the voice of rumour screamed aloud.

John of Bavaria was dead of an English poison—and the poisoner, husband to my own bastard sister whom I kept by me and cherished still. Who then had set the murder afoot? Why, the one that had most to gain by the man's death.

Jacqueline; Jacqueline, Countess of Holland.

'The rumour's cooking your goose,' my mother said. 'And Philip will see it's done to a turn. He's at the Hague again plotting with Brabant.'

I stared at her in dismay.

Philip and Brabant friends still! In spite of his promise to Philip, my uncle had made Brabant his heir after all; his sole heir—and Philip cut out of everything! I had been so sure this must result in a quarrel between the two, so split my enemies and bring Philip over to me. And now—friends and allies still!

She said, shrugging a little, 'You undervalue my nephew's subtlety. Brabant's a sick man and Philip's content to wait a little. Why not? He's Brabant's heir—and that means Bavaria's heir, too. It's all signed and sealed. And that includes everything that belongs to you!'

And when I opened my mouth to protest that it was not Brabant's to give, she said, drily, 'Argue that with your cousin.' She paused; and then she said, 'They say Brabant's dying; can hardly sit a horse, so I hear. It's a pity you didn't wait a little longer before getting yourself tangled up with Gloucester—you'd have been free to marry where you chose!'

'Dying, not he! We've heard that before. It's the rotten branch that hangs longest.'

'But it falls in the end. Brabant can't last long. And he's willed everything to Philip—everything he *can* will; not his duchy, of course, that goes to his brother St Pol. But Philip is to have your inheritance—titles and lands down to the smallest island, the meanest farm.'

The vicious fool had become an adversary indeed! Now Philip would fight to the death against me. Fortune played cat to my mouse; but Philip was her darling!

Gloucester came striding in, all gall and verjuice.

'Courage, dear heart!' I told him, hiding my own griefs and fears. 'Hainault has sworn allegiance to you; soon Holland and Zealand will swear, yes and Friesland, too! Why should they accept the Burgundian, that foreigner, to grind them beneath his heel? I am my father's child and rightful sovereign. Now my uncle is dead, and Brabant's dying; and there's no one left with a shadow of claim. If Philip comes, sword in hand, why then we'll beat him to his knees.'

And so keeping his courage high, I kept my own high also; and courage we needed. For, though the Estates of Hainault had declared my English marriage good, still in every city in Holland and Zealand they preached against us from the pulpit; yes, and in some cities of my beloved Hainault, too.

But we were gathering our forces. As always, the first to come were my kinsmen the van Brederodes; and with them those bastard brothers of mine that had not fought before William of Medemblik and Adrian of Dordrecht to stand with Everhard and Lewis, for their sister. And there came flocking all my friends tried and true—the de Montforts and Etienne d'Istre and Arent of Ghent à Geldrois and more than I can name here. And there were Gloucester's captains—the de la Porte brothers and Jean du Bois; and with them the raw Scot Macart, worth any three captains.

I was sitting with old Brederode and the Lord of Montfort, captains of my divisions, waiting for Gloucester, when he strode in smiling out of his mouth but his eyes were bitter.

'Before God, Madam!' And he thrust a paper beneath my nose, 'I stand, so it seems with Turks and heretics.

'Burgundy, God damn him, has summoned every man in my three countships'—and I could not but notice the word, not *our* but *my*—'to bear arms against me—a crusade! Crusade. He actually calls it so! He's published lies about me to be nailed to every church door. By God, I will hang every man that carries the broadsheet and I will burn every church that publishes such lies!'

'That will hardly make you more beloved, son of Gloucester,' my mother said, drily.

He ignored her. 'I shall write to Burgundy and tell him so!' He hit fist against palm till I thought the bones must crack. 'Let no man say I did not give full warning!' He roared aloud for his clerk and, as the man came wheyfaced and hurrying, I signed to my captains to go. My husband was past caring what he said or who heard him speak; he might well regret it later.

'High and mighty Prince Philip, Duke of Burgundy, Earl of Flanders and of Artois...'

His mouth was sour about the titles ; suddenly his impatience got the better of him; he snatched the quill and pushing the man aside, began to write himself. In spite of his impatience he did not spare himself a single honour—Son, brother and uncle of Kings; Protector of England; Duke of this, earl of that! It was all there. And, having set himself out in full, he started that long train of letters, each more bitter than the last, that served no end but to exacerbate each man against the other.

He found it hard to believe, he wrote, that the broadsheets could have come from Burgundy since they were so full of lies! Then, having called Philip a liar—and I saw my mother's mouth tighten at this insult to de Charolais honour—he proceeded to praise his own good faith and generosity in the affair.

I ask for nothing but what is my own. I am content to have nothing but what belongs to me by right of my dear wife and companion. And those things, by the help of God, I shall guard and keep as long as she shall live.

Should, however, your intention remain unaltered, God, from whom nothing is hidden, will defend my just rights ...

There was a good deal more of it; and it ended,

Written in my good town of Mons, under my seal this twelfth day of January, fourteen hundred and twenty-four.

My town of Mons! A mode of signing not likely to soothe Philip!

'Now we shall hear what the little Philip has to say!' He swaggered a little. 'I have pressed for a speedy reply. That's at least a courtesy he must grant!'

'He'll answer when he chooses!' my mother said and there was more than a hint of complacency about her mouth. 'You must be patient, son of Gloucester.'

It was a patience that had to last nearly two months.

Now it was my cousin's turn to accuse my husband of lying.

I am perfectly aware of all you are attempting against my cousin of Brabant and very displeasing it is to me. But even more unpleasing is the way you seek to tarnish my honour. And that I will not endure from you or anyone. And so I demand that you take back your accusation of lying; every word!

If you refuse to do this then I am ready to fight against you in single combat, at once, trusting in the help of God and of our Lady.

Have the goodness to answer me immediately for I am impatient that anything touching my honour shall be settled as soon as possible ...

'Now it is your cousin of Burgundy that grows impatient!' Gloucester cried out, furious.

'You don't know my nephew!' my mother warned him. 'A show of anger at the right time—*at the right time*, son of Gloucester—may work miracles!'

'I work no miracles for him. I'll answer when it pleases me!'

He went about repeating the letter he would write; I listened while he altered this and that, shaped and reshaped. A fortnight later the letter was ready.

I, Humphrey, Duke of Gloucester, son, brother and uncle to Kings ...

Again the flamboyant beginning, as though he were not quite sure of himself. And then to prick Philip further,

> ... Count of Hainault, of Holland, of Zealand, Lord of Friesland.
> The contents of your letter concern me little—except in one thing. You say I refused to agree to the terms of peace suggested between me and our cousin of Brabant; and that is utterly untrue.

This fresh accusation of lying could only add fuel to the flame. But he would not listen.

> Nor shall you or anyone else force me to eat my words. With the help of God and our Lady and St George, I will meet you in single combat and force you to eat your words. Believe me, I am as anxious as you to bring this matter to a speedy end.

And he named the day—St George's day. In vain I pleaded with him not to stake everything on single combat; my armies were gathering, and my cause was great. He would not listen.

'It's impossible for Burgundy to win with all the weight of his lies heavy on him!' he declared and proceeded to underline what he had already said.

> With regard to our cousin of Brabant, if you still dare to say his rights are better than mine, I am ready to add this too, to the cause of our combat; and to fight you body to body, as I have already said; and by the favour of God, our Lady and St George, prove I have the better right.
> Written in my town of Soignies, the sixteenth day of March, in the year of our Lord fourteen hundred and twenty-four.

I think he really did expect Philip to eat his words, which is odd knowing Philip. But Humphrey had always the idea that if one said a thing often enough and loud enough, it became the truth. He was genuinely surprised when Philip accepted the challenge at once.

And so all was set. A duel between two of the greatest princes in Christendom—a scandal and a disgrace; and a very great danger to me.

XXII

A scandal and a disgrace ... and a very great danger to me.

'Must I endure this fresh burden?' I asked my mother, impatient. 'Have I not enough already? My captains wait while Gloucester disports himself with my cousin of Burgundy and my inheritance slips from my hand.'

'There will be no duel,' she said. 'You should know both men better. Each is too calculating to hazard everything upon a single throw.'

'Gloucester's calculating up to a point. When he's angry he charges like a bull.'

'Then he'll charge at empty air.'

'Philip has ordered his armour,' I said.

'A gesture, only. They'll let the matter drop. Oh, each will find a good reason. And, if they don't—then Bedford will. Bedford won't allow it. He needs them both. Mark me well, the duel will drop.'

And with that I tried to be content.

For the moment it seemed she was right. My husband stopped talking of the combat; he had something else to talk about. He was rehearsing his address to the Estates of Hainault—his first speech as Hainault's accepted lord. He had a gift for words; and his golden voice knew well how to draw the heart. And he was handsome and bore himself kingly; he honoured his blood, this son, brother and uncle to kings.

I was filled with pride, overflowing with pride, when I sat listening in the great chamber of the Estates at Mons; the man's splendour blinded the eye to every fault.

'Will you, a free people, allow the foreigner to tread you down, to be a province of Burgundy or a hanger-on of Brabant?' And he played his voice like an instrument, now heavy with anger, now light with scorn. 'To drive away the foreigner is your sacred duty; and to do that duty, no man is too humble or too weak.

'And I that am not unskilled in warfare shall lead you—if you will take me for your leader—together with my beloved wife your true prince, who though she be a woman has yet the courage of a man...'

They listened, well-pleased; but the pleasure was damped when he requested the sum of forty thousand crowns to pay his men.

His first mistake. A prudent man would have waited. There was much heat and more bitterness before it was grudgingly granted.

'And can you wonder?' my mother said. 'My son of Gloucester speaks honey-words; but he cannot, or will not, control his men. They run wild taking what they please, and no questions asked. Let a virgin cross their path—and she doesn't go home a virgin. It does you no good; it breeds only bitterness. You had best be plain with that husband of yours.'

I made no answer. It was St Alban's all over again—the slackness of discipline, the wildness of his men. But then when anger took him—he had made an example, punishing the offender, sometimes out of all proportion. Now he did not punish; he was afraid of losing popularity with his men. So now I could say nothing. But for all that the blood was in my cheeks.

'No need to flush and flare!' she said. 'Listen, my girl. When Hainault decided for Gloucester, it was by no means with one voice—you saw that for yourself. If he hadn't got those armies of his planted on our doorsteps, I doubt they would have accepted him at all. And even then some stood out; Engilbert d'Edlingen for one; and the Lord of Jeumont for another. You're by no means finished with the van Vliet affair. Oh, people see you young and innocent but that doesn't stop the tongues of slander—especially tongues that have been paid to slander. They say openly that if you didn't plan the poisoning yourself, then Gloucester did—while you stood by and said no word. And now you keep van Vliet's widow about you. Daughter, you must send her away. I am warning you.'

I shook an obstinate head; it was a thing I could not do.

'This is no time for woman's whims,' she said. 'Now you must play a prince's part.'

'I'll play my part, never fear. We march at once for Braine-le-Comte.'

'Not you,' she said at once; and again, 'not you. There's no need. The town holds strongly for us. St Pol besieges it for Brabant and he'll never reduce it. But it will be a most bloody fight; no quarter asked or given!' She put a hand on my shoulder in an unaccustomed caress. 'If you're killed that's the end of you and your cause. They'll send Gloucester packing—never doubt it! And Philip takes all. You should stay at home till you've bred us an heir.'

Again the tell-tale red came up into my face; I remembered the nights my husband lay from my bed.

She shrugged. 'You had best send that slant-eyed baggage packing,' she said.

I got up and went out of the room.

'Ill-luck dogs us,' my husband said and threw down his helmet so that it rolled across the stool and clashed to the ground. 'Here's a town that loves you—or so we hear! It's strongly held, with enough food to last six months or more. And within a week—it yields.'

'There were three thousand of your own English in Braine,' my mother reminded him drily.

'No one doubts the loyalty of any man—English or Hainaulter,' I said quickly; the air was heavy with their anger. 'Yielding had nothing to do with disloyalty.' And I sighed for the dire penalty the town had paid for resistance. 'It was fear that made them surrender—a very proper fear; fear of Heaven. You cannot blame them. They had no thought of surrender; things were going well for us. And then, suddenly, there was St George himself riding at the head of the enemy and waving them on. Who can hope to stand against God?'

Gloucester's laugh had a cutting edge. 'And it was no one but a Brabanter on a white horse and a red cross to his shield!'

'I suppose,' my mother said, 'we may say Heaven was against us since misfortune was permitted. And if we don't, then Philip will. Be sure he'll make the most of it!'

So we rode sadly home again in the early March weather. I suppose the sun must have shone, but I remember nothing except dust stinging my eyes and the wind like a knife cutting through my soldier's cloak. And I remember my mother's face set and dark; and I knew she was angry because I had chosen Gloucester to be my husband. She had taken his measure, she said. Any man rather than this one whose handsome face could not win my people's heart. He was a foreigner; and his men the terror of the countryside.

And now—all downcast as I was with the unexpected loss of Braine-le-Comte, and the dislike of my people for my husband—the blow fell, bitter, unexpected.

The Pope spoke at last.

I must leave Gloucester. Until the matter of my marriage was finally decided I must put myself under the protection of my cousin ... of *Burgundy*!

Philip's hand was only too clear in this.

Leave my husband. Put myself under Burgundy's protection. His prisoner, neither more nor less.

The letter dropped from my hand; my world span darkly and bitterness was in my mouth.

And Gloucester. Irritable with defeat at Braine, sour with knowledge that here in my country he was neither liked nor trusted, he spared me nothing.

'The Pope brands you strumpet, my dear!' he said, all pleasant-smiling. 'As long as you stay with me you can't hope to keep your men together.'

Not *we* but *you* ... *you.* Already he had separated himself from me.

I put out my two hands and they were shaking. To be parted. It was the thing he had sworn should never happen. Let the Pope, let all Christendom say otherwise, I was his wife and he would keep me so! He had sworn it.

He must have seen the shock in my eyes for he said more kindly, 'Never fear. I will never give you into the hands of Burgundy, or any other. You shall stay here, in your own land amongst your own friends. It is I that shall go.'

I tried to speak; I could only implore him with my eyes.

'That's the way it must be,' he said. 'I return to England. I shall come back, I swear it, as soon as the Pope speaks.'

'And if it isn't in our favour?' And in spite of myself the tears ran salt into my mouth.

'Amazons don't cry,' he said lightly. 'Indeed, I love better to see you armed cap-à-pied than weeping like a Niobe. Yes, I shall go; must go, indeed. I am, after all, Protector of England; I have some duty there.'

'And me? What of me? Have you no duty to me?' I had not meant, for pride, to press him further; but my grief was greater than any pride.

'That duty will be my pleasure ... when I am allowed,' he said, very smooth; but it was a courtesy and nothing more.

He would have taken my hand but I pulled it from him.

'You grow like that harridan your mother,' he said, still pleasant. 'I cannot endure harridans; I would hang them all.'

He turned and left me there in the empty room. I remember that I put a hand to my heart and held it there as though to still its pain. I dared not move. It was as if a cord bound him to my living heart, dragged upon my living heart, so that the pain was beyond enduring.

Soon the cord must snap and I bleed to death.

I am no coward. Indeed, I have much physical courage. I had shown it at Gorcum and at Braine where I rode amongst the arrows and gunstones; and on the long marches knee-deep in water, or slipping and sliding upon the frozen ground. But now, the wounding to my heart was agony not to be endured.

I knew he meant what he said. The loss of Braine—to any other man no more than a setback—was to him a crushing blow. Now he was sick of the whole affair; and more sick of me that was the cause of it! I loved him too much and could not hide it. I would have gone into exile with him or into prison; I would have died with him. Without him there was little meaning to my life. But he was already tired of me.

And there was more to it than tiring of me as a woman. He was tired of the responsibilities that went with me; tired of my courage, my willingness to endure. A woman showing her sweet shape was one thing; that same woman hidden beneath unyielding armour— another.

And most of all he was tired of that strong Burgundian blood of mine. How often, looking into the face he thought he loved, had he seen instead the hated face of Philip? Or, remembering my mother whom he feared and detested, had he recognized in me the same energy, the same determination, the same dominant character? It might well be so. Determined and dominant I could be; but not with him, never with him. Yet he was not wise enough to know it; he did not care enough to know it.

In England there had been something appealing about me—a young woman friendless. Here in the mud and blood of a foreign land where no one liked him, and with friends to prosecute my cause, the thing was different.

I did not know all this at the time. Wisdom came too late. But all the love and wisdom in the world wouldn't have helped me then. His mind was set. He believed the Pope would go on refusing consent to our marriage; and he hoped it with all his heart. He was anxious to wash his hands of the whole affair; nothing to be gained by it! If, however, by some miracle my forces were successful—why then there was always time to think again. Meanwhile the highest honours awaited him in England. That my own honour had been blown upon was, perhaps, a pity but nothing could be done about it. Life was too short.

In Hainault there was rejoicing. The foreigner was going, taking with him his accursed soldiers. Now no good man need fear a broken head when he went abroad, nor any virgin for her honour. Thanks be to His Holiness and to the good duke of Burgundy! And it was not only my enemies that thought thus. My friends thought so too, that loved me and sought only my good. It added to my grief. Desolate and lonely, I could not and would not allow myself to be abandoned. He was my husband and I must go with him.

But I was a prince. For me men had fought and died. I must remain with the armies. The Council at Mons, urged strongly by my mother, refused to let me go.

'What shall I do?' I cried out, arguing not my woman's heart but my need for protection. 'Where shall I find safety, my husband gone?'

'In your own city,' my mother said. 'Mons will protect you to the last drop of its blood. The city has sworn it.'

Gloucester wasted no time. It was moving towards April; the canals were as blue as the sky and the streams ran full, their banks already misty with myosotis that the English call forget-me-not and that are—strange irony—an emblem of his house, when my husband rode away.

My mother and I, together with sixteen horsemen, were to ride with him as far as St Ghislain; and so we set forth from Mons that fine spring morning, he at the head of his troops, banners waving, lances lifted—a victorious army you might have thought, instead of a defeated captain ingloriously returning home.

But as for me, my heart lay within me like a dead child. My eyes kept sliding to the tossed bright hair beneath the chaperon, for he wore no armour; and to the smiling mouth that had so often kissed mine. And, every step lowered my sad heart further so that my horse, feeling the weight, dropped into a slow pace and would not quicken until Gloucester leaned sideways and brought his whip across its neck. The lash caught me once, biting through the glove to the hand beneath but I gave no sign; and I treasured the pain since he had given it—it would be with me longer than his kisses; and, indeed, I wore the weal for many a day.

And so we rode into St Ghislain, but I could not bring myself to turn for home. I must ride with him to St Crespin at least. I would have ridden with him through the sea to England had I been let. At that moment I would have been content to let Philip take all if I might ride with Gloucester for the rest of my life. But God knows best. Heavy lies the crown; but heavier still the head that once wearing it, is robbed of that weight. Should I have been content disinherited, a pensioner of my husband? I think not, even had Gloucester been loving and faithful; but faithfulness was not in him.

Parting between lovers is always grief, even if they know they are to meet again and soon. But I had no assurance. I felt in my blood this was the last time.

What we said in that moment of parting I do not know; for my eyes were blind and my ears deaf with my misery. I suppose he promised that we should meet again, that all would be well. I know he kissed me but the touch of his lips helped my misery not at all. And I know I sat my horse and would not move for all my mother's urging while Gloucester and his men grew smaller and fainter and vanished at last in the dust of the road.

And so we turned for home. We must have rested, we must have eaten; but I remember nothing ... except that every step carried me further from my love.

In my apartments—and how grim and sad they seemed, bereft of him!—Beatrix waited. She wore a dark, dejected look; I found it natural for her mood to chime with mine.

She longed, I knew, to comfort me, to take me in her arms; but she did not dare. I stood there playing with my gloves, obstinate with my grief and with my weariness. She took my hat and cloak, but when she was about to unlace me, I pulled myself away, bidding her send for Cobham.

I needed, I knew not why since I liked her no better, to see the woman again. Nor did I stop to question myself as to the reason. I only knew that I must see her, and see her now.

Agnes van der Poele answered the summons; I stared at her in surprise. It was Cobham's duty to lace and unlace my gowns.

'Go!' I told her sharply. 'Send Cobham at once—I am in no mood to be kept waiting.'

She made her curtsey, her eyes not upon me but upon Beatrix.

When the door had shut behind her, Beatrix came over and knelt by me.

'Jacque,' she said, 'Jacque my dear! ... Cobham is not in her chamber.'

'Then search for her! She has no permission to be absent.'

'No need to search ... unless we search as far as England. Her clothes are gone, jewels, furs ... everything.'

I had known ... I had known. Bitterness like gall came up into my mouth because the thing I had known was true.

XXIII

I said no word then on the matter, or ever again; not even to Beatrix. But night and day beneath the increasing burden of my affairs the wound festered. To keep my husband faithful I no longer hoped; but I had expected some remaining affection, some respect for us both, would have lent him discretion in his sinning. That he would betray me shamelessly where every eye could behold, was a thing I had not expected and it shook me to the soul. Even when I wrote to him—as write I must—I made no mention of the insult. It was as though I must hide it even from the eye of him that dealt it.

April moved on; arrows of rain slanting beneath a bright sun, birds wheeling and calling joyously in their mating. But for me there was neither brightness nor joy.

Twelve days since my husband had left me; but I had heard nothing beyond his safe arrival and a message for my welfare; though how in the face of all my difficulties and lacking his help, it was to be achieved, he did not enquire.

Philip's armies grew daily. My country groaned beneath the feet of his horses, the feet of his men. Now there marched under his banner not only his own forces and those of Brabant, but also a great host of Picards together with many other mercenaries. For Brabant's spoken promise to make him heir to all my lands had been written down, signed and sealed. And Brabant was growing weaker every day; he could no longer sit within a litter, so they said; and so Philip was taking no chances. Now he was attacking openly and ruthlessly those cities that had sworn obedience to me; and, with news of the slaughter that he made, many did not wait to spill their blood but left my obedience for his.

My heart bled for my poor torn country, trampled in blood. And, for myself, my heart bled also.

There came no further word from my husband. He had forgotten me. He was living openly with the dark witch that had been my servant; and all Christendom blazed with the story. *Gloucester has gotten him another strumpet!*

The new bond between my mother and me was broken. She openly rejoiced in Gloucester's absence and I could trust her no longer. And my distrust was the more because she was forever riding out to meet my cousin of Burgundy. Trying to make all smooth between Philip and me; doing her uttermost on my behalf—so she said.

Van Brederode had no use for conversations with Philip; a snake, in his opinion; to be knocked on the head and not to be reasoned with. He was all for fighting. But de Montfort thought we should wait yet a little. My mother, he pointed out, had given proof of her love by coming openly to my side. If now she seemed to show friendship for my cousin, mightn't it be to serve me better?

And, while we pondered, the blow fell; a blow to shatter still further my trust in my mother and to cut the ground from my feet.

What my mother had been about with Cousin Philip was suddenly clear.

It was van Brederode, the network of veins standing out purple against the whiteness of his face, that brought me the news.

'Hainault has gone over to the enemy!' And while I stared, not making sense of the thing I heard, he said, 'The snake of Burgundy and the weasel of Brabant have made a pact here, in this very Mons; signed and sealed and all good friends together! Hainault recognizes Brabant as its sovereign, and that means Burgundy. You stand on enemy soil!'

'No,' I cried out. 'No!' But even while I spoke, my heart knew the unbelievable truth. 'Not Hainault. Mons is sworn to protect me. Mons would not let me go when I might have gone in safety. Mons will not break its pledged word.'

'The word is broken,' he said. 'Mons was not unwilling; nor the lady your mother, neither; she stood as mediator. But, indeed, I think the city could not help itself. Burgundy threatened to put it to the sword.'

'Then what becomes of me? Where shall I run? Whither shall I fly?'

'They will put you under Burgundy's wardship ... to be taken to such place as he decides until Rome speaks.'

'Until Rome speaks! Then for ever!' I cried out. And then, 'When?'

'In two weeks or three.' And he could not look at me.

I flew to find my mother, crying out against her false Burgundian blood. She denied all part in the matter. I longed to believe her, to find in all this treachery one true heart. But I could not believe her. I could not.

'Child,' she said, 'all will yet turn to good, you will see it. Instead of bloodshed—peace. Philip will forgive your Hainaulters; there will be no punishment.'

'Forgive!' I cried out. 'Forgive them for not shutting their gates in my face when I came home again? Is it my mother that speaks?'

She nodded. 'Princes more than other men must bow to circumstances. You should rejoice that Mons is to be spared. Now all will be quiet...'

'Quiet?' And I thought my heart must burst. 'Oh yes! quiet for me! Quiet in the prison cell.'

She said, gently, 'Philip will treat you with all courtesy; he has sworn it.'

'When my own people break the oath and my mother countenances it, who can expect honour from the enemy?'

'Philip is not your enemy but your protector,' she said, 'until Rome speaks.'

'And then?' I cried out. 'And then?'

'Then all good Christians will welcome their duty...'

'What duty?' I interrupted, very fierce.

'To obey God's Vicar on earth.'

I went out and left her without a word. The grief I had known till now seemed little indeed. That my own husband lived openly with his paramour, had lost its sting. That Hainault had cast me off, broke my heart. But even that I might endure—men have lived with their hearts broken before now—if I might be free. I wanted nothing in this world but to be free. Like a wild thing that smells the cage I was mad for freedom.

I sat all that day my head within my hands wondering what to do. I could think of one thing only; to go, myself, and implore the Council for their help. They had sworn to protect me; they could not turn a deaf ear.

But it was cold comfort I got! An answer so dreadful I dream about it even now so that I awake crying out in the quiet of the night.

'Sirs,' I said, 'it was at your most earnest entreaty that my lord and husband left me in your protection. And, before he agreed to do this, you swore to be my true and loyal subjects and to hold me in your greatest care. I do implore you now to remember that oath that you may give a good account to my lord when he returns.'

The leader of the Estates rose at once; and it was that same man who had looked at me with kindness, promising that the oath with Brabant should be broken; but there was no kindness in him now.

'Madam,' he answered, 'we are not strong enough to protect you. We cannot, it seems, protect ourselves, even, from those men my Lord of Gloucester left behind!'

At this there was a great stamping and a crying out that the handful my husband had left behind meant to murder them. *Death! Death!* They shouted the word again and again, and would not be quieted until the leader held up his hand and gave his orders. And at his words my heart shrivelled and the sickness came up into my throat.

All my husband's men were to be seized—both common men and captains. And all of them, to the full number of two hundred, to be hanged at once. But by God's mercy some of them escaped.

But one did not escape for he had come with me, to be my bodyguard—Macart, my husband's faithful servant; and one that, for all his quick temper, had not lifted a hand against any man since Gloucester left. But they seized him where he stood at my side and they took him away and beheaded him in the courtyard, and no prayer for his soul.

And that is the thing that makes me cry out in my dreams. For I left the Council chamber and there in the courtyard his headless body lay in blood; and the executioner was holding the head aloft ... and there was a surprised look in the dead eyes. And the blood spurted and fell upon my hand; and it was as though I, myself, had murdered him. I have seen men die in battle; and I have been myself prepared to die, fighting. But to seize a man that has done no wrong and, in cold blood, take off his head—and no prayer for his soul—it is a thing that must haunt me to my own dying.

Nor was this all.

Sickened by the faithlessness and the hatred, heaving at the smell of blood and the sight of death, I made my way back as best I could to find my apartments empty, save for the women. The officers of my household had been arrested—every man they could lay hands upon, peaceful men that went quiet about their business.

My Hainaulters had done this, my Hainaulters that had sworn to cherish me. They had murdered good men whose only fault was friendship to me; and others they had carried away. They had left me friendless. They darkened my world that day.

And now in my dire peril my thoughts flew to Gloucester—my last hope. Love me he might not; but he was still my husband. Both as husband and soldier his faith was pledged. I had, by God's mercy, a messenger. In all the horror of this day there had been one stroke of luck. Louis de Montfort had been absent; he had returned after the ransackers had left; even now he lay hidden in my chamber. I would send him with my letter.

I remember how I sat, head between my hands, wondering what I must write; and how, every now and then, the bloody head of Macart would rise between me and my shielding hands so that I must stiffen myself against the rising vomit.

That letter. How could mere words bear the weight of the horror and the grief and the fear?

I told him how the city had risen against me, of his men hanged for no fault; and especially I told him of Macart whom he valued above all men. Surely that treachery, that senseless murder must move his anger if nothing else could. I told him that unless he came at once they would carry me away—God alone knew where—Philip's prisoner.

> ... I write this that am the most unhappy, the most ruined, the most betrayed and falsely treated woman alive ...

And remembering how I had been betrayed by friend and by lover alike, I had to stop writing because of the shaking of my whole body. I forced myself to quiet, I took up the pen again.

> ... unless you come to my help at once ... at once, I think you will never see me again. Most dear lord and husband, all my hope is in you and all my joy; all I suffer is from love of you. And so I beseech you, most humbly and very tenderly, for the love of God to have compassion upon me in all my miseries, and with the utmost speed, come to your forlorn creature if you do not want to lose me for ever ...

I put down my pen and stared at the paper. Would this move him? To remind him of our marriage vows—and he living openly with another woman—was that wise? I crossed out the word *husband* and wrote *father* instead. If there was any tenderness in him, any pity, then I might move him by a sense of duty; the duty of a man towards a woman that had given up everything for his sake, a woman ten years younger than himself.

He loved me no longer; he did not believe now that he could pull any chestnut for himself out of my oven. If anything at all could move him it would be an appeal to his maturity from my youthfulness.

I took up my pen again.

...Dear lord and father, I pray you will do this for me. I have never behaved ill to you in my life and I never will. If you do not come I think I shall die. You are my only comfort and my last hope.

And then for all my care, bitterness came breaking through.

It seems that you have utterly forgotten me. And now I have nothing more to write except to commend to your kindness my servant Louis de Montfort that is in grave danger for my sake. He will tell you all the things I cannot write. I beg you, dear lord and father, be a good master to him. As for myself, let me but know your wish and whatever it may be I will obey with my whole heart; and my witness to this is the blessed Son of God. May He give you a long and happy life.

...Written in your false and treacherous city of Mons with a deeply sorrowful heart,

Your unhappy and loving child that suffers unspeakably for your sake.

I folded the paper that was blistered with my tears and sealed it; and I called to de Montfort to come forth.

He stood fingering the letter. 'I will deliver it, with God's help,' he said. And then he said, 'Lady, do not count overmuch on your answer. My Lord of Gloucester—however much his heart be set—will not find it easy to come to your help. The English Parliament reproaches him because he set his wife's affairs before that of his country. They say that his fingers itching for a crown of his own, he has all but let his own King's French crown slip.'

'Their Parliament did not forbid him when there was a rich prize to be won! I am friendless, with neither husband nor father to stand by me. Yet God does not forsake me. He has given me a most true friend. How can God be less true than man?' And I kissed him upon both cheeks.

These days I could not rest; I could neither sit nor stand, nor sleep, nor eat. How long before I would be given into Philip's hands? Two weeks van Brederode thought. Time enough; enough to bring Gloucester sailing with his troops. He could not for shame's sake let me fall into the 'protection' of my cousin.

Protection. I laughed aloud; and how dreary it sounded in the lonely sunlight of my chamber. Philip's protection would take me to my death. Dead before Brabant, I! The sound limb cut from the tree before the rotten branch could drop. Yet so it would happen. Philip would make an end of me. Let Christendom whisper; his smooth tongue would make all right again. I should be dead; and my country ground beneath the Burgundian heel.

And so the slow days passed. I wandered the empty rooms and deserted gardens of this sad Naasterhof I had entered with so high a hope. I was virtually a prisoner now with none but Beatrix to share my imprisonment—but her I would have chosen from the whole world. And still no answer from England. And I knew what I had known in my heart from the beginning—how it must end.

And so I came to the last day. I had been warned to be ready at ten in the morning. But time came and went while I stood waiting; I looked down upon the Market Place and the free people coming and going in the June sunshine and I wondered whether I should walk the streets again—a free woman.

Courtesy, it seems, is not required to fallen princes. It was two o'clock when we left the Naasterhof; and in that time I lived through a dozen mad hopes, died a dozen wild despairs. All about me rode five hundred troops; by my litter rode the captain himself, the Prince of Orange, looking neither to right nor left. A man to do his duty and not to be turned aside by any woman's grief.

From the hot gloom of the litter I could hear behind me the roll and rumble of wagons heavy with the weight of my treasures—sure sign I should never return. Philip would take all; except—if I were fortunate—the bare furnishings of my room; my bed perhaps, a stool, or a press. I could not comfort myself with the thought that he would allow me the dignities of my station; he had already dismissed my household. I was much concerned though for this second carefully garnered treasure of mine. Brabant had stolen all he could when I had run from Valenciennes. But there were furnishings in my own houses he had not been able to lay hands upon, the jewels Gloucester had given me together with furs and gowns; and I had also the gold I had saved from Henry of England's gift. Now I was stripped of all but the few silver pieces in my pocket; and, if one seeks any comfort in prison, one must pay and pay again.

So there I rode in the dark litter, a prisoner, deserted by my husband and all but penniless. By my side Beatrix sat, her face as white as her coif. Once she sent me a smile—and God knows what it cost her! I could not send it back again, but sat dry-eyed and stony. Nor had I wept this morning when I bade Farewell to my mother, knowing, as she did, that this might well be for the last time. I had not meant to bid her Goodbye whose treachery had helped bring me to this pass. But, at the last moment I could not go without seeing her. She had sold me to Burgundy ... but she was my mother.

Suddenly, with no warning, the litter stopped, throwing me upon Beatrix. There was a confused roar of voices crying aloud, the irregular clatter of hooves strange after the measured beat of my escort; and then the clash of steel upon steel.

Ears astrain, I made out a cry and dared not believe it. I looked at Beatrix and she nodded. And now the tears so long denied were running down her face. *A Jacque, Jacque, Jacqueline!* My name was a battlecry.

Gloucester had come at last!

My heart threw itself about like a bird in a cage. I pulled open the curtains of the litter, nor would I close them again for all Beatrix pulled at my cloak, crying out that if a stray arrow found its mark, then all rescue was in vain!

And, as I looked, my heart died.

There was no Gloucester, nor any ordered troops. A handful of friends, only, desperate for my rescue. Gallant they were; but the escort of five hundred would make short work of them.

And so it proved. And, as my captors closed about me again, and we resumed our steady march into Flanders, there was an added sorrow in my heart for the faithful hearts that lay still; hearts I could ill spare.

In the darkness of the litter, Beatrix and I folded our hands and prayed for the passing of their souls.

XXIV

The unexpected hope and the crushing of that hope was almost more than I could bear. And, added to my sorrow for friends uselessly dead, was bitterness that Gloucester had made no move. And all the time I was shaken by my fear. Where were they taking me? And what should I find when I arrived?

It was getting on for six of the clock, if I could judge by the shadows, when they brought us our supper there in the litter—and a rough supper it was! A strong hard cheese, a manchet of black bread and a skin of rough wine. I ate what I could of this coarse fare; it augured ill for our reception, wherever that might be.

And now we quickened our pace, for the skirmish had set us back. Orange must have had his orders not to delay, for we stopped only to change horses, and then Beatrix and I were allowed to come forth to stretch our limbs and to relieve ourselves. Then whips cracked again; the horses were lashed without mercy.

The long summer day passed into twilight and then into night. I slept fitfully, lulled by the stale air and the beat of horses' feet, only to be pricked awake again and again by my fears and my griefs ... Gloucester had forsaken me. Well, I would care little for that, so I could go free; free to come and go where I would. Without love I could live; without freedom I must die. There in the dark night, carried steadily towards my prison, I remembered that when my young French husband had died, my mother had tied a black riband about my arm. Would she pay the same tribute when Philip had done with me? And I wondered whether it was true that Brabant lay dying in his airless room. And now—though he had humiliated me and betrayed me—I felt pity for a young life wasted and spoilt.

I might have spared my pity.

It was early morning when the spires of a city rose against the red sky. Orange turned in his saddle and for the first time spoke. 'Ghent,' he said. 'And the end of our journey.'

It was full daylight when we clattered through the city gates. The streets were busy; and I envied most passionately the meanest fellow that went free about his business.

Past a very great hostelry we went; and, Orange, relieved now that his guardianship was all but over, told me it was the Cour de St Georges, renowned for its wines and its cookery; my Lord Duke of Burgundy held his feasts there. Down a narrow street, past the little market square where the horses were tethered and already the air acrid with their droppings to the long, low Buttermarket, its stalls already set out with articles both homely and fine—linens and fine silks, silverware and household pots. But I had no thought for them, then, though afterwards I strained my eyes to catch the corning and going of dear, common household affairs. Now my eyes were fixed upon the great fortress that towered black to the sky. The Gravenstein fortress. My heart that I had thought past sorrow fainted within me.

Philip was taking no chances.

Once this had been a royal residence and even then it must have been a forbidding place with its blank walls and its gaunt watching towers and its great keep high as a church steeple. And, as if one such fortress was not enough, the black walls and towers lay reflected in the oily waters of the river that flowed about it on three sides.

The drawbridge to the street fell with a clang; the great iron-studded gate within the wall closed behind us.

The courtyard was empty save for the men-at-arms who looked at me with a grinning curiosity. Orange gave me his hand and I stumbled a little from the cramping of my limbs. One of the fellows tittered; and Orange turned upon him such a look that the laughter scorched in his mouth. Another fellow with keys jangling from his belt came across the courtyard and bade us follow. Up a narrow staircase we went and into a pleasant set of rooms comfortably furnished. Torches flamed in cressets and a great fire burned; for all it was sweet summer without, within it was dark and cold. These pleasant rooms were not, alas, for me; but for the Governor who rose now to receive me.

Orange presented me, took a receipt for my safe arrival, bowed, and with the scantest farewell took his leave. He had been neither friendly nor careful for my comfort; yet I grieved to see him go—this last link with the free world and no corruption of prison on him.

I stood there, Beatrix behind me; and though my heart was low, my head was high. Madam the Duchess of Gloucester, Countess of Holland, of Hainault and of Zealand in her own right.

'Madam,' he said, 'if you will keep faith with my lord the Count of Flanders,'—and that title, it seemed was greater in his eyes than the proud name of Burgundy—'then he will keep faith with you. My lord allows that you move freely within this tower; and you may walk in the garden below. It is a small garden but it will serve. You may have your woman about you if she behave with discretion. And you may write your letters ...'

'And will they be delivered?'

'It depends—as Madam the Duchess of Brabant knows for herself.' And the old discarded name fell upon me like an insult. 'It depends upon what the letters contain. And for the rest, if Madam lacks for anything, she has but to speak.'

'And if it's freedom I lack?'

'Madam knows the answer to that!'

He made a slight bow and ordered the fellow with the keys to conduct me to my apartments. Up another staircase we went, very dark and the stairs so worn and narrow I could scarce find foothold. The man threw open a door and, with a grudging bow, left us.

It was not as bad as it might have been; nor yet was it as good. I might have expected some comfort—my own cook, my own servants, my own furnishings. I had done no wrong and my birth entitled me to some attention, but Philip was too mean for that!

The rooms were a fair size; the furniture was of the plainest but sufficient. There were neither curtains nor cushions nor bedhangings. These made their appearance later, after my repeated demands, together with my drinking cup, some books and my writing materials. And that was all I ever got from my twenty-eight wagon loads!

And yet I had solace enough. I had Beatrix.

'If I were a lady in an old tale,' I said and I tried to sound cheerful, 'why then the gaoler would fall in love with me and I would cozen him and so escape. But this is life and no romance. And I have shed so many tears I doubt there's anything in my face to delight a man.'

'Your face is well enough!' she said. 'And at your age—scarce twenty-four—the world is not lost ... until life be lost!' And she sighed, thinking no doubt of her Jan.

It was gloomy in the Gravenstein; but apart from the fact I was a prisoner, with all the frustrations and the depressions prison must bring, I was treated well enough. When the governor paid his daily visit to receive any complaint, I had none to make. I had enough to eat and I walked in the air when I would. The garden was certainly tiny, but the grass was green and a little rose-tree filled the air with its fragrance, so that shutting my eyes I could dream myself out of prison and into freedom—and I think that garden saved my reason.

When I was not walking in the air, or lying restless in my bed, I was writing my letters. Writing, writing; asking for news, asking for help, seeking desperately for comfort. Some answers I did receive; but though I wrote again and again, there was never a word from Gloucester. Even now, with pain and despair long past, I must make myself believe he never received them.

Philip, of course, saw every letter before it was sent to its destination; and, I believe, he allowed me only those answers that would lower my courage and add to my griefs.

It did not help me to know that Mons—my city—was *en fête* for its new lords, Burgundy and Brabant; nor that my name had already disappeared from the town records. Nor did it cheer me to know that the swearing of eternal friendship between England and Burgundy was the order of the day.

My weary life dragged itself on. In spite of Philip I was not entirely without comfortable news. Beatrix was allowed to shop for me market-days—though my dwindling purse must soon call a halt to that. And she never failed to return without some piece of gossip ... She came back one day with a tale that was going about everywhere—England was angry at my treatment and a vast army was coming to rescue me. And, even while I looked at her all flushed with hope, she shook her head. 'Never believe it, Jacque my dear. England will do nothing for you.'

'The Parliament perhaps not. But ... Gloucester. Do they speak of Gloucester?'

She did not answer; nor did she meet my eyes.

'This tale of an army marching to set me free! If there's no truth in it, where does it come from?'

She said, slowly, 'It could be a tale put about by Burgundy himself. Such a tale could be ... useful.'

I looked at her. I saw the point.

'An excuse to ... kill me?'

She threw out her hands. 'What's to stop him? Neither truth nor compassion. Oh, there'd be questions asked! But none his lying tongue couldn't answer.'

So I must no longer believe in the army from England; I must no longer *want* to believe it. It could mean my death.

But there was another tale I was forced to believe.

Brabant, that dying man, was not yet dead. There was enough life in him to work me further mischief; and Philip was using him while he could.

It was actually on my birthday—I was just twenty-four and wearing my heart out in prison—when the news came; and to distress me beyond all hope, the governor himself vouched for the truth.

Brabant had taken it upon himself to issue letters patent commanding my subjects —Hainaulters and Hollanders, Zealanders and Frieslanders—all, all, to obey Philip as lord and master.

Now he was not only heir to all my lands—he was now the ruler... *I, Philip, Ruward and heir of Holland, of Hainault and Zealand...*

A pleasant birthday gift —and plenty of time to savour it. But worse was to come.

Beatrix came back from her marketing with a white and troubled face.

'They are saying everywhere that you're a cause of danger to their lord—and of course you are! Your friends can't be expected to sit idle under this new piece of wickedness. Jacque ... they are gathering!'

And when I cried out in joy, she said, very sombre, 'Jacque, Jacque, why won't you understand? You're a danger to Burgundy and to peace. To *peace*! Burgundy has his excuse at last. They say he means to carry you away—no one knows where. And it will be prison—and prison, indeed. A most rigorous confinement.'

My heart dropped. I actually felt the drop of my heart. And now there was no anger left in me, only a fear that shook me, soul and body. I would not allow myself to sleep at night for the fear of a hand sudden upon my shoulder. Or, fallen asleep in spite of myself, I would dream of being carried away into the darkness to some unknown place. The beat of hooves shuddered throughout my body; and I would awake, and the beating of the hooves was the beating of my heart. And I would cry out for Beatrix. And, when I saw her face, kind in the candlelight, I would think, Soon, soon I shall call to her ... and there will be no answer.

And now, as if to prepare me for this cruel confinement, no more letters came for me; nor could I believe that any I wrote—and they were desperate enough—were ever delivered, except into Philip's hands.

Beatrix however was still a source of news.

My cousin was setting out on his Joyous Entries. But, prudent man, he was gathering men and ships in case his new subjects were not as pleased to greet him as he to greet them! 'Yet he does his best to make all sweet!' she said. 'Promises, promises, promises by the sackful. Promises of peace, of favour; promises to confirm old charters, to give new charters; promises to remit taxes; to pay all debts left by your uncle of Bavaria and by you, yourself ...'

'Money buys honey!' I said.

'But not faithful hearts!' And she said it not as a hope but as a certainty. And when I pressed her, she said, 'I had meant not to breathe a word till all was certain. But hope keeps us alive!' And she brought her lips close to my ear.

XXV

It was a full month after my unhappy birthday that Beatrix went to market to buy me a warm cloak and a petticoat; and I stood upon the lower platform to see her pass through the courtyard. And, so watching, I thought that when I came to my new prison, Philip would have no need to kill me. Lacking her dear company I should fall into a melancholy and die.

I saw her halt at the gatehouse for her escort. It was always the same man and I gathered he found his duty pleasant. A very nice lady, though not so young as she might be! Beatrix had often heard him express his opinion. A lady free with her money; that liked wine with a good body—and a man to match it! When my commissions were done—and they didn't take long, I had little to spend—those two would make for the Cour de St Georges and there they would sit and gossip and drink.

The fellow, Jan Stein was his name, was never in haste to return. He liked nothing better than to sit in this great inn, where but for Beatrix he had never dared thrust his nose, and watch the wealthy and the great go about their business. And he would confide, for the hundredth time, that he was growing sick with rheum and with the pains in his joints. It got a man sooner or later, that cursed Gravenstein did. His dream was to buy his way out. 'Out of that devil of a place and into some jolly little inn, and a jolly partner along with him!' And he would nudge her in the ribs. 'A man would be his own master then. And good money to be made—except you need money first. Money makes money and I'll wager you're not short!' And he would leer into her smiling face.

She would smile back at him and pat her pocket as though there were an understanding between them.

And so it happened, this particular day—the cloak having been bought and the petticoat also—that they made their way to their favourite tavern. A stranger was lounging near but they paid no heed to him. Beatrix was too busy filling her friend's glass and flattering him; and he was too busy swallowing both wine and flattery and pressing his knee against hers. In the end she had to help him home.

'You're to be sent away at once!' she cried out of breath and throwing down the bundle she carried. 'Ghent's too near Holland! And what's more, some of our people—and not a few—are already asking by what right Burgundy makes his Joyous Entries. Let his foot slip never so slightly and they'll rise; rise for you. That's what they're saying down in the market.'

I felt the blood leave my heart. I said, 'So this is the end.'

'No,' she brought her mouth close to my ear. 'The beginning. Everything's ready. I spoke with Vos this morning; and Spierinck will be here within the hour. They'll be waiting for us with four horses ...'

'Four horses—and two riders! Every eye will mark them!' I said.

She shook her head. 'Those two are disguised as merchants; the extra horses are laden with goods. We meet this evening at the North Gate.'

'Where I shall be recognized and brought back!' Already I felt upon my forehead the sweat of that anguish.

'Come now,' she said, 'you were never one to play the coward—though prison air doesn't favour courage, I admit. Look!' She unrolled the bundle to show me two complete suits of men's clothing. 'I exchanged these under the very eye of my admirer!' And her mouth twisted with disgust. 'He was too drunk to see what I was doing. Quick, let me hide them!' And she stuffed them into a press and turned the key.

The blood came back to my heart. 'You've done so much, lost so much for me,' I said. 'What have I done to deserve your love?'

'That I should serve you was my father's wish; and my dear lord's wish; and it is my wish, too. And ... you are not hard to love, Jacque.'

Friday night, last day in August, fourteen hundred and twenty-five. A night I shall never forget; a night of terror and of hope.

The lamps burned in the bath-house. Stein was on guard; we had chosen this night for that very reason.

'And I hope he hangs for it!' Beatrix said. 'I am sick to the stomach of his love-making.'

I shared her disgust. I had heard some of it for myself as she crossed the courtyard to the bath-house carrying towels and fresh linen and a warm cloak to put about me after the heat of the steam.

'Let's have a peek!' He was very jolly. 'I've never seen a lady, not what you'd call a high-up lady, without a stitch to her nakedness.'

'A lady, be she never so fine, is made the same as any other woman! A fine fellow like you has no need of spying to see a naked woman.' And there was a world of meaning in her voice.

'You're woman enough for me, my girl; yes and lady enough too! Don't you think you've kept me waiting overlong?' And I heard the saliva wet in his mouth.

'Yes,' she said, 'and myself also!' And her voice was honey. 'Tonight then! What about tonight?' I heard him swallow.

He was a lusty fellow and there were few opportunities for love-play in the Gravenstein.

'Why not?' she said.

'When?'

'When my lady's abed.'

'In the garden then? It's soft on the grass.'

'Yes,' she said and laughed. 'Dew's thick, though. I'd best bring a cloak.'

'I'll warm you quick enough, cloak or no cloak!' His laugh scratched on the air.

'The dirty lout!' she said coming into the bath-house. 'I hope he hangs for this! He's been watching the bath-house ever since you went in—enjoying himself with the thought of a naked woman! He says you're having a pretty long bath and that you'd best make the most of it because it'll be long before you get another where you're going.' She stopped. She said, very low, 'It's time ... Jacque, are you ready?'

I nodded, and she went over to the door. 'Hist!' she said and brought the fellow running.

'Fetch me another towel for my lady!' she wheedled. 'See!'

And she held out the sodden cloth she had thrown into the bath. He must have hesitated, for she said, 'If you want your fun you must save my legs! Look. I'll leave the door ajar—so. Just push the dry towel inside; and if your eyes follow your hands, it's all you'll see of any woman tonight!'

'If I can't set eyes on that proud madam in there, I'll take my revenge on you, my beauty—and that's a promise!' And I heard the wet smack of a kiss.

She watched him out of sight. 'Now!' she whispered.

The bath-house stood in an angle of the courtyard near a wicket that opened on to the road. This wicket—whether the governor knew it or not—was always open a full hour after the great gates were locked; belated supplies might come in this way, or a servant slip out on an errand.

In the half-darkness of the summer night two men—a burgher and a younger man, his son maybe—hardly discernible in their grey suits, slipped through the wicket. The stench of refuse trodden into the muck of the Buttermarket was sweet to their senses, the jostling of crowds a protection. And crowds there were! It was that busy hour when country folk are clearing away their stalls and making for home; and with them those that have come in from neighbouring villages to buy. There was a steady stream flowing out of the city gates.

Mingling with the press the two men walked at their ease—or so it seemed. But how they longed to run, run, run to the North Gate.

The soft dirt of the road muffled out horsebeats; but nothing could muffle the thumping of my heart that shook my body and sounded in my ears loud enough to deafen me. Soon we left the road to cut across stubble fields where the corn had been harvested, and over flat clover meadows whose sweetness breathed out upon the darkening air; and with the coming dark my heart a little quietened.

'How long before they miss you?' Arnold Spierinck asked.

'A couple of hours,' Beatrix thought. 'Those fellows have dim wits. Stein will thrust his towel through the door, but he won't look inside; he's been warned—under penalty!' And her laughter was edged. 'A few minutes later the other fellow takes over. He'll see the light and be satisfied ... for a while. It'll take some time to penetrate his thick head that the bird's flown. By the time he's found the sergeant—and he won't be in a hurry about that; by the time they find the governor and the enquiry's finished; by the time the chase begins—two hours at least. Yes, we can be certain of two hours!'

Two hours. We made the most of them, riding the long night through. Excitement gave us strength, fear gave us wings. Dawn came up and found us on the bank of the Scheldt. Brabant country. I caught my breath.

'Courage, Madam!' Vos said. 'The van Brederodes are waiting at Vianen.'

But we had to get through Antwerp first.

We rode carefully now, along the river bank, and soon, against the skyline, rose the walls and towers of Antwerp.

A great and crowded city—I knew it well! Should we ever get through it in broad daylight?

'They won't have heard of your escape yet,' Spierinck said very cheerful. 'Two hours' start and the shortest route! With luck we'll show a clean pair of heels everywhere.'

Now, as we rode onward, I saw that the river flowed between us and the city, a deep wide river—and no bridge. I said nothing; but I must have looked my despair.

'Courage, Madam,' Vos said again, 'we didn't open the cage to let the bird be taken again!' He slipped a leg over his horse and slid to the ground. He helped me to dismount and Spierinck did the same by Beatrix. He made fast the horses and we walked steadily for a hundred paces or so. Where a great willow dipped green hair to green water, Vos ran down to the river's edge. He bent, straightened himself and beckoned.

Deep in the rushes lay a small boat; and beneath the seat, two gowns such as tradesmen's wives might use.

The oars dipped, the boat moved and we were safe on the other side. We tied up the boat lest it should float empty and tell the tale.

Through Antwerp we walked, two burghers and their wives, very quiet and sober. And, all the time, in spite of Vos, I wondered that no hand fell upon my shoulder, nor any eye notice the high beat of my heart beneath the grey stuff gown.

Through Antwerp and out again; and into a two-wheeled cart that jolted us up and down until we were black and blue. But I had no complaint of that, for we moved at a good pace. And so north to Breda—Breda, first town in my own Holland. Here, more than ever, a burgher's wife must walk wary; Burgundy's spies were everywhere.

And through Breda.

Our hearts rose.

That night Beatrix and I slept within the cart, well hidden in a wood, while Vos and Spierinck took it in turns to keep watch. We slept little, as you may believe; and before sunrise we were on our way.

Unresting, weary and dirty, but in good heart, we bumped along; the cart hid us even better than our gowns. For though by now our flight was known and the roads were being watched, the harmless cart went unobserved; so common a sight as to be unseen!

The fourth day saw us at our journey's end. I remember the sky all wine-stained with dawn above the towers of Vianen. We were safe, God be thanked!

And now the Lord of Vianen, Reynolde van Brederode, came out from the castle and knelt at my feet and brought me within his house. And his lady came hastening, a gown of silk across her arms. The silk was grateful to me after the sorry makeshifts I had been forced to wear.

In the best chamber a fire burned; for though it was but scarce September, the early summer hours were chill and we stiff with our jolting. Two serving-men staggered in beneath a great tub and as the hot water steamed upward I laughed remembering that last bath of mine. And the laughter mounted and I could not stop myself. 'I have robbed you of a lover!' I told Beatrix, while tears of laughter ran down my face.

Beatrix all-but spat.

XXVI

And now the tale of my imprisoning and how I was to have been carried far away and murdered, perhaps; and how I had escaped stirred many hearts. Some of my cities returned to me before ever a blow was struck; Dordrecht, to my deep joy, cast off the Burgundian yoke, sending its homage to me by my father's son Adrian; Dordrecht that Brabant had lost for me before I fled into England.

And now they came marching to join my standard, my Hook nobles, and their men behind them.

Gouda I made my headquarters; loyal Gouda with its gentle river and its great church, and its stadthouse all red-and-white that looks upon the Market Square as though to protect all comings and goings. And there came marching the van Brederodes and the de Montforts—my loyal Louis come from England to fight again beneath my banner. And there were new friends also; that great captain William Nagel with the men of Kennemar and Alkmaar streaming behind him; and Philip of Leyden with his son John; and there came also Didier van de Merwen and the Lord of Sevenbergen; and, most cheerful to my heart, my faithful clerk William de Bye and I made him my steward in place of Baudoin that Philip had carried away from Mons. And there were more; men more than pen can write and that heart can ever forget.

But Philip was not less busy. To him came pouring in the traitors. First and foremost the Egmonts—Arnold of Marenstein at their head with both his sons, and all the great host of their false blood. And there came also Gerard Boel, a man after Philip's own heart, sly and smiling and without bowels of mercy; and that insolent Lord of Jeumont that had shut up his city of Hal against Gloucester and me; and Engilbert d'Edlingen, a good gentleman and a bonny fighter whom I would have given much to win.

All these and more. And not least amongst them the Lord Frank van Borselen; and him I would not have won if I could. After my cousin Philip I hated him most. He had been my father's bitterest enemy; and he and his brother Floris had sentenced van Vliet to death. A just sentence; but they had not enquired how they had come by his confession, nor why he had been half-carried, dragging his broken limbs into the court. And my heart remembered it.

And so I was rich in friends and in enemies, too. But in this world's wealth I was poor indeed. I could barely feed and clothe my men. Between them Philip and Brabant had stolen my treasure and harvested my income. I was forever forced to borrow of those from whom I had already taken too much. I am a giver rather than a taker; and to be forever taking shamed me to the heart.

Yet I comforted myself a little that, one day, I should make all good; paying back all debts and with interest. For now, to add to my fighting-strength, there would be Gloucester. I was at the peak of the struggle; he stood to gain with me. Surely he must come!

'He must help us,' I told van Brederode, 'for his own honour. And if that won't move him, then his own gain will. *Humphrey count of Holland, of Hainault, of Zealand* and the rest! He'll never stand by and see Philip take all!'

'He has his hands full in England,' van Brederode said drily. 'It's one constant struggle with his uncle Beaufort of Winchester.'

'Then let him leave the struggle and come and take his crown! And, if he cannot, or will not, then surely he will help us with his English gold. How long can I stand against the wealth of Burgundy?'

And when my old captain made no answer but stood looking steadfast and sad upon me, I said, 'If England shuts up her purse, why then we'll do without! I have captains the bravest; and councillors the shrewdest; I have nobles the loyalest; and commons the lovingest. And, if Philip has caught some cities in the snare of his promises, there are still some that know how little to value his word. This Gouda of mine: and Schoonhoven and Zieriksee and Dordrecht, too, have all refused homage to him. And more will throw off his yoke, more and more. While hearts are full of love I will not grieve overmuch that my purse is empty.'

And, as though God meant to give us a sign, while we were actually speaking together, Louis de Montfort brought in the letter from England. And I remember how I lifted my head and said, 'Gloucester will be with us soon. If Gloucester's ready to try his luck with us, then things look bright, indeed!'

'We should be glad of Gloucester's help—we need it, God knows! But you must not count upon it,' van Brederode said. 'Bedford will stop him!'

'Never! Bedford's a just man. I have been cast into prison, I have been robbed of my rights; they are mine to be won again. Christian justice must admit it.'

'Bedford's desire is for justice,' van Brederode said troubled. 'But he has an even greater desire—to keep the French crown safe for England. And for that he needs Burgundy. If Gloucester comes to your help then the old anger between him and Burgundy will flame fiercer than before. There are signs ... there are signs. They say the long-talked-of duel will be fought at last.'

'I've heard that too, but I don't believe it.'

'No,' he said, 'neither do I. Bedford won't allow it. He'll move heaven and earth to stop it. And that means stopping Gloucester from giving us help.'

'It won't be fought—but not because of Bedford,' I said. 'They've each got bigger fish to fry—and the fish is my inheritance. Both mean to have it. And that's why, let Bedford do what he will, Gloucester will come to our help.'

We were both right. His Holiness, egged on by Bedford, forebade the duel which neither had meant to fight; each man was saving his steel to fight on a far greater scale. For I was certain that, now all things promised well for me, Gloucester would surely come.

It was clear, as men joined me or turned their backs, that it was still party against party; for me the Hooks; for Philip the Cods.

Civil war—than which nothing is more hurtful, since win who will, still the country must lose—had already begun. The gutters ran with the blood of those slain in useless quarrel. Blood. You saw it, smelled it ... and the dogs smelled it, too.

Violence and treachery blackened the sky.

It wounded me to the heart, this wounding of my country by itself. Nor was Philip minded to see his strength wasted in futile quarrels. We hastened our preparations. From le Quesnoy, my mother made no sign. She would wait, as always, to see which way the cat jumped.

These days though I grieved at this wild violence, my heart was high. I was free; I was young; I was strong. My husband was coming to my help and I had my good captains.

Philip was on the march. 'He rides already like a conqueror,' van Brederode said. 'In every city he takes homage; his gold wins men to his banner.'

'It is a very great army,' I said. 'And ours is small. But our cause is just and our men in good heart. And any day must bring help from England.'

He said nothing. Only his grizzled brows shot up; it was clear he had no faith in Gloucester's promises.

Louis de Montfort came in, not stopping to bend the knee. 'Burgundy marches towards us by way of the Rhine!' he said, and leant against the table to catch his breath.

'Alphen!' van Brederode cried out in his great voice, 'Alphen he must have!' He struck upon the outspread map with his fist.

No need to tell me why Philip must take Alphen. There it sat commanding the waterways at all points—north, east, south and west.

'Alphen let it be!' I said. 'We ride at once to meet him!'

'Not you!' he said as my mother had said before. 'The battle will be bloody; you must stay behind. If you are taken, then all is lost. We cannot do without you—our leader.'

'A leader must lead. I ride where I may be seen ... as I have ridden before; yes, and won my victory, too.'

So there I was riding again at the head of my men—helmet and crown, breastplate and sword. No skulking within safe walls for me. Whatever my captains faced, I would face, too. I had no desire for death; but I preferred it to the long dying within a prison cell. And, as I rode, I would not let myself be afraid because our forces were small. My cause was great; and God was good.

Nor, indeed, was there time for fear. The long forced marches in the bitter weather took an undivided mind; hour after hour picking our slow way across ploughed fields, watchful lest the horses fall upon the hard and slippery ground. It was a cruel October with night frosts, and in the daytime, rain turning to sleet. Not until the long day drew to its end could I, weary and wet to the bone, seek my damp pallet.

We found Burgundy's troops ringed round the city and we attacked at once, our van taking the full weight of his troops. At once the difference in numbers told. My small force began to break and scatter.

Before I knew what I was about, I had spurred on my horse, striking at those that would have held me back, and who were now forced to follow. Above the din of the battle—the splitting of gunstones, the clash of steel, the brute cries of rage, the dim crying of the wounded, both man and beast, I sent out my voice. *A moi ... à Jacque, Jacque, Jacqueline ...*

At the sight of me, at the sound of me, those that were running away, turned back again. We rallied. The ranks of Burgundy fled before our madly screaming hordes. Old van Brederode said I was like the angel of Death that day.

Hair streaming, for I had lost my helmet, I rode back to Gouda. Behind me rode our forces, flying banners—our own and those of the enemy. And, in the great church, I knelt offering the banners of my enemy.

'Now you will see some fighting!' old van Brederode said. 'How they will fight! They must win their banners again; without their banners they are disgraced.'

'Let them come!' And I remember how I laughed and my young captains with me; but there was no laughter in the old man.

I had won more than a battle. I had turned waverers into believers that God was with me—I, a mere woman, had turned the tide of Burgundian power! So the story went; and those that told it and those that heard it, forgot alike the wisdom of my captains and the courage of my men. They remembered only the crowned helmet, the figure-head. And many that to save further bloodshed were ready to submit to Philip came over to my side. I was a prince, they said, worth any man's sword!

Worth any man's sword—but not Gloucester's! Not for me did he leave playing with the long hair of his dark witch, but to carve himself a kingdom in the Lowlands—his old delightful dream. Now with news of my victory, he was truly mustering men and ships; and the thought of them stirred my blood.

But what of Gloucester himself?

I told myself this was no time to dream of love. A soldier's pallet for me that must rise early and bed late stiff with the day's work, stained with sweat—and lucky if it were nothing more.

I told myself I loved him no longer. I *had* to make myself free of the pain he could still inflict.

'I have waited too long for the letter that never came, for the help that was never planned,' I told Beatrix.

'But still he has power to shake your heart,' she said. 'With anger and with shame; with those only!'

'That could be true ... if you never loved him' she said, 'if you were taken by a debonair face and a gay tongue, by the glory and the glamour of him. I think, perhaps you never loved him.'

Never loved him! And I longing for the sight of him, the touch of him ...

'Dear little Jacque,' she said, very gentle, 'neither the sickness of disappointment nor the anguish of shame, no, nor even the grave itself can quiet the heart that truly loves.'

I looked her in the face, and for all her sorrows, I envied her the certainty of her own heart.

'Let me alone,' I cried out. 'I don't know ... I don't *know*.'

'You will know,' she said, 'when you meet him face-to-face.'

October gave way to November. The wind whistled over the flats of Holland, the creeks of Zealand, the woods of Hainault. But not icy winds nor waterlogged fields could cool my spirit. For Gloucester was coming; in love a broken reed, he was yet soldier enough to trouble Burgundy.

My cousin Philip was redoubling his forces, redoubling his ships, redoubling his efforts to win hearts. He was bidding high for the friendship of those still to win. He was sending from city to city confirming their privileges, extending their privileges. He knew, none better, the bait of prosperity to win hearts away from honour. So now he published his plan for trade between my three countships to knot them into one prosperous whole—to be guaranteed by his strong arm. Even I could see how that must win them.

I could offer nothing like it. My mind was not set upon home comforts—I had to win my fireside first. Nor were my captains disposed to put prosperity before honour. But, had we wished to meet Philip plan for plan, we had not the means; at best we could only limp after him.

'We're soldiers not piddling pedlars,' old van Brederode said, his cheeks hanging like those of a St Bernard dog. Philip's cunning in commerce, though he would never admit it, worried him.

'Then we must learn to peddle, too!' I said.

'With what?' he asked and his sorrowful look startled me.

'There's news?' I cried out sharply.

He came and stood by me. 'Child!' And the name shook me, so long since I had heard it. 'Dordrecht has gone back to the enemy.'

I took in my breath. Dordrecht; city so urgent to my cause, city that had been lost to me and won again. Was this an omen? I turned to the window. The great spire thrusting upwards—as it might be to God—steadied me.

I said, 'Dordrecht is faithful at the heart, but it cannot help itself. Soon my husband will be here; and Dordrecht will return to us again.'

But I no longer believed in either event. I was desperate for all my fine words.

Still Gloucester did not come. And Philip took a further step. He boycotted all those towns that still held to me. Starve or come to his side!

Christmas was drawing near and I sent young de Montfort to beseech Gloucester hurry, hurry!

Waiting, I made use of every smallest thing to enlarge my prestige to keep the courage firm of those that still believed in me. There was a great fish, I remember, caught off the coast of Zealand, greater than any man had seen—a whale, maybe. 'A sign of victory to us, great as this fish!' I said and caused the story to be spread, so desperate I was.

'There'll be no victory; I doubt there'll be fighting, even, unless Gloucester comes and comes soon!' van Brederode said. 'Courage is high still with the victory at Alphen; but like any other fire, it dies for lack of fuel!'

'This Burgundy forgets nothing!' Reynolde of Vianen broke in upon us. 'He's flirting with God as well as with cities. He's making a round of the most eye-taking pilgrimages—on foot if you please! Barefoot, in all this mud and ice! Even God may find it impressive. Men certainly do.'

'God is not deceived,' I said. 'Nor are my true friends deceived. Burgundy cannot win either with his wickedness. God will see to it!'

Van Brederode and Reynolde looked at each other, father and son, and said no word. But their faces spoke for them.

From Leyden and Gouda, Philip and I watched each other.

In the new year de Montfort returned.

The fleet had sailed from England. And, even while I thanked God, the blow fell.

The fleet. But not Gloucester. Gloucester was not yet ready.

'The Lord Fitzwalter is a gallant captain' ... old van Brederode began but I would not listen. I could take no comfort. Gloucester thought so little of me or of my chances that he would not risk himself!

I turned and left the Council chamber without a word.

XXVII

The fourth day of January. Two o'clock of a dark and bitter night; and I, in spite of the heaped rugs upon my bed unable to sleep for the weight of my responsibilities, and for grief that my husband cared nothing for the love that had put my country into his hands, a free gift. Well, if punishment were deserved, I was punished ... I was punished.

Beatrix, hearing me stir, came in softly with a hot drink, but even the spiced wine could not stay the shivering. And, even while I drank and shivered, there came the blow upon my chamber door. Beatrix handed me my bedgown and drew the bolt.

Van Brederode strode in armed and radiant; each fold and wrinkle in that old face seemed to hold his joy.

'The English fleet is sighted. Oh Jacque, my dear, my child, my prince!' And he was not ashamed of the tears that poured down his cheeks.

'God be thanked!' I said. And then, since bitterness will out, 'Since Gloucester can bring me happiness no more, God grant he send good help!'

'Amen!' the old man said; he stooped to my hand and was gone.

Beatrix brought me a warm gown; and, as I dressed, though the wind blew between door and window sharp as a knife and my heart was cold with its sorrow, I felt excitement stir in my blood. I cou'd see, as I leaned out into the night, how the dark camp outside the city walls broke into points of light; in the torchlight dark shapes stirred—men and horses already on the march.

Now, as I went below to join my Council, the messengers came posting in.

Philip had sighted the English fleet before we did. Already in the bitter dark of the morning he was riding with his troops, riding towards Rotterdam.

Hourly the messengers rode in.

Philip was in Rotterdam. As he marched, cities had opened their gates to him, men streamed to him, bells pealed for him.

Philip was sailing down the Maas, his proud ships following; by road and by waterway his vast troops moving.

In Gouda I sat, the map forever unrolled, now striking out those towns that had betrayed me, now ringing in those that were loyal … and the crosses outnumbered the rings.

And yet there was hope; surely there was hope! The fine English ships bore forces three thousand strong. And though Gloucester had not come, Fitzwalter was a good captain; van Brederode had said so.

Van Brederode brought me news of defeat.

'The English ships draw too much water. They couldn't land. Two grounded at the beginning of the battle; they were seized at once. As for the rest—they made off. Goodness knows where! To the north, it seemed.'

I could not speak. What was there to say? I looked at him for comfort but there was none; there was none at all.

'This Gloucester, this rash know-all—saving your pardon, Madam—should have taken advice! Lighter ships would have reached Zieriksee before the gates closed. Zieriksee was ready and waiting to welcome them. Now ... now...' He paced about, came to a halt. 'Oh Jacque, Jacque, my child. It's more than the loss of a couple of ships, more than the loss of a battle. It's Zieriksee. Zieriksee, I think, will not stay loyal. Without English help it *can't* stay loyal ...'

It was a thing I had not expected. I had taken blow after blow and kept my courage high. When Dordrecht had returned again to the enemy, I had comforted myself with Zieriksee. Zieriksee would take the place of Dordrecht in our plans. And now ... now ...

I threw out my hopeless hands.

'They haven't declared against us, yet,' the old man held out his crumb of comfort. 'They declare themselves neutral—for the present.'

'Neutral, that's no good; no good at all!' And his last words passed me by. 'We *need* Zieriksee; we depend upon it for food.'

'We'll get food—if we pay enough. The town's free to sell to both sides. But we'll have to pay through the nose.'

It was as bad, almost, as if the town had gone over to the enemy. Victory for me must depend to a great extent on the length of my purse—and that was lean enough without this further strain upon it.

But even while I sighed and worried, God smiled. He sent us a victory.

The English fleet, reported to be sailing north after the disaster, had bypassed sly Zieriksee and besieged Browershaven, six miles further along the coast. The town, strongly held by the enemy, had been taken by surprise and the hated Cods thrown out. It was being held for me.

A small victory; but still a victory. And, like all success, it brought men to join us. From all parts of my three courtships they came to me, in Gouda; not in great numbers but enough to put heart into my captains, my forces, and me. And so heartened, I would ride about the city and through the camp outside and I would talk with the men. They strengthened me with their love and I gave them my heart's thanks.

And then, when things seemed set fair, my hopes came tumbling.

The English decided to join me at Gouda that we might attack the enemy together; and a portion of the fleet moved up the river.

It was the old story all over again.

The ships grounded on the sandbanks; and there they stuck—the fine ships—helpless. Philip's light, small boats, hundreds of them, piloted by men who knew the channels followed, relentless.

The English were caught. Rats in a trap. Oh they gave a good account of themselves. Bonny fighters! They fought hand-to-hand on decks all slippery with their blood; and in the shallow water all red with their blood. But you cannot fight long in a trap and there was precious little left of the English. Their bodies, hooked from the water, were left to rot on the banks; and the few that lived were carried away prisoner.

In my heart I blamed Gloucester most bitterly. How like him to dilly-dally; and then rush madly ahead without taking advice. Little good I had got from my English husband! And even then I guessed there would be no more.

January rains swept over Holland; the ground was sodden; the wind whistling over the low land stung like arrows. Within my camp the men shivered, crouching close to the smouldering fires, trying to bring warmth to their starved bodies. Philip's men were in better trim. Mercenaries for the most part, well pickled in war-fare, they knew how to pluck comfort from hardship. They knew how to find food and warmth, yes and wine, too; their pockets were lined with Burgundian gold. And above all, their faith in their captain was steady; Burgundy was foremost amongst the captains of Christendom ... and I was a weak woman. The odds against me were too heavy—unless God sent a miracle.

We had fought the old year out and the new year in; but the weather was hopeless now. Men cannot fight slipping and sliding upon ice, nor yet clogged in mud. From Leyden Philip kept a sharp eye on Gouda; he would see that no further help came to me from road or river.

January went slowly by. There was no sign of a miracle; nothing but the deadly cold and the heavy odds. Yet I kept my courage steady; I think now, looking back, that was a miracle. I would sit within my chamber rubbing my raw hands; or I would rise and walk the room to bring the blood back to my numbed feet. I kept my courage steady ... but I put my mirror away. I did not want to look upon the woman with dull hair, eyes and skin reddened in the wind. Hard to believe she was that Jacqueline once beloved of Gloucester, a man careful in his choosing of a woman!

My mind was obsessed with him, forever turning upon the way he had treated me. He had left me for his low mistress; he had let me fall a prisoner to Philip's hand and had left me to eat out my heart in captivity. He had sent no help until it was too late and that help ill-organized, useless. He had not come himself. Had he come, the splendour of his person and the glory of his name might have won us through ... but he had not come. And grief would sweep over me, and bitterness. And, drowning beneath those waves, I would try to drive away the thought of him in prayer; but even while I prayed I would see that debonair face before me and the miserable tears would roll down my cheeks; and I could not for the life of me have said did I love or hate him.

These days it seemed to me that God had turned away His Face.

I prayed in secret; but Philip prayed wherever eye might see. Wet weather or fine, he walked, the Sacrament carried before him, head bowed, hands folded—proud head, cruel hands. And, within the churches of every town beneath his obedience, God and his saints were badgered for the success of the Burgundian arms.

And all the time Zieriksee grew fat, providing me with food at famine prices ... and our men grew lean.

Towards the end of January the weather cleared; a watery sun actually shone in the sullen sky. A messenger came in at the gallop—a Saturday it was. Philip making the most of the rare sunshine was bringing his fleet into line, assembling his armies. Across our own camp the fife and trumpet shrilled their summons. The remnant of the English army, brooding still upon the loss of their comrades and the disaster to their fleet, leaped at the sound; my own men more soberly looked to their harness.

It was an army well-found that rode out, I and my captains riding each with his division. And the men were in good heart, eager to fight after the long days of inaction.

We chose a fine position at the top of a dyke where the enemy must climb to us; and it had the further advantage that we could see for miles around. Now, waiting for the attack, I rode about the troops, with encouragement and thanks.

The English showed a most grim courage. Leave their bones to rot in this bleak land? Not they! They were for home again when fighting was done. And my own men stood steady, knowing full well how many must find their graves in this sandy dune.

The struggle was unequal from the start. And because of that, more bitter. The Burgundians and the Flemings outnumbered us three to one. And yet, for one brief moment I thought we must win.

My men leaped upon the enemy, crying out so that the sound echoed and re-echoed across the plain to the sea. Such was the force of our attack, that the enemy hesitated and began to retreat. Philip, in the midst of his men, cried to them to advance—and nearly lost his life from a chance arrow. It was a miracle he did not get his death-wound. It was in that moment I thought we must win. But, maybe, those clamourings to the saints were remembered now.

Philip received no death-blow; but I did—death-blow to my hopes.

I sat my horse unmoving while Burgundian and Fleming and traitor Dutch fell upon my forces. And there I must have stayed had not de Montfort seized my bridle and galloped me from that bitter place and saved me from the hands of my cousin.

Good Philip, pious Philip, sanctimonious Philip!

Anger at his near-defeat stirred him—never patient—to bloody vengeance. There was no talk of ransom or of pardon; and few English and fewer Hooks limped back to tell the tale.

XXVIII

Death to all prisoners! Smiling Philip, pious Philip had made victory secure. He had suffered great losses, but in mercenaries, chiefly; nothing that could not be put right with gold. But mine was a different story. I had lost my own people—my own nobles, my own burghers, my own peasants—my friends. Had I the money to replace body for body still I could not make those losses good.

Yes, Philip might well be satisfied. He had forgotten, so it seemed, his duties to his English allies; the French wars dragged on without him, while he stayed to wring every ounce out of his victories.

Holland was quiet for the moment. He left his lieutenant—a bull-dog of a man—to deal with any possible disturbance and marched into Zealand; and there Frank van Borselen had made all smooth for the victory. As for Hainault, letters from Brabant—not yet dead, alas—commanded his loving subjects to obey Burgundy as himself!

'*His* loving subjects! Mine, Mine!' I stormed to de Montfort, my governor in Holland. 'Oh I am well-served between my two hus-bands. One takes all—and the other lifts no finger to stop him. The wretched Brabant filches my rights and hands them to my cousin. He's actually handed over Mons to Burgundy; given it to him—a gift. Mons my capital. Mine!'

'Brabant's got all the Cods behind him!' de Montfort said. 'His letters bear their seals; and the first seal is that of van Borselen.'

'Van Borselen. It's a name I know well. I shall remember it for my father's sake and for Beatrix van Vliet's sake ... and for my own sake.'

God hearing me then, must have smiled.

Zieriksee surrendered—and how could I blame it? It had held out for three whole months; the last of my cities to submit. Now Hainault and Holland and Zealand lay beneath Burgundy's heel.

Life had turned to ashes in my mouth; my lips were stiff with smiling above the taste.

And still I could not lay down my arms; and still I went on hoping. Here I would besiege a city; there I would fight a pitched battle. Sometimes I won; but, more often I lost. But, win or lose, still it was loss. Little to show for all the blood and all the sweat, all the dear friends slain ... and the ever-growing debt.

And now all was quiet beneath his heel, Philip returned to France to pursue those duties he had shamefully neglected. In Holland, van Uutkerke watched with a merciless eye; in Zealand, van Borselen; in Hainault, Brabant was sufficiently alive to serve my cousin's interests that were his own.

Shut up in Gouda with my ever-lessening forces, there were days when I thought I must surrender, make what terms I could. I was a woman and twenty-five; I had had but little joy out of my woman's life. I had fought enough. Now I would live my life, enjoy it while I might. Then I would remember those that had died for me; and those that had impoverished themselves for me, and the farmers and the fisherfolk tireless in their love, bringing me the harvest of their own hard lives to feed my cause. And I would go doggedly on.

Yet in the end I must yield and I knew it. There were not enough of us ... there were not enough.

There was one more victory before the end.

It was at Alphen where I had won my first. First victory and last. And there, my heart lifted with success, I knighted seven gentlemen, and among them Everhard of Hoochtwoude my father's bastard that had served me as lovingly as any trueborn brother; and I was glad to honour him for my father's sake.

Van Borselen laughed when he heard of it. Two things I should never make, he declared—an heir since he was made already; and a knight, since I was none myself.

I laughed as loud as he.

'Knights I will make, as many as I choose, by right of sovereign prince. An heir I will make when I have driven Burgundy from my land.'

My last victory ... but I did not know it then. Still I fought untiring for my cause. And all the time the weight of the army, the constant anxiety for food and money lay heavy on my heart, but heavier still lay the punishments I must command. For, in spite of captains and councillors, the responsibility of each man's death was ultimately mine.

And especially one death ... and that death I will remember even when I come to my own.

There is little kindness in warfare and I was not such a fool as to strive for it; but justice I held before my eyes. Yet there were times when I failed even there; weary and distraught it is not always easy to see things clear. The justice I did not give to Jan Knuypf cost me more than any loss in battle; and it led, in the end, to my defeat.

A pleasant young man, little more than a boy with his smooth cheeks and his blue eyes and his fair hair. He had come to Gouda on his father's business and there he had seen me about the camp—a soldier's cloak above my shoulders, skirts kilted above the muck, walking and talking with the men. It is shameful for a sovereign to drag about the camp like a strumpet, he had said—or so it was reported to me. I believe now that the words were twisted and turned about to serve my enemies; but certainly they were brought to me in a bad moment. Harassed by news that Gloucester would not come because they could not tear him from his dark witch, unreasonable with fatigue, I was overthrown by anger. 'The boy's your friend,' van Brederode said. 'Then the more reason for him to die,' I told him. 'How would it seem if those that call themselves my friend—even those—spit upon me unchecked?'

They brought the boy to me. I see him now, the young bewildered face; I hear the stammered words of innocence. He had never said the shame was mine, but the shame of those that let me, a fair young woman, drag about among the men. Nor had the word *strumpet* passed his lips.

But I would not listen. Had any word but strumpet been reported I doubt my anger would have been so dire. But strumpet was the word they used; and strumpet was the word they would go on using. Even her own friends brand her strumpet! I knew how the whisper went. And against it Gloucester had left me defenceless. Strumpet. It was a word I had heard too often!

Old Knuypf came hastening from Hoorn offering a king's ransom. But I hardened my heart against his grey hairs ... and against the gold he offered for his only son, gold I was desperate to have.

'How should I look in the eyes of honest men if I covered my stained honour with your gold? The stain must be wiped out and nothing but death can do it.'

But still the old man knelt and would not suffer them to take him away.

'My son is innocent, by Christ's Blood I swear it. And by that same Blood, I beseech you, save the innocent. But, since for the sake of example he is judged worthy to die, then, at the last moment, I implore you, lift your hand. Spare him and add mercy to your glory.'

I said nothing. I nodded to de Robbesart to take him away; and the old man, mistaking the nod, besought me no further and let himself be taken.

I dream even now of the old head and of the young—so honest and so frank. But time teaches us all; if we are capable of learning. It was that one word that blinded me. Any other word would have commanded, if not my mercy, then commonsense. But—*strumpet!*—the name the greater part of Christendom flung at me. Gloucester's strumpet since the Pope had not spoken even yet to clear my honour.

That was the only time I turned a deaf ear to the counsel of my friends; and I paid for it. One after another they came, advising me to spare the boy—van Brederode, obstinate and angry; and his son the Lord of Vianen who had sheltered me at his own hearth; and de Montfort who had sought only my good; and de Robbesart who had risked all when I fled into England—these and more with them.

I should have listened. I should have listened if not in the name of justice then in the name of commonsense. But that word bled like an inward wound not to be staunched until the one that had dealt it was dead.

And so he died, I standing to see it; and his father too. And though the old man saw the cart move from the scaffold he could not believe his eyes. Madam the Countess had promised; she had stood by the scaffold herself to stay the hangman. She had promised ...

I did not sleep that night; nor for many nights after. And the days that followed were full of the noise of that hanging.

'Knuypf's making untold mischief,' van Brederode said troubled. 'He's saying everywhere you swore to save his son. He's telling everyone how the boy stood, the rope about his neck and you ...'

He stopped. 'You may tell all,' I said. 'Keep nothing back.'

'... you, perjured liar and cruel heart stood by and did not lift your hand in common justice. He utters his threats and cares not who hears. He says they are more than threats and so you shall find to your bitter cost.'

As I did ... I did.

'He says you shall pay for it with your crown. Never in Hoorn where he leads opinion—or elsewhere, if it be in his power—shall you find friends. The king's ransom he collected for his son, and his great wealth besides, he means to spend like water to bring about your defeat.'

I should have had Knuypf's head; it was pure treason that he spoke. But I pitied an old man's sorrows; I could not add death to death. I had withheld mercy where it was folly to do so; I showed mercy where it was even more folly. And I paid for both. Well, we are as we are made!

Hoorn declared for Philip. The town that had loved me now hated me. 'I will take it by force!' I cried out and beat with my fist upon the Council table.

My captains said nothing; no need. I knew their thoughts. I was a fool. I would throw away lives and gold to win back, if I could, what I had wantonly cast away.

Their silence angered me. 'Throw armies about the walls, bring engines and guns, I will take the city; I will hang Knuypf and the chief citizens. Hoorn, I will have!'

And so I made bad worse. I should have confessed my fault, offered such recompense as might be accepted; above all I should have cleared the name of an innocent man that had died a traitor's death.

The same bad blood as her uncle the Pitiless. We will cast her out, the Bavarian! So Hoorn said and so my enemies repeated. And thus I lost not only the town but my people's love.

Fourteen hundred and twenty-six. A bad, bad year.

I was losing my last foothold in Holland as I had already lost it in Hainault and in Zealand with its islands. Losing foot-hold; losing hearts. And the news from England was bitter.

No more help.

The slaughter on the dykes, the fine ships lost—and all in a useless cause—had shocked the English Parliament. And worse; the help already given was making bad blood with Burgundy, they said. The matter must come to an end. Bedford came from France to make it clear to his brother. He might have spared himself the trouble. I doubt

Gloucester would have stirred from the side of his witch, no, not if by so doing he could put the crown back on my head.

For now he lived openly with her as though she were his wife. She that had been my servant now ruled my household, sat in my place, slept in my bed. She was accepted everywhere—she and her spotted honour. She had more power than any woman in the land. If Queen Catharine and Queen Johanne, like many another, desired not to meet Madam Eleanor, why then they were welcome to stay at home.

She was duchess in all but name.

'Yet she can never be his wife,' I raged to Beatrix, 'not while I live! My one comfort—if a poor one. *I am Gloucester's wife.* Let the Pope dilly-dally, their Parliament acknowledges it; and the little King acknowledges it. And Gloucester himself—whether he will or no—must acknowledge it! His honour and mine are bound together. He cannot put me aside.'

Beatrix said, gentle, 'Then go back to England before it's too late. It's been in your heart this long time! I know it well; I've heard you sighing out in your sleep, sighing and crying. Stay no longer eating out your heart in this country that will have none of you!'

She lifted her head, all streaked with grey, Beatrix old before her time, her life ruined in my sorrows. 'Life waits for no man; and the life you lead—constant warfare, constant anxiety, out in all weathers good and bad alike—isn't kind to women. Go back to my Lord of Gloucester while you may.'

'It's too late!' I lifted the mirror I had not used for many days, and stared at the face worn to the bone, the chapped skin, the sunken eyes. 'Do you see what I see?' I asked.

'I see nothing but what rest and a little care won't put right. You could win any man if you put your mind to it.'

'Even Gloucester?' I asked, bitter.

'Even him. Jacque, my dear, I must speak plain. You loved him and he loved you; in the face of all opposition he loved you. And what opposition! In the face of my lords of Bedford and Burgundy; yes, in the face of the Pope himself! He risked excommunication and his immortal soul for love of you. And you were happy together. You were happy with him once?'

'I ask no more of heaven.'

'He loved you as long as he was let—'

I would have spoken then, but she paid no heed; she went steadily on.

'As long as he was *let*; as long as you were woman to his man. But—when you forgot you were a woman, when you made yourself a soldier and a captain of men—what then? Your mind was on your armies, your battles, your gains and your losses, in bed and out. Some men—though none would relish it—might remain faithful. But not that man. He likes womanhood in women; he likes grace and beauty. That he left you is, in part, your own fault.'

My hand lifted to strike her. She, of all people, knew how I had suffered; and now she took it upon herself to blame me. She held me with her eyes; my hand dropped—and my eyes, too. I was ashamed.

She said, steady but gentle, too, 'It's true—though none dare tell you but me ... you are not easy to live with these days, my dear.'

'No,' I said, 'no! And you are right, maybe. But, I will not go back like a whipped dog. That's no way to win Gloucester. Winning back the lands I have lost, I win him, too. The only way.'

Day after day shut up in Gouda which I had entered with so high a heart and which held me now like a prison! I saw that Beatrix had been right.

'I shall go back to England,' I told her. 'I am an English national, to come and go as I choose. There's no man can refuse me leave to depart and none to deny me entrance.'

She said nothing; but her sigh echoed the doubt in my own heart. I had left it too long. Let my rights as an English national be what they might, Burgundy would never let me go, nor Bedford welcome me. And if they would? How would Gloucester himself receive me, all battle-worn and with my empty hands?

Fate that had rained so many blows upon me had yet another in store.

The Pope spoke again. Better for me had he kept silent. For though, even now, the final word was not said, it was easy to guess what that word must be; his letter foreshadowed it.

I had violated the laws of God and man. I had deserted my Lord of Brabant to live with Gloucester while Rome's judgment remained unspoken. Until that judgment was spoken I must return to Brabant; or, I must put myself under the protection of Burgundy. Frying pan or fire; it mattered not!

And now tales about my husband and his harlot came thick and fast. He said, openly, that he had no doubt what the final judgment would be. As soon as the word was spoken he intended to make his mistress his wife.

'Never!' I told Beatrix and I remember how I laughed. 'Gloucester, son, brother and uncle to kings! Proud Lancaster make his low-born strumpet his wife! Birth and custom alike forbid it. Treat her as his wife—maybe; he's infatuated. Marry her—no!'

'Infatuated!' Beatrix repeated. 'It was yourself that said the word.'

And it was the truth. I must wait no longer. I must get to England before the Pope's last word set Gloucester free—before I fell once more into Philip's hand. For then it would be the prison he had sworn; not even the scant liberty of the Gravenstein, but a living tomb … if not the tomb itself.

I saw now that freedom—freedom to breathe the sweet air, to see a friend's face, hear a friend's voice, outweighed the thing called love. Let Gloucester protect me—and I would not ask for love. Give me but shelter of his name and I would make myself content.

But I knew him; how useless to appeal to him for whose sake I had lost all. Yet I was still an English national; it was to the King himself I must appeal. And so, for the first time, I wrote to my little godson.

> … Your Grace has been pleased to name me dearest aunt. But I am more than that. I am your mother in God. It was my arms that held you at the font. In the name of God, and in the name of your great father that promised me help and friendship I implore your protection…

And while I waited for the answer that never came, the thing happened; the thing so long expected, we expected it no longer.

XXIX

John of Brabant, who had been so long a-dying that we feared him immortal in his sickness, was dead.

Now I could pray for him because he had found his freedom; and, finding it, had given me back mine. There were tales in plenty of the manner of his dying. Some said he died as he had lived—vicious, rotten; others that he had remembered his God at the last and I prayed it might be true, that God might have mercy upon his sinful soul.

But when I heard that he had died forgiving me all he wrongs I had done him, then the old bitterness rose in me. Ten years of misery—of humiliation, of unkindness, of poverty! Impotent, he had robbed me of my woman's right to children; treacherous, he had robbed me of my sovereign's right to rule.

Well let it go! He was dead. And the barrier between Gloucester and me was gone. No need now for any Pope to speak. God had spoken. God had set me free.

For the first time in long months of misery I knew a little hope. Love me or not, for very shame's sake Gloucester must come; if not as my lover, then as my true husband.

But when I looked into my mirror I saw little to please either. Beatrix brought her lotions and her unguents; she was forever washing my hair and shining it with a cloth. 'You've forgotten the feel of a silk gown,' she said. 'Yes, I know a breastplate suits your purpose; but there are times when a woman has need to be a woman!' And she sent for the merchants.

She was right. I looked at the rolls of silk and longed; and, though I have any woman's love of finery, I chose one and one only. But what a one! Of richest silk it was, lozenged all over in blue—since blue signifies constancy in love—and gold; and in each golden lozenge I had them embroider a spray of myosotis—device of the house of Lancaster; and in each blue lozenge my own cypher set beneath a crown. And, since my jewels had long fallen into enemy hands I sought an ornament to hold my girdle—a flower of little pearls. 'Not a jewel for a great lady!' Beatrix said throwing up her hands. But I have never been one to spend on finery where I cannot pay and the little flower must serve.

Beatrix's ministrations and my own new hope were bringing back something of my looks. When Gloucester came, he would find me, perhaps, not so different from the Jacqueline he had loved. And I? Though I could never love him again, I could live with him as his wife and enjoy it too. He was a man well made and debonair; and he was witty above most men; and he could be kind. Yes, I could live with him as his wife and thank God for the chance. With a man's arm to do man's work I should give myself to woman's work—an heir to make my poor torn land whole again.

Day after day. And no sign of Gloucester, nor any message. Well, I had learned to be patient; but, dear God, let him not stay too long!

Gloucester did not come.

If Gloucester was slow to move, the same could not be said of Philip.

June was drawing to its close and Brabant had not been dead three months; the trees were all hung with green and the river was blue as the Virgin's scarf. From my chamber I could hear the bustle of the Market Place; I had but to put my head out of the window to smell the salt fish of herrings, the sour smell of cucumbers; see the bright bunches of picotees and roses laid amongst cabbages and turnips.

A gay day, fine and warm; but for me, a day of darkness and grief.

My mother had come at long last, bringing with her the copy of letters Philip had sent to every town in my three countships.

'So!' I said and lifted my shocked face. 'I'm a poor and friendless widow, am I? Gloucester will choke that lie down cousin Philip's throat!'

She did not answer. No need; the answer was clear in her eyes.

'I need a man's strong arm to guard me, he says! And by Christ's Sweet Face that's true! I trust my cousin will enjoy that strength when it falls upon him! So, my Lord of Burgundy, out of the goodness of his Christian heart, undertakes to rule my lands on my behalf! It's the duty of the good man to protect the widow, he says. The good man and the widow! One's as true as the other; and may God choke the words in his lying throat!'

She said, 'Leave railing! Philip holds his hand—with the master card in it! He could claim possession, actual possession, by right of Brabant's will.'

'There's no right!' I said quickly. 'And he knows it. And you know it, too; Brabant had no right, not even the shadow of right, he was never my husband.'

'Leave railing, I say, and think what's best to be done. Philip met the Estates at Mons ...'

'At Mons? Already? Why didn't you send to tell me, why didn't you summon me?' But I knew my answer; it lay in her de Charolais blood.

She said, shrugging, 'What use? The Estates themselves entreated him to rule.'

'To rule—*Philip?* But I am sovereign.'

She said nothing.

'Was nothing said of me?'

'Something was said.' And she avoided my eyes—as well she might. 'Philip will rule for you, since, so they say, you are little able to rule for yourself.'

I tried to speak but rage rose in my throat to choke me. Had I the power in that moment I should have struck Philip dead. I stood, eyes upon my mother, forcing her to tell me how such treachery had come about.

'It was a week ago ...' she began.

'A week, a whole week!' I cried out and beat my hands together.

'... they exchanged oaths, he and the Estates; and not only for Mons but for all Hainault. It is bitter for you and bitter indeed! But a man's strength is needful; you cannot altogether blame them.'

'Can I not?' I cried out in a terrible voice. 'And you—my mother, my father's wife—condone ...'

'I did not condone,' she cried out very sharp. 'I protested. I protested with all my might; but it takes a dyke to keep the sea back not one woman's finger! Philip's a man and he's a soldier. And he promises protection and peace. Can you promise either of these things? All I got in answer to my protests was the old business of your marriage with Gloucester. They say—and there's reason in it—that when you made Gloucester your heir you set aside, wrongly and wilfully, your nearest of kin!' And I knew she meant my cousin Philip.

'My husband is my nearest of kin,' I said, very quick.

'We doubt very much he is your husband. You may well find he is not! The Estates said, plump and plain, you shall not remain in possession of lands you propose to alienate to foreigners.'

'And the Burgundian?' I broke in passionate. 'What's he but a foreigner?'

'He isn't as foreign as your Englishman. His lands march with yours; he and your people understand each other. And, above all, he's wise where Gloucester's a fool. You may hate your cousin, my girl, but he rules well; even you must admit it. Wherever his hand falls there's peace and prosperity. Can you say the same of Gloucester? For the great good of the land—so the pact runs—Philip is entreated to govern in your place. *For the great good of the land!*' she said again.

'No!' I cried out. 'No! To me the oath was sworn, the homage given. To me, to me!'

'Oaths may be broken—you, yourself showed the way! The oath between Brabant and Mons was broken, at your request, that it might be made instead to Gloucester. It's not surprising, then, that when it suits them, they do the same by you.'

'There's a difference—and you know it! The difference between right and wrong. I am their prince. To me the oath is due. It was sworn to Brabant by right of me ... of *me*.'

She shook her head. 'An oath broken is an oath broken. Never before had it been broken—the oath of the Joyous Entry—until you showed them the way. You showed them the way when it pleased you; they follow when it pleases them. Well, as for rights and wrongs, that's all one now! The new oath has been sworn to Philip, the homage taken, the promise made, the pact signed ...'

'And does no one remember me, no one at all? Have I no friend in Mons, not one?'

'You have no money! And money speaks with a sweet voice. Philip has both friend and enemy in his pocket along with his gold.'

'Then let him keep them—false friend and true enemy! I have other help. You have forgotten it; and Mons has forgotten it; and Philip has forgotten it! But they will remember again when Gloucester comes!'

'You must not count on that,' she said, slowly. 'For let him come— which I must doubt—still it would not help you. I would not say this unless I must; yet you should know it for yourself. It's Gloucester's the stumbling block. Gloucester himself strengthens Philip's arm. Listen, daughter, and listen well! It is expressly stated in the pact that Philip reigns not in his own right, but for you. For you! He's governor and heir only until you deny your marriage with Gloucester.'

'Never!' And I could not at first get the word past my throat so strangled I was with anger. 'They steal my rights and they steal my treasure. Now they would steal the last thing that's left to me—my honour. But that they shall not have. I would die first!'

'Jacque,' she said; and it was long since she had called me by my little name. 'Give up all thought of Gloucester. He's brought you nothing but pain and disgrace and bitter loss. And he will bring you more—if you let him. He took what he could and then cast you aside. If you've more to give, he'll take that, too; and then again you are cast aside. Cast him aside first! So you cast out Philip. So you win back the love of your people; and, with it, your titles, your lands ... and your Christian honour. Jacque, listen to me; you must listen to me; I'm your mother and what I say is true.'

'My mother you may be!' I said, very bitter. 'But when did you ever keep faith with me?'

I saw her wince at that. She only said, 'Forswear Gloucester before he forswears you. There's but one hope and that's in Philip. You cannot stand against him. Lay your arms aside and take instead the love of your people. You were meant for a woman's life; it's written all over you! You need a man to cherish you that you may bear your children in happiness.'

'Children? In happiness?' I cried out! 'They are robbed before ever they're conceived. What inheritance shall I give them? You who are so clever, tell me that!'

She said, 'Philip's your heir only until you forswear Gloucester. Have you forgotten so soon?'

'Gloucester's my husband. I will not spot my honour to save my crown; it is you that forget oversoon!'

'Then all your hope's in Gloucester—and it's a poor hope!'

And her sigh was real enough. But I could not trust her—it was part of my tragedy. God knows I had need of that shrewd brain but her loyalties were not with me. She had proved it again and again and I dared not trust her.

And yet, looking back, I know that is not the whole truth—though very near it. Maybe she did, indeed, believe my only safety lay in sitting dumb within Philip's shadow. Yes, it may well be that she desired my happiness—if it might come that way.

There was no one in whose advice I could trust. My captains and my councillors were fighting-men, shrewd in warfare, blunt in policies. They saw nothing but the armed struggle. I had been dispossessed; the matter must be set right with blood.

The days came and went. And no sign from Gloucester. I wrote to him no more. I bade Beatrix put away the fine gown I had ordered with such hope. When she would dress my hair I would snatch myself from her hands—there was no one to find me desirable. I was twenty-six; and I felt old and bitter and wasted.

There was a lull now. Shut within Gouda I had neither men nor money to fight further. But I had one last hope. I was an English national; it was to the King of England I must appeal—to him and his Privy Council. I spent my nights and days writing, turning this phrase and that, seeking the words to melt cold hearts to pity.

Those letters. When I look over the rough drafts now, it is as though I look upon the sorrows of some other woman. I see the crossings-out and the rewriting; I see the faint marks of blistering tears ... and I wonder any heart could refuse that long-ago girl.

But all I received in return were letters urging me to make my peace with Burgundy.

Anger dried my tears; I flung myself, all hot blood, to answer the insult sealed with the royal seal of England.

... I will never in this life make peace with my cousin of Burgundy who seeks to thrust me from my inheritance, no, not though Christian blood should flow. With all my heart and soul I wish your royal father were alive. I should not then find myself in such bitter need ...

And when this letter to the King of England brought me no reply, I wrote and wrote again ... but there was never an answer. I gave up writing to my little godson; I wrote to the Privy Council—my last hope.

> ... I am left, a sorrowful woman, to endure miseries and to suffer poverty and fear; and these I have borne without hope or cheer. Your late good King promised to cherish me and to help me, his kinswoman. He welcomed me to England; he promised me a father's help in all my affairs. Yet today I stand despised and condemned by the whole world, deprived of all comfort and counsel.
>
> And so I implore you to urge my dear brother of Bedford, your Regent; and also my lord and husband to help me that am in such sore need. Weary, grieving, I am left to wonder why God summoned my father to Him so early, leaving so noble an inheritance to me, his daughter once a happy child, and now condemned to lose all by a most cruel injustice. My nearest kinsman, my cousin of Burgundy, is my most bitter enemy and I know not which way to turn ...

I put this last letter, together with my last hope, into the hands of my faithful secretary. 'Speak for me, Grenier, dear friend. Tell them my cousin of Burgundy demands that I deny my husband or renounce all. Tell them I will never agree. Ask them why no army is being gathered for my cause. Tell them I am the most unhappy lady in the world, the most forlorn. Tell them, Grenier, tell them! Let your voice speak louder than mine, for mine is choked with tears.'

Whether it was that last letter of mine, or Grenier's golden tongue, I do not know. But England was moving at last. Help was coming; the little King had issued a decree.

> ... and because of the great troubles and distresses sustained by Madam the Duchess of Gloucester, our very dear aunt ...

Madam the Duchess of Gloucester our very dear aunt... So he proclaimed my marriage and kinship. My honour shone clear.

> ... and because of the affection I bear her; and on account of the many prayers made to the Council by my dear uncle the Duke of Gloucester...

So he had tried. Gloucester had tried! If he no longer loved me, he had not denied our marriage. I could read no further for the blinding tears. It was Grenier who read the rest.

... and we have decided to provide for the said Duke of Gloucester the sum of twenty thousand marks and also men-at-arms to garrison the towns obedient to the said Duke and Duchess and to escort Madam the Duchess into England ...

'Take me into England! In God's Name, why, Grenier, why? Before ever a blow is struck do we prepare for failure?'

He lifted his head from the King of England's decree.

'The English army is not to fight save in self-defence; that and that alone. The men are to remain inside the garrison until such time as they may conduct you to England.'

I threw out my hands all bewildered as I was. He said, 'You must not attempt to regain any city or castle you have lost. It is the condition.'

It was a thing I had never imagined. I could not speak; only my hands, upturned and empty, spoke for me.

'You have no choice,' he said, gentle. 'It is that—or nothing.'

And, now, indeed, there was yet another battle to be fought—and this time with myself; myself alone.

Duty bade ... me stay and fight to the finish, whatever ill that might bring; and death would be the least. Commonsense and great weariness urged me to England, there to wait until my friends were ready to march again. I should heal myself in England's peace, gather strength to my weary body, wash out the stains of war, know what it was to be a woman again.

'You must return your answer, and soon!' Grenier broke in upon my thoughts.

'What answer? Grenier, tell me, tell me!'

'I think,' he said, slow and troubled, 'we should spill no more useless blood.'

'Perhaps ... perhaps,' I said. And then, 'Yet a principle drives me to fight to the end.'

'A principle?' he questioned me gently. 'What is a principle beside safety? Safety is sweet and must be paid for.'

'It could be paid for too dear. The principle is rooted here.' And my hand went up to my heart. 'Uproot it and I should die.'

My mother came hurrying at the news. 'Who would be fool

enough to trust England's offer? Have you not had enough of English promises, promises given and broken?'

'Not broken; honoured!' I said. 'But there are other promises—sworn and sworn again that will never be made good.'

'If you mean my nephew of Burgundy, you are wrong. He will honour his promise—your people will see to it.' She was silent for a while, wandering the room, touching this and that. At last she said, 'If you go now, you will never come back; you will not be let to come back; your people will see to that, too! Will you wear out your life an unwanted stranger in a foreign land when you might be wearing a crown in your own?'

I looked at her very steady. The hard grey eyes stared back giving nothing away. Was she advising me to refuse for Burgundy's good, lest Gloucester, with soldiers at his command, disobey his orders and raise his standard? Or did she truly desire to save me further grief?

I could not tell. When most I needed that cool brain I must set it aside, come at the right as best I could.

And so I wavered first to this side and then to that; and, in the end, it was duty drove me. Duty in princes is greater than any desire for happiness.

XXX

England meant well by me; not only her nobles but her common people. The Privy Council wrote to Bedford in France saying that the whole country was set to rescue Madam the Duchess of Gloucester. Would my Lord of Bedford beseech my Lord of Burgundy to set the wrong right?

I sought out my mother, all triumphant with my news.

'And how if my nephew recognize no wrong?' She was half-amused, half-pitying. 'Well that's a question you needn't trouble to consider. Bedford will not breathe a word on the matter. You may believe me in that!'

'Bedford's a just man,' I said. 'His justice is renowned in Christendom.'

'He's a man wedded to his responsibilities,' she said, 'and you are not one of them!'

I dared not believe her. I needed this hope so much. But she was right. She knew how expediency may drive the just man to injustice—and no shame in the matter.

I have a copy of Bedford's reply before me.

> ... I have neither the wish nor the power to urge my brother of
> Burgundy to relinquish his conquests in Holland. The validity of
> Madam Jacqueline's marriage lies with the Pope; her inheritance with
> the Emperor. It does not lie within the jurisdiction of our lord the
> King and he is free of all responsibility in the matter. Even if Madam
> Jacqueline be aunt to the King—a thing of which we are by no means
> certain—still her complaints must not be allowed to bring the welfare
> of our country into danger...

But even then I would not allow myself to believe that England
would send no help. The English people pitied my wrongs; how
could Bedford stand against them?

And so again I waited and the long summer passed. Shut up in
Gouda, so beleaguered that I dared not set foot outside the town, I
yet had my moments of hope. Van Brederode, best of captains, truest
of friends, old though he was, took the brunt of ten men. He had
taken Texel—a marvel of fighting against heavy odds; now he was
marching to Wieringen. 'The man's a lion,' my mother said.

My old, my faithful lion was taken in the net and lay in prison. He
was weeping when they took him, the grand old man. 'I can serve my
lady no more,' he said. 'Do what you will with this old carcase.'

And now autumn had passed and winter shut down upon us. Philip
had left the Lowlands; we would fight no more until the spring.
Nothing to do now but wait ... and go on waiting.

And still no word from England.

'And yet this Gloucester—' and my mother no longer called him
son, 'could make all right with a word. Brabant's dead. If the man's so
occupied he can't come himself—' and her words made light of him
and me, 'why then, a marriage by proxy and you're his undoubted
wife. No tongue to say you Nay!'

'Go through the ceremony a second time! Admit that all these
years I had been his harlot! I would not hold my honour so cheap,
not though all Christendom lent me countenance and aid.'

'Deceive yourself if you can, daughter, don't try to deceive
me!' And she shrugged. 'Willing enough you would be—like any
woman in your place. It's Gloucester that won't consent. He'll
never consent to be tied to you save at a price; and that price you

can no longer pay. Your inheritance will never fall into his hands and he knows it. Royal Gloucester is not one to let himself go cheap. And so honesty and loyalty, common decency even—to the dunghill all three!'

And when for very shame I could not speak because the thing was true, she said, quite gently, 'The surgeon's knife is bitter but it cuts clean. We have cut to the bone and come at the truth. The wound will heal ... it will heal!'

Shut up in Gouda, hampered by my poverty, I wrote no more letters; nor did I make my further prayer to the Pope. But if I made no move towards Rome, others were working fast to pluck advantage from my dishonour.

Noble Bedford, just Bedford, was moving heaven and earth to get the matter settled. Once he had made a fine show of imploring the Pope to sanction my marriage; now he flung all his power in the balance against me.

I must say—though I would rather not—that he did not work for his own hand; but your good man is more to be feared than your evil. Bedford was working for England and for his little King. And he was desperate.

And with reason. Things were going badly in France; and badly indeed. Defeat after defeat, and the tide of favour flowing towards France's uncrowned King—my cousin the Dauphin who called himself, and rightly, King of France. The French were beginning to ask themselves why they should put their necks beneath the heel of the foreigner—and that foreigner a child?

And they were being pricked on to their answer by a girl; an ignorant girl from the country. She had raised her standard for the Dauphin—Christ among the lilies. She was gathering her armies and fighting her battles; and winning them, too. She would, she swore it, see her King crowned in Rheims.

'If she drags Charles to Rheims and gets him crowned,' my mother said thoughtful, 'it's the death-blow to the English in France. Do you wonder Bedford cares not a jot for you or your rights?'

'If Bedford needs Philip, Philip needs Bedford!'

'Philip needs no man!' She spoke with her de Charolais pride. 'His irons are in both fires and Bedford knows it! If Gloucester turns his back on you, then the friendship with England stands—and Philip's the most powerful man in France. If Gloucester annoys Philip further in the matter of your marriage, then Philip breaks with England and throws in his lot with the Dauphin ... on terms;

terms the idiotic boy can't afford to refuse. And those terms will make Philip master in France. Either way he stands to win!'

So Bedford and Burgundy went about behaving like brothers; and Philip's messengers joined Bedford's in Rome praying His Holiness to denounce my English marriage. It was essential, they said, to the peace of Christendom. That it was essential to their own plans they did not say.

When two of the most powerful princes in Christendom unite to demand a thing, how shall a mere Pope—God's Mouthpiece though he be—refuse them?

It was the second week in January, a cold, bleak day, that the answer came. For all the two braziers burning in my room, I could not get warm. And, when the messengers, kneeling, handed me the letter with the papal seal, my hand trembled and I all-but dropped it.

My mother caught it before it fell. She dismissed the men, broke the seal and, without a word, handed me the document.

My eye flew across the wide paper that trembled in my hand, darted here and there, could not take in one word or another. My mother took it again and read me its contents.

'The Brabant marriage was a true marriage,' and she gave no sign of her triumph; nor of pity, neither. 'You have lived adulterously with Gloucester, so it stands. You are not, and never have been, his wife.'

And never shall be. For the rest of my life dishonoured ... And I wished the earth would open and swallow me.

'What kind of dishclout is this Pope?' I cried out. 'He robs me of my honour; and with it, all comfort, all aid!'

'He's God's Mouthpiece,' she reminded me drily. 'And you had best remember it!'

'God will not allow it!' I cried out and my mouth shook. 'The Pope has not understood. They have made him believe their lies! I will send to him again; and again and again, until his mouth declare my honour or my own be stopped with dust.'

'As it may well be ... if you are so unwise,' she said. 'My nephew of Burgundy is not a patient man!'

She got up and went to the door and there she paused. 'Child,' she said, 'the Pope has but two ears—Bedford's at one; Burgundy at the other. How shall he listen to you? Be advised. I *beg* you to be advised!' And was gone from the room.

I sat there, the letter hanging from my hand, the seal on its bright ribands adangle.

The end. For long there had been no love in Gloucester for me; now there was no duty. Until today one bond alone might hold him; the duty of a man to protect his wife—even an unloved wife. Now this last bond was broken. Gloucester was free of me for ever.

I was twenty-six; and my world lay in pieces about me.

It was Beatrix that found me shivering in my chair. She picked up the fallen letter and put it away where I might not see it. She brought me a fur cloak—and how thin and moulting it was! She brought me a cup of hot wine. I tried to drink; the wine fell spotting the bosom of my gown. I looked at the place to wipe the stain away; and it struck me sharply how thin I was that had been so sweetly rounded. Plump delicious Jacque, Gloucester used to call me.

I said, 'I am sucked dry of honour; of rights and of riches. And I am sucked dry also of such beauties as I had. Battle-scarred—and nothing to show for it!'

'There were victories,' she said, 'and will be again. The world doesn't end at twenty-six.'

'The world ends when hope ends ... and I am nearer twenty-seven.'

She nodded. Hope had ended for her and she had the look of an old woman, she that was but ten years older than I. It was not so much the grey in the dark of her hair, nor yet the lines about the eyes and mouth. It was a thing that came from the spirit; the acceptance of age when hope is gone.

How long before I, too, wore the accepting look of age?

Never! I will never give way. I am not one to accept disgrace, come what may!

June had come again and the air was sweet with roses. They lay with picotee and phlox on the market stalls at Gouda.

I had thought, with the Pope's letter, to have suffered the last of fate's blows. How simple I was! When fate has you upon her anvil, there you remain until she has done with you. I know that now.

When I took that latest blow darkness fell upon sweet summer; the world whirled black.

Gloucester was married.

He had married his dark witch. He had cast me off. He had cast me off, not for any advantage he might gain, that I could have endured; it was his nature. He had cast me off for his low-born strumpet; the strumpet he had enjoyed for years. No need to marry her ... no need! It was as though he meant to show Christendom that he spat again upon my honour.

The darkness stopped whirling. I was lying on my bed and Beatrix cradling me as though I were a child again.

The light came back sudden and hurtful to my eyes; the memory to my heart.

'Oh Gloucester, Gloucester!' And my voice came out in a wail. 'Son of Kings, royal Gloucester to defile me with this marriage!'

'Hush,' she said, 'oh hush! Jacque my sweet, no man can shame you, nor break your pride while you hold fast to courage. Shame there is–but not for you. All Christendom must hold him cheap; *him*–not you. Show Christendom how cheap you hold him, too.' And then, because I trembled still, she said, 'I thought my heart broke when Jan died; now, it breaks again to see your courage gone!'

I set my chattering teeth at that—as she had meant. By the time my mother came marching into my chamber there was little to be seen of grief.

'He shall pay for this, royal Gloucester!' she cried out. 'Philip shall see to it!' Now that all danger from Gloucester was passed she could afford to show concern for me. 'By God's Face I could whip him with my own hands. As for the witch—she shall burn!'

'They hang them in England!' And I shrugged. 'But not such a witch as Madam the Duchess of Gloucester; never such a witch as that!' And though I strove to make my voice careless it came out harsh and bitter naming her with the name that had been mine.

All the passion I had thought dead came flooding back.

'How did she win him when I failed? I was comely; beautiful they said; and I was kind; and I was royal, his equal in blood. How does she hold him who laughs in every woman's face, who slips from every woman's arms?'

'She has had schooling enough!' And until my mother spoke I did not know I had declared my tormented mind. 'All things to all men! With this one yielding, with that one coy; with this one merry, with that one very still in her smiling. Oh I watched her when she was in Mons with you. Very modest; but for all those down-cast eyes a mouth that promises.'

'Yet he will leave her as he left me!' I cried out.

She shook her head. 'You play a man's part in battle; and so you lose him. She plays her woman's part in bed; and so she keeps him.'

'Still he will leave her!' And I turned my face away remembering those early days of our marriage. I had not played a man's part then!

209

'Never!' my mother said. 'She holds him with more than beauty, more than her cunning.' She stopped; she said, slowly, 'She holds him with the children she has borne him.'

So cruel a thrust, so unexpected! I all but cried out. She was using the knife again. She pitied me; but still she must wound. It was her nature.

'You have nothing more to hope from Gloucester, save that he come to his just punishment. And so he shall—if you will make your peace with Philip. And you can do no other. Philip's your man.' And she was gone with a great sweeping of skirts.

Beatrix that had stood so silent we had all-but forgotten her, came over and knelt by me.

'This Cobham is indeed a witch! Oh, we have called her so in anger, and we spoke truer than we knew. She has dealings with the devil. There are tales—great folk would be slow to hear them since they start in the kitchen. There's a fellow down there now, come with the messengers. This new duchess—duchess, God save us!—gave my lord a love-potion she got from a witch; common knowledge he says. And this potion has made my lord sick.'

'But not too sick to marry. Talk no more to me of witchcraft! What need of witchcraft, she with her secret eyes and her full breasts and her narrow waist, she with her willing body ...' and my mother's knife had cut deep, 'her fruitful body!'

But there was more to this marriage with a low slut than a fruitful body, or love-potions, either. I knew that well! Enjoy her he might; but marry in the dunghill unless Bedford gave him the nod—never! He would not dare. And why should royal Bedford give him the nod?

And suddenly I had my answer.

It was to make sure that Gloucester would never return to me, never think again to possess the fine lands that were mine, never cross swords with Philip on my account. It was to mend England's sick friendship with Burgundy.

Yes, Bedford would be satisfied! I must have spoken aloud, for Beatrix said at once, 'Whoever is satisfied, the common folk are not! There's yet another tale the fellow tells. The Londoners are angry with their *good duke*. They are hot against him for his treatment of you.'

'It's overlate for anger now!' I said bitter.

'It's well to know that good folk hold by your honour. The fellow has a tale; he swears by Christ it's true. The women from some market near St Paul's, decent women of good repute, marched to Westminster. They besought the English Parliament to command the Duke of Gloucester to put his whore away and take his own true wife again. A scandal to his honour, they said, harmful to the holy state of matrimony, and injurious to the State to keep by him a woman of ill-fame.'

'When honour falls from the hands of those in high places,' I said, 'then it is for the humble to pick it up and, like a jewel, cherish it.'

XXXI

My love, my inheritance, my honour lost; all lost. And I was penniless.

From Delft, that sweet town once my own, Philip, with loving words, invited me to visit him that we might discuss a truce. Well, why not? He was my enemy; but had he worked me more harm than Gloucester, my lover, my husband and my friend? Let Philip have his way. How could one poor young woman stand against the might, the wealth of Burgundy? My stronghold Gouda, beleaguered as it was, had become my prison. Let me make an end. Finished the weariness and the fear, finished the pain and the bloodshed. Finished everything!

It would have been courteous for him to come to me. For all his fine manners he could not show a conqueror's grace.

There was nothing to complain of in my reception—on the face of it. It was like the old days of the Joyous Entry—so you might think. But the banners and the garlands were not for me; nor the flowers looped high over the canals and reflecting bright garlands in the green water; nor the little boats at night all lit with lanterns that the dark water sent back again; nor the singing nor the cheering. They were for Philip; all for Philip. It needed no signature of mine to make him master here in Delft.

And master he was. Gone was the coldness to me, the hostility; he was smiling and gracious, free and friendly. I liked him better the old way; the old way was safer.

I took the first bitter step. Beneath his smiling eyes I signed the short truce. Three weeks' breathing space; three weeks to consider the treaty he had already drafted, the final treaty ending all.

Three weeks. And every day heavy with its burden of thought; and every hour flying by, lost beyond recall ... every hour to the last hour.

I sat pen in hand. No need to read the papers now; for three weeks, with de Montfort and with Grenier, I had agonized over each word.

Now, sitting here, it was as though this moment concerned some other woman and not myself, some long-dead Countess of Holland, of Zealand and of Hainault, of Friesland and its islands. Yes, every title wrote fair. Philip would recognize them now, Philip my own personal guardian and governor of all my lands. My signature would make him both. And without my signature? He would be *Ruward* and *Mambour* still. Already dispossessed, I could no longer allow my country to bleed in a useless struggle.

I lifted my hand to sign.

I, *Jacqueline* ... And it was no longer some woman dead and gone. It was myself, I ... I ... I.

I put down the pen, biting my lips upon the pain. I would not let Philip see my pain, God damn him!

My lips I could discipline but not my eyes. He turned smiling towards me; he said catlike and soft, 'Cousin, there's no tragedy here. Your guardian and governor I am; but only till you choose to marry.'

In that moment I hated him more than I had hated anyone in all my life; more than his father, or my uncle of Bavaria; more even than Gloucester that had made me the shame of Christendom. For, *Who would take you all battle-scarred, naked of inheritance, and your honour stained?* his smiling eyes asked.

He was taking no chances. He had guarded against that miracle, if God should see fit to show it to me. For I must not marry without his permission; it was writ clear in the treaty. And if I did? By that very act I set my people free of all obedience to me. And to whom must they give obedience then?

Obedience to Philip Duke of Burgundy. Philip guardian and governor of me and my lands. Philip, Philip, Philip!

And, sitting there, blood from my lips, salt upon my tongue I remembered, as how often these ten years—my father's dying wish. Twice I had disobeyed; once persuaded by crafty tongues, once by my own foolish heart. There would be no third chance.

No more marriage for me. He would always forbid it.

He had me both ways. If I obeyed his *No* then he remained my guardian and governor of all my lands until I died. If I disobeyed I was at once dispossessed, and he take my crown not as guardian nor governor but in his own right.

I kept my eyes down upon the papers that he might not read the hatred in my eyes.

I was to be robbed not only of my lands and every right to rule, but of the best part of my revenues, also. Bare-faced robbery on Philip's part was no new thing; yet I had thought some Christian shame might restrain him now. But Philip knew no such weakness. Two thirds of all my revenues he thought needful to pay 'old debts'. Whose debts—his or mine? What of old friends that had beggared themselves for me—like old Sevenbergen destitute in a foreign land? Would some of the money go to them, or into Philip's own pockets? As for the remaining third, it was to be halved between him and me.

Of all my father's wealth, one sixth only, to meet all my needs. How should I pay back even a tithe to those that had given everything for me? I could not think Philip's notion of 'old debts' would reach so far. And what of my houses? How to keep them up, not in state, but in bare wood and stone? Some of them were badly in need of repair. And what of my own household, however humble? Where find wages for a steward, a cook, a serving-man, a tiring-woman? Even my faithful Beatrix must eat! And how keep myself in shoe-leather however coarse, in clothes however plain, in bread-and-cheese if nothing else?

And still I kept my eyes upon the document with its long-stretching clauses; and each one giving power to Philip. Power to nominate six members of every council in all my countships. Six out of every nine! Lickspittle to pass or veto every act at his nod. Power to Philip over every soul in my lands, rich and poor, gentle and simple; power over me that was now the poorest ... power over me.

And so I came to the last clause of all, so simple-seeming, so innocent, so right! The names *Hook* and *Cod* to be abolished under threat of direst punishment. Clever Philip! He had sucked every advantage from those quarrels, had hoisted himself into power over the dead bodies of Cods and Hooks. Now he would proclaim the common good–and suck advantage out of that, too! He would take no chance of a Hook rising in my favour. Clever, clever Philip!

It spelt the end of me, that last clause.

I took up the pen. I signed my name. Philip lifted the Bible towards me, and, hand upon it, I swore to keep my oath; swore at his command, by God and by Christ and by His Mother, swore by my Christian faith and my honour as a prince.

And God did not lean from his heaven to strike the man that

bade me call upon His Name, even while he robbed the widow and the orphan.

It was later that same day when a knock fell upon my door, and before I could say *Yea* or *Nay*, Philip was in my chamber, a paper rolled within his hand.

'You may stay, mistress,' he told Beatrix and it was a command. 'But first summon Master Grenier.'

So he had not finished with me even yet! What more had I to give?

He left me in no doubt.

'Cousin,' he said, 'you have neither husband nor child. Should you die, your heir unnamed, there would be war and ruin to your land and people. You must name your heir and name him now.'

I said, holding myself quiet that he might not see my anger and fear, 'You go too fast, Cousin Philip. I am not so old nor yet so ill-favoured that I cannot find me a husband and beget a child.'

'Still you should make all safe!' And his smile reminded me that without his *Yea*, there could be no marriage.

'And whom shall I name?' I asked and my smile matched his.

His bow answered mockery with mockery.

I turned my back on him and went over to the window. I should have expected it, this last demand; it was the reasoned outcome of his every act. But, I had thought that after this morning, he would leave me awhile to lick my wounds.

And now he was here with his new subtle, this outrageous demand! Philip, my heir! Philip to rule not as governor, accepted by me only until I could gather my strength again, but in his own right—the heir's right—given to him by my own hand. What would become of my country? And what would become of me? Help me, sweet Mother of God. Blessed St James intercede for me!

But the air was quiet between us.

Beatrix and Grenier came in together.

Philip said, 'You are to witness your lady's signature,' and smiled into their startled faces.

Grenier would have taken up the paper but Philip covered it with an impatient hand. 'It is enough that you witness her signature. Let no man say the thing was done by force.'

Their faces swung towards me and I nodded. They came and stood one each side of me and I signed ... and they after me.

When he had bowed himself out, I picked up my seal and stood staring at it. Virgin with child ... woman with child. But for me, there would be no child ever—Philip would see to it! I was but twenty-six; but already we reckoned both of us on my death and childless dying. Anguish fell upon me that I, myself, had made Philip my heir; that I had given my people to the heel of the conqueror.

And now, having performed my tricks to the satisfaction of my master, I was to receive my sweetmeat—Philip's grace and favour; a sweetmeat enclosing a bitter pill. But the full bitterness I did not taste until Philip went to take homage of my cities. Then, then, I truly understood the full extent of my loss.

It was August when we made our progress in royal state, and, to make things more palatable to those that were still loyal to me, he carried my mother with us. She had not been hard to persuade to the winning side. So there she was, riding along with us, cozening the people with her nods and smiles to believe me willing for this new, hateful order of things.

Philip rode, armour laid aside, all supple elegance in cloth-of-gold. The proud head and the long narrow face with its green-blue eyes smiling beneath fine arched brows; and the obstinate chin masking itself in smiles—though all his smiling could not hide the harshness of that narrow upper lip. Philip handsome and gallant—the darling of women's eyes. And my mother, equal in arrogance if not in beauty; with her nods and her smiles and her gracious unbending, she might have been his mother rather than mine. And I, too, in the blue and gold gown made, alas, for a quite other occasion, bending and bowing by Philip's command that I might not spoil the show nor let the people see to what state he had reduced me.

Obedient I rode by his side, walked by his side. I bowed when it was proper, gave my hand to be kissed when it was proper and smiled when it was proper ... when it was not proper. Smiling even when the oath was sworn to Philip—the oath of my own people, the pledge to stand with him against all who questioned these new rights of his—to stand with him even against me.

August dragged on. A month I shall remember, even dying, I think. Riding in the heat and the dust; dust upon my shoes and upon my head and upon my heart.

The army England had promised did not come. And, though I gave up hope, I still prayed, beseeching God that it might yet appear and carry me where no eye could see my smiling shame. In England there would be humiliation enough, dispossessed as I was; and cast off by the man I must call my husband no more—a beggar alike in lands as in love. But I need not ride in the public gaze; I need no longer smile and smile. To hide alone with my grief; I asked no more of life.

August moved into September heat. Nothing stirred in Hainault except dust in the wind; and, in my heart, nothing but dust, also.

Mid-September. And I was in Mons again. Mons most beloved of cities, most treacherous of cities. But now it was neither one nor the other; it was an alien city; that and nothing more.

In St Waltrude's church where, I, a girl, had taken homage to myself alone; and where Gloucester, standing at my side, had received the obedience of the city—a gift of love from me—Mons offered its obedience to my cousin. For me the empty form of homage, the scanted courtesy; for Philip the true, full homage due to my governor, my guardian and my heir.

And how gladly did they give it, weary of the bloodshed, ejoicing in the strong shelter of his shield!

And I endured it; I endured it all. Only Beatrix, undressing me at night, laying aside the empty crown, knew my exhaustion and my empty heart. Exhaustion was the one mercy heaven showed me then; else I must have destroyed the high ceremony, crying to heaven my useless denial. But, numb with my weariness, I moved with a quiet that deceived even my friends.

And so from city to city. High pomp of the swearing of the oath, procession and progress, feasts and fêtes. Month after month until winter shut down upon my land ... and upon my heart.

But even now Philip had not done with me; nor would be done until the last tatter of seeming-power had been dragged from me.

Out of every nine councillors he had the right to name six; I, to name three. Smiling and friendly, he waited to snatch even that shadow of power from me. He had not long to wait.

I was desperately poor—he had seen to it. My wretched allowance was not enough to remember even in scantest recompense the half of those that had beggared themselves in my cause. I was pricked with guilt when I thought of them—rich men reduced to poverty, poor folk lacking the horse they had lent, or the bit of silver in a pot—all enduring hardships for my sake. Something must be done and at once.

When I opened my mind to de Bye, my faithful steward cried out that I had given enough already—enough and enough! My purse was empty.

'Then it must be filled again!' I said.

'Gold is not picked from every dunghill,' he answered, severe.

'It might be picked from Cousin Heir's dunghill. I think I could come to some arrangement. Let him keep my revenues, every penny; he has the best part already. I know not from one day to another what is due or whether he returns a true account. Yes, let him keep it all, if he will give me a fixed sum in exchange. Oh I know very well,' and I silenced de Bye's protest, 'he won't give me fair value knowing me hard-pressed, but I would sell my revenues for ... yes, for twenty thousand crowns a year.'

He threw up his hands. 'That beggarly sum! For you, Madam, hereditary prince of three lands.'

'It's as well someone remembers it ... though much good it has brought me! Twenty thousand's a beggarly sum. All the more reason to hope I'll squeeze it out of him. I could manage on it—we live simply enough. With twenty thousand crowns' steady income, I could begin to pay my debts; and what I could not pay, I could promise, yes and keep my word. It would at least be a beginning.'

'It would be the end. Hasn't Burgundy taken enough that you must give him more? For every guilder he gives—though it be your own—he'll press the last hairsbreadth of advantage to weigh against you in the end.'

'The unpaid debt weighs harder. How shall I live before God, keeping even the poorest state—and nothing in my purse left for its true purpose? No, money I must have!'

I sent for Philip and he came all smiles; he could afford to smile!

'Dear beloved cousin,' he said, 'you are wise! A pretty woman should not live from hand to mouth, nor rack her charming head—' and he smiled into my worn face, 'to know where the next guilder may come from. Certainly you shall have your income ... if you will be reasonable!' And he proceeded to abate me by one half. Ten thousand; he was not ashamed to name it! Thence crawling upward by unwilling stages ... eleven, twelve, thirteen to sixteen thousand; and higher than that he would not go. Had I looked carefree, he had not dared. But I was hard-pressed and I was anxious; and I have never been one to wear a mask.

But even then he was not finished.

The money I should have, paid each quarter-day without fail; but I must give up my right to name my three councillors.

The pill was bitter and unexpected; but, after all the bitterness I had swallowed from his hands, little enough! Besides, what would my three councillors avail against his six?

And now having bated me down and robbed me of even the smallest finger-stirring in my own pot, he could afford to be generous.

'Out of my own pocket I will keep your houses in good repair,' he said. But he did not add that he himself would be using such of my houses as pleased him.

He bent over my hand in farewell. 'Dear cousin,' he said, 'I have a gift for you and I give it with a glad heart. You have always had great joy in the chase; and so I give you freedom to hunt wheresoever you choose, be it Holland or Hainault, or Zealand. Every corner of these lands is free for your pleasure.'

I looked at him, seeing his crafty thought clear as a pebble in a clear stream. He meant to catch me by my pleasures, so that I might forget the struggle and my lost rights.

'I thank you, cousin,' I said. And then, since my bitterness must out, 'Our Lord was sold for less ... a good deal less.'

He gave me his dark smile and was gone. Beatrix came from the inner room all white with her anger.

'The new coins!' And she flung a guilder upon the table.

I nodded—it was no news to me. I picked up the coin and looked upon Philip's face side-by-side with my own. Philip's head upon my country's coins! That silent head spoke louder than any voice.

'How long before one picture disappears altogether, how long?' And she beat her hands together. I did not answer; I sat spinning the coin with idle fingers.

'Like any cuckoo he's pushed you from your nest!' she cried out. 'And now he's feathered it well, he can afford to show himself kind. Everywhere smiling, everywhere courteous, everywhere generous. And the people run to let themselves be cheated! But let them beware! Let them displease him, be it never so little, and they'll see. They'll see the mailed fist, and the dead rotting in the streets, and the harvest fields running in blood.'

'God forbid!' I said. 'For the guilt is mine, mine, too. I failed. And the land that was mine is lost to the foreigner.'

'It's oversoon to speak of failure,' she said very quick. 'Dear, dearest Jacque, you're young and your spirit is great. And the people will not tolerate the foreign yoke for long. You will see!'

I saw, I saw.

I saw my country so quiet that Philip could return to France; the tide was flowing more strong than ever to the Dauphin that honest men called the King. And the English were desperate. In the streets of my cities men went steady about their business; in the field they sowed and harvested as though no foreigner held a free people within his grip.

Peace and prosperity, how long would it last?

As long as my cousin chose—and no more. The hand that seemed to shield them now, would brandish the whip and the sword.

I saw now, walking the woods of Hainault, that I had thrown away my last rights for a few miserable crowns. When I sold my rights to name any councillor within my realms, I had sold my country's last hope. I saw it now; now that it was too late.

'I should have gone on fighting to the end!' I told Beatrix. 'Who can say when the battle will turn and God give the victory? I've been a coward and a fool!'

She would have spoken then, given me some comfort, but I was in no mood to be smoothed with kindness.

'There's a girl in France,' I said, 'very ignorant and poor. But she is rich in the grace of God; and all France is her inheritance. She will have no friendly speech with thieves that would steal it. She would lose life itself rather than her inheritance.'

Beatrix looked at, me. 'You mean ...? Oh no you cannot mean the girl from Lorraine, the one they call Joan! Not the strumpet that goes about with soldiers!'

'So a man said of me once. But I was a prince; and so he died for it!'

'And deserved to die. As for the wench that goes about like a man shameless ...'

'Had I done the same no man had picked me out to call me strumpet. A young man would not have died and I lost a fine city ... no, nor my cause, neither.'

She shrugged away such nonsense. 'We talk now not of the past but the present; not of a dead young man but of a living woman—the French witch. Witch they call her, and no wonder! To get the French to fight at all, let alone to win victories, to get that miserable King of theirs crowned—it reeks of witchcraft!'

'Or of miracles. She carries Christ upon her banner. Had I shown myself worthy, God, maybe, had worked a miracle of me.'

'You blame yourself overmuch,' she said. 'You find excuses for that girl because your heart is kind.'

'Kind?' I said. 'That girl's my living conscience. She is all I should be and am not. She goes on fighting; I laid down my arms. She has no truck with the enemy; I bartered and sold my people. She sees nothing but the cause; I was distracted and blind. My living conscience with a vengeance. I pray night and day for her safety.'

'Then you'd best pray hard. For if she's caught to the fire she shall go. Your cousin of Burgundy has sworn it.'

I felt my flesh shrink as though the fire waited for me also. There was a bond between the girl and me—the bond of leaders in a just cause. But she was steadfast and I had failed.

'Saint or witch to the fire she must come,' Beatrix said again; and she said it with no regret. I found it strange in so gentle a creature. 'If she's a witch then good Christians should rejoice. And if she's a saint, why then she knows her end. She will not shrink from the fire; and God will take her to His Bosom.'

'Before that same God you are too easy, delivering the body of another to the fire!'

'If it be to uphold God's laws then it is right; and if the church allows it, dare anyone of us deny that right? Jacque, Jacque, beware how you speak. You are half a heretic—God forfend; or so it seems!'

'Then I shall be out of favour with God as well as with my good Hainaulters. Here, in my own city, the people are weary of me. Or, maybe Philip has said the word—I would rather think it! I am to be sent packing.'

She stared; she could not speak; it was as though she did not understand and I could not blame her.

I nodded. 'Yes, it's true. Mons, my own city, turns me out. I cost too much! I am to have six thousand pounds—minted in England, mark you!—to take myself hence like a bad servant the good master pays in full.'

'May God blast Philip of Burgundy!' she said; and she said it gently as though she prayed. 'To send you from your own town! What would your father have said?' And she did not lift a hand to wipe the tear that ran down her cheeks.

'His sword would have spoken for him. But Philip has clipped me, wings and claw; and I can neither fight nor fly. So it's the cage for me; a fine cage gilded to the tune of six thousand English pounds. And it is wide. I am free of my three courtships—if they don't follow Mons and turn me out. We leave for Holland within three days. Bid them pack everything; there isn't much! Oh Beatrix, Beatrix, I have loved this town above all earthly places ... and I shall come back no more.'

XXXII

The Hague received me with courtesy—and nothing more I was a visiting prince; I was no longer their lady.

It was hurtful to be so treated in the house where I was born, in whose gardens I had played—the Child of Holland.

My friends came to see me. Old van Brederode, old indeed now, stiff and frail from his Leyden prison; and the de Montforts; and my bastard brothers. They were admitted with the barest of courtesies. We would sit talking of the past and thinking of the future—the hopeless future; and they would get up to go. Soon they stopped coming.

Now that there was no state business for my attention, no more fights and stratagems, I found time heavy upon my hands. Needlework is a pastime for which I have never cared, nor to read overmuch; and to hunt I had not the heart. But there was a thing I could do—I could set about paying my debts.

Again de Bye shook his warning head. 'Madam, think well before you throw good money after bad! You have all-but beggared yourself.'

'I have given here and there, thoughtless, as is my way!' I told him. 'Now is the time for thought. I have been thinking one should give not only to those that have done a great kindness but to those that have done no kindness at all. We should give, maybe, not in return for service received, but a freewill offering. As for my poverty; not I, but my cousin of Burgundy beggars me. So, like any beggar—I shall beg!'

And when he lifted his puzzled brows, I said, 'I am not ashamed to beg for God's poor.' And then I said, 'I remember Valenciennes; it sheltered me all unknowing when I fled into England. And, though it afterwards shut its gates upon me, yet I remember that unwitting kindness. J shall build a hospital there. Yes, a hospital! Never stand there gaping, old friend. Fetch me Grenier; I shall need you both.'

And so the plans for my hospital grew. St Jacque it should be called, after my patron saint. I was content that it should be small; yet the modest sums we set down grew at an alarming rate. Grenier and de

Bye were alarmed and begged me to put the project by; but I would not listen. God would help His poor.

And now, thinking of others and their needs, I could not be satisfied doing this one thing to the Glory of God. There were so many in need of comfort and of help.

I had seen—and still do see—poor scholars eating their hearts out that they can get no learning. I must find money to admit such, if only a few, to the university. And then there was the church I had built to my father's memory; if it was to fulfil its purpose there must be endowments; even priests must live!

And there were other plans dear to my heart; but, as the list grew, one project after another must be set aside for happier days. But my three darling charities remained—the hospital, the church, the university. When de Bye or Grenier would have struck one of these from the list I thrust my fingers into my ears and would not listen. 'I told you I am not ashamed to beg; I shall get the money somehow. Those that would refuse me will not refuse God.'

So Grenier and I wrote our letters—to Mons, to Valenciennes, to Rotterdam and Amsterdam, to Utrecht and Haarlem and Delft and to all the cities that had been mine. And some were generous and some were mean and some ignored me; but there was sufficient to make a beginning upon my hospital, to help a student here and there, to provide masses for my father's soul. And, the supply, though it might be small, never failed. God did not abandon His Work.

As the walls of my hospital grew, as some student came to thank me that he had got his chance, I was just that little bit less unhappy. If my life could bring no more happiness to myself, it could yet bring happiness to others. But there were yet times when I would wander restless, remembering how my life had been laid waste. For the truth is, a nature like mine, ardent and impulsive, cannot live on the happiness doled out to others. I was twenty-nine; no longer young as women go. Like many another I had been put into the bridebed at fourteen; and the years thereafter had not been kind. Now, all worn with my sorrows and very poor, it was unlikely that any man should seek to cherish me. But in spite of that, my body's rhythm shouted a different tune. Surely something was left that a man might love. But ... love! What love had I known even when I was young and comely?

'Beatrix,' I said one day when, more restless than usual I could endure neither to sit nor stand, 'I was accounted a beauty once; yet what man ever cherished me as a man cherishes a woman? I have been thrice married—to a child; to a fool; to a knave.'

'The child loved you,' she said.

'As a child, not a man. With the fool I knew the rubs of dirty living.'

'The seeds of corruption were in that marriage before ever you saw each other's face.'

'And with the third marriage—scandal and shame. But Gloucester loved me, if only for a little while. And though he shamed me in the eyes of Christendom, yet there was glory, too. For the love I once had of him, I thank God.'

'Are you so beaten, Jacque, that you can thank God to be a man's leavings?'

'Look at me! And answer that question for yourself.'

'Beauty goes quickly over—and a wise man knows it,' she said. 'But the gifts of the heart—'

'Much men care for that!'

'More than you think! Yet if it were not so. You are worn to the bones; but they are good bones. And the eyes, if they will smile a little, are good. And the mouth is good. A little happiness, a little care for your looks and a great deal of rest ...'

'And shall I be beautiful again? *So beautiful a lady* ... he said that the young man from Hoorn. Are those words on which a man should hang?'

'There were other words,' she said. 'One other word. Have you forgotten? Besides, the thing is done and you have paid for it!'

'And will that bring him back to life? Oh Beatrix, he was little more than a boy. *So beautiful a lady...* How strange! The words for which he died have become a precious balm.'

I could no longer stay at the Hague. I had not been happy there, but coldness alone would not have driven me out. I would have stayed—had I been able; but I was not able. I could not support the upkeep of so great a house. I had given with both hands, not only all I had begged and borrowed, but from my own purse also. Now that purse was empty. More than once my steward had warned me to pay out no more, or to wait, at least, until my allowance fell due; but I had not listened.

Now he stood before me again. 'I have nothing left. Sour looks behind our back have turned to sour looks before our face. We must go to some smaller house until your allowance is paid again. And even then we must count our pence. Madam, we are very much in debt.'

Pride must give way to necessity. Within the week we were settled in Zealand where I have a small hunting-seat; Ostende it is called. It lies inland where the air is salt still from the sea; and the nearest town is Goes. My father had built the house and he had loved the town; indeed, he had given Goes its first charter. There had always been kindness between Goes and our house; and this kindness was the breath of life to me after the coldness at the Hague. Here in the house my father had built I felt something of his spirit linger. It was as though I had come home.

My spirits were often low, but I was happier here than I had been at the Hague or at Mons, for the people of Goes showed their love plainly. At first Goes would have shown me royal ceremony, but it was not fitting, I thought, to my present state. And soon they got used to seeing me ride through the little town with only de Bye or Grenier in attendance; or come into church my two women behind me and no barrier at all between them and their prince. The kindness of the common people. I had never felt it so warm, so close. My pinched heart began to open, to blossom again. Truly I had come home.

Dear Goes. Much of the little happiness I have ever known came from within your walls. I remember how, all unasked—out of love certainly and perhaps because my poverty was clear enough—you sent me a box of gold pieces. Six hundred gold pieces. A very great sum indeed. But it was soon gone—and I shabby as ever; for I cannot keep money by me when there are those with a better right to it.

I was slowly settling down to a quiet not unhappy existence. But it was hard to forget what I had been—and was no more. And, moreover, I was constantly dragged back by the mention of a name; the name of my old, my bitter enemy.

I suppose it was to be expected. Frank van Borselen lived a few miles away at St Martensdijk castle. That he was a comely man in his cold Dutch way, I had seen for myself. But that he was also a kind man, and generous was a thing I refused to believe. How could I believe anything good of van Borselenfriend and lackey to my cousin Philip, captain to Philip, Stadtholder and deputy to Philip? He had thrown all the weight of his influence against me when my father died. He could—had he desired it—have brought the Cods to my side. He might have married me, had he chosen, but he did not choose; and the bluntness of his refusal was not the least of his slights. He had chosen, at all times, to set his strength against an untried girl. Save for Philip himself, he was the first of my enemies.

Yet even so I could not escape hearing—overhearing is the better word—praise of the man; he was much loved in Goes. It was Beatrix who first took it upon herself to name him to me in my own house.

'I saw him in Goes this morning. They call him proud. But there he was walking about on two legs like any other man—and handsome legs they were!'

If I ignored her speech she ignored my silence.

'Wherever he went,' she continued, 'bonnets swept the ground. Curtseys and smiles everywhere! And not because he's a great lord but because he's a good one—so they say!'

'Is that so?' And I was goaded that she spoke so of him that was her enemy as well as mine. 'He was one of the judges that sentenced your Jan to death ... Jan whose legs were broken. Or have you forgotten that in view of the handsome legs you saw this morning?'

I was taken with shame before ever the words were out—I have a hateful tongue when I am angered. I put out a hand towards her; she moved gently but certainly away.

'I forget nothing,' she said. 'It was a bitter judgment but a true one.' She said no more but busied herself about my gowns; so poor they were, so few. They needed her constant attention.

She sat herself upon a stool and took up her needle. I saw how slow she was, how fumbling, so that the thread could not find the hole and I knew her eyes were blind with tears. She sewed in silence; then, lest I should grieve, I that had wounded her with my cruel taunt, she said, 'Your father liked to see you fine—and you but a child! He would weep could he see this!' And she held up the gown so that the light came through where the stuff had worn thin.

He would weep for my ungrateful tongue and I with him! I must not say that; it would grieve her yet further. I said, 'My gowns are not worth a single tear—his or yours. Who is there to see? I grieve, though, that my friends go poorer because of me. I have bad dreams because of it.'

'You have done what you could; and more, more! There's no man alive—not even your greatest enemy—can call you a mean spirit.'

'God forbid they should! And yet, I take such dreams to be a sort of warning. I am afraid, Beatrix ... I am very much afraid. One day there'll be a service done and payment to be made. No one will press me but I shall be disgraced ... disgraced and shamed.'

'You fret too much! Well, here's the darn finished, though how long the stuff will hold it, goodness knows. Heaven send you a new gown soon!'

Whatever my enemies might say they could not say I fattened on the poverty of my friends. Life was pared to the bone at Ostende. Our food was simple and there was not overmuch; my gowns were mended and faded, even the blue-and-gold, ordered with so much joy at Gouda, had suffered in the dust of that weary progress. I would laugh, sometimes, twirling about to catch sight of the latest darn, I that had been a great heiress in Christendom ... but sometimes I did not laugh. I had grown thin these days; my gowns hung loose so that Beatrix was forced to take them in at the seams. And at night I would cough a little so that I was disturbed in my sleeping. It was the damp air blowing from the sea, or the lack of fires since we must conserve our wood. But September was all-but passed; soon we should light our fires, and, if the cough was tiresome still, I would send for a physician—though I was loth to do that; it would make too deep a hole in my pocket. I, that was a hearty spender, now sought for new ways to save this and that, though the value be little more than a pin's head. For the fear was constant with me—some service rendered and my hands be empty.

My evil dreams had caught up with me. The thing I had feared fell upon me.

I was sitting within my chamber with Beatrix, I was thinking that for all the sunshine this fine morning, the air was sharp and though we were not quite into October we must light our fires, when there came the sharp jangle of the outer bell and then the beat of hooves upon the cobbles of my courtyard. Presently de Bye stood before me; my mother had sent two gentlemen to enquire of my health. I was glad of this gesture on the part of my mother. She had played me false many a time; but she was my mother ... and I very much alone in the world.

One of the gentlemen carried a small parcel wrapped about with linen and heavily sealed. When I had greeted them and enquired after my mother—whom nothing ever ailed—Beatrix took them away for meat and drink. And, though I welcomed this break of the outer world into the isolation of my little house, yet I hoped they would not make too long a stay; feeding them and their servants, we were likely to go short many a day.

When they were gone I sat alone looking at my parcel. I am, as a rule, much pleased when a present arrives—especially if it be unexpected; and at Ostende that happened so seldom. And yet I was unwilling to open my parcel. I had, indeed, to force myself to the task. At last I cut the seals and spread out the linen.

The moment was upon me; the moment of my fear.

And yet any woman must have delighted in the little heap of sparkling gems. I took up my mother's letter. Since I lacked jewels she wrote—and did not mention who had stripped me—and because these ornaments must come to me some day, she sent them that I might have the pleasure of wearing them now.

Pleasure! The precious stones winked spitefully at me. It was clear she did not know the full measure of my poverty. Had she done so she would not have sent the jewels at all; or she would have enclosed the money with which to thank her gentlemen. For to reward such messengers in proportion to the gift is a custom and an obligation and a courtesy.

So there I sat, the gems pushed from me and not daring to look at them, as though the very glance at them dishonoured me. I am a woman, like any other, and dearly love a fine jewel. Had my circumstances been happier I should at once have tried on a brooch or a ring. Now it seemed wrong to touch them.

Beatrix, returning alone, found me sitting, head in my hands.

'My dream has caught up with me!' I said and pushed the jewels yet further from me.

She leaned over, frowning, picked up a ring and put it upon my thumb. It lay upon my hand like blood.

'It is right you should have a jewel or so!' she said. 'William de Bye must find a way out of this!'

'You cannot squeeze blood from a stone,' I said and put the ring from my hand.

My steward came in wearing his thin look. These sparkling vanities were not worth the heartache of these faithful friends. Yet keep them or no, the jewels had been brought, the messengers must be rewarded.

Beatrix sent de Bye a dark glance. 'The shame is certainly yours!' she said.

He nodded taking it upon his own shoulders. 'My lady's allowance is not due for a full two month. The gentlemen must return home long before then—and, indeed, we have not food for them.'

'We must send them back satisfied as soon as may be!' I cried out. 'But—*how?* How?'

'My lady has friends,' Beatrix said.

De Bye said nothing.

'The Lord of Brederode?' she asked.

He shook his head. 'Neither he nor his son; nor any of their house.

Oh, they would give and give gladly. But their purse is empty as my lady's here.'

'The Lord of Montfort?' she persisted. 'Of all friends the dearest.' Again he shook his head.

'Like all my friends, beggared in my service!' and I bowed my head.

'No!' de Bye cried out; and it was as though anger burst from him against his will. 'The Lord of Montfort has paid himself well! He's laid hands on such of your father's treasure as he could come by. You made him Stadtholder of Holland—who should refuse him? You must count no more on his kindness.'

'No!' I said and my voice came out in a whisper. 'I cannot nor will I believe it. Think shame to say such a thing!'

'Yet it is true.' And he was humble as though he himself were at fault. 'Madam, I asked the Lord of Montfort once before—he has the means; and the answer was *No!* Let not my lady grieve overmuch; let her remember instead that as long as there was need he was most faithful to her cause.'

I gave no sign lest I betray myself with tears. I would have staked my life on de Montfort's love. Here was a wounding that went deep.

'There are others!' Beatrix shrugged. 'The Lord of Wassenaar—'

'Not he,' de Bye said quickly—'though he, too, have the means; and there are plenty like him. Men—and good men—will lay down their life but not their gold. Gold. I have seen it eat into a man's honour like acid.'

'It is easier to die than to go hungry!' I said.

De Bye said, 'To ask a friend and be refused, is to lose that friend.'

'For myself I would rather ask an enemy,' Beatrix said; she sent de Bye a glance. I had the strange feeling that they had rehearsed this conversation.

'My friends have refused,' I said; and it seemed to me so great a wonder that I must say it again. 'My friends have refused—and you talk of help from an enemy. Such things happen only in old tales.'

'And if an enemy should help?' he asked.

'Then you may take him at his word!' And I laughed. De Bye bowed himself out.

I sat restless within my chamber, not able to leave it for shame of facing those gentlemen I must send away empty-handed. Well, at least they should have a good supper—though feast day for them turn to fast day for me!

And now, with time hanging heavy upon me, I found myself
pricked by the memory of that glance Beatrix had exchanged with
my steward; the words of our speech together came back to me. *If
an enemy should help?* And my answer, *Then you may take him at his
word.*

But I had laughed; surely de Bye must have known I spoke in jest.
Now it seemed no joking matter. De Bye had meant it! *He had meant
it.* But whom, in heaven's name, had he in mind?

There could be but one answer; an answer so shameful I could
not name it. No! It could not be possible for my faithful friend to
heap such shame upon me.

'Beatrix!' Her name called sharp and loud brought her hurrying.
'The enemy of whom de Bye spoke it was a real person?'

She nodded. 'But you knew!' Her voice faltered, 'Surely you
knew!'

'I know now,' I said, quiet and bitter. 'Have you lost your wits, both
of you, to shame me before van Borselen?'

'There's no shame!' she said. 'A good man the Lord of Borselen
and no meanness in him.'

'A man need not be mean to refuse his enemy. But to help me, he
must be beyond words generous.'

'The Lord Frank is beyond words generous—when the heart moves
him. It has moved him, de Bye says, towards a most brave lady.'

I said, very slowly, 'De Bye is mad to think of such a thing, and
you, also. In your right minds you would not dare!'

'We would dare very much to ease your heart,' she said. 'Your
friends have been asked and they have refused. Lord Frank will not
refuse.'

'*I* refuse!' I cried out. 'I *refuse*! Between you, you have given my
enemy one more cause for laughter.'

She said, 'Let an enemy do a kindness and we turn him to a
friend.'

'You are mad—de Bye and you together! My father's enemy
and mine! Van Borselen would not offer, nor I take, the hand of
Burgundy's lackey.'

'The Lord of Borselen is no man's lackey,' she said.

'Borselen, Borselen!' I cried out. 'Has he seduced you, too, with
his charms? I am sick to the heart of the sound of his name. He
poisons the air I breathe. You and de Bye have done me an ill turn
this day!'

The short October day wore on. Beatrix brought me the candles; we sat there in the half-gloom while the cheap tallow guttered and stank.

'You have shamed me—and all to no purpose!' I said at last. 'That most chivalrous gentleman, that most noble enemy has refused; and de Bye is afraid—and with reason—to come and tell me so.'

I went down to supper and sat smiling between my guests. It was an excellent supper, such as I had not tasted this long while; but it was wasted upon me, so hard it was to force each morsel down my gullet. Now I should not only have the shame of sending away my guests unrewarded; I should have the double shame of suing to my enemy and being refused.

I excused myself early and went back to my chamber.

Night had long fallen, that silent darkness in which no traveller cares to be abroad when, sitting in stony silence, Beatrix and I heard the sound of horses; and then, feet, eager upon the stairs.

It was de Bye all breathless with his haste. Beneath his arm he carried a casket and this casket he set upon the table. Then, kneeling, he offered me the key.

And all the time he said nothing; and I asked no question.

I took the key and my fingers trembled so that the key fell clattering and Beatrix picked it up. I nodded to her to open the box. She turned the key and lifted the lid.

The box was stuffed full with gold pieces.

De Bye said, very softly, 'The lord of Borselen bids me tell my lady to take what she needs and to stint nothing. Where this comes from, there is plenty more. And, if my lady should, at any time, find herself hard-pressed, he prays her of her gentleness to send to him again. For, he said, I count it an honour that she should ask this favour of me.'

I tried to speak and could not speak. It was not only because of this generous giving when all my friends had failed; it was because of that grace in giving that made the taking less hard.

I said, 'The Lord of Borselen has taught me a lesson this day!'

XXXIII

But what lesson?

The money accepted, the messengers departed, I had leisure to consider the matter. I had been mad to take money from my bitter enemy. Why had he offered it? And how should I look now in the eyes of my friends?

The grateful mood broke; distrust of the man came flooding back.

'Men like van Borselen don't give freely—and nothing in return!' I told Beatrix. 'What will he ask of me now?'

'You show yourself less generous than he!' she said.

'Should that surprise you? Two men swore to cherish me; and each thought of himself alone—Brabant and Gloucester! And others that swore to protect me—my uncles and my cousin Philip. What faith did these men keep with me, what kindness show? And this van Borselen. Why should he be better than they? What will he ask in return for his handful of gold? He's a man and I a woman; a woman with empty hands. There can be but one payment. And if he demand it, must I not pay, lest I shame myself further? When the Lord of Borselen sent his gold and when I took it, the bargain was made between us.'

She would have spoken then but I was in no mood to listen; I must rid myself of the bitterness that scalded within me.

'Oh you may well ask what honour's left to Gloucester's whore? And Gloucester's whore I am since I signed away my title as his wife. You will ask me, perhaps, what pleasure any man may get from this poor body of mine? And you may well ask, seeing I am close upon thirty and have lost my looks; and this man in the flower of his manhood, rich and handsome. What pleasure? To take his payment despising while he takes. To enjoy his enemy; to make me still further a laughing-stock in the eyes of Christendom. Desire is sweet; revenge, sweeter.

But she could not see beyond the fact that he had come to my aid. 'The Lord of Borselen is a noble gentleman,' she said.

'So now you excuse him for leaving what's not worth taking?'

'Nothing will satisfy you in this mood,' she said. 'I know you of old! It's the naughty child your mother commanded us to whip; but we never did. A pity now I see! Oh Jacque, you do yourself, no less than him, injustice. You're well enough for any man that likes a lady delicate and fine. You've lost the fat from off your bones and the roses from your cheeks. What then? The bones are good; and a lily colour becomes you. But all that's by the way! We talk now of a gentleman of honour. Consider! De Bye loves you as a father. If there were any question of such a payment, would that old man have let you accept the gold, much less suggest the thing himself?'

I said, 'Tongues have wagged too long about me; too long and too loud. Maybe I see evil where none is.'

She said, 'How they have hurt you! Don't let them hurt you any more, don't, Jacque! When they rob you of your faith in goodness, they rob you of your greatest treasure.'

'It's too late,' I said.

There was no word from Martensdijk and I tried to put the matter from my mind. But it was not easy. Beatrix was forever talking of van Borselen. A handsome gentleman—fair in our good Dutch fashion. And rich. Richer than many a prince! The right sort of gentleman—quick with his sword and slow with his tongue. A kind heart not to be worn upon the sleeve …

It was strange to hear her praising the man that had condemned her husband to a cruel death. Forgetful with age, I would tell myself. But it was not true and I knew it. She was old with sorrow not with years. She was one that grief frees from blindness; purged of all bitterness she saw life's pattern clear.

The days went on. Sometimes I would meet van Borselen face-to-face in Goes; and he would bow to me across the mare's neck, sweeping his bonnet the length of his arm. I would return his salutation but I would never smile. To me a smile is the small coin of friendship and for such friendship he had shown no desire. Nor, on my side, was I willing for him to think that friendship could be bought with a handful of gold.

Days lengthened into weeks. Not for all our salutations did the Lord of Borselen make a move towards acquaintance. And though I breathed freely that he asked nothing of me, still I was pricked. He despised me. He had given me gold as one might throw a bone to a dog. Brabant had hated me, Gloucester had deserted me; and this man despised me. What was I less than any other woman?

My mirror told me. A bag of bones. Useless the attempt to paint me into beauty. But, for all that, I called once more for the lotions, the powders, the oils and the paint. And Beatrix, seeing this new interest in my looks, went closely through my wardrobe. 'I might have saved myself the trouble!' She sighed deeply. 'A dreary, faded lot they are!'

'Still they must serve. My first charge is to those that have a claim upon me.'

'Then you are like to go threadbare for the rest of your life!' she answered, sour.

All through the fine autumn the Lord of Martensdijk and I would meet in Goes; and still I would take his smiling salute, and he my smileless answer. And now though my anger was not less that—beyond those first flowery words—he had shown no kindness with his gift, there crept into it something like regret for the coldness that lay between the man and me. I would not admit it—least of all to myself; yet it was not surprising. I was lonely and over at Martensdijk there was always good company.

Once the days had been overful of my affairs; now they were empty. I thought with longing of the music and the singing over at Martensdijk. And now with winter shut down upon us, and each day stretching empty and endless, I began to think of Gloucester again. I loved him no longer; passion had burned my heart out and nothing was left but the scar of that burning. But alone in the windswept house with no one to share the things I loved, I began to miss him—his wit, and the way he could tell a tale; and his delight in a new poem, a new picture, a new gown, even. I missed him more deeply than ever before in my life. He was my mind's need, not my body's—I was beyond that. It was not my love I wanted but my gay companion. Once I bade Beatrix bring me my books. But at the sight of the words his eyes had seen, and the notes his own hand had written, I bade her take them away.

Desolate and disconsolate, lacking the will to ride even the short distance to Goes along the frozen, rutted road, I sat within my house and read; but not in any book Gloucester had given me. And though it was a discourse I read that should have set my thoughts upon heaven, they flew instead across the few miles of frost-bound country that lay between me and Martensdijk ... Great fires in the hearth, savours of rich foods, musicians in the gallery, dancers in the hall. My house seemed lonely and comfortless as the grave.

Spring hung out her first banners—swelling of bud, pennons of catkin; my steward thought we should leave Ostende for a more comfortable house. There was Theilingen for instance; a good house and excellent hunting. But though Ostende lacked all comfort, I could not bring myself to leave it.

And now it was full spring. Along the bare branches of yesterday, leaves ran like green fire and birds sang as though their hearts must burst with joy. There was a cuckoo, I remember; I counted his call a hundred times, until, in the end, I gave up … and he still calling.

And after spring, summer; a summer I shall remember as long as I live—and that is not so long now. For in the early days of that summer I knew a great sorrow and a greater joy.

Sorrow came first. It was the death of the girl Joan in France. You may think it strange that I, who never saw her, should have felt so deep a grief. But there was a sisterhood between us, though she knew it not, stronger than any tie of blood. We had led our troops, she and I; had known the glory of the battle and the heart-break of defeat. We had seen our friends grow weary and leave us; the same hand had snared us both—the hand of my cousin Philip. They said she defied her church; and of me they said it also. But her cause was great and she came to her death in the fire. But I had little cause beyond the delights of the flesh … and I lived. And in that we were different. To me, all unworthy, God showed His kindness and brought me to my joy.

I have seen a butterfly or some such creature, come from its winter sleep. First there is a faint movement, hardly to be perceived; and then another and another, very faint and slow; and after that a quickening and a thrust into life. And so it was with me.

Goes was holding its archery festival and the good people pressed me to honour it by taking part. I did not need much pressing. I dearly love the sport; and the sweet summer was giving me back a little of my youth.

When I arrived on the ground, the overseer of the festival would have had me shoot first; but I had been delayed and would keep the archers no longer. I know well how disagreeable it is to wait before a contest, how the pulse flutters and the throat dries. I had arrived last, and last I would take my turn. It was, I suppose, a sort of pride in me.

The target was difficult, being set at an awkward angle; and, though all were skilled marksmen, few managed to score three hits out of five. And, as man after man took his place at the butts not one found the mark with four hits.

I remember the silence in which I took my turn. I think there was not one man or woman but wished me well—a douceur for my misfortunes.

I fitted the first arrow, and, as I bent the bow, I saw, head and shoulders above the others, the Lord of Borselen.

My hand trembled, the arrow flew, landed quivering … beyond the mark. The blood burned in my cheeks. He had seen me go wide of the mark! Now he could add another reason to his light opinion of me!

I gritted jaw against jaw. I longed to acquit myself well, as desperately as ever I longed on any field of battle.

I fitted the second arrow, sent it flying. I dared not look to see if it had found the mark. In silence I fitted the third, the fourth. I heard the indrawn breath of those that watched. I saw the amused eye of Frank van Borselen. I fitted the fifth arrow and the last. And still I dared not look. It was only when I heard the cheering that I dared raise my eyes.

Four arrows hung within the innermost ring.

So I, the uncrowned lady, was crowned Queen of the day.

And it was the Lord of Borselen that put the crown upon my head—the crown of laurel and spring flowers—he that should have set it upon it the crown of gold.

It was shortly after this that he made his first move. His servant knelt at my feet—and the stuff of his livery was finer than my best gown. My most humble servant the Lord van Borselen begged the honour of receiving Madam the Countess at Martensdijk castle.

I thanked his master, I said, and would send my answer soon. But even while he was bowing himself out, I was, like any child, hardly to be stopped from calling him back and naming the day. I, that had made my progresses and my Joyous Entries, was overcome at the prospect of visiting a man in his country estate—and that man cold to me. But when delights are rare the smallest pleasure shines bright.

De Bye rode over with my acceptance; and that done, my mind was at its old trick of seesaw. Why had he asked me? Was it to pay my debt at long last? He was, after all, no friend to give his gold freely; he was my declared enemy.

But de Bye had said he was a man of honour. Then, if not his payment, what did he want with me—he, Philip's friend and servant, Stadtholder of Holland? I would not go to Martensdijk. Let the debt remain unpaid; it would not be the first! But a debt unpaid to the enemy? Certainly it would be the first; I could not sink so low. Come what might I would go!

'I think he asks you in simple kindness because he pities your sad life,' Beatrix said looking over my wardrobe; and she might have spared herself the trouble since we both knew its meagreness. I must have a new gown, she declared. And when I shook my head, though I longed for a new gown, God knows, she said a new cote at least I must have and held up the old lozenged blue and gold, the silk cracked, the worked flowers and cyphers rubbed with all the progresses forced upon me by Philip.

'The sleeves will pass,' she said. 'The silk shows little wear and the sable's good. As for the rest—it is not to be endured that my lady should go to Martensdijk so meanly dressed.'

And so I sent de Bye into Flanders with a link of my father's chain—since other gold I had none—to buy me a length of velvet. Green velvet I told him; the best my link could buy. While he was gone Beatrix cleaned and pressed the golden sleeves and brushed the sable well. She took an old gown to pieces for a pattern, crying out when she measured it upon me that she must take it in more than a little since I had grown so thin.

De Bye came back with a good piece of velvet—forester green, a colour I have always favoured; and they sat sewing, Beatrix, and my old friend Ermgart van Rituelt that had lately come to serve me since Beatrix tired easily these days.

The gown was finished and it became me well. I agreed with Beatrix and Ermgart that green was a most kind colour; but, in my heart, I knew the cloth was not good enough. There was no pattern—neither embroidered nor interwoven; and how could I forget that once the looms of Italy had woven my royal pattern about my cypher and my crown?

The day had come; the horses waited and I was ready. I stood, admiring the sweet backward flow of the gown; and then—surprising even myself—I commanded Beatrix to unlace me and bring me the old lozenged silk.

I caught Ermgart's look, shocked, unbelieving. But Beatrix gave no sign. She went, face quiet, and brought me the old gown. And presently, ready to cry at my own foolishness, I rode out. Why had I behaved so? Was it that the old gown, worn though it was and tarnished, spoke of the glory that had been mine, demanded its own respect? Or was it something quite different? Was it that I could not endure him to think I had made myself fine for his sake? He had never seen me but in a shabby gown.

I do not know; I know only that pride and pride alone drove me.

I would not wear the green gown now or ever. Beatrix might have it, or Ermgart.

XXXIV

And now, my small and shabby train at my heels, I rode through the great gateway of St Martensdijk. Why had he invited me? I should soon know.

In spite of my agitation I could not but notice the ordered cleanliness of everything—no grass springing between the cobbles, no rusted hinges nor rotted woodwork; how different from my own Ostende! Philip had guaranteed to keep my houses in good repair; it was a promise easy to forget when he himself had no use for a house.

The Lord of Martensdijk came from his place at the great door and himself stooped to help me from the saddle—as though I were still that sovereign he had pulled from her high place. At the thought, I was tempted to take back my hand; but he was my host. And, as I went with him between the bowed ranks of his servants, I felt once more—for all my poor gown—Jacqueline countess of Holland, of Hainault, of Zealand, and of Friesland with all her isles. And for that moment I put away my anger against him, remembering only that I was his honoured guest.

There were two great fireplaces, one at each end of the great hall; the bright flames leaped, casting their warmth, for even on a summer's day stone walls strike chill. I had shivered in the chill of my own house and presently should do again. By one of the fireplaces stood a great chair all cushioned and hung with needlework; and, spread upon fresh rushes, a little carpet for my feet.

A young boy brought wine in a silver cup; and, like any cupbearer, the lord of the house took it and tasted; then he turned the cup about and offered it upon his knees. The wine was of a quality I had all but forgotten; and there were small cakes upon a dish all spiced and sugared such as are to be found in rich houses only.

When I was a little rested, he offered to show me his house and I followed him up the narrow staircase, where, at every curve, he turned to give me his hand; and I felt it warm and steady about my own.

The solar was light with windows and warm with summer; it was comfortable with cushioned seats in the embrasures, and here, too, carpets were spread upon the stone of the floor. It was hung with green—summer within as well as without—and all worked with hunting scenes which gave me an especial pleasure.

The first chamber that opened from the solar was the master's room—so much was clear. On a peg hung his cloak and chaperon; his tall boots stood by them and his riding-whip. This room was hung in red sewn with strange beasts—gentle unicorns and a fierce phoenix rising from the flames, and lions and tigers such as I have seen in the Tower at London. There was a great curtained bed with white fur coverings spread orderly; and I thought it must be pleasant to sleep all snug amongst the bright coloured beasts. And then I remembered whose bed this was; and I remembered the question to which I had found no answer and I could not come quickly enough from the room.

Next to the red room was a blue chamber where white-and-gold angels played in a blue-and-gold heaven. There was a couch whose blue-and-gold covering swept to the floor; upon a carved stool stood a ewer and a basin of chased silver, and leaning against a stool, a lute tied with ribands of blue and gold. There was a comeliness and a homeliness about this room, that caught at my heart and I could not speak.

'The lady's bower,' the master said. 'Some call it the Paradise chamber!' And, indeed, after my own house with its bare walls and its whistling winds, it was paradise indeed.

And so we came back into the solar and found a table spread with linen of Damascus as fine as silk; and on the cloth, two silver cups and two knives, the handles of ivory finely worked. In the middle of the table stood a subtlety—two figures carved in sugar as though from marble. And, when I looked, one figure was myself with a crown upon my head; and, kneeling at my feet, the Lord of Martensdijk that had helped me to lose that same crown.

I would have turned then from this mockery but the rich smells floating upward, took me with a most fierce hunger; it was long since we had ridden out from Ostende.

And now the servants came carrying the food already jointed into portions, and pages took the dishes and brought them first to their lord; and when he had nodded, brought them to me and then back again to him. There was—so stupidly do such small things stick—a dish of pigling snug beneath its blanket of anchovy sauce.

And, suddenly, savouring the rich fat food, such as I had not seen for many a day—and was not likely to see for many more—I remembered again the part this man had played in my poverty. And I looked again at the sugar countess with a crown upon her head, and at the kneeling man, and the food stuck in my throat; and I wished I had kept his gold by me that I might fling it into his false face. And all my distrust came sweeping back so that the food stuck in my throat and I sat there, my gorge rising as though with a nausea.

So, seeing I could not eat, he laid down his own knife and the servants took away the food and left us two together.

He came over and stood by me but I would not look at him. It was as though he blotted out the daylight; and all my old hatred came sweeping back—hatred and distrust.

He knelt down then and I saw his lifted face. There was no pride in it nor any greed but a kindness only. And this kindness on the face of my enemy all-but defeated me. The world I knew so well, the world where men press each to his own advantage and there is no pity, fell from me. This was a new world and I had lost my way.

And, while I sat trying to find it again, to save myself from this man that sought to ensnare me with his false gentleness, my eyes, wandering as though for help, caught something I had seen before—seen but not truly marked.

The garlands of fresh green that hung everywhere were looped every now and then with a cipher—and that cypher the letter *D*. It stood, I thought, for a family name or motto; it held no interest for me; but to give myself a little moment to come to terms with myself, I asked him what *D* might mean.

He looked me full in the face. 'What I long to say and dare not say, this letter says for me.' He stopped; he said, very humble, 'Dijn dienaar.'

My servant!

For a moment I could not speak. Then, 'Words are easy!' I said; and I had hold of myself again. 'Your services come too late. You gave me into the hands of my enemy; you betrayed me ...'

He shook his head. 'I never swore the oath. I never betrayed you. I was your father's avowed enemy and your own enemy ... until now.'

'And now?' I asked, bitter. 'Now?'

'Now I see you face-to-face and it is different.'

'How different? I am still myself and you are you. As for seeing me face-to-face, you did that more than once.' And I remembered the tear-stained girl holding out her hands for help—hands that came back empty. 'And one of those times, at least, you should not forget. We stood face-to-face, my lord, when I asked the honour of your hand in marriage.'

He said, and his mouth was wry about my mockery, 'I have not forgotten. I remember it daily, wishing I might have said *Yes*. But I could not say it then; I could not in honour say it.'

'Oh,' I said and wrung my hands, 'why were you my enemy? What wrong did I ever do you?'

'Got yourself born a foreigner.' And his sigh was deep.

'I am in the direct line of your own Margaret of Holland that was countess in her own right. My grandfather—her son, lest you forget that fact—was born in your own Hague where all true counts of Holland are born; and my father after him. And I—I was born there also.'

'It takes more than two generations or three to make a Dutchman. And, in proof of that, what do men call you? Jacqueline of Bavaria, von Bayern, de Bavare ... Bavaria, *Bavaria*, your name throughout Christendom. You and your father and his grandfather before him, foreigners all! Van Borselens have lived in Zealand three hundred years and more; and we don't take kindly to foreigners. And such foreigners! Foreigners with their hearts in Bavaria or ... in England.'

'Or in Burgundy?' I said quickly.

He went on as though he had not heard me.

'Do you know what they say of you, of you yourself? That you cared nothing for this country save to milk it dry for your Englishman. And it's true, isn't it? You would have made him master of us all. Do you think we could stomach that? We are a free people, not slaves to be passed from this master to that at a woman's whim. How could we go on accepting you—our liege?'

'Yet I am your liege whether you will or not. And there are plenty that loved me—and love me still. As for you, do not blind yourself with fine words, my lord. You and your friends set yourselves against me not for any fault of mine—though faults I have in plenty, God knows! Before the last breath was out of my father's body you set yourself against me as you had set yourself against him. Yet he was a good lord—and well you know it!'

'Friends may sing his praises,' he said, 'but others sing a different tune. He was not for these new times of ours! Old-fashioned; his head stuffed with nonsense about chivalry. Chivalry is not life. His feet stood not upon good Dutch soil but upon Cockayne or some such place. And like chivalrous knights of old he held women cheap.

I am a man that does not count lightness with women a little thing. Oh, you may flash at me with your angry eyes, but it's true—and you know it. The land is sown with his bastards.'

'And I thank God for them!' I cried out. 'They were loyal when true-begotten men betrayed me. Oh, you make fine talk about bastards and foreigners. Is Burgundy no foreigner? And is not France and Flanders and Holland and wherever his foot has trod, sown with his bastards? But what does that matter to you, since Burgundy makes you Stadtholder of Holland? But take care, my lord. It is Burgundy calls the tune! Take one step, one little step away from his piping and proud as you are and strong as you are, it's the end of you!'

He said nothing. He got up and paced about the room and stood staring through the window. At last he turned about. 'Some of the things you say are true. In the beginning I did stand out against you because you were your father's daughter; and because you were a woman. Weakness in rulers leads to disorder and to bloodshed. But had you not married Brabant then you might have won me to your side. But Brabant! Another foreigner to squeeze Holland to feed his vices. That was the end for others besides me. Why? Why?' His voice came out full and strong. 'Why did you not marry one of us—your own people?'

'It is a question that comes well from *you*. You would not marry me, my lord—light daughter of a light father—not for all my asking.' And the words were bitter in my smiling mouth.

'No,' he said. 'I did not like your house—nor do I now.'

'Then what do you want with me? And why did you send me your gold? To drag me yet lower than I have fallen? Make me eat from the hand of my enemy? I cannot think there is any other thing in me to give you pleasure.'

He looked at me then; he said, very slow, 'Why did I send you the gold? Because your courage was high and your fortunes low. When de Bye asked me, I was proud ...'

'Oh yes, you were proud! It pleased your arrogance to throw me your gold.'

'Not throw—share,' he said. 'And not until I was asked. I sent it—as it might be—a gift between friends.'

'Friends! What friendship between enemies, and those enemies a man and a woman? Had you asked for your payment like an honest man I would have paid, whatever it might be; yes, even with my poor body. So much of honesty I have. But you chose to take your pleasure in a baser fashion, humbling not the body but the spirit. You have made of me a beggar that cannot pay you again, that must be forever mindful of her debt. Your charity, my lord, has turned to bitterness.'

'Charity?' he said as though he were puzzled. And then, 'Charity? Why not? Charity and love, they are the same word—or so I learned in my Latin. I sent you the gold because I loved you ... but I did not know it then. There was nothing clear in my mind except to help you a little, if that might be done.' And then he said, very slow, 'You are right. A man does not give away his gold for nothing. I sent you mine because I loved you.'

I did not answer; the thing made no sense, no sense at all. I looked at him, asking without words, whether I deserved this mockery at his hands. But he looked not at all like a man that mocked. He looked very humble kneeling there and beseeching me with his eyes.

'I did not ask you here,' he said, very slow, 'to rake up old quarrels; but to honour my house. It is you, my love, proud and quick, that cannot leave well alone. See!' And he smiled so that it was sunshine on the coldness of his face, 'see how I must speak the truth to you to the last hairsbreadth, though it cost me your favour. I might have kept silent about so many things ... lied a little. But I cannot lie to you, not even to win your favour that is all the world to me. And so you must listen now and you must believe me.'

I wanted to believe him; for one precious moment I think I did believe him. But how could I not remember that for all his kneeling and all his honeyed words, he was yet Philip's lackey? And how could he love me that hated still my house?

I found my tongue at last.

'Is this a trick to shame me further, or to serve some purpose of your master of Burgundy? You like neither me not my house—and now this sudden turnabout! I am not fool enough to believe you!'

'And yet you do believe me,' he said, 'though it is as strange to me as it can be to you. I do not like your house; but you—you I love! And that is the truth as my Saviour hears me.'

He was not a man to take his Saviour's Name lightly. And yet, how often had my poor wits battled against the subtlety of enemies!

I said, 'Do not confound me with the name of our Saviour. Why should I believe you, seeing you might have had me ten years ago when I was better worth taking!'

'As to that I cannnot agree with you. Ten years ago you were ignorant and headstrong—your father's child and your mother's. Passion of Bavaria, pride of Burgundy. But now the tears have washed away the dross and you shine through, pure gold. Oh you're proud still, but it's a good pride, a most proper pride; and passion has turned to compassion.

'And so your face, all worn with your tears, is lovelier to me than the roundness of youth; and your sorrow, my love, dearer to me than the happiness of youth. And I am now and forever your servant.'

He all-but broke me with his tenderness; but I would be caught in no more traps.

'My faithful servant!' And I made my lips smile. 'Well, faithful servant, will you win me my crown again?'

'No,' he said at once. 'I will not be the one to start blood flowing again. But I would wait and I would watch; and, when the time came—*if* the time came—I would stand by your side and my party with me.'

So that was it! Ambition. Ambition and not love. The thing was clear.

'The pendulum swings,' I said, 'and there are hearts that love me still. Lord of my inheritance—husband and heir! Yes, it's worth taking me for, bad blood and all! But you are not clever enough, my lord. Do you think your master would allow it—a marriage that loses him the lands he's schemed for so long; a marriage, moreover, to please my people, to unite them? And if he would allow it, I would not. I am a tired woman and can fight no more. Your sword and your ambition—you must let them rust together. I have nothing to do with either.'

'My sword is already put by,' he said. 'But not my ambition. For my ambition is to serve you and cherish you as long as I live; and that is all the ambition I have. So, since you will not marry to please your people, will you marry to please yourself?'

'You offer too much for the body of Gloucester's whore!' I said, bitter, and I made my lips smile.

I saw pain run across his face but I would not be stopped.

'How often did you not name me so, you, yourself, my lord; and all Christendom with you? Would you mix the proud blood of van Borselens, good Zealanders this three hundred years, with the base blood of Gloucester's whore?'

I saw the tears in his eyes then—a man's tears and they could not lie. 'Before God, Madam, when you speak so, you cut the heart from out my breast.' And then he said, and he was smiling a little, 'And what can a man do lacking his heart? So give me your heart in exchange and make me a whole man.'

'I have no heart to give,' I said. 'It was broken long ago.'

'I will mend it.'

'I doubt God Himself could do that. I am a tired woman and there's no strength in me. Give your heart to someone that will better serve your ambitions and your body.'

He said, 'If you are tired, I will give you strength. And if you are sad I will make you laugh. And soon you shall be well again. I am not a man to marry for ambition, for I might have done that long ago—and that you know for yourself. As for your body, though I love it and desire it as a proper man should, I will cherish you and serve you, asking nothing until you love me back again.'

'Then your service will be long,' I said. 'And it will be fruitless. For I have been humiliated in marriage and I have been betrayed and there is no love left in me.'

And even while I said it, I knew it was not true.

XXXV

The thing I thought could never happen again, had happened.

I rode back in the summer evening pondering the miracle. God, having taken so much away, sent me now of His kindness this greatest of gifts.

Frank van Borselen loved me. I felt my whole self, like a plant long starved of light, turn towards him. It was a most sweet feeling—a gratitude, a great trust. But it was not love—if love be the wild passion I had known for Gloucester.

Gloucester. At the thought of him my hands shook upon the reins; the sweet countryside dimmed in my tears. Why did I weep for Gloucester? I was no longer his wife ... but he had been my husband. Yet remembering that, I must remember too, that he had deserted me for his dark slut; that he had let my name be blown upon; that he had lifted no finger when help could have spelt salvation. But he had been my husband. If he whistled, could I be sure I would not go running to his call? A fruitless question; he wanted no more of me. And a burnt child fears the fire.

If—if?

Lord Frank's face rose before me—the noble head, the clean honesty of the man. No passion here; but the heart's kindness.

My question was answered.

I wanted no more passion. I was a sick woman and I wanted to be made whole again. I was the tree Gloucester had uprooted and left to die. Lord Frank would plant me again, spreading my roots in the kind earth. He would be my sun and my shade and I should grow again, blossom and fruit.

Then—did I intend to marry him?

A difficult question, too much was involved. I put it from me. I was loved; and surely, I must love again. For the moment it was enough.

It was not until I was back again in my own chamber, coughing a little from my fatigue and with the cold—for summer nights are chill at Ostende—that I set myself to consider the matter in all its complexity.

Beatrix said nothing about our day at Martensdijk, as she had said nothing the long way home; she had always the delicacy to wait for a confidence; and then she would listen with a whole heart. Now she stood regarding me, plainly troubled.

'You've done nothing about that cough,' she said. 'It's been with you all the winter though I've begged you to send for the physician. You're reaping the harvest of the hard times—up to the knees in water, little rest and less food. *Don't neglect it*—I kept saying so. But you would do nothing. *Summer will bring its own cure*—you said that every time. Well, summer is here and still you cough; and still you do nothing!'

'I shall be better soon ... I promise,' I told her. 'Undress me, Beatrix, and let Ermgart bring me a cup of wine; and then come back and let us talk a little.'

But, as I lay shivering in bed, waiting for the hot drink, I knew I had been foolish to let the cough fasten on me. For Beatrix had spoken truer than she knew. She had heard me cough; but she had never seen me lean against a wall, all racked with my coughing; nor did she know there were times when, taking my fingers from my mouth, I found them smeared with blood. I wonder now—when I long so much to live—that I could have been so foolish. But there had been a carelessness in me because of my griefs. Now, now, I did care. I would look to myself; soon the cough would mend and I be strong again.

I saw again—as I was to see at every crisis in my life—how wise my father had been. He had warned me against the Brabant marriage and the Gloucester marriage. And I had not heeded him. Now I would marry as he desired—but not for his reasons. I would marry the Lord of Borselen not that he might put me back upon my throne—I no longer desired it; I desired nothing but to grow strong again beneath my husband's cherishing and the full life of a woman.

Beatrix came back with the wine and stood leaning against the bedpost, looking down at me.

I said. 'You know what happened at Martensdijk?' She nodded. 'I've guessed this long time.'

'Then you're cleverer than I! I never thought, never dreamed—how should I?'

'You value yourself too low; I've always said so.'

'You were always too partial. It's a tangle—and I know not what to do.'

'You know very well what you're going to do! But for all that it *is* a tangle—and one we must unravel with care if more than yourself are not to be caught in it.'

'Lord Frank? There'll be danger for him—there's my cousin of Burgundy to reckon with! I'm pledged never to marry without his consent.'

'That he'll never give, choose whom you may! And to the Lord of Borselen least of all. Why should you desire to marry your life-long enemy? That's the question Burgundy's bound to ask himself—and you must expect it.'

'The answer's simple. Because Lord Frank is kind and I love his kindness.'

'And himself?'

'I don't know, Beatrix, I don't know. That I can come to love him, I do believe. I want to marry him because he's kind; and because I'm tired and alone.'

'Burgundy's too subtle to believe the simple truth,' she said.

'Dishonest is the better word! And what does he know of the kindness between men and women? I doubt he's ever known it for all his marriages and all his bastards. You're right. He won't believe the truth; he'll forbid the marriage.'

'Could you pray Madam your mother to speak for you?' she asked, doubtful.

I had a sudden picture of my mother, fierce brows lifted to the edge of her coif. Her implacable pride would never accept that an enemy could become a friend. *Your pride, your pride.* Upon that string she would play. But it would be her own pride that would not let me mate with lesser blood nor allow my inheritance to pass out of de Charolais hands.

Desolation flooded my heart like sea-water bursting through a dike. I must have this man or die; and die indeed ... The sickness in nay lungs only his cherishing could cure.

I said, 'I must know the tenderness that is between married people. It's a thing that, for all my three marriages, I have never known.'

'You shall know it,' she promised. 'And now you must sleep. The Lord Frank will not thank me to find you with so white a face.'

Frank. I had been thinking of myself alone—*my* needs, *my* happiness. But what of him? What danger might this spell for him?

He came riding next morning to answer that question.

'I'm a man, dear heart; and I'm a soldier. I can look to myself.'

And I believed him. How should I not believe him seeing him so upright and quiet and strong? And for myself, Philip had stripped me naked; what more could he do?

As long as I live—and the time is short enough now—I shall not forget Frank's courtship, so tender, so cherishing, and so gay. I had not thought he had in him to be gay, the grave, big man. He was my lover and my father—the father I had so bitterly missed. He gave me back my youth, that youth lost in the years of hardship. And though the earth close upon me and I lie cold in my narrow bed, I shall remember that other bed—my marriage-night so simple and so secret, lacking the pomp of drums, the garlands and the feasting of my first two marriages, lacking the wild passion, the ecstasy of my third marriage. It was all a gentleness and a sweetness and a cherishing.

We were married secretly at Ostende, judging it safer than Martensdijk, which is so great a house. It was July and the summer air blowing from the sea brought a tang of salt mixed with the scent of wild roses. I was glad to be wed in the summer that the poverty of my bed-coverings be not felt.

I remember how I went into my chamber all sweet with herbs and Beatrix waited to undress me. She had sent Ermgart away, and I saw again how the face of this sister of mine took, in the flickering cresset-light, the features of my father—his eyes, his mouth. And, remembering how twice I had disobeyed him and the evil that had come of it, I could not believe that now, though I married according to his wish, any good would come of it. For I had waited until all was lost; and it was not obedience that had driven me nor love of my people; but love of myself, myself alone.

'Beatrix,' I cried out, 'I have done wrong to bind this proud man to me—I that have failed and failed again. No good can come of it.'

She cradled my head as though I had been a child.

'Much good will come of it,' she said. 'Happiness to you and to your lord; and above all happiness to your people. A son of Holland, God grant it; and the Burgundian driven out.'

'No good, no good,' I said and would not be comforted. 'What good ever came from three marriages that I must try a fourth?'

'That is a question you must answer for yourself,' she said, grave.

'My first husband was without fault. Had I borne him a child that child would even now be King of France ... it is a strange thought. But, be that as it may, we were both young and there was no time and nothing of that marriage is left.'

'Understanding, forbearance, tenderness. Is that nothing?'

'My second marriage. A child would have been my salvation; yet, as my Redeemer hears me, I am glad there is no child. Brabant brought me sorrow enough; but he, too, has gone down into the grave and all is forgiven; and of that marriage, too, nothing is left.'

'To learn to forgive—that is not nothing,' she said. I fell to silence then and she waited patient.

At last, 'Your third marriage?' she asked. And when still I did not speak, said, 'Jacque, my little one, if your mind is not clear and your heart clean tonight, this marriage will be wrecked also. Then you will break your heart past all mending ... and mine, too.'

I said, 'Must you remind me again, again? Let me forget the pains and the shames Gloucester put upon me.'

'And the love that was between you? You must forget that, too. If you long for it still no good can come from this marriage.'

And, waiting for this new husband of mine, I remembered that wedding night at Hadleigh ... handsome, laughing Gloucester, light and greedy Gloucester.

'It was not love he gave me, it was lust,' I said.

'Whether he loved or lusted is all one now; with him we are finished. But you? What of you?' And there was authority about her.

'I loved him as a wife; but he took me as a mistress.'

She said, 'There's a thing I must say—though your own mother would not dare. And yet it is a thing that comes well from woman to woman when there is love between them. And it must be said now; and never again. Shall I say it, Jacque?'

She looked at me very steadfast.

'Say it,' I said.

'You loved Gloucester as a wife loves her husband—so you say and so you think. But *was* it as a wife you loved him or as a ... mistress? No, never flush and flare! Two things every mistress desires from her lover—delight for her body and the reward in her hand. Did you not desire these things, also—his fine body and what his strong arm could win for you?'

'A wife?' I cried out. 'Does not a wife desire these things, too?'

'She desires them differently, so they are different things; and that I think you understand very well. Did you love Gloucester as a mistress or as a wife? That is the question you must answer and answer now.'

I said, soft and bitter with the blow she had dealt, 'Truly you dare overmuch and it is hard to forgive you. Are you jealous that you must spoil this night with memories and with questions?'

She looked at me then and I was ashamed before the love in her face.

'I would give the heart out of my body to make you happy,' she said. 'But happy you will never be until you have faced the truth for yourself. For the memories have never left you; and never will till you yourself send them packing. And the questions are thorns in your heart and there they will stay until you yourself pluck them out. And so I must ask you again, Was it love you gave to Gloucester or was it lust?'

I turned my face from her. 'Who can tell from the ashes what went into the fire?'

'It seems I must answer the question as well as ask it.' She put out a hand and gently turned my head again. 'This love of yours for Gloucester! Did you ever speak together friend to friend? Did you ever dare to tell him your mind when he was wrong? Did he ever consult you on this or that, be it ever so small a thing? Your love for him! I'll tell you what it was. A constant flattering lest you lose him. A constant offering of your body to be taken or left as he chose. A wife? Then wife turned strumpet!'

The hateful word, so unexpected, shocked me into knowledge of the truth; and because I faced the truth at last, and because of that word my anger flared—anger that bade fair to part us for ever. I looked at her; pale and steadfast she looked back. Must all her long love of me, long patience, long kindness to go up in flame before a little word—and that word true? But it was a word rooted in my pain and in my shame; in a young man's cruel dying and an old man's sorrow.

Yet it was true and I must say so. Whatever happened between us, so much she deserved of me.

'It was not love,' I said at last.

'How do you know?' she asked out of a still face.

'There was nothing of the spirit between us. I loved his body, not for his sake but for my own. I humbled myself that I might enjoy it. I was as lustful as he and more, more. And yet—' and it burst from me like a cry, or a prayer perhaps, 'I was happy ... I was happy.'

'For so short a happiness so long a sorrow! You have paid the price.'

'And must Lord Frank pay also? I have spoilt my own life. I will not spoil his!' And, in my distress, I would have risen from the bed but her hand upon my shoulder forbade it.

'His life and yours are one now,' she said. 'Because he is good you will be good; because he is honourable and gentle and loving so you will be also. Now that you have faced the truth about Gloucester he will never trouble your heart again.'

She bent over and drew the sheet up to my chin. 'I have hurt you, Jacque, but the bad place is healed and there's nothing but cleanness left. May Christ and His Sweet Mother give you happiness.'

And I was happy; I thought of my cousin Philip hardly at all. And of Gloucester less; had he come to me with a crown in each hand, still I would not have looked at him. For what traveller, putting into harbour storm-tossed and sick, would venture again the hazards of the sea? A younger one, perhaps; but I was thirty and I thanked God for my safe harbour and the sweet certainty of land.

For this marriage was a true marriage such as I had never known. In my husband's cherishing, his tender care of me, I grew stronger. I put on a little weight; I coughed less; I surprised myself with the sound of my own laughing. If God would now grant me the thing long withheld! A child. I had known that precious hope once with Gloucester but the hope had miscarried and thereafter had come warfare and parting. If now the hope were given once again, my life would be crowned.

Crowned. With returning strength, ambition I had thought dead began to stir. If God gave me a child I would fight again. I would fight for my rights and for the rights of my child. With my husband beside me, a united country would drive the Burgundian away. A true child of Holland would bless the land again.

I underestimated Philip.

Strange, considering how much I had already suffered at his hands. But I was so happy, so sure in the strength and authority of my husband, that I was inclined to think less of my cousin's dark cunning.

I should not have forgotten for a single moment that he must be told about this marriage and told soon. And I should have remembered that a child born of my body would be the direst menace to him; a menace so dire that it must never happen.

I should have remembered.

And, indeed, we had meant to tell Philip, catching the right moment, sweetening him with gold and yet more gold. But with Philip there was no right moment, and our happiness so new, so threatened, we dared not speak.

My husband's duties took him to the Hague; and since I dared not travel with him, I followed a few days later. For I could no longer endure to be far from him; he was my sun that coaxed me back to health.

I took up my old apartments, I could afford it now; and though the Stadtholder of Holland has his own apartments within the palace, Frank preferred to occupy a house he had within the city.

And so the sweet summer passed into autumn. I no longer regretted that Philip's man governed Holland—he was my man, too.

And then, suddenly, the news! Philip had left Paris. He was on his way to the Hague bringing with him his new wife.

'Why does he leave Paris so suddenly?' I was badly frightened.

'Half a dozen reasons. To show off his new wife. She's a pretty piece! To make a routine visit ...'

'Routine visit—when everything goes well here? When he's needed in Paris and needed badly? The English need him and every man he's got. No, there's another reason ...' And I felt myself go cold in the sunshine.

'Dear heart,' he said, 'leave your worries to me.' He turned up my chin and smiled into my face. 'Come, never look so white. You should walk in the garden this fine morning—there'll not be many such. Winter will be on us before we know it!'

And so it was ... it was.

They were troubled lonely days and I must deal with my fears as best I could. I saw little of my husband; his hands, always full, were now, with Philip expected daily, fuller than ever. Nor did I catch more than a glimpse of him in his scant leisure moments; we had decided not to see each other alone until Philip had come and gone.

If I had thought little about Philip before, I made up for it now. Restless during the day, I could not sleep at night. I lay alone in my wide bed and gave myself up to my fears—and my fears were all for my dear lord.

It was full November before my cousin arrived, bringing with him his pretty bride ... bringing with him his horsemen and his bowmen.

I waited in the great hall to receive them. I wore the old blue lozenged gown, lest from a richer dress he might pluck confirmation of my changed fortunes. I stood there quiet and smiling that was all sick with my fears.

Why had he come? Why?

But Philip was kind. Smiling and debonair, he presented me to his bride—lesser to greater. I was sovereign in name only; and inferior to Madam the Duchess of Burgundy.

I looked at pretty Isobel of Portugal and envied her charming youth. But how long would she remain a gay and pretty child? And I remembered his unkindness to his first wife my cousin Michelle; and how quickly he had taken a second and then a third. And I remembered all the women who had loved him and the broken hearts he left wherever he went. Lecherous, treacherous Philip. These days I feared him more than at any time during my life. I had more cause. I feared now for my dear lord.

But Philip continued easy, friendly ... and no more to be trusted than any other snake. I entertained the young bride, careful of every word that rose to my lips; I did my duties towards Philip. And all the time I was afraid. Frank I saw only at a distance or in Philip's company and dared not acknowledge him by more than the cold greeting bestowed upon an enemy to whom one must show courtesy.

Philip rallied me on that. 'Come now, Cousin, the past is past. There are no more Hooks and Cods. And if there were—why then we must love our enemies. It is our Christian duty. You are too good a Christian, I hope, to forego that duty.' And he smiled with his mouth; but his eyes did not smile.

Fear. I lived night and day with it. I could not carry it to Frank to find comfort there; but in the quiet of my chamber I whispered to Beatrix lest Philip's spy listen, ear flattened at the keyhole.

Beatrix tried to comfort me but she herself was alarmed. 'My Lord of Burgundy talking of loving one's enemy! You had best walk wary, Jacque my dear.'

And Philip continued to show himself kind; and kinder to none than to the Lord Frank van Borselens He would walk, an arm thrown about my husband's neck; and I wondered how soon that grip would tighten.

And the days passed on.

The days passed on; and now it was towards the end of November, the twenty-fifth day. I have good cause to remember it.

XXXVI

Yes, I have good reason to remember. The mark of that day is upon my heart.

My husband was supping in my cousin's chamber; there had been business to discuss and Philip had declared himself much pleased with Frank's stewardship—as well he might! And now, business being over, Philip kept Frank by him.

My cousin poured more wine, laughing and slapping his knee. 'They tell me you're a virgin, Frank, but I don't believe it!' he said.

It was then Frank began to doubt his master's good faith.

Burgundy went on rallying him. 'A man of your years—forty if a day! The thing's outside nature.'

Frank laughed with his master; but his doubts were hardening.

'Why, man, it's time you begot yourself an heir. Since you're so bashful we must look about and find you a pretty partner.' Frank bowed. 'Your grace is kind.'

'Oh, we're kind enough, never doubt it! We know how to reward faithful service—you shall see! But it grows late. My bride will be waiting. It's a pity you can't say the same—eh, man?' And he all-but thrust Frank from the room.

Frank stood on the other side of the door. It was late—as Philip had said—and he should be making for home. Yet he felt in his bones that things were wrong. He had the strongest desire to see that all was well with me. And at the thought that I might have come to harm, he could no longer restrain himself.

At the door of my chamber they took him. So swift, so stealthy the taking, that I, fallen asleep at long last, knew nothing. My very door—and I knew nothing!

Hustled along in the dark of the morning—I have pieced the story together since—he tormented himself wondering what new miseries he had brought upon me. And it came to him that once he had played his part in my misfortunes because he had been my enemy; now he would go on playing it because he loved me. At this irony he groaned.

The Scheldt was flowing dark and oily; cold stars reflected in cold depths. The small boat rocked as he stepped in. Behind him the guards sat; de Ternant faced him in the stern, naked sword across his knees. The water slapped against the side of the boat; it was the only sound in the still night. Frank sat upright, stiff with his misery; he did not even know that his hands had swollen beneath the cords until afterwards when he came to himself and felt the pain. He thought about his own danger and wondered where they were taking him; but chiefly he thought about me. He would willingly have died for the part he had played in the new troubles he had brought upon me. And, though he walked in the shadow of death, it never occurred to him that I and I alone was to blame. For, wilfully and in the face of all promises, I had married him; and through me he went now to his death.

Dawn was breaking when they reached Rotterdam and there, in the milky light, he was hustled ashore and into yet another boat that waited.

The sun came up pale in November mist; there was little difference between dawn and full day. Where they were taking him he could not know; but it would be where he had no friends—Flanders, perhaps. Yes, certainly Flanders, under the close guard of Burgundy's own subjects, under Burgundy's own eye.

When the towers of his prison rose before him, he knew without any doubt, that he was in Flanders; and, staring at the high dark walls manned by men-at-arms, seeing the water black and deep in the wide moat, seeing the drawbridge rise and then hearing it fall clattering behind him, hearing the lock turn in the narrow barred door that closed instantly behind him, he knew that Burgundy did not mean him to leave this place alive.

And all the time I tossed and turned in sleep; and woke whimpering and longing for Frank's kind arms; and knew nothing until Beatrix came to me in the morning.

Ermgart was dressing my hair; and I was thinking that Beatrix should make me a camomile wash and the yoke of eggs in it to bring back the brightness, when she herself came in.

I cried out at her stricken face; but I was silent enough when I heard the news. She put out a hand to me lest I slip from my chair but I stiffened myself against even her loving touch. And so I sat and listened while anger and fear curdled within me. And when she had finished, I cried out, 'I have taken enough from the hands of my cousin; enough, enough, enough!' And I heard how my voice came out in a wail. 'I will take no more, no more! All my life these Burgundies have been a blackness upon my heart—father and son, both. All my griefs come from them, all my losses. Let Philip keep what he has taken, let him keep them all! But not this, not this!' And I beat one hand upon the other. 'The world is too poor lacking so good a man; and I, I am poorer still ... too poor, too poor. Philip must not take this one last thing. God will not allow it. God will punish! Philip had best give back my husband to sweeten the years that remain ... the few years. By God's sweet Mother, Philip must give him back ...'

And then, suddenly, I was quiet again. I knew what I must do.

'Send to my Lord of Burgundy—let Grenier go,' I told Beatrix. 'I must speak with him at once.'

'My Lord Duke left the Hague,' she said. 'He followed ... the first party, so they say. Gone into Flanders.'

'*Where* in Flanders?'

She said very low, 'Rupelmonde, so they say. But it may not be true.'

'Rupelmonde.' And my voice came out in a dreadful sound. And it was true; I knew it. Rupelmonde. From that dread fortress of despair no prisoner ever issued alive.

'Bid Grenier make ready a boat.' And now I was surprised at the steadiness of my voice. 'And tell de Bye I am for Rupelmonde. He goes with me and Grenier and you also. Ermgart, make ready a bundle—a change of linen and whatever I require. We sail within the half-hour.'

Ermgart busied herself about the bundles; but first she brought me a cup of wine. I sat there, mouth and hand shaking so that I was forced to set down the cup.

De Bye came in hatted and cloaked. 'Within fifteen minutes the boat will be ready—Grenier has sent word. But—' and he looked troubled, 'what will Madam do if my Lord of Burgundy refuse to admit her?'

'Batter at his gates with my bare hands, until he does! No, never look so grim, he'll not refuse. We understand each other, he and I. He knows I would not come and no gift in my hand—a gift he covets. Tell me, friend, what did he say before he left? What was his mood?'

'A cold anger; very quiet. He said he needed no baggage. He would not be absent long.'

Not absent long. The words fell cold as death. Philip meant to make short work of the business.

'And, Madam—he knows about your marriage; has known this long while. That was why he came.'

I nodded. It was a thing I had always known.

'But how?' de Bye asked puzzled. 'How? He has his spies everywhere, that's true. Yet of the three of us that knew, not one but would have gone to his death rather than tell.'

'That I know well. But, a look, a touch of the hand, maybe; and the tale is told.' And at the thought of Frank's look, Frank's touch, I could speak no more.

'There's a thing I should say ...' he stopped.

'You may say it—though indeed I can guess. I am no green bride to hide my face for blushes.'

'Burgundy swears there shall never be a child born of you and my Lord of Borselen. If you are already with child, then you will die before ever you give it birth.'

No news to me! Yet, spoken aloud, the calculated wickedness added to my fears. For the first time I thanked God I had conceived no child by Frank.

Beatrix knocked upon the door. All was ready.

I sat upright, hearing the water slip from the keel. I drew about me the fine new cloak my husband had given me—scarlet-cloth lined with grey fur. I was glad of its warmth, for I sat shivering more with fear than with weather, though we were but two days off December. And I was gladder still of the fine red colour, for hurry and grief had brought on a cruel fit of coughing; and, before I could bring my hand to my mouth, there was a wet stain upon my cloak. Now I sat kerchief to lips and the blood salt in my mouth; blood rising warm from the cavern of my breast.

I did not let it distress me overmuch. There had been blood before and there were more important things to deal with now! I thought, maybe, the blood had cleared my head, for my mind was clear, my thoughts sharp as the little knife hidden in my pocket.

I knew exactly what I must do.

I must bargain for my husband's life. Though Philip had stripped me bare, I had yet something to bargain with; something I, and only I, could give. What I offered now was the crowning-piece of all his ambitions—and crowning piece indeed.

And if he refused?

My hand closed upon the sharp thing in my pocket. If he refused he should pay for it—I cared nothing what happened to myself. But I knew my Philip. He would not refuse.

At Rotterdam it was easy enough to follow in his wake. Gossip spoke true; he had taken boat for Rupelmonde. And de Bye, chatting to the sailors and slipping a guilder into a bronzed palm, heard the story of the fine gentleman the soldiers had hustled along early this morning ... very pale and tall he was and his fair hair all dark with the rain and his two hands tied together.

And my heart broke for the fine gentleman that could not put up a hand to wipe away the rain that fell upon his face.

And so we took ship again. I must have slept with the slow rhythm of the boat and the fatigue of my coughing, for I started suddenly at the jarring of the boat. It was pitch-dark; and the cold stars pricking in the black sky. In the darkness I could see nothing but dark river and dark flats of the watermeadows.

Grenier strode forward and pulled upon the hidden bell; its rusty clang went echoing over the dark river and a heron that had been sleeping, head tucked upon its breast, flew up with a flapping of wings. And now, my eyes, accustomed to the dark night, saw what Frank had seen this morning—the walls and bastions of Rupelmonde.

And now, waiting there in the cold night, it occurred to me for the first time that Philip would not see me. Why should he? He had Frank under his hand; and me in that corner to which he had driven me. I must have been holding my breath; for I remember how it came out in a great, tearing sigh—as though I had been running—when the bridge fell and the great doors opened.

But of course, I said to myself, of course! Philip would not deny himself the sight of my fears and my weakness and my grief. And I blessed him for his cruelty—a thing I had never thought to do.

He was half lying in a great chair, his feet upon a stool and a fur cloak upon his shoulders. There was a fire blazing on the hearth and a brazier flamed at one elbow; at the other a table stood with wine and bread and dishes of meat.

It was long since I had eaten and the savour of food filled my mouth with water; yet I could not have eaten had he offered me food, because of the sickness of my fear. But he did not offer.

He made no movement to rise, nor did he give me any greeting; and that, I thought, ominous. For though he could betray and murder, yes and torture, too, his manners were the fine flower of his training. He must, indeed, do violence to himself to show such rudeness.

His rudeness rather than the heat of the room brought the blood to my face. He said, with that sly smile of his, 'You are in looks today, Cousin. Sorrow becomes you.'

'Then I should be the world's beauty,' I flashed out, 'seeing all the griefs you have put upon me.'

'Every grief you have put upon yourself!' He nodded so that the great jewel in his black velvet bonnet sent out spears of light. 'You and van Borselen between you have served me a double treachery. He has broken the oath to me, his lord; you have broken the oath you swore at Delft. You are dishonoured, the pair of you, and must take what comes of it!' And there was no more smiling in his face. 'Had you chosen another man I might have forgiven it. But you seduced the man I put to govern, the man that was your enemy and my friend ... I have not so many friends I can afford to lose one. You have done me great wrong, Cousin.'

It is a strange thing that, with all my fears upon me, I half-pitied Philip. For it was the truth he spoke—and we both knew it. Conqueror and master of men; and no man his friend.

'Love the man I did; but for all that he must die—and you know it!' And there was no mistaking the truth of the sigh that burst from his lips. 'No other way. He's powerful, he's knowledgeable, he's danger-ous. Why did you choose this man and no other? You will tell me, no doubt,' and he was smiling again, 'that you love him. Love!' And he all-but spat. 'An itching boy's desire, a green girl's dream. But you have no such excuse, neither you nor he. You're thirty if a day; and he'll not see forty again. Never talk to me of love. You knew well what you were about, by Christ's blood you did! Treachery. Treachery to rob me of my lawful gains—gains won in battle and by treaty, too. Treachery; double treachery. The man must die.'

Must die ... The words that should be a dagger in my heart were yet a gleam of hope. Frank was alive. His time was all-but run—save for me and my bargain. But he was alive; he was still alive.

I said, 'Cousin, I have come to make a bargain.'

'What have you left to bargain with?' His smile belittled me; but his eyes were alert beneath hooded lids.

'Something that's worth more to you than any man's life.'

'No need for me to bargain. I take what I want.'

'This thing you cannot take. No one can take it. It can be given only; and only I can give it.'

'Do you offer ... yourself, Cousin?' His eye, raking me from head to foot, mocked at my sad charms.

'I could not aspire to great Burgundy,' I said. 'All Christendom knows he likes his women plump and tender.' I dropped my banter. I looked him full in the face. 'You know well what I am offering.'

He nodded. 'I know. But why should I trust you?'

'Because the thing I want is too precious to lose.'

'Love?' And this time he laughed outright. 'This man or that—what does it matter? All cats are grey in the dark! Come now, I forgive you. When van Borselen is out of the way, I will find you a man as pretty.'

Now, in this moment, when most of all I needed a cool head to deal with this sly and cruel man, I lost my temper. 'Do not mock at me, Cousin!' I cried out, 'or by God, I shall kill you. All my life I have been robbed of the love that should be between a man and a woman—and it is you that have robbed me.'

'You talk like a kitchen slut,', he said. 'Princes do not wed to satisfy the itch of the flesh—that may be satisfied elsewhere. Policy moves us into marriage—'

'Policy has moved me once too often. And I am not minded to go empty for the rest of my life.'

He said, 'Flaming eye and flaming cheek! No wonder that fool of Brabant was afraid of you. As for Gloucester, he may thank his God—and me, too—for robbing him of a termagant. And yet anger becomes you. When the blood is up you have all the air of a pretty woman. It was a pity, maybe, to bed you with that vicious fool. I am half-sorry I did not take you myself. It would have saved us both much trouble.'

'There are two to every bargain!' I told him.

'But one of them is not always in a position to bargain. Well, it is a bargain we are to discuss now. Will you sit, Cousin?'

It was the first time he had offered me the courtesy. Now he took his feet from the stool and nodded me towards it. He meant to show me which of us had lost the power to bargain. We both knew it.

'I had rather stand,' I said.

'I had rather you sat.'

I stood for a moment defiant; I sat down in my low place at his feet.

'Well now,' he said. 'This talk of bargains. You have nothing to bargain with!'

'You know better than that!' I said. 'You know these people of mine. Their loyalties are not your loyalties and you cannot make them so by chopping off a head, or half a dozen heads or half a hundred! You have got my people beneath your heel, Cousin Philip; but you haven't got their hearts. You don't rule by love, Cousin.'

'Love! Love again!' And he laughed. 'Will you never be taught?'

'It is the only way to keep a people true; and it is you that need the lesson.'

'You are hardly the one to teach it!' And he was frankly jeering. 'These people of yours—how true have they been to you?'

'The heart returns to its own. And there are signs. If you would stop my people from turning back to me then you must take my offer. But I will not make it until I have seen my husband.'

'Nothing you can offer will move my mind. Keep your bargains to lessen your own punishment. The man must die. You spoke just now about a chopping-off of heads. It will not be so simple, cousin Jacqueline.' And he was smiling again. 'For such treachery, betrayal of both lord and friend, it will be burial ... alive.'

I stared at him then and I could not speak. I could not believe him in earnest. This cruel death; this shameful death ... a woman's death. And Frank. Frank that was everything brave and noble and true. For his honour Philip could not mean it. Men would spit upon his name wherever it was spoken.

My voice came out in a whisper and there was no more courage in me. For he meant it; no doubt about it. He meant it. 'You would not dare ...'

'You dare rather much yourself, Cousin, when you take that tone with me. Van Borselen is to die that way and no other. But let no man say I am not merciful. You shall see him first. No!' and he dashed my last, poor hope. 'I would not have you help him to an easy death. You shall see him from a distance.'

'How shall I see from a distance whether you trick me or no? He might be dead ... already dead ... and I not know.'

'Then love is as blind as they say! How you shall know him I care not a fig. Take my offer or leave it.'

'I take it,' I said. 'And when I have seen my husband and know he is alive, then, Cousin, let us talk again. I swear to you by the Blood of Jesus that the thing I offer is the thing you need to seat you now and forever on the throne of my fathers.'

'There's nothing I cannot take for myself! Must I tell you again? As for van Borselen, have no fear, it's the man himself you shall see; van Borselen, and no other. And, for talking further, why not? You intrigue me with your nonsense, Cousin. And, besides, I have always time for a pretty woman.' He smiled, mocking my tears and my wasted looks.

He rose up then and struck upon a bell and gave his orders. I made my stiff farewell and, a man-at-arms each side of me, went out and left him there. And, as I went, I saw that he smiled no longer, but his brows were bent as though upon a matter of some importance. I knew then that, for all his denial, he would listen to me; yes, and bargain with me, too.

I went between my escorts down the stone passage that would not be warm even in summer, for no sun ever came there; and now I shook so that I could hardly walk ... but it was not with cold. It was because I was to see him I loved above all earthly things; and because of what Philip had said about the way he was to die.

It was full daylight when we came into the courtyard; I had been longer matching my poor wits against Philip than I knew. The raw air of winter cut through my cloak and my feet slid in the muck and the ice. But the day was crystalline and the sky showed a patch of clear blue—and blue is the colour of hope.

I started violently at a touch upon my shoulder; one of the men pointed upwards. The tower was empty; and the long line of battlements also. I went on staring. I bit my lips that the tears might not rob me when the moment came.

And suddenly he was there. Three figures black against the pale sky. Two men-at-arms; and between them a figure I should know had I been blind; know by the leaping of my heart and the beat through all my pulses.

But I was not blind. And so I saw again the high carriage of his head and the fine set of the shoulders, and the whole proud elegance of the man. And I knew that, though I could not see them, his eyes would be smiling at me—those true Dutch eyes. And I saw his arms go up in greeting, both arms rising together against the sky. A strange posture ... and then I saw his hands were chained one to the other.

Then indeed, my world did swim in tears; and I called out his name. I had meant it for a message of hope but the wailing sound beat upon the enclosing walls and carne back to me in hopeless longing.

Frank ... Frank.

I would not lift a hand to wipe away my tears; he must not know I wept though the tears ran salt into my mouth.

One of the men touched me upon the arm. I think he must have spoken and I had not heard.

I turned about and went with my escort back again into the fortress.

XXXVII

I found Philip exactly as I had left him. He sat upright, coldly alert, as though he had not moved. The stool, too, was where I had left it; and, without rising, he signified that I should be seated. I said, still standing, 'Send your men away. What I have to say is between us two.'

'And what of the knife?' He was smiling again. 'But, of course there is a knife!' And he was all lazy good-humour. 'It is the proper thing, is it not, when you go a-visiting?' He nodded dismissal to the men. 'Oh, cousin Jacqueline, you are not very clever. Did you truly think I would treat this as a friendly call?' He tapped lightly upon his silken doublet, and I heard the ring of metal.

I took the knife from my pocket and laid it upon the table between us.

'A pretty thing,' he said and ran his finger along the edge. 'And no toy, neither. Toledo, as I guess. Valuable! I shall keep it, cousin—since after all it was meant for me. There is, I trust, no poison upon it.'

I held out my hand for the knife and drew it lightly across my wrist; the blood welled in bright beads. 'If a man must die, I should give him a clean death,' I said and handed him the knife again.

'Your uncle of Bavaria thought different. And now, cousin, for this great offer of yours.'

'You are guardian and regent for me until I marry—and only till then. Well, I am married now.'

'You will soon be husbandless again,' he said gently. 'And, besides, there's a thing you have forgotten. Marry without my consent—and that very act frees your subjects from your obedience and brings them to mine. So it stands in the treaty we two made at Delft. You have no more subjects, cousin; they are already mine.'

'On paper, on paper only. And there are those that will never accept you. And, if you kill the Lord van Borselen, a true man and much loved, there will be many more, believe me!'

'Now, cousin, you are not only my guardian, you are my heir—until I provide one of my own making. For all the sorrows you have put upon me I am not yet beyond the age of childbearing.'

'You have not been overforward in the matter,' he said.

'No need to dwell upon that now. You must take it that I am not beyond providing an heir of my own body.'

'Is it wise to stress that point?' And there was venom in his eyes.

'Yes,' I said, 'since it must be reckoned with. And besides you know it already. But what you don't know is this. I am a tired woman. Suppose I give up my throne, the throne itself; every title, every right, give them to you for ever?'

'And what good should I get from that, seeing I have already sole power?' His smile was lazy enough but the look in his eyes gave him away.

'You know better than to ask that! Regent you are, and heir you may be. But you are not sovereign ... *You are not sovereign*. And, even should I bear no child still I am younger by several years; why should I die before you?'

'Why not?' And though he smiled still, his eyes threatened.

'Make an end of me? Then you make an end of yourself and your claims. For you make a martyr of me that have done no wrong. The people would rise like a nest of hornets. You think you have them under your heel; but you have never won their hearts; and without my goodwill never shall. They accepted you as regent and heir because I accepted you. I hid my bitterness beneath a smiling face for the sake of peace. But it is not a peace a country can accept with honour. When men live under such a peace, they think not so badly of war—especially when war drives the tyrant away. Let your foot slip never so little and they will rise and drive you out.'

'And why should my foot slip?'

'Because you are a foreigner; and because you are a tyrant. You look first to fill your own pockets. You may remit a tax here and there; but you slip on another as heavy. Oh it's all very sly! But men know full well when their pockets are empty; the yoke bears hard upon the galled shoulder.'

He would have spoken then but my hand uplifted, stopped him—stopped great Philip Duke of Burgundy, Count of Flanders and of Namur, Duke of Brabant, Regent of all my lands, even those inches where my feet stood—I penniless and powerless with my empty titles.

'Believe me, cousin, though you should forsake your own Burgundy and forego your ambitions in France; though you turn your back upon Flanders and upon Brabant, you will always be what you are now—*the foreigner*, until I, of my own will, acknowledge you friend and sovereign. And that I am prepared to do.'

'I do not need your offer. My grip is firm—heel and hand. Van Borselen dies today. And you I will put where you can make no more mischief. Do you forget the Gravenstein?'

'It is you that forget!' And though my smile matched his, my heart sickened within me. 'The Gravenstein could not hold me.'

'Then you shall stay here—with van Borselen's ghost for company. No bird escapes the cage of Rupelmonde.'

'My people will break open the cage. I tell you again there's no real peace in this land. Here and there anger flies upward like a spark—a very small spark. But one spark and another and your peace goes up in flames. People may crawl on their bellies before you—but love you? Never think it! Last year, you were all-but murdered, here in this country of mine. Have you forgotten it? Oh, you dealt with the assassin and he'll trouble you no more. But there will be others, always others ... more and more. And what will you do then? Kill me you may; but kill all your enemies? Never think it! They're too many! For, cousin, you must reckon on this! When you brought your "peace" to my land you forbade the names *Hook* and *Cod*. You set your heart on a nation united to support you. Well, there are no more *Hooks* and *Cods* and it is a united nation. But how if that nation rise against you? Kill my husband; kill me; kill my mother—if you can. There are others to take our place and always will be. A united nation.

'But I could make everything easy for you. If, of my own free will, I give away my crown, then there is no anger against you for taking it. The anger is all against me that gave into your hands the lives of my people.'

He said nothing. He got up from his chair and paced the room. And even then, my husband's life hanging by a thread, some part of me stood by and noted his elegance and his grace—the perfection of the black doublet slashed with gold and the golden chain about his neck with the great jewel, and the silken legs and the jewelled cap.

He halted and swung upon his heel. 'You argue well, cousin Jacqueline, but why should I believe you? You have your own axe to grind!'

'I do not argue. I tell what we both know. You can keep this land of mine by right and right only. And that right no one can give but me. And that right I offer you now.'

He said, 'You have fought against me more bitterly than any man. Who can trust this turnabout?'

'*You* can trust it,' I said. 'Warfare is not a woman's work. Though the spirit be strong, the body is weak; and in the end the body conquers. When I first marched against you I was young and I was strong. I marched through heat and through cold; I stood breast high in mud and in blood. I slept upon the hard ground—or slept not at all. Those years have taken their toll. I am older now; and I am older than my years. Cousin, I am a sick woman.'

He said, 'As for being older—we are all older. And for the rest, there's colour in your cheeks, brightness in your eyes...'

'The colour's the colour of sickness, the brightness the brightness of fever. I have few years left. But, with eternity at my door, I would give my soul to be a woman and not a soldier. No more a soldier, no more. I have not the strength nor the heart. I long for nothing in this world but to live a woman's way—order my house, sleep quiet at night ...'

'... with your husband!' He interrupted, brutal. 'Bear your children ...'

I would have answered him then but the dreaded cough began in my throat and my hand went up to ease the pain in my chest. I tried to keep back the coughing but I was worn with so much speaking and with my journey and with my grief; and the coughing would not be stayed. I turned away my head; no one had seen me yet upon the rack of my sickness. I had no wish for Philip to be the first. There was the old sickly taste in my mouth—iron and salt.

And it came to me, standing there, that this last shame too, I must conquer if I meant to save my husband.

I brought my hand from my mouth and held it out to him.

'You see, cousin, you see!' And I was coughing still. 'You have nothing to fear from me and very much to gain. Give me back my husband alive and well, and I will give you everything in return. All my rights; my countships together with every town great and small, castles and manors, tithes and incomes; not one thing, be it great or small, will I keep back. And further—do you listen, Cousin?—let it be written down. I swear to give you these things for ever, as my Saviour hears me. And, if I should bear a child, I swear for him also. But—' and I looked at my hand with the blood upon it, 'You are right; and I think there will never be a child for me.'

It was the blood upon my hand convinced him; the sickness that must kill me, saved Frank's life and so I cannot grudge payment now.

But still he said nothing. I held up my hand again, the blood bright upon it. 'You see, Cousin,' I said, 'it is not hard to give up every right for myself and for my descendants, as long as Christendom shall stand.' And I stood there very still, and the winter sunshine fell upon the bright blood as though to show him how short my time.

How long the silence lasted I do not know. I stood there, soul and body withdrawn in supplication, not to him but to God.

At last he nodded.

I said, 'Sweet Christ be thanked! Keep faith with me and I will keep faith with you. Send them to deliver my lord.'

'You must wait a little, cousin,' he said, a little sour, 'the law does not move as quick as woman's desire. We must have documents drawn, every point writ clear so that *Yes* is *Yes*, and *No* is *No*; and neither is *Maybe*. And it is not a matter for me alone; there are the cities of the three countships to be convened, our arguments presented, their obedience obtained. Not until all this is done can our bargain be signed and sealed. Until all is right and tight, van Borselen stays where he is.'

I should have expected that; it was reasonable. But my disappointment was almost more than I could bear. I looked at my cousin. I said, 'Do not make me wait too long. I am a sick woman.'

I might have spoken to the wind. Philip meant to risk no right that the slow procession of law would give. January came in, dark with snow, and February with its bitter winds. March went out in a scutter of rain. In early April when the willows are golden by my rivers, he declared himself satisfied; all had been ratified by law. Nothing for me now but to sign.

And now—we are made as we are made—the thing did not seem so simple. I might yet have a child, my physician had said so. It was not uncommon, he said, for a woman wasted by a consumption, to bear a child and thereby to recover her strength. What right then had I to sign my rights away for ever? It was the thing that had troubled me these weary months.

I looked at Philip coiled like a spring beneath his quiet smiling. That smile reminded me that if I did not sign, there would be no husband to give me a child.

I looked at my mother that stood beside him. Nothing to be gleaned from the mask of her face.

But, if Philip played me false in this, as so often before?

I put down the pen. 'I will not sign,' I said, 'until with my own eyes I see my dear lord safe and well.'

He said, pale eyes ablaze with anger, 'I have sworn by Christ Jesus ...'

'It does not say so here!' And I tapped upon the paper.

'As I hope for salvation,' he said, 'the man is safe.'

'You may believe so! But how if an accident has already befallen—and you not know? A push from the battlements; food tainted a little, perhaps; a stone loosened from its mortar as he walks below. Such accidents are not unknown. No, Cousin, I must see my husband before I sign your papers.' And I pushed at them with a seeming-careless hand.

He bowed, biting back his anger. 'You shall see him within the half-hour,' he said.

'Then within the half-hour I will sign.'

He turned on his heels and the long procession of his friends with him. At the door, my mother turned and came back to me. She stood looking down at me and now there was no mistaking the pity in her face.

She said, 'You would do well not to provoke him. For whether you will or not, still you must sign. This agreement, made between you, has been read the length and breadth of the land; read and considered and accepted. If van Borselen should die—' and she shrugged as though it were no great matter, 'still you would have no cause to complain; for there's no word anywhere as to his safety. There's word only of your desire to be free of your burden and of your unworthiness to rule.'

She picked up the paper and read,

'... and I, Jacqueline, countess of Holland, of Hainault and of Zealand, together with Friesland and the islands thereof, seeing that I am a weak woman and cannot command obedience nor administer government in peace and tranquillity; and because above all things I desire the good of my people, do here declare that no man is so perfectly able to render my people happy nor serve their good, as our dear. brother of Burgundy my true heir and next blood. Therefore out of perfect love and natural affection, without the least compulsion...

'*Without compulsion!* So you see, if now, at this last you refuse to sign, your people will say, A sick woman, changing with every gust of wind. We cannot, with safety, leave ourselves in her hand! Sign or not—your cousin of Burgundy takes all.'

I had no cause to trust her; yet the words made sense, I turned to Grenier and he nodded grave.

'Yet read the rest,' I said, 'though I should know well what's there. I've read it through again and again, with every fresh demand—and

267

God knows there's been enough! My cousin forgets nothing how-ever small, not so small a thing as will sit on a pin's head. All, all written down—except the one thing for which all is given! Yet read it, Grenier.'

He looked at me with the compassion I had learned to fear; and then, as though he needed more light, went across to the window taking the papers with him ... I think he could not endure to see my face while he read, nor to let me see his own.

... without the least compulsion, and beyond any power of revocation on our part, we give and bestow all the powers of sovereignty high and low, territories, cities, castles and peoples of our countships of Holland, Hainault, Zealand and Friesland together with all garrisons, rights, liberties, revenues and aids; also gifts from any estates ecclesiasti-cal or otherwise, without reservation of anything that has accrued to us from our dear father...

And now it came, the full list! Everything to be handed over to my cousin—nothing forgotten, not one manor, not one due, not one pin's head.

... and I hereby release my subjects each and all, from their oaths and I swear to enter into no bond of friendship with the enemies of my cousin, the said Philip Duke of Burgundy ...

Grenier laid down the page, took up a second and a third; he laid down the eighth and last page; and each page a catalogue of my gifts to Philip!

I said, and I was smiling though my mouth shook, 'A very great price to pay for the life of one man—and that life not even men-tioned!'

Grenier said, 'Nor is there mention of your marriage, Madam; no word of consent given—or to be given.'

My mother said, 'My daughter is simple and my nephew most subtle. He guards her good name. For, how would it appear in Christendom that she sold her inheritance and her people for lust of this one man?'

I ignored that last taunt, I said, 'Does cousin Philip guard my good name? I think, rather, he forces me, for all his fine words, to write myself down unfit to rule.'

She said, 'The people will be happier, believe it. And you will be happier; you are too much of a woman—all impulse and passion—to rule. You have no nature for it. I'm your mother and I speak the truth. And indeed, had you the nature you have not the strength.' And she looked with pity upon my wasted frame. 'As for the understanding about van Borselen, you may trust your cousin in this.'

'May I indeed! A man that fears nothing in this world ... 'But he fears the next. He is afraid of God.'

'He thinks he has God in his pocket. But, if he deceives me in this, then God Himself will strike him down.'

'God grant it!' Grenier said and met her stare unflinching.

For the first time she smiled. 'I love loyalty,' she told him, 'wherever it may be found. Come now—' and she turned her smile upon me and it was a true smile, 'were your cousin to return now and declare himself unwilling to sign—what then?'

'I should want to die,' I said. 'Yet, so perverse are we poor creatures, it is still a grief and a bitterness to set my hand to it.'

'You will live to be glad of it!' she promised.

And now there were steps along the stone passage; and amongst them a step I knew by the leaping of my heart. I stood up and my eyes were on the door.

From his place between his guards Frank looked back at me. Alive he was; but well? Four months in prison had left their mark. Yet from their hollow sockets his blue eyes looked very steady into mine, and his mouth smiled.

I took a step forward; the guards crossed their halberds between us.

Frank said, 'Dearest heart, think well before you sign. I am not worth the price.'

'The world is too poor to lose you,' I said. 'And I am too poor also.'

I turned to my mother. 'Go tell your nephew I am ready.'

XXXVIII

I was no longer Madam the Countess, hereditary Prince of Holland, of Hainault and of Zealand. But my love was safe. He was pale from his imprisoning, but it was a pallor that must yield to freedom; for we were into May now and the sun like a blessing upon the world. For myself, my cough troubled me still; yet I was hopeful of my husband's cherishing to make me well.

These early summer months I was happy with my dear love. I held my proud place no longer; nor had I yet taken my prouder place—Frank's wife in the eyes of Christendom. For Philip would not give the word.

'My love, my love,' Frank cried out once, 'you have lost everything for me; and I am not worth the sacrifice.'

'I would give up my heavenly crown to be your wife, let alone an earthly one. I am a woman; I ask no more than to lead a woman's life ... in honour. If he keeps his promise, I am content.'

And now, having robbed me of my rightful titles, my cousin bestowed upon me a new one—and a curious one. I have never been a patient woman and the old Eve in me dies hard.

'So I am Madam the Duchess of Ostrevant!' I told Frank. 'And my cousin laughs in his sleeve. We have changed places he and I—and he means Christendom to know it. He takes the ruler's title, I the heir's. Yes, he may well laugh.'

'He may laugh too soon. He makes you his heir—why not? In spite of his four wives he has no heir. And you are young, my heart, younger than he.'

I did not answer him. My sickness had not fastened upon me further, but it had not retreated neither. And, since I could find no word, I gave him my hand; I saw him look at it before taking it into the warmth of his own; it looked very thin—translucent, almost, in the sunshine.

'You are not very fat, certainly,' he said. 'I shall feed you on cream until you're as fat as a little pig and all Christendom will envy me my beautiful fat wife!'

I tried to smile but the smile came hard with me. He said—and there was no smiling in him either, now, 'Beloved child, I will care for you and you shall soon be well again.'

I came into his arms and was glad to feel his strength about me. To be a child and cherished! Sweet and sweet, indeed! Good to know for a little while that sweetness; the bitterness was soon to come.

Philip had not done with me. It was early in June when he made known his pleasure.

I must ride with him through all the chief cities of my three count-ships, and, standing by his side, must, myself, release my people from their vows.

It was a humiliation and a pain I had not bargained for. I saw Frank's face when he read the letter; I put my own pain aside. 'I would give my heavenly crown to be your wife,' I said, 'but all I gave was an earthly one. And given ... it is given. Why should I shrink from saying so?'

But for all my fine words the ordeal to come drove away sleep. I brooded over it lying sleepless, a hand at my throat to keep back the coughing lest it disturb Frank that was so tender of my comfort. This last demand, the public showing of myself, the public renunciation, was a bitterness and a humbling I knew not how to endure.

And yet I must endure it.

And so began the long and mocking progress—the heralds and the knights, the banners and the trumpets, the garlands and the gifts. But not for me; no more for me. For Philip, only for Philip.

Riding with Philip through the Hague my proud city, through Rotterdam and Amsterdam, through Haarlem, through Delft—Delft with its flowers and its harbour and its memories! And all the time sitting erect and smiling out of my painted face. Walking with Philip the length of a council chamber, the length of a church ... and all the time remembering that had I obeyed my father I should not have found myself in this plight. Had I been a little patient I might have married Frank in the first flush of my youth, Frank for whose dear sake I had given all. I might still have been confirmed in every title, every honour, my children growing up about my knees. I might have been young still, and strong; not barren and burned with the wasting sickness.

The long riding, the long humiliation, ate further into my poor strength; the sickness fastened upon me no more to be shaken off.

Towards the end of our progress even my cousin could see I was a sick woman. Maybe he feared I might die upon the way; maybe he feared my wasted looks would turn hearts towards me. I might release the rest of my cities by letter, he said, if I so desired.

If I desired! And we riding to Hainault—Hainault so loving and so loved, Hainault, so loyal and treacherous. I thanked my sickness that it had spared me this one thing—the riding through Mons for the breaking of the oath. At all cost, I was grateful to be spared that!

And so we returned to the Hague, I lying exhausted within the charette, he all aglitter with triumph.

'Now all is done,' I said, 'let me go away. But first your promise—your consent to my marriage with the Lord of Borselen. I have waited long and long enough!'

'Not so fast, cousin,' he said. 'And, indeed, what haste? You have enjoyed the man long enough!'

I bit back my anger. I had given up everything, endured everything.

No sense in angering him now.

He said, 'There is a thing, a small thing. You have told your own people how gladly you give everything into my hands.' And he smiled. 'But that is not enough. To save anger and bitterness and the shedding of blood, you must tell all Christendom. See here are the letters; you have but to sign. And when it is done I will give consent to your marriage.'

I said, 'You have promised and promised! And always there is one more step to be taken, one more thing to be done. I will do nothing further until I hold in my hand your consent to my marriage, written, signed and sealed. Then I will sign those letters. Until then you get no more of me!'

He smiled; and the smile was honest. 'Had you always been so cautious, Cousin, you had not ended thus!'

'I am satisfied with the ending—if you play fair!' I said.

'By God, there's a pride in you a man could love,' he said. 'You had every gift heart could desire—beauty and wit and a great inheritance.'

'And a great enemy,' I said.

'The enemy is within yourself—your own nature; you are too quick, too rash. But the spirit, the spirit is great! When I think of what you were, it pricks me a little, that I did not marry you myself.'

'So you said once before! But I would not have been your wife, not for all the crowns in Christendom. I want nothing of you but the keeping of a promise for which I have waited long and paid dear.'

It was late in July, in the year of our Lord fourteen hundred and thirty-four that my cousin and I stood for the last time face-to-face. The letters he had bade me send out to the Kings of Christendom lay unsigned upon the table.

To my dear Cousin the most puissant Charles VII of France ... To my dear nephew, the most puissant King of England, Henry VI ... To my dear Father in God, His Holiness Pope Martin ... Philip's own letter lay beside them.

I, Philip, Duke of Burgundy, Count of Flanders, Count of Holland, of Hainault and Zealand, together with Friesland and her islands, do hereby empower my dear cousin Jacqueline, Duchess of Ostrevant, for the love I bear her, to marry with the noble and powerful knight, Frank Lord of Borselen, Seigneur of Zealand of St Martensdijk and of Cortgène. And both the said Countess Jacqueline and the said Lord Frank of Borselen shall incur neither blame nor reproach concerning this marriage from me or any other ...

I watched him bend to the table, saw his hand move across the paper. I took up the pen after him.

And now it was done. Having declared my unfitness to rule before the whole of Christendom, I might, at long last and without reproach, live with my dear love. Philip and I saluted each other with a kiss—a last kiss. And now all was finished between us of enmity or friendship. I counted no more in his proud scheme. We should meet in this life no more.

'We have been married above eighteen months in the sight of God,' I told Frank, my mouth all wry with my smiling, 'but still I face Christendom as a strumpet for the second time, until you make an honest woman of me, my love!'

And so in the Castle of Martensdijk, that castle where *D* entwined amongst the garland had first spoken of Frank's love, we were married at last in the sight of Christendom.

Were this a *conte*, you might well believe our happiness unblemished and enduring. Enduring it is, but not unblemished; for this is life and no romance. My bright sky is shadowed by the constant cloud of my sickness; and, at the beginning also, there were the fleeting clouds of my own regret. For there were times—in my own heart let me admit it when, in spite of myself I must remember the great place I had lost and the noble titles I had borne. Now I bore my empty titles, fine-sounding in the ears of fools—Jacqueline Duchess in Holland; not *of* but *in*—a little word and the world's difference between them. Jacqueline Duchess of Ostrevant—yet another empty name; for it meant nothing, nothing at all. There is another heir now, another Child of Holland—Philip's infant son. Another de Charolais launched upon an unsuspecting world!

Satisfied, at last, that my lands were secured to his line, Philip threw me a final, careless title—*Lady Forester*. So he made me warden of the woodlands in those lands that had been mine, where justice and life and death had lain in my own hands. I returned my thanks for his favour; this most scarifying favour.

I am satisfied … I am satisfied, I told myself those first days of utter renunciation. I would awake whispering it in my mind; but I never told Frank how deep that last insult had cut. There were days when I went about praying God to strike down my cousin and his infant son together.

But the days went by and the galled shoulders began to take the burden with more ease. Perhaps because my sickness did not mend, I began to see earthly titles as not important; my soul accepted the renunciation.

But the sickness in my lungs I could not accept. Yet, if I did not mend—there was some coughing, some blood and much weariness—I grew, I thought, no worse. I was forever telling myself that soon I would be with child; and, being pregnant, I should grow strong again. But I do not think I ever quite believed it—my cousin Philip's taunt had struck deep. Yet it was a hope I must carry in my heart; for, with that hope, I need not acknowledge even to myself the seriousness of my sickness, need see no physician, need discuss it with no one, not even with Frank. Frank himself barely recovered from his imprisonment. But Beatrix saw those things I could not bring myself to say. She showed her love of me a thousand ways; and most of all by never mentioning the matter. She knew I desired the thing unspoken; as though, the word unsaid, I might buy a little further time.

There are no words to tell of Frank's goodness, his loving kindness. Sometimes I would think myself a liar and cruel with it, to leave him in his fool's paradise; and, sometimes I would think that, for all my careful covering of my sickness, he must know. Was he not a little too quick to understand my excuses when I could not ride, too quick to invent them when my own invention failed? I think he, like Beatrix, has the merciful gift of silence.

Of all our houses I love Martensdijk best—as you can understand. But we do not stay there often. It is too close to the sea and the damp wind chokes in my breast so that I cannot even cough but must stand gasping for air—and death's hand upon my heart. Most of the year we live at Theilingen in the woods of Haarlem where trees break the sharp wind and the smell of pine is grateful to my lungs. Here I breathe more freely and there have been days when I told myself that I am, after all, not so ill; and that, by God's Grace I shall be well again.

Once I went to the Hague where some occasion called my husband. It was a bitter thing. To be a lady amongst others—to be even a great lady—where one has been greatest; to make my curtsey to the governor's wife that had bent her back to me often enough. Bitter and bitter indeed!

And there at the Hague I remembered how Frank had been taken by treachery and must have come to his death but for my bargaining. And more than once I awoke crying out, 'I must go home. I will come here no more ... no more.' And, all wild with my fears I cried out, 'I will not come again alive or dead. I will not be buried here though every count of Holland lies here. I could not rest in this place that stinks of treachery and fear.'

Frank quieted me and bade me not talk of death for I was but a child; but still I wept and entreated not to lie in the Hague, until he swore to remember my request and to keep it.

But at Theilingen all is quiet and gentle. Now I am too weary to sit a horse or even to sit upright at a feast, I lie in my chamber remembering my childhood. Do you remember? I ask Beatrix, *Do you remember?* And we talk of my father and the courts he held when he was free of his duties.

'Do you remember the guests at le Quesnoy and the feasting and the music?' I asked her once.

'And the hunting parties?' she asked in her turn. 'Oh those hunts! You would be wild with excitement; there would be no holding you. I would bring you down to the courtyard holding you by the hand and you would weep to be off with the hunters.'

Though I weep myself into the grave I shall ride no more with the hunters. I turned my face away lest she read the thought and she went on, 'And the day they sat you on the great horse because you would not be done weeping; and you rode out with your father ...'

'And I was not afraid. And he brought me back and set me next to him at the head of the table because he loved my courage. And I reached out my hand for this thing and that on the table and my mother looked all daggers; but my father and I laughed one to the other.'

'He laughs best that laughs last! You were sick and must be taken away; but you would let no one handle you but me. So I was sent for ...'

'And I carried ingloriously away!'

And we laughed together, remembering.

Perhaps because my sickness reminded me too much of the darkness to come, I yearned towards the bright days of my childhood. And I thought if I could fashion Theilingen upon my father's court, I might—if I could not cheat him altogether—forget death a little. Of my old friends few could come; poverty kept some back, age or sickness others; but their sons came and their daughters. They did not help me to forget the grave. Watching those bright creatures, I would think, How short a time since I myself was thus! I was after all but thirty-three. I wanted to cry out to them, *Laugh while you may; life goes quickly over!* And I would plan new diversions, speed up the merriment ... I was never a godly person!

Frank delighted in my little court. He is a rich man and generous and he loves beautiful things. So he had his merchants search for stuffs and jewels; and I that had gone threadbare, counting myself lucky to have two pairs of sleeves to one poor gown, now have my fill of cloth-of-gold, of silks of Damascus, of fine English cloth. Gowns and furs and jewels—my coffers overflow.

Once—and it not long ago—when Beatrix was dressing me for supper, Frank came in tossing a leather pouch from hand to hand. 'Catch!' he cried out and tossed it in my lap where I sat beneath my woman's hands.

It was a rope of pearls, fine in colour and perfectly matched. I sat there looking at the lovely thing; and it was nothing to me but a reminder how short my time must be to know the loving kindness of this husband of mine. The pearls slid through my fingers and the choking came up in my throat.

Frank said sharply, 'Time presses; and there's some little matter to do before supper!' I could not see his face clearly for he spoke over his shoulders, his head turned from me. Between us the pearls lay upon the floor.

In spite of myself my hand went out to call him back; but even then I would not let him see how sick I was. Between the paroxysms I gasped out, 'Oh, who will comfort him when I am gone?'

Beatrix said nothing; she stood beside me a frail old woman— though she was not yet fifty—all drawn with grief. It is my mother, I thought with sudden longing, that should be with me now, my mother hale for all her sixty years. She was neither a loving nor a comfortable woman ... yet she was still my mother. But most of all I longed for my father dead these many years, longed beyond all understanding. It is strange, how, in our troubles—however old we may be—we long for the touch of a mother's hands ... or a father's perhaps; someone older and wiser than we. Is that why we turn to God—if not at the beginning—then at the end? *Our Father ...*

Well, if I may not live—though less than half my years are told— then I must die with courage. It is all that is left. So Beatrix put the red upon my lips and upon my cheeks, painting the mask of health on my sick face; and soon I was sitting in my place at supper in my fine gown, the pearls too-heavy about my neck; smiling and upright for all the weariness that ate into my very bones.

When our days are numbered we turn more closely to God, beseeching His mercy, redoubling our prayers and our charities in His Name. But this comfort I must not take. I must deny myself for

Frank's sake, take my part in feast and frolic, show a smiling face ... and all the time my chest hollow with its pain and the blood salt in my mouth. How often do I clap at the tumblers when my hands should be folded in prayer? And these prayers I say while I lie sleepless in the long nights. And the charities I long to give must wait until I am dead. They are written in a book that all may be done when I, myself, cannot do them. And I think God will understand.

XXXIX

Two years since Philip gave me permission to marry. Two years in which to live with my love, my kind and cherishing love. Two years. And they have melted away and I have little time left. I have tried to resign myself into God's Hands; I have agonized to resign myself. But still I fight against my sickness, crying to Him to grant me a little longer.

Every day this past year Beatrix painted my face when I rose; and I went to bed bedaubed like any harlot. But now there is no more need; everything is open between my husband and me. And Beatrix is dead. I think my slow dying hastened her own—she was not yet fifty. Beloved Beatrix. Ermgart is good; but I miss your kindness and your gentle hands every hour of the day.

Summer has come again. It is the year of our Lord fourteen hundred and thirty-six and I am just thirty-five. I was born in June; the Rose of Holland my father used to call me; I am glad he cannot see me now in my cankered blooming. These last weeks I could not keep my secret from Frank any longer ... because I can no longer walk. He did not wait for me to speak; he had already sent for John of Leyden and Gysbrecht of Rotterdam—but it is all useless, useless. Had I thought there was any help in man I would myself have sent, but Floris of Dordrecht, than whom there is no more skilled physician in Christendom, told me long ago there was no hope for me except to bear a child; and that it seems I cannot do. These learned gentlemen sweat me—that sweat enough of my fever; and they let my blood—that spit blood enough. We must let out the sickness before we can let in health again, they say and they smile; but for all their smiling their eyes slide from me.

Frank is constantly with me; he uses the little chamber that belonged to Beatrix so that he may be for ever within call. He says I am his beloved child; and this morning he brought me a mirror that I might see how young I looked. And indeed, this wasting sickness has given me back something of the look of a child. I am all rosy with fever and bright-eyed with fever; and I am glad to die looking not uncomely. Frank laughs with me and jokes with me; but when his eyes are unguarded, I see his passionate pity and his loneliness. Could he open his heart and pour the pure blood into my sick lungs he would do it. How good is God that gives us no choice. Men like Frank are needed in this poor country of mine.

And so I lie here the long summer through, my windows sealed lest the air breed more strongly the sickness in my body. I am so weak I cannot, without help, stand, nor sit upright in my bed. But I do not want to die ... I do not want to die. Even now I cannot say *Thy will be done.* My own will fights against this last Farewell. Why must I die in the midst of the only true happiness I have ever known? How can I leave my dear lord to his loneliness? Though I shut my eyes against the sight of his face, still it comes between me and my prayers.

... between me and God. Make me well, oh God; if not wholly well, then a little well, a very little ... as well as I was last year, last month, last week even...

God does not hear me.

I must make my last testament, I know it. Yet, the words said, the name signed for the last time signed—it is an invitation to Death. Invitation? It is Death commands ... and I must obey. Yet I am but thirty-five. It is not so old. And God is good. If I beseech him long enough and humbly enough surely He will let me ride the woods again; or, if not to ride, to walk, to walk a few steps; and, if not that, then to let me lie here a little longer where our eyes may see each other—Frank's eyes and mine.

Summer has gone and taken the roses and I shall not see them again. And September has gone; and there's no more green upon the trees; the woods of Theilingen are hung with gold. And soon there will be no leaves at all; the trees will lift their naked arms, save where the laurel hangs dark and shining like witches' candles.

And still I lie in bed and, for the most part my eyes are closed; do what I will, they drop of themselves. Frank thinks I sleep but I do not sleep. There are so many memories to call home ... and so little time.

I dwell so much upon these memories that things about me are not always clear; and sometimes it takes a little while before I know where I am. My mind darts this way and that, as though it were a bird flying through cloud; and what I will find behind that cloud I do not know. Sometimes there are clouds behind clouds and I am not in Theilingen at all, but in some childhood place. Time melts and lets me through. It is all very confusing and so I have sent for Grenier and I try to tell him the thoughts in my mind. At these times I send Frank away; for though each parting is like a little death, I know he has other duties than that of a sick wife; and I know, also, he needs air other than that of my sick chamber.

I lie back on my pillow and talk to this dear friend. When I cannot draw the air into my sick lungs or choke upon the pillow, then he lifts me gently and moistens my lips with wine. I tell him my thoughts and he writes down the things I say that Frank may know my thoughts when I am gone. For time has been short between my husband and me; and I want him to know everything about me ... until the end.

I lie here and Frank holds my hands in his, as though to keep me safe. I try to keep my mind here in this room where I can feel the safety of his hands; but I cannot always command my mind. Back it goes, back ... back ... like the bird I spoke of flying blind through the clouds.

This morning I dreamed I was a child again. The Hope of Holland; and every back bending as I passed. I was walking in the gardens at le Quesnoy and the birds were flying and calling. There was a sound of a lute and a voice singing. And it was John, young French John, walking with me and singing. I thought you were dead, I told him; but he turned and smiled and his face was clear as though a painter had caught it in a lozenge of light to hold it forever. I put out my hand but he turned away. I wanted to cry out *wait ... wait* ... But he was gone; he did not wait for me.

'He is waiting,' Grenier said.

Master Grenier writes quickly and steadily. Sometimes as I watch him, the room disappears and he with it; and when it comes back again I think I have been dreaming. But I am not quite sure. The place the bird flies to is dear and bright; and the chamber dim ... and I do not always know which is real. And I do not always know people ... at the first. Sometimes I think Frank is my father ...

I have slept a long time today. And now, in my dim chamber I am telling Grenier about my dream.

I was in the throne room at the Hague ... where now another sits in my place. I was ten years old, I think; for Master van Eyck was there and his palette all ready. I was wearing my best gown—my father brought it from England—my white gown of stiff silk embroidered all over with red roses.

I was tired and I did not want to stand. Master van Eyck said if I was good and patient now and let him paint this little picture my father desired so much, then he would put me in a great canvas and I should be an angel with wings; or a saint, perhaps. I told him I should like that—though I was neither saint nor angel; my mother who cared little about me and Beatrix who cared much were agreed in that one thing.

And so I stood ... I stood. I grew weary of standing ... I tried to tell him so but my throat would not let me speak. I looked down at my gown. The red was not roses at all. *Blood*, I cried out, *blood*. Master van Eyck put down his palette and came over to me. And it was not Master Jan at all. It was a tall, tall man and the sun was shining about his hair as it might be a halo. I said, *Father?* But it was not my father. It was my husband ... or so I think. I am not sure now ... it is all very confusing. And yet since these are the two I love best in the world, all is well.

All is well, Grenier, since the sun shines ... it does shine, I think, though I cannot see it; nor can I feel it warm upon my hand ... my cold hand. But I know it is there; and the good doctors will make me well again. The bird has come home from a far place and the sun shines ...

Written in the hand of Frank van Borselen, Lord of Zealand and of Cortgène.

Sunday, the ninth of October, this year of Grace, fourteen hundred and thirty-five.

This day died my beloved wife Jacqueline, sometime Countess of Holland, of Hainault and Zealand. And I write, that Christendom which so cruelly slandered her may know her courage and her sweetness and her truth.

I should not grieve that she is dead since these two years have been for her a long dying. But nature is too much for me; and I long for her that was my wife and my companion and my darling child.

Her courage was always great; she led her armies, won her battles, accepted defeat. But the courage she has shown these two years out-tops all.

She was dying and she knew it. But it was her wish I should not know and I respected her silence. Why not? I had spoken constantly with physicians ... and there was no hope.

But for me, also, it has not been easy. To hear her cough in the night so that you might think her lungs must burst—and to make no move, not even to give her a draught to ease her pain nor even a sip of wine! To lie there pretending to sleep while she lay tormented! I have heard her weep in the night, very quietly; and I have given no sign. And I have seen her painted to the eyes to hide the tell-tale colour—the pallor with the fever-spot burning upon the cheek-bones, and the shocking thinness of her face.

And all the time she used her failing strength to deceive me further—riding when she should have been in her bed. How often have I seen her upright in the saddle denying her disease with the strength of her will! And how often have I seen her lifted from her horse and half-carried to her chamber by the faithful Beatrix—Beatrix watching for the moment of return. And I must close my eyes and see nothing. And then, when she could ride no longer I must hear her smiling excuses, accept them, smiling.

I must accept it all though I saw her burn her life away. I must accept it lest I break her spirit along with her body—a thing I had been warned against. And so I played my part. I sent for stuffs rich enough for a queen, for furs, for jewels; for all those things that women love, knowing she could not wear the half of them. But, I think, seeing them gave her a sort of hope. We have had so little time together—and that spoilt by sickness; but I have tried to make her life rich and gay, her life that has been so poor and sad. It is an irony of fate—and I think she felt it too—that I, who might have cherished her in the sweet flowering of her youth strove to cherish her when it was too late. And this adds to my burden; and this, too, I must carry.

This last week I have known the end must come. The priests have been by her side and the good sisters also. She was, for the most part, away from her mind, and did not, I think, fully understand why they were there.

She had made no legal testament, and I would not distress her. I will see all disposed as I think she would have wished.

But, though I would not trouble her her mother was not so nice. All unwilling I sent for Madam Margaret; she has never made things easy for my poor child. I need not have troubled to send. She was already on her way, bringing with her van Arbele and van Egmont, Burgundy's councillors in Holland. There they were, already in black; crows all eager for the picking. I was angry and did not hide my anger. Did they think I would allow them to frighten my child at such a time? 'Between you, you have taken all,' I said. Did they think there was something yet to snatch from my dying child?

I was not reasonable, perhaps. I think I hated Madam Margaret because she had never been a mother to my girl; and because she is hale and hearty—and will be long after my girl is dust.

I kept my unbidden guests from the sick-room but Madam Margaret I could not forbid. My girl lay there, sleeping, I thought. She did not open her eyes when her mother came in; but she sensed, I think, the unwelcome visitor, for she made a movement with her hand, a rejecting movement. And she made a sighing sound; and *blood*, she whispered, all surprised, *blood*. And the blood flowed out of her mouth and stained the white linen. I took Madam Margaret out of the room; unless my child ask for her, she should not be allowed to enter again. I think Madam Margaret suffered, seeing the child; and I was not ill-pleased.

For a week my girl lay, eyes closed for the most part. Sometimes her eyes opened but she did not always know me. Father she said; and there was a smile on her lips as though she were a child and happy. And sometimes she said my name; and then she smiled as though she were a woman and happy. And I thank God I have brought a little gladness to her life, though it be at the end.

Yesterday she came from her dreaming and her mind was clear. I might have hoped then had I not been warned—a flicker of light before the darkness. She said, very slow in a thin voice, 'I am stronger. I could sit up in bed if I choose ... but I do not choose.'

I tried to smile at that; it must have been a good smile, because she smiled, too. 'Take my hand and keep it,' she said. 'As long as you hold my hand I think I cannot die.'

And then she said, and her voice though faint was clear enough, 'I have been dreaming ... of John ... French John. So young ... so good, so gentle ... and I a spoilt and wilful child.'

She sighed as though her heart must break and I said, 'Leave talking, now, my heart. Let us speak again later.' But Master Gysbrecht nodded to let her talk and she went whispering on.

'I never dream of Brabant; my mind rejects him; runs on other thoughts and turns him out. Once I thought I could not forgive him ever; now I forgive him as I pray God will forgive me all I have done amiss, and it is not a little.'

She stopped, fighting a little for breath; at last she said, 'And then ... *he* came.'

I knew whom she meant for she lay smiling upon the thought;

and, dying as she was, I felt the anguish of jealousy; and hatred because he had used her so ill.

'There was a glory all about him … a false glory but I. did not know it. I loved him … so much; and I suffered so much. I could not believe he had deserted me… I kept writing and writing … and then I stopped.'

Tears spilled upon her cheek; and as I wiped them away, I felt upon my hand the ghost of her kiss, faint and very cold.

'But he loved me once, … I must think it. It makes my shame a little less. Did he love me, do you think?'

It was a hard moment for me. I wanted to cry out *No*; to wipe him from her dying mind. But I could not do it.

'He loved you,' I said.

'Yes,' she said, 'yes. But it did not last. It *could* not last. He was beautiful and glorious. And I, a woman scarred in warfare and very poor.'

Her mouth shook; she lay still for a while and then the smile came again to her lips and I marvelled at its sweetness.

'And then … you, my love. Of all men the best, the kindest … most noble. He shone like gold; but it was base metal. And you, my love … pure gold. Lover and friend and husband and father. So many sorrows … so many; yet were all to do again I would welcome them … all, if in the end it brought me you.'

Suddenly the lids dropped and she was asleep and in her sleep she smiled still.

I sat by her side her hand in mine and watched the face that had known a thousand sorrows and so few joys, that I might remember it as long as I lived.

How long I sat there I do not know. Perhaps I slept also. I came awake at a light tap upon the door and since I would not unloose her hand, signed to one of the sisters to answer it.

It was Grenier; and, behind him, Madam Margaret and her precious friends. I rose and gently loosed my hand. I did not look at them. I spoke only to Grenier. 'Bid the black crows be off!' I said, very low. 'It is not yet time to pick the bones!'

The slight movement, or my voice, perhaps, aroused my girl.

'It is Greasier,' I said, 'come to pay his duty.' And shut the door against the birds of ill-omen.

'Dear Grenier,' she said in that voiceless whispering. And then, 'Have you brought your pens? I am better, see!' And she lifted a wasted hand. 'But one should be ready… I have left things too long!' She shook her head slightly from side to side. 'I was always a feckless thing ... yet I have a grateful heart. So many kindnesses to remember ... so little to remember them with! My jewels ... Philip took them long ago. And my gowns so poor ... my furs so shabby.' She sighed; and then I saw her smile. 'But the gifts you gave me ... the lovely gowns I never wore, the jewels ... may I have them? Will you sell them for me? Will you?' And her thin hand burned in mine. I nodded. I could not speak.

'My books,' she said and a little frown puckered her brows. 'My English books ... give them away. But my Froissart in which we have read together ... for you, my love ... to remember me.'

She stopped, waiting for her breath.

'To Beatrix my silk hoods, my cloaks and a pension ... six hundred guilders.' She stopped again. 'Oh,' she said, 'Beatrix has no need of anything ...' and she was smiling. 'She is waiting for me; I shall get to heaven, maybe, on the tail of her skirts. As for the cloaks and hoods, give them to Ermgart; and a pension also of two hundred guilders. For Agnes Hastgen my chest of kitties and shifts ...

'There's a certain Kerstine dwelling at Utrecht that claims to be my sister ... and I think it is true. For her a black gown of fine wool and two hundred and fifty guilders that her daughter be admitted——as she much desires—into a sisterhood ...'

She was stopped by coughing; the bright drops flecked her chin and the white shift.

'To my church at Bouchain, where the heart of my father lies, a sum to pay perpetual masses for his soul. And to every church throughout my three lands a sum that they may say perpetual masses for mine.' She looked at me then; she said, and there was a ghost of laughter in her sunken eyes, 'I need those prayers if I am to scramble into heaven ... but it's a lot of money. Am I worth it, do you think?'

I made myself smile; I nodded. For a while she said no more but lay back upon the pillow. And though she did not speak her mind was at work.

'There's a student,' she said at last, 'very poor. I promised him a fine supper when he should become a doctor. For him fifty guilders ...'

'His name?' Jan Grenier asked.

She shook her head. 'But—' and again the little smile of mischief moved on her mouth, 'He will remember. He will tell you ... I make no doubt.'

She fell to silence again. I sat and watched the late autumn sunlight gild her wasted face. At long last she spoke.

'So many have served me, poor as well as rich and I forget their names. I forget ... but it is written down ... my little book. Ermgart knows. Every name ... old servants, priests that have prayed for me, old soldiers wounded for me ... and others, others. Pay them. Pay them all or I cannot rest. And, if any claim payment and his name be not set down, pay him, pay him also.'

Towards evening her eyes opened. 'Pay ... all,' she said.

'All,' I told her. 'I promise.'

'I was too poor,' she said, 'too poor.' And my heart was broken that, dying, the years of her poverty were with her still.

She nodded; her mind at rest, she seemed to doze again.

Towards evening her eyes opened for the last time; she turned their darkened light to where I sat. 'Father?' she said. And then, very joyous, 'Oh father!'

The bright blood gushed.

Monday, October 24th.

We buried my girl this morning. Even her last wish was not granted. Her mother and her cousin over-ruled it—as they have over-ruled everything her life long. Her body must lie in the burying-place of the Counts of Holland—Philip had always a sardonic humour. I marvel that the long-dead counts did not rise from their graves to drive away the foreigner that wears their crown.

Well then, her body must lie in the Hague. I thought, at first, to demand her heart, that it might lie beside me in Martensdijk when my time comes. It would seem a pretty thought; but I am a plain man and no poet. Cut the dead heart from her wasted body! I cannot do it. Well, if I am not to have her heart, then I will, at least, have her image. I have ordered Master Joris, that has great skill in this matter, to carve her portrait in wood; not wasted, as in these last days, but very young—as when I first saw her.

It is late and I cannot sleep. I miss my love, my dearest child; and I am burdened with a guilt because I did not carry out her last wish ... even dying they denied her. I have asked Ermgart to bring the book of which she spoke before she died and it lies before me.

I turn page after page. She was a long time a-dying ... a long time remembering.

Church and university and hospital—one might expect that from a prince; and great names—one might expect that, too. But it is the unknown names, the poor, little names that move the heart with her goodness. I loved her and was humble before her courage; yet I never knew the dearest thing about her; the way she would reach out beyond her own sorrows—and they were heavy enough, God knows—to the needs of others, their smallest needs.

… For Jan de Bruyn the gift of a gown because he is such a shabby fellow…

Yes, she would remember shabbiness and pity it.

…A new cloak, warm and of sober hue to the poor young chorister of St Goes. And to Jan that bled me so gently in my sickness, such a cloak also, and with it a hood that his ears may not prick with the cold …

There is one entry at which I stare and cannot leave staring.

…To the family of William van der Berg a sum to be paid to the treasury of Brabant that shall complete the amount of the fine still due from the family of his murderer …

Oh child, child, this terrible generosity of yours! I am tempted to leave this one thing undone. Must you set tongues wagging again? Your last mercy towards the man that humiliated you, that made you the laughing-stock of Brabant's court. But who will believe that? She was no saint—as she knew full well; but mercy never died in her. And I am sworn to her commands. Let the thing stand.

There was a knock just now upon my door. De Bye. The birds flock for the feeding-sparrow and carrion, too. All those that ask—though their names be not set down—to receive largesse. So she prayed with her dying breath. And so they gather with little thought for my grief. There is a priest that swears he lent her money and another priest with him—the one very fat, the other very lean; and both of them shifty fellows, de Bye says, and asks permission to kick them downstairs. Let them be paid up courteously, I tell him. It is her wish. And there are old servants declaring that they lent her this or that. De Bye would question when and where; but the sums are small enough, let them be paid.

And so they come in a steady stream.

This fellow lost his horse ten years ago in his lady's service; that one wore his shoes to holes journeying from one shrine to another to pray for her success. The poor student who was promised a fine supper has received his doctorate. She was right; he did not forget.

And so it goes on and on. Pay them all and do not abate one jot of their claims. For while the procession lasts of those that served her, or even speak her name, then she is not dead, but when the procession stops and I am left alone in my empty house … it is a thing I cannot face as yet. I dread the moment when I am left alone bereft of her I loved so late … dying in what should have been the fine flower of her womanhood.

She was my enemy and she became my love. I might have saved her; I might have known her joyous as was her true nature, but I was too late.

Everyone has gone now, satisfied. And I am left to ponder the puzzle that was Jacqueline. She was loving and longsuffering; she was fierce and she was swift ... a young man hanged for a careless word, the one word she could not forgive. And she paid for it; not only with tears for her lost cause, but with the bitterer tears of remorse. She could not forgive herself. 'Though I weep tears of blood, it cannot bring him back,' she said.

They spoke against her when her uncle died because she did not send Beatrix van Vliet away and because she shed no tear. But van Vliet had come to his just death and his wife was innocent. And for the tears—why should she weep for the man that would have dishonoured her with an incestuous marriage, the treacherous man that having sworn the oath to her, laid immediate hands upon her inheritance?

She could not weep; she had a shining honesty. And she had a filial devotion to God; though—like the best of us—she forgot, at times, her duty towards Him. She had a most loving and passionate heart; and with it, a tenderness and a humility. Her father knew it; and I knew it; and Beatrix knew it; and Grenier and de Bye and every meanest servant in her household. She had a deep humility and a high pride.

She had a hard life and the courage to match it. She endured more than women are called upon to endure; and when she did aught amiss she repented with tears. And to those tears God Himself will bend and He will wipe them away.

Some Books Consulted

Biographie Nationale. 28 vols. 1866–1944.

Blok, P.J. *A History of the People of the Netherlands.* (Translated by O.A. Bierstadt and R. Putnam.) 1898–1912.

Calendar of Patent Rolls. Henry VI. 1422–29. 1901.

Camden Society. *English Chronicles, 1377–1461.* (O.S. 64.) 1856.

Camden Society. *The Historical Collections of a Citizen of London.* (N.S. 17.) 1876.

Cartellieri, O. *La Cour des Ducs de Bourgogne.* 1946.

Chastellain, G. *Oeuvres* (ed. Kervyn de Lettenhove). 8 vols. 1863.

Denton, W. *England in the Fifteenth Century.* 1888.

Devillers, L. *Cartulaire des Comtes de Hainaut.* 7 vols. 1881–96.

Dictionary of National Biography. 22 vols. 1908–9.

Grimstone, E. *A Generall Historie of the Netherlands.* 1627.

Kingsford, C.L. (ed.) *Chronicles of London.* 1905.

Michelet, J. *Histoire de France.* 2 vols. 1851.

Monstrelet, E. de. *Chronicles of Monstrelet.* (Translated T. Johnes.) 5 vols. 1809.

Nicolas, Sir N.H. (ed.) *A Chronicle of London.* 1827.

Nicolas, Sir N.H. (ed.) *Proceedings and Ordinances of the Privy Council of England.* Vols. 2–4. (Record Commission.) 1845.

Pirenne, H. *Histoire de Belgique.* Vol. 2. 1905.

Putnam, R. *A Mediaeval Princess.* 1904.

Ramsay, Sir J.H. *Lancaster and York.* Vol. 1. 1892.

Rapin–Thoyras, P. de *Acta Regia.* (Translated S. Whatley.) Vol. 2. 1726.

Rymer, T. (ed.) *Foedera.* 20 vols. 1704–35

Scufflaire, A. *Les serments d'inauguration des comtes de Hainaut.* 1272–1427. (*In* Standen en Landen. 1. 1950. Pp. 79–132.)

Stevenson, J. (ed.) *Letters and papers … during the Reign of Henry VI.* Vol. 2 (Rolls Series). 1864.

Strickland, A. *Lives of the Queens of England.* Vol. 2. 1851.

Vickers, K.H. *Humphrey, Duke of Gloucester.* 1907.

Wylie, J.H. *The Reign of Henry V.* 3 vols. 1914–29.